Under Torn Paper Mountains

A (sort of) Novel by

Perry Robert Wilkes

Liberación Press

ISBN 978-1-7350115-1-6
1. Fiction, General
2. 1960s Generation, hippies
3. Southwestern history
4. Travel, Mexico

Published by Liberación Press
P.O.Box 6460
Nogales, AZ 85628

Cover design by Carolyn Kinsman
Printed in the United States of America by IngramSpark.

"You don't know about me,
without you have read a book by
the name of *The Adventures of Tom
Sawyer*, but that ain't no matter.
That book was made by Mr Mark
Twain, and he told the truth,
mainly. There was things which
he stretched, but mainly he told
the truth."

—Huckleberry Finn, 1884

DEDICATION

During the 1800s the novel began to supplant and eventually kill the oral tradition, the ancient custom of storytelling around the fire, around the comforting hearth. And then the distractions of television programing, and now the ubiquitous computer, did much to seal the casket.

But in a novel the storyteller can perfect the story, can get it right. Hemingway and Pound spent much time debating "le mot juste," the exact right and proper word to convey the true essence of a sentence, a phrase, a thought. Yet, lest we praise the novelist too highly, Sartre observed that, "A writer promises the moon for a gold piece, but ends up showing his backside for a sou."

This is an adventure told in its own peculiar way, a novelization of true stories, the early years of wanderings and musings and pain and passion in the southwestern deserts, with a few lessons learned along the way. This is not a suggestion for others to follow, but some nuggets may lie among the slag heaps and ruins left behind. And much of it is true.

It's dedicated to Carolyn, my partner, my muse.

And to the members of my family, but especially the nieces, the nephews, the grandkids, who follow in our tracks. To Rachael, Elyse Anna, Bo, Luke, and Sam. To Kai and Carson and Kaylie and Dominic. And to Alec and Eliot, who will never read this. May their memory endure and may they rest in peace.

1   **HEADING SOUTH**

*My soul was born in the deep purple shadow of
torn paper mountains. There is a mythic and
heroic quality to the west, especially as the sun
sets and distant desert peaks go flat against a
brilliant horizon.* — PRW

The news hit me hard. Much harder than I ever could have imagined. I felt as if the life had been suddenly forced out of me as I slumped heavily into an old chair with the phone still pressed to my ear. It was Carin on the other end, and she was calling to tell me that Annie was dead.

Early details were sketchy, as they always are when something like this happens. Annie had fallen and hit her head, or something like that. She had died in the car on the way to the closest hospital. Rob, her sometime live-in boyfriend, had found her by the stairs of their remote cabin late in the afternoon when he returned from work. The police were questioning Rob before they released any more details. Because parts of it didn't seem to add up. They had fought often.

Carin and I spoke for a few minutes more and then I thanked her and hung up the phone. There was nothing more to say. Whatever relationship Annie and I once had long ago was over. And in a way, I was now finally and tragically free. I stared through a window at a small tree swaying in a stiff spring wind, its naked branches bearing the rich and promising buds of another summer, a summer that Annie would not be part of. I thought again of those days when we were younger, and of Annie as I wanted to remember her.

We were young then, in a time when it seemed that youth was its own reward and there were no meaningful consequences to it all. Yet there was so much that seemed to be of tremendous importance among the events of those days, much of it wonderful, much of it merely confusing, all of it part of a generational movement that swept over us and across the entire country and that carried us along with it; and it changed each of us in ways that we could only begin to imagine then as we embraced it, astounded with ourselves, in a place that we somehow felt was very near the center of it all. It was a time of great promise, of hope undiminished by the cynicisms of age, and yet still clouded by youth and our individual histories. Out of this circling storm and the continual sweep of massive events beyond our making, it was left to us to begin the task of crafting our lives, our community, our world in the best way we knew how.

I looked back and remembered it all once more and I searched again through the rubble for answers. Then my thoughts turned again to Annie, and our divorce. It was June of 1974, over a year since everything had fallen apart, and I couldn't believe I was still being consumed by this. Annie had died on a cold day in February, and I was still reeling from the news.

I suddenly realized I had been staring for some time at a dirty plastered wall just beyond the edge of my old wooden kitchen table. My right hand was still wrapped around the cold remains of a cup of coffee. An open box of cereal sat beside a clean and empty bowl. A large spoon with a bent handle lay beside the bowl on the chipped white painted wooden table. I had been spending a lot of time lately just staring at one wall or another in this small adobe house that occupied one bend of a winding dirt road in the Rio Grande Valley. I usually began each morning staring at this particular wall. Staring at it but not seeing it, really. Somehow it seemed that the promise of an entire generation had managed to elude me up to this point in my life.

It was the beginning of another day, a Tuesday in early June, and the long hot days of early summer in the southwest desert had begun to stretch endlessly and mercilessly before me, as they always do at this time of year. A burning sun was rising over the highest peaks of the mountains that etched the eastern horizon and it flooded through my window, washing across the ridges and valleys and missing pieces of the old plaster wall. It was going to be another hot day and I was glad I wasn't going to be around here for it. I pushed away from the table and dumped the cold dregs of coffee into the sink. Then I put the coffeepot back onto the burner and I watched until the grounds just began to foam again with the rising heat. The rich smell of hot coffee, slightly burned this time, filled the air once more.

There had been no rain or snow since some time back in February and the snowcaps had quickly melted, first from the mountaintops just to the east of town and then from peaks in the distance farther to the north. As the last of the snow disappeared, each day grew steadily warmer under a brilliant, lapidary, and flawless blue desert sky. Spring was wonderful, as it usually is, but too short this year. The heat built with each new day until mid-June and now the hottest days of summer were upon us. In July, the colossal and architecturally magnificent forms we call thunderheads would begin to build over distant mountains with a promise of cooling and life-giving late-summer rains for the few plants and animals that were strong enough to survive the baking brutality of June. And the desert would come to life again.

It was this way every year, a part of life, the cruelty and the promise. It was part of my own life. It was something I always relied on, and now I needed something I could rely on. But this year was different. This year I was sick of the heat, and I realized that I was sick of this town and all the tragic memories it held. I poured some cereal into the bowl and finished breakfast, and then I sat for a few more minutes and looked out my dirty kitchen window with another cup of coffee. And I waited.

A pair of finches scratched in the dirt outside near a pile of salvaged construction materials. The sun was already starting to heat the inside of the kitchen as it streamed across the table and onto the floor. This day had finally come and I hoped it would change things in my life, a lot of things that needed changing. I rose from the table and washed the dishes. My bags were packed. It was time to go.

Mark pulled off the washboard dirt road and onto my gravel driveway. From inside the cool thick adobe walls, leaky windows, and sagging front door, I heard the roar of an old VW bus engine, the chatter of tires on gravel, and the raucous laughing voices of Mark and Linda above it all. Mark's gleeful and obnoxious honking of the horn was totally gratuitous, and yet not at all unexpected. I needed them to be here now. I needed to get myself out of what had become a seriously whiney mood—and I needed to stop thinking about Annie.

Mark killed the engine and they were out of the bus, laughing as they ran across the desolate space that passed for a front yard, and they were through the door before I could open it. My opening the door would have been a ridiculous formality anyway, under the circumstances. They spilled into the only reasonably livable room in the tiny old adobe house I was still renovating, and almost tripped over the mattress and box spring that were resting on the worn wooden floor. A war surplus Army trunk beside the bed served as a nightstand, holding three half-read novels and a secondhand gooseneck lamp. A small table and two chairs stood along the opposite wall near an old freestanding wood stove. They edged around the mattress, and past most of my belongings stacked in cardboard boxes, toward the kitchen.

"This place still looks awful." Linda laughed as she glanced around my never-ending construction project and across a floor that hadn't been swept in a while. It didn't deserve more than a quick glance because there wasn't all that much to look at. "Do you think you'll ever actually finish moving in?" she asked with a skeptical smile and a shake of her head. She stared at another large pile of boxes stacked in one corner.

"Someday it'll look a lot better than this." I grinned, but without much conviction; I was hoping the pain wasn't real obvious so early in the morning. This renovation project was just the next logical step in the rest of my turbulent life. I hadn't had much time to think things out when Annie and I got divorced more than a year ago. At the time I just needed a cheap place to live. The whole thing happened so quickly, I didn't have a clue what I was going to do next. Our parting really shouldn't have come as much of a surprise, but it had anyway. These things probably never happen in such a way that you can plan out the next phase of what's left of your life.

I ended up buying this three-room adobe shack with no real plumbing on 3/4 of an acre for only $5000. It seemed like a good purchase to me, but none of my friends or family saw it that way. There was an outhouse at the back of the lot and a kitchen sink inside with water but no sewer connection, so the sink drained onto the ground behind the house just outside my kitchen window. I got a phone installed in the kitchen and I wrote phone numbers on the wall beside it, inspired by a line in a Chuck Berry song. I liked to think of the place as charmingly rustic although no potential girlfriends seemed to agree. But it was a start, another start among several I'd been through so far, and at least I could afford this one. Now I just had to make the place livable whenever I managed to get some money together, and maybe this time around I'd figure out some way not to have to go through all this again real soon.

Mark grabbed my tattered leather suitcase off the bed while I finished stuffing a few last things into a smaller one. "C'mon, man, let's go!" he laughed. " At this rate it'll be dark before we get to the border!"

We had about seven hours driving time ahead of us on our way to Ciudad Juarez, Mexico. Actually, it might be more like eight hours in a fully loaded Volkswagen Bus— and maybe longer when you added in a lunch break and some pit stops. I grabbed my jacket and we headed for the bus. It was 7:00a.m. The sun had already begun to cook the desert floor, but maybe we'd miss the worst of the afternoon heat if we left now. And we needed to make an early start if I was going to catch one of the afternoon buses to Chihuahua. I had never been south of Juarez before and I didn't want to miss anything by traveling at night. I wanted to know Mexico instead of remaining just another gringo bystander.

I stood for a moment on the crumbling stoop of my little adobe home and locked the door while Mark stowed my old leather bag in that space above the engine behind the back seat of the bus. There wasn't much of anything in the house worth stealing, but I didn't want anyone messing with what little I had. I was leaving with friends on what promised to be a beautiful and endless summer day, and I didn't want to come back to a ransacked house. I was beginning an adventure that I had been waiting several months for and I was hoping to, I don't know, lose myself in the exuberant essence of Mexico, I guess.

Linda and Mark climbed onto the front bench seat of the old VW Bus and slammed the tinny doors shut. I stepped up into the back seat, stowed my other bag, and pulled the rolling side door shut. Mark shoved his key into the ignition and the old reliable 36-horsepower engine rattled into life. He shifted into first and we pulled away from my endless construction project, passing a motley collection of other small homes and barren windblown yards that lined the street on our way to the stop sign on the corner. Then we turned right and headed for the closest freeway on-ramp.

I had expectations for this trip south beyond the border, but I also had a feeling they were unrealistic. That's a trait that had defined much of the arc of my life. I was hoping for deep insights about Mexico and some answers among the scattered remains of my life. I wanted to leave the confusion behind for a while and try to clear my head. Maybe a clean slate would make things simple again, like the days I seemed to remember before Annie and I first met. It's true, isn't it, that most of us like to think things were simpler and made more sense somewhere "back then" in some imagined past. I'm good at rewriting my own past to make it more palatable. But back before Annie brought her excitements and her complications into my life, at least back then I had lower expectations.

I didn't own much of any real value before we met, and I still didn't, so I didn't have to worry a whole lot about losing it. Having little of material value defined my life then, as it did now. And it gave me a lot of freedom, from responsibilities mostly, but maybe also from a real sense of happiness. I had my worn tool belt, a couple of good hammers, a good power saw, and some other essential tools. I could walk onto one of the new subdivisions that were springing up everywhere at the edge of town and I'd have a decent-paying job that started first thing in the morning. The work was hard, but the air was clean, and I slept well every night. The weather was just about perfect during the months of spring and fall, although summers and winters were rough. But I could usually save enough money to take time off and get out of the weather for a while every year during the worst of it.

We rolled down city streets, past too many old memories, and finally onto the freeway. Mark and Linda concentrated on merging the old slow Microbus into the horsepower-dominated world of modern freeway America. And soon we were on our way to a distant horizon.

The far edge of town was visible to the west and I recalled sitting out there last winter in the cab of a warm, idling truck with an old contractor who I was working for at the time. It was a cold early morning just before the day's work began. We listened to some guy babbling on the radio over the roar of a heater fan as we looked through a misty windshield at the windswept icy landscape before us. Patches of refrozen snow and dirty ice hid in shadows along the north side of the building we were constructing. A cruel north wind blew across the hood of the truck and buffeted the doors. We were sipping the last of our hot coffee and waiting for his dashboard clock to read 8:00a.m. He stared straight ahead, his watery eyes reaching deep into the frozen windblown scene, while the last wisps of steam curled upward from his cup into the air and he contemplated his many years in the construction industry. Then he said quietly, and with a touch of sadness in his eyes, "You know, it's a great life if you don't weaken." He'd spent almost all his life outdoors in the freezing mornings of winter and the blistering afternoons of summer. His haunted eyes now told me that was all he'd ever known, and I could sense it was all he had to look forward to for the rest of his life. I still think he was right, about it being a great life that is, but I also knew, even as young as I was at the time, that I was starting to weaken. I was starting to look for a way out, a maybe easier way through life.

During those hardest days of winter I often thought I'd like to work in a comfortable office somewhere. Behind a desk in a place that was warm in the winter and cool in the summer. But I just couldn't imagine what those people do in there all day, hidden from the sunshine, away from fresh air, without the unlimited horizons I had become accustomed to every day and all day. I could stop working for a moment whenever I needed to straighten my back and I'd look up at long wispy cirrus mare's tails painted across the sky like streamers of sand swept up and tossed upon a vast blue beach. And I understood the message they were whispering. I knew as well as any weatherman that we'd have a change in the weather in a day or maybe two.

After all those years of working beneath an open sky I wasn't sure I could stand the cloistered myopia of an insulated office somewhere. I wasn't even sure I could manage to shave and get myself into a white shirt and tie every day. And I knew it wouldn't take long before my new co-workers saw through the disguise anyway, and I was exposed as an interloper in their private world. And there was another thing I couldn't figure out about that lifestyle. How do those people dress up to go some—place special, like to a wedding or a funeral or something? Do they just wear the same clothes?

In those days, I had nobody special to share my home with, and share my life with, but still, each new day brought a feeling of freedom. My life then was so much less complicated than it had become recently. In the past I had done alright with how the next day might turn out. It was pretty straightforward. But with Annie I was never able to tell. She was compelling and she was a constant challenge.

The old Microbus rolled onward and southward, its

faded red and black paint soaking up the early heat of another day, and I thought about the long and empty road ahead of us. There was not a cloud in the sky, just endless dry desert mountains. There would be at least another month of burning skies before the rains brought blessed relief. I knew that we were heading toward a hot Mexican desert, but I hoped that maybe the rains would arrive early this year somewhere farther to the south, in a place beyond the border.

Soon, the freeway took us past another poor section of town where I'd had a tiny apartment many years ago and I thought about my life there.

February 1968

It was a cheap and shabby one-room apartment in a Black and Hispanic neighborhood wedged between South Broadway and the Freeway. I lived there for a few years just before I met Annie. When Annie first saw the place she must have been feeling benevolent. She said it was charming in its way, and somehow maybe even authentic. "Authentic" is one of those words we use to describe poverty. She was correct, although she liked to romanticize the concept. She told me she was tired of slick-talking coffee house philosophers, the guys who hung around the campus and talked nonstop about quitting their phony ivory tower intellectual ghetto to go live the simple and honest life of the working world. To Annie, I was already doing that, and not just talking about it. My cheap dirty apartment on the wrong side of town gave me a sort of credibility in her eyes. As far as I could tell, she even assumed that my basic naiveté was some mark of dignified honesty. I had an actual skill, doing hard outdoor work bringing in an honest paycheck, and I wasn't living off my parents or off some trust fund. Not like those guys with plenty of time to hang around the coffee houses.

Annie had worked when she was in high school and never expected to receive any money from her folks. Now she was working her way through college as a waitress. I had managed to pay my own way through two years of philosophy classes, until I was worn out by also maintaining the constant working grind and I decided to quit school for a while. There seemed to be a genuine cultural commonality between the two of us. I could feel it somehow. She came from modest working class people and she respected that quality in others, like me. I respected that quality in her, although she seemed to think it was a lot more romantic lifestyle than I did at the time. But Annie, I would come to realize, fell in love easily. And she was easily betrayed by it.

As the miles passed by outside Mark's VW bus I realized I was spending too much time thinking about how pathetic my life had been up to now and I should think about some of the good things that happened. There were plenty of people who had it way worse in life than I did. I had lived in some dodgy places but it had mostly been my choice and it had given me a lot of freedom to do so many other things with my time and my limited money. This trip to the border was already giving me time to think about those things. I could almost see that shabby apartment on a dead-end street that backed up to the freeway as we passed by. And I even had fond memories of it, at this many years of distance.

The general noise level from freeway traffic and the frequent high-pitched tire-scream of heavy-loaded cross-country trucks provided a kind of nightly lullaby and I got used to it after a while, although I never learned to love it.

My front door opened straight off the sidewalk, and the sagging door had scraped deep gouges in an arc as it swung inward across a worn vinyl tile floor. A combination lock that hooked over an old bent and battered hasp kept the door shut from the outside. There was a rusted throw bolt on the inside. Cheap faded and stained cotton curtains hung limp in a fixed pane of glass mounted just high enough in the wall beside the door to keep people from looking in and high enough to keep me from looking out very much. Whenever the wind blew, the glass rattled in its frame against an accumulation of old dried-out putty and paint.

The entire apartment was one single room about eleven feet square, with a small dark bathroom added at the back. There was a metal kitchenette unit, and a stove and refrigerator arrayed along two walls. As far as I could tell, the bathroom was an old outhouse that had been nailed to the back of the place and "upgraded" with a rusty steel shower stall and a toilet. The bathroom was so cramped that Vince, the landlord, had hacked a hole in the side of the shower stall to allow enough space for the toilet handle. I had to reach into the shower to flush the toilet or risk cutting my fingers on the jagged, rusty edges of the crudely-cut hole. An old dirty curtain covered the bathroom doorway to provide minimal privacy if someone came to visit. There was a bare bulb hanging from the bathroom ceiling, and there was no bathroom window or any other kind of ventilation other than the wind leaking through cracks in the old wooden walls.

There was no window in the apartment that could be opened. I opened the front and back doors whenever I needed some fresh air, and whenever I wanted to have a view of something other than the four walls of the place without standing up to look out. But generally the apartment was a good place to sleep and to store my few things, and to read or otherwise keep the mind occupied since there were few esthetic distractions. There was an old wooden table with a chair on each side. One cold winter's day I drew two eyes, a nose, and a mouth in magic marker on the face of the chair that stood just across the table from where I usually sat so that the place wouldn't feel so damn lonely. But at sixty dollars a month —utilities paid—it was affordable and it gave me the economic freedom I wanted at the time. I was spending some time prospecting in southern Arizona in those days trying to strike it rich with an old geezer who seemed to know what he was doing, as far as I could tell. Or at least he talked a good game. It was another wonderful crazy time after a winter I spent with lots of extra people in a commune up in Taos, and I loved the freedom this cheap little apartment gave me. As long as I paid the rent in advance I could spend as much time as I wanted on some adventure, and I never felt that I had to worry about anybody breaking in. Surely the thieves who lived in the neighborhood had better things to do than rob my shabby little hovel. They couldn't be that desperate.

My landlord's mother, Mrs. Garcia, lived in a little house at the back of the lot. Now and then, I'd hear her tapping on my back door and calling my name. When I opened the door, she'd be standing there in her well-worn cotton apron, holding a small plastic bowl of freshly-made red chile, or maybe a little plastic plate with a slice of homemade white cake. Her son Vince, who was in his mid-forties, had finally gotten married a few years back and he left the old barrio for a home in the heights, so Mrs. Garcia bestowed her motherly ways upon whoever was renting the little apartment by the street. It surprised me at first and I wasn't very happy about the intrusions into my solitude. I had rented the apartment as a kind of hideout, but gradually I learned to accept Mrs. Garcia's visits, and later I didn't really mind the attention. Eventually I even came to enjoy seeing her, although it was an independent and rebellious period of my life and I didn't see my own family for months at a time. I even came to welcome the comforting sound of old Mrs. Garcia tapping at my back door and calling out my name.

I often wondered how the Garcias got to this part of the Rio Grande Valley, but Vince didn't seem to know.

"You should of asked my grandfather," Vince told me one day as we stood outside the back door under a spindly old elm tree. Vince was a friendly guy and he liked to talk. "He would of known. He was always full of stories about the old days growin' up on the ranch out east of here near Vaughn. Life was rough out there chasin' those cattle around. Tryin' to keep 'em from freezin' in the winter and dyin' of thirst in the summer. Cattle are really pretty stupid and you have to take care of them. You know how cold it gets out there in a blizzard. I remember he told me how one time they lost half the herd in a blizzard. They just froze to death out there where they stood. It was a rough life out there on that ranch. He finally moved the family here to town when he lost the ranch in the Depression. No, I don't really know how we got here. I guess we came in with the conquistadors or something a long time ago."

"You mean you think your family came into New Mexico with De Vargas about three or four centuries ago? Or maybe even Oñate?" I asked.

"Yeah. Prob'ly with one of those guys. But I don't know. My grandfather would of known but he died about fifteen years ago. He was real old. I wish I'd of listened more to all his stories but I was real young and I wasn't really interested in those old stories then."

Vince seemed to live almost completely in the moment and I wasn't sure he even had any particularly deep well of curiosity about how his family got here so long ago. All that stuff probably didn't matter much to him. He and his family were here now and that's what mattered most, and that's probably normal for most people. I wasn't even sure that I could track my own family back farther than my great grandfather, and I had no clear idea when they arrived on this continent from Germany or England or wherever they came from.

When I asked Mrs. Garcia she answered me in her heavily-accented English. "Oh, I don't know. You should ask Vince. He's real smart. He knows all that stuff. He learned it all in school."

Mrs. Garcia was much more comfortable speaking in Spanish. I often heard her talking with the other older women in the neighborhood who came by to visit, and I could hear her radio tuned to her favorite Spanish station when I opened the back door. And she always spoke to Vince in Spanish. But, since my Spanish was inadequate to carry on any real conversation, Mrs. Garcia and I spoke in very simple English. And our exchanges were short. She and her friends were the last remnant of a generation that grew up speaking fluent Spanish and only learned basic English at school. Vince's Spanish was only a little better than mine and his kids didn't speak it at all. I could feel that we were on the verge of losing an important part of the history of New Mexico with the passing of that older generation, and Mrs. Garcia was a rare link to that past.

Whatever Mrs. Garcia may have known about her family's history was not for me to learn, but I was still very curious about how the Garcias, and the Trujillos, the Martinezes, the Barelas, and all the other families on the street who were here long before my arrival, had managed to get this far inland through the desert so very long ago. They were strong people and I enjoyed hearing or reading their stories. I usually had several books on the subject, old personal accounts and diaries of New Mexico history, lying around on the floor by the mattress I slept on.

The apartment met my needs although it was tiny and shabby, and my housekeeping was so minimal that most of my friends joked about the place. In fact they joked quite a bit about it. Rebecca, a former girlfriend worked for the New Mexico State Department of Welfare. One day she dropped by to tell me about another place she'd seen that was even cheaper than mine. It was a dirt-floored, three-sided room with an old ragged carpet nailed across the open side. They were actually renting it to Mexican immigrants for ten dollars a month! Other than a bare bulb with a pull-chain hanging from the ceiling and an outhouse by the back fence, there were no modern facilities at all. Rebecca thought it had a certain Stone Age charm. She thought it would be perfect for me.

My living arrangements didn't meet with my father's approval, either. He decided to stop by the apartment for a visit one day to see how his oldest son was doing. I showed him where to step to avoid tripping over the scattered oily parts of a disassembled Triumph motorcycle engine. As soon as I could afford the replacement parts, I planned to reassemble the motorcycle and get it out of the way because I needed space to work on the balky carburetor from my ratty old Austin Healey Sprite. Dad and I sat down across from each other at my small kitchen table, and I reached behind me to grab the coffee pot from the stove and pour out two cups of relatively fresh and very strong boiled brew.

The true purpose of Dad's visit was to get me thinking about my future. He had developed a, well, you'd have to call it a "life plan," for me. The years were carefully hand printed along the bottom of a page of graph paper, with potential salary levels up one side. Across the middle of the page he had plotted a gracefully upsweeping curve that showed where I could be in, say, five or ten years. This, of course, would require a shorter haircut on my part and daily shaving. I feigned politeness and listened quietly as Dad, the engineer, explained all the better possibilities that lay ahead in the logical progression of my life. To him, it was all mathematical. A person's life could be graphed out and planned for success. He had lived his own life this way and saw himself as proof of the indelible reasoning behind the process. He wanted me to have a life with all the modest advantages that he had managed to gain through hard work and devotion. But later in his own life, the logical process would fail him. He and my mother would be divorced and they would each go in very different ways. Dad would spend several years in a sort of emotional purgatory of pain and confusion, and even poverty. And then we would have a lot in common. But neither of us could foresee it as we sat across the table from one another in my ratty apartment.

When it was time for Dad to leave, he paused by the door and briefly surveyed the place one more time. His eyes swept from the motorcycle engine to the dirty dishes in the sink, to a pile of dirty clothes lying in one corner on the floor. Then he said, "You know, you really should put a doormat here so people can wipe their feet on the way out." I always appreciated my Father's humor.

I thought those days were far behind me. I thought I had left my freewheeling, and lonely, single life, and that crummy apartment, far behind when Annie and I got married and rented a nicer place next to open irrigated fields in the far South Valley. It was a new life, a new adventure, for each of us, but it was a life that neither of us was capable of living. Now I was alone again and still living a minimal existence in another small, dilapidated hovel of a place. And Annie had moved to another small place by the university near where she lived when we met. That's where she met Rob, the guy who probably killed her. We had each come full circle in our own way, and now there was no possibility we could ever come back together. And I didn't want to think about it anymore. It would be good to leave all that behind for a while.

Mark looked at me in the rear view mirror and smiled as a dry wind poured in through the side windows of the old VW Van. It was too loud inside the van for much talking, so I smiled back as I considered the prospects of our trip to the border. But my mind raced back to the long dark days of the divorce. It had been bothering me all morning as usual, just as it had for the past several months. Mark could see that I needed a little more time to think and he kept driving without trying to engage me in the moment.

It was in the dead of winter, that cruelest season of all, when things between Annie and me finally came apart. There is nothing quite like doing hard work on a construction job in the middle of a cold winter's day and knowing that tonight there's nobody at home to welcome you when you finally get there, frozen and exhausted. A cold dry northwestern wind can chill you to the very core of your being. I spent my working life out there. Outside in it all day. Everyday. When friends invited me away for a weekend skiing trip I could only laugh. All I could think of was staying inside my shabby little house by the stove, or in a warm coffeehouse with a hot cup of Java warming my hands, waiting to see if any friends showed up. Soon enough it would be eight o'clock Monday morning and I'd be freezing my ass again, swinging a hammer and building a warm home for someone else to live in. And by the time we got the place ready to insulate, our crew would be off again to some other cold and windswept concrete slab starting the whole process all over. And on top of it all I was too distracted by the divorce to finish the long-neglected repair work that cried for attention around my own shabby house. By the time I got back to my empty home each night, cold, exhausted, distracted and lonely, I didn't feel much like working on the place.

As we neared the tail end of winter I was frozen to the bone. It happened this way every year. Every damned year. But this time I was completely sick of it. I wanted to go someplace warm for the next month or so, until the pleasant gentle kiss of springtime settled once again upon the Rio Grande Valley. But, as the long winter ground onward into spring, I hadn't been able to put enough money away to pay the mortgage for a few months ahead. Any chance of leaving for a while was going to have to wait until early summer and I was a little further out of debt. I found myself wishing again for the days when I was only renting that cheap apartment and I had no significant responsibilities.

By the time I was able to leave town, the blistering days of June were upon us. I knew it was crazy, but now I was heading south, into the heat of the Mexican desert, in early summer.

From the freeway I looked out across rows of small and decrepit homes in the southern part of my old neighborhood and I saw the shiny new corrugated metal roof of Jimmie Romero's house in the distance. I smiled and realized I hadn't seen Jimmie in about a month. Jimmie was usually up to something interesting, or even bizarre, and he was the kind of guy who could always bring a smile. He was a hard-working guy and he really wasn't any more unusual than most of the other people I hung around with, but most of his "projects" seemed to end up with unexpected results. I remembered when he was pouring a concrete floor for a garage in his backyard off the alley. It was a Friday morning and I had to be at work. Four of his drinking buddies had promised to show up and help out, but three of them got so drunk the night before that they were too sick to be of any use. Federico, the only one who actually showed up, started drinking the large supply of beer that Jimmie had bought as bait to get them all there, and by the time they'd poured half the concrete he was worthless, too.

Jimmie was left standing there by himself with a truck full of concrete turning and idling in the alley. The truck driver helped out for a little while as Jimmie kept hoping his amigos would show up. But soon the driver had to leave and Jimmie was stuck there, completely exhausted, with a large pile of slowly congealing concrete in the middle of the floor. I stopped by on Saturday morning and saw the mess he was in and the two of us spent a couple of hours busting up the pile with picks, sledge hammers and chisels before it was completely hardened. He was surprised that I didn't drink any of his beer until the job was done, but I get sluggish after a beer or two and I decided to wait. And he was surprised that I was the only one who would help him out of this jam without looking for a payback of some kind. Back then we hadn't known each other very long, and Jimmie thought this new gringo friend of his was alright after that. It was a long time ago.

When I decided to leave for Mexico on this trip I got together with Jimmie for a few beers and we talked about it. At first, he sounded excited about the adventures I was going to have and then I asked him if he'd like to go at least part of the way with me. He spoke good Spanish and the spring semester was over now, so he could put those biology books away. It was amusing to think that Jimmie had become an elementary science teacher. We had joked about it when he got the job.

"Hey," he said with that easy laugh of his, "I figured out that all I have to do is stay one lesson ahead of a bunch of fourth graders. I think even I can do that!"

I knew that Jimmie and I would have a great time down south where the air was warm and the beer was cheap. He could talk to the girls for both of us, those beautiful girls with their legendary dark eyes and flowing black hair. And there were *ejidos* to visit, the communal farms that *Presidente* Lázaro Cárdenas had set up after the Revolution. We could check out the leftist legacy of the Revolution and the inspiring murals that graced the walls of every city, town, and village.

Jimmie came from a working-class family with deep roots in the community and although he was the first in his family to attend college, he had an abiding respect for the workers who keep society going. He grew up doing manual labor with his father, who had never finished the eighth grade. When he was young his father told him, "M'ijo, yo *quiero que tú no trabajas como un burro. Como yo.*" His father knew there was more to life than just hard physical labor, than just working like a *burro* for an entire lifetime, and he saw to it that Jimmie finished high school. And then he was delighted to see his son in college.

This trip would be a good way for Jimmie to extend his education beyond the horizons of the valley we both lived in. That's how I felt and I told him so. But Jimmie said no, it would be just like visiting a bunch of his relatives, and probably the ones he didn't really like all that much anyway. The girls, and everybody else, would look about like the people he'd grown up with around here. For him it wouldn't be the same exotic experience that I was looking forward to. We joked about it some more and I pressed him further until he reluctantly told me about an experience he had a few years ago in Juarez. He was drinking with some guys down there in a bar and they quickly figured out he was an American because of his accent and by some of the words he used. But that was okay. He was having a good time with his new compadres as a blazing afternoon sun baked the land outside the door.

But the guy who'd been drinking the heaviest finally decided he didn't like Jimmie much. In a drunken slur he said, "You think you're better than us just because you're an American and you've got money. You think we're just a bunch of dirty poor Mexicans down here because we live on the other side of the border. You come down here and buy our cheap beer, but we can't do that in your country because we don't have enough money and our clothes are dirty. They don't want a bunch of dirty Mexicans in their bars, and they don't want our dirty pesos, either. But you're not any better than us! You're just another fockeen Mexican too, and you'll never be anything better than us!"

Jimmie was stunned by the guy's sudden bitterness. Up until then he'd had a warm feeling of brotherhood with these guys. The others at the table sat looking at their beers, and glancing at Jimmie and his accuser to see what would happen next. One of them turned to console his drunken friend, but any feeling of commonality was gone. The truth of it all was plainly evident in the old clothes they wore, the pesos in their pockets, the lost sense of opportunity in their dark eyes.

Jimmie wasn't ready for this. He'd never thought of the implications of their life below the border like this before. He considered himself basically Mexican, too. He tried to tell them how his family had come up through Mexico by foot back when it was New Spain and they'd worked the land with their hands to survive in a harsh desert far from their homes. He hated gringos as much as the rest of them because of the way they had stolen property from the *pobres Chicanos* of the southwestern states. (He paused at this point in the story to say that I was one of the few exceptions.) But all the amity they had shared was gone.

After a short interval Jimmie made his exit from the bar and walked back down dusty streets to the border where a couple of White Immigration agents hassled him for a while because of his brown skin and his accent until he produced enough ID to show he was American. They were a couple of ignorant lifer types who'd been given some limited degree of power. They'd learned how to abuse it and liked hassling young Chicano guys. I had never been treated like that at the border. I was a tall Anglo, and they had always waved me through. But Jimmie couldn't even get back over to the north side of the border without hearing a lot of racist crap. He was used to dealing with gringos. It was just part of life in the southwest. But on this trip he'd gotten slammed from both sides and the dark reality of it had finally hit him pretty hard.

That was the last time Jimmie went to Mexico. He didn't need any more of the resentment, and the stupidity.

I wanted to say something that might fill the silence that descended as Jimmie finished his story and as we both stared at the beers we were cradling with our hands. There were patterns of interlocking wet rings shining on the Formica table top. Beer rings. I wanted to say something like "Yeah, I know how you feel." But I had no idea what it felt like to deal with racist crap when you're the one who inhabits the underside of some alien-dominated culture. When you're the one who's in the underclass. I'd been called a gringo a few times, but it was always amusing and it never really bothered me. I was in the dominant role in this cultural mix that defines the southwestern states and racist slurs always seemed irrelevant, and even a mark of desperation when they were hurled at me.

I have also never mastered the art of saying the right thing in a sensitive situation, so I kept my mouth shut, hoping maybe that this would all go away. Jimmie was staring out the window at his dust-blown yard and at a couple of old dead cars that had been parked in his neighbor's yard across the street for most of the past decade.

"I guess I'll never understand this gringo fascination with Mexico," he went on. He stared out the window and his voice was soft now, and with an edge of profound sorrow. "Those people are just a bunch of poor Mexicans like me and like almost everybody else I know—and they're even poorer than we are! Why would I want to go see that? I just don't think that's charming. I guess it reminds me of how close I am to their situation. That could have been me living over there in a dirt floor house with no money and no future. I don't need to
see it to know that it's true."

Jimmie turned to me as I tried to enjoy the rest of my beer at his kitchen table.

"You know, you've got it lucky," he said. "You can travel wherever you want to without all this double racism that I have to put up with." He left it there and stopped to stare at that cheap Formica table. I watched the bubbles that were rising in my beer; They slowly reached the top and burst into the air. Dammit Jimmie, I thought to myself, you sure know how to stop a conversation. We both sat there for a while until I managed to change the subject to something less controversial. Something we could both agree on. Like stupid ex-girlfriends.

Still, I wished Jimmie was going with me on this trip. Maybe things would have been different once we got well south of the border and into the heart of "real Mexico." Whatever that was.

We rattled our way onward to the city limits, to the junkyards of south Broadway. It was taking longer than I hoped just to leave the city behind, and it was stirring far too many memories. And why was I heading deep into the Mexican heartland anyway, avoiding the tourist trail along the coast? Was it to somehow test myself? To find a mythic land that was still raw and wild and emotionally revolutionary? I had a small amount of money, a Spanish-English dictionary, and an old tattered guidebook, and no real idea where I was going.

Out the window I saw Al Lemon's Tire Shop down on south Broadway, with his big plywood tripod sign standing out by the road like any other morning of the year and it looked like the world was going about its business whether I was going to be part of it or not. There was something about Al Lemon that always brought a smile and I shook my head as I saw his tire shop down there in the distance. It was nice to think of Al and not to feel morose for a while. Al's sign stood there in the dirt like a big sandwich board with two long strap hinges at the top and there was a chain that connected the two bottom edges to keep them from slipping and leaving the sign lying flat on the ground. That had actually happened once before Al figured out he needed to put the chain on it. A wind caught it and lifted it just enough so that one side started sliding away and the sign had collapsed in a puff of dust. Then someone absent-mindedly ran over the flattened sign without stopping and left two big black tire tracks right across it ("...rat acrost it," was the way Al described it). Al was outraged and tried to figure out if he could match the tread pattern and track down the perpetrator but it was from a very common Goodyear truck tire. Things like this always seemed to happen to Al and his response was always remarkably the same. Someone had done this to him. The fact that he hadn't actually built the sign well enough to stand up never seemed to occur to him.

So, Al repainted his sign. There were only four words on the sign, in large red letters. Big and unavoidable, like Al Lemon himself. The sign read, "Charge Bateries Fix Flates." There were only four words on the sign and Al had managed to misspell half of them. He had misspelled them on the original sign and now he misspelled the same two words on his new repainted version. It's nice to know some things in life are constant, that there are things that you can rely on. Like Al Lemon.

I turned away from the sad and dilapidated junkyards of south Albuquerque, and looked down the long tongue of black highway that stretched before us into the southwestern desert. The distinctive craggy silhouette of the Sierra Ladrones loomed far to the southwest embraced by the clear morning air like a marker pointing our way south, like the large battered hulk of a derelict ship full of *bandidos* that had been stranded in the desert some time long ago.

ANNIE

A cool morning breeze whistled past the open sliding side windows as Mark's old VW Bus rolled further down the freeway and picked up speed. The sky was clear, deep, rich, the color of turquoise. It was going to be another hot June day and soon the morning sun—and our sweating bodies—began to heat the rolling tin Microbus that carried us slowly and steadily south toward the border.

Mark was driving Linda to Juarez to catch an express bus to Mexico City. She was working on a book about women's issues in Latin America and needed to do several weeks of research "in country." They both thought it was time I got my sorry butt out of town for a while, and Mark suggested I go along with them. After we crossed the border into Juarez, I would catch a big southbound bus and just stop when I thought I had gone far enough, or when the money ran out. He was right. It was what I needed. I have never had trouble with the idea of running away from problems instead of trying to face them, trying to deal with them. Sometimes, running away is a really good idea.

Mark and Linda had lived and worked in Venezuela for several years and they were both fluent in Spanish. A couple of months ago they shared an old Spanish *dicho* with me: "*Un clavo nuevo saca otro clavo.*" It's a very Spanish way of looking at love. Instead of pulling the last nail out of your heart, just drive another one in after it, replacing the old pain with a new one. At the moment I didn't have any new nails in my heart, only the dull throbbing ache of the last one, still there, still festering, the one driven in so deeply by Annie. I needed something else to be meaningful in my life. But mostly I just needed to get away for a while.

Mark slipped a joint from his pocket, lit it, and passed it over to Linda. Might as well start the day off right, with a well-rolled joint, in a hippie bus rolling through the heart of redneck country. What could go wrong with that? I watched as Linda took a long sensuous drag and then I took the joint and I noticed how well-rolled it was, tight and neat, with no wasted effort. Not at all like that one I tried to roll a couple of months ago. With someone else's dope.

I had dropped by to see a guy I knew. He was about four years younger than me and there were a couple of his friends sitting at the kitchen table. They all deferred to me because I was a little older and they assumed I was that much hipper than they were. It was heady stuff, all that adulation from a bunch of young guys. One of them pulled out a small plastic bag of grass and some papers and put it on the table. Then he slid it over to me. It was a moment of honor and respect in a newly-evolving culture. I was the ranking hippie. I had hippie seniority here. I had the most time in grade. I glanced nervously at each of these guys and saw expectation in their eyes, and then I opened the bag. I had never actually rolled a joint before and I was going to have to fake my way through this test or lose a lot of face in the process.

Three pairs of adoring young eyeballs watched my every move as I pulled a paper from the pack and held it between my thumb and second finger with my index finger lying in the middle of the fold. So far I'd copied the moves I'd seen by countless cool guys at countless parties over the years, where I had never actually needed to roll one myself. I poured a healthy line of marijuana in the trough and its skunky fragrance filled the air. I set the bag to one side. Then I carefully licked the gummed edge of the paper and tried to roll it smoothly into a respectable joint, but it kind of got away from me somehow, and leaves of precious marijuana rained onto the table and onto the floor. My young audience followed this extraordinary exhibition of basic incompetence in an essential generational lifeskill with little amusement as they scrambled to recover each tiny leaf. They looked at me for an explanation and I mumbled something about not having my favorite brand of papers with me. I slid the whole mess back across the table and cracked a few jokes to distract them from my disgraceful performance. One of them rolled a beautiful joint and we engaged in the hippie rite of communion. After a few more minutes of faked nonchalance, I made my exit.

I was glad that Mark had done the rolling early this morning and stuck the joints into his shirt pocket, but I was preoccupied with my thoughts and I wasn't sure this gift from the earth would do much to raise my spirits. So far I had been unable to muster the carefree cheerful mood that might fit this happy moment. I didn't really care if we all got totally loaded and ran off into a ditch somewhere. It was an overwrought and exaggerated grief I was feeling, but the thought of dying, broken and bloody beside the road, somehow seemed better than what I was going through inside. Staring out the window, I had a sort of "cheap novel moment" as I saw my devastated relationship with Annie reflected in the auto-wrecking yards and industrial wastelands of South Albuquerque. It was almost funny that we had to drive past this stuff on the way out of town. The clean unsullied and sun-drenched hills of the "promised lands" lay beyond this trashy gauntlet. The symbolism was just too bizarre.

I had some questions to ask myself. Did I need to embellish the pain? How had it all gotten so ugly so fast after starting out so well? Had it really started out all that well, or was it another one of my shattered delusions? It had been more than a year since the divorce and I still didn't have any answers.

Each of us was soon enveloped in a quiet foggy world of our own as the golden morning sun slowly melted down dark dry canyons. Sunlight filled the folds and rivulets creasing the tall mountains standing to the east of us. Soon the very land itself would lie fully open and exposed to the intensity of the day. Soon, there'd be no place left to hide.

The tree-covered granite and limestone spine of the southern Rocky Mountains knifes across a crystal sky along the eastern edge of the Rio Grande Valley at Albuquerque. On the opposite horizon, five ancient volcanoes stand as markers along the valley's western boundary. Down the center, a lacy flow of muddy river nurtures a linear forest of towering cottonwoods—the *bosque*, an ancient verdant brushstroke across a mixed dry landscape of high desert grasslands, cool mountains, and rugged lava fields. It's an especially dramatic scene driving into town from the vast deserts lying to the west when you crest that last hill and the entire valley lies open before you like a revelation, with a range of tall mountains, the Sandia mountains, glowing pink in the sunset, standing just beyond to the east. Over the years I've lived here I have increasingly become part of this valley and part of those rugged rimming mountains. And the history of the West has become my own history.

There was a time, not long ago, when this part of the Rio Grande Valley had a more special quality to it. It had a simple beauty then, when the city itself was much smaller and rested more lightly on the ground. Albuquerque has grown far too quickly in recent years. Everything is moving so much faster now, maybe ten thousand or so years after the earliest native people arrived, and several centuries after the first Spanish settlements were established in this part of the fertile valley of the Rio Bravo del Norte. In those days, the Rio Grande was known as the Wild River of the North for its violent raging floods in springtime when early rains melted deep snowcaps too quickly from the northern mountains and waves of icy water surged over their banks, carving new paths and reshaping the ancient valley. New lakes and wetlands were formed. Tiny adobe homes and fields were destroyed. Sections of forest were carved away and new open habitat was created. Sometimes the entire valley was rearranged by the terrible and renewing floods of spring.

And sometimes, people were swept away in the spring torrents, their bodies buried deep in layers of sandy silt. The community mourned its dead, and families who lost their men to the waters prayed for God's help through the hardships of the coming year. There was a terrible and beautiful balance to life in those early days. It was a balance rigidly imposed by an immutable natural process. During times of good weather, the fertile lands yielded bountiful crops of *maize, chile, y frijol.* The Spanish learned to grow these crops and adapt themselves to this river from the Pueblo peoples whose ancestors had settled in this valley a millennium before, drawn by the reliable and abundant water source. During good times their crops flourished and the population grew. During times of flooding, or drought and famine, people perished. And in the end the balance was maintained. The natural world demanded, and received, a great deal of respect then.

But now the river was dammed and tamed and the land was made safe for those who chose to live in the bed of the old river. And they came by thousands to build their homes on ancient farmlands that had given life for so many years. And now most of the fields were gone. Asphalt and concrete fills this once fertile valley, leaving only remnants of the past.

La Villita Real de Alburquerque. With two Rs. That's how the name of the town was originally spelled in 1706, when the Spanish Crown authorized the governor of this portion of New Spain, Don Francisco Cuervo y Valdéz, to establish a small administrative center, a *villa*, here in the valley. He named this little settlement in the New World in honor of his distant Spanish patron, the Duke of Alburquerque, from a small city in western Spain. Cuervo y Valdéz proclaimed San Francisco de Xavier as the patron saint of the new villa, but the *Real Audiencia* in Mexico City changed the patron saint to *San Felipe de Neri* in honor of the devout and ascetic Spanish King, and the old adobe church on the original plaza still carries that name to this day.

There were other small farming villages in the area, but Alburquerque would become the new administrative center for the middle valley. Alburquerque was only the third villa in this vast and empty section of New Spain. Santa Fe was the old traditional capital, and Santa Cruz was farther to the north, to deal with issues in the *Rio Arriba*—the upper river. But Santa Fe was a two-day ride by horseback, in good weather, from these southerly farming communities. The growing population in scattered small settlements along the middle valley required a more immediate governmental presence.

The Villita de Alburquerque soon became a trading center as well, and it grew slowly but steadily over the next two and a half centuries as it passed from Spanish to Mexican rule after their own War of Independence in 1821. And then it passed into American hands after the Mexican American War of 1845. The arrival of the railroad in the 1880s brought a new wave of Anglo settlers from the East and the town grew steadily larger. But this new wave of largely Protestant Anglo residents who followed the railroad west settled apart from the old Spanish town and established their New Town beside the steel tracks that would continue to bring new economic life to the community.

And eventually there came the massive gringo invasion that followed the new economic realities of American life after the Second World War. My own family was part of this invasion, arriving from the Midwest during the mid-1950s in a 1949 Ford two-door sedan traveling along Route 66 as it snaked across America down the main street of each small town along the way. I was the oldest of four children traveling west in the large bin that was created when our father built a folding wooden structure to fill the foot-space behind the front seat. We spent several days—I don't remember how many—wondering when this trip would end and when "The West" would suddenly appear just outside our windows. I was ten years old at the time, with dreams of cowboys and rodeos and rugged mountains, but all I saw out the window was dry grassland and a few stunted trees.

Then we rounded that last bend through the mountains and the entire valley unfolded before us. It was a revelation. We were in the desert. And there were mountains and volcanoes in the distance.

In the early years after our arrival it took all of us a while to adapt to the dry brown desert landscape, but now I saw in its crystalline skies and jagged eroded mountains a dramatic beauty unattainable in wet climates where the weight of heavy air enshrouds and hides the land. At some point along the way I had finally evolved into a westerner with a visceral love of the land and a kinship with the open and unspoiled wildness of it all. The depth of its history became the depth of my own history.

Over time the sleepy little western town of Albuquerque, the one I remember, grew from a population of less than a hundred thousand to almost half a million. And the change was hardly graceful. Entire blocks of charming and historic older buildings were demolished to make room for some of the cheapest and worst new architecture in the West. Ancient adobes, with priceless stories to tell, fell before the blade of the bulldozer, replaced with ugly boxy commercial buildings and cheap project housing. In my imperfect memory, a graceful old Pueblo-style City Hall was destroyed along with most of the rest of the early charming core of the city, and the downtown landscape was soon dominated by an egg crate-looking City Hall devoid of personality facing a brutally ugly Convention Center across a sterile Civic Plaza that somehow actually managed to discourage human usage. It was a poor mockery of the city's once-exuberant old plaza and its rich Spanish heritage, a gracious way of being that revolved around plaza life.

And most of my friends and acquaintances seemed to disappear, replaced—or absorbed—by crowds of people I didn't know. These new people built upon the ancient land and disturbed the very memory of the dead, and a brash and growing city filled the entire valley like a surging reservoir of insensate beings, with speeding cars, and cheap houses and miles of glaring neon that washed upward to the base of rugged mountains on the eastern side, and to the foot of reddish-black volcanoes along the west, spilling out of open ends of the valley to the north and to the south. It was all moving faster now—too fast, sweeping me before it in an endless flood tide of humanity, threatening to bury me in its concrete grasp. I was an alien in my own land and longing for a way out. For a simpler time, a quieter time.

My world had become too complex. And my recent divorce from Annie was another grating manifestation of the onrushing and overpowering machinery of this modern world. And I needed to get away to…somewhere. Like I had done a few times before. Before I ever met Annie.

I thought of the times I'd spent prospecting down in the oppressive summer heat of the Mohave desert with crazy old Ted. My eyes drifted westward in a marijuana haze, out the window of the old VW Microbus toward distant Arizona.

August 1968

The intense midday heat of July rose from a shattered and baked Arizona landscape as I stood near the crest of a small hill and looked southwest across an endless sweep of dry desolation toward ranges of parched mountains standing in rows of gray and blue in the distance. I took off my old straw hat and wiped my forehead as shimmering waves of superheated air rose from the desert floor, distorting the dry and tortured land. An afternoon furnace breath swept up the hillside to dry the remaining salty sweat from my forehead and provide a small measure of cooling relief. On the distant two-lane highway that sliced across the desert floor, a lone car headed northwest toward Parker, a small town on the banks of the Colorado River. I had seen only two or three others pass by all day.

At my feet stood a crude rock cairn, a stubborn pile of random, football-sized rocks, haphazardly piled up a couple of decades ago in the desert sun. "Cairn" is a fancy word for a pile of rocks baking on the side of a hill in the desert to serve as a sort of marker, but that's what the prospectors call them around here.

Buried under those rocks was an old rusted Prince Albert tobacco can with a simple note inside marking one of the corners of a claim. "I, Ed Baker," it read, "declare this to be the Northeast corner of claim no 3 as registered in the courthouse at Yuma, Arizona, May 14, 1949." It was just as we had found it when we looked in the registry books at Yuma last week. Ed Baker had staked his claims—he had quite a few in the area—after the war. He was probably a returned war veteran nurtured by delusions of wealth while he carried an M-1 rifle through endless miles of dust and mud in some other country halfway around the world. And hoping he would survive the war. I could understand Ed Baker. As far as delusions of wealth were concerned, he was a lot like Ted and me.

According to the records, Ed Baker renewed his claims several times over the years, and then his entries ended about a decade ago. Maybe he was dead now. Or maybe his wife got tired of watching her husband in the grip of whatever particular lunacy it is that draws men to the desert, and maybe she demanded they do something more productive with their time, and their resources. Or maybe he just stopped pouring out good money and wasting his vacation time grubbing around out here looking for something that probably didn't even exist in enough quantity or quality to interest anybody with real money who could back him in a mining venture. Maybe he finally shook that sickness and moved on with his life. And it is a sickness. Even Barry Goldwater once said that the Arizona heat breeds two things: right-wing politics and gold fever.

We didn't know what Ed Baker was looking for in these hills but, from down on the valley floor looking back in this direction, you could clearly see the greenish, reddish colors of mineralization up here along these hills. It was a slim promise, but one any decent prospector would be willing to stake some time and money on. Our own samples from a previous trip had assayed out with small traces of lead, copper, even a little silver. Sometimes a mine will show just enough silver, or even gold, to pay the expenses, and the real profit is made from something as mundane as lead. But so far, our samples were a long way from showing any pay dirt. So far we had come up empty out here looking for a rich mineral vein of some sort, probably just like Ed Baker and every other damned fool who had ever trekked these hills before us.

But besides those traces of silver and copper, the assay report had shown something called gallium. Neither of us knew what it was or what it was used for, but a couple of research books described it as a "rare earth" and said it was used in the space industry. Whatever it was sounded promising, so we returned to the desert, Ted and I, to see if we could come up with some more of it.

After hours of sweating in the hills gathering bags of samples, we got back into Ted's old 1954 International pickup truck with its faded red paint and we headed about twenty miles down the highway to the town of Salome and an air-conditioned bar/restaurant that kept a good supply of ice-cold beer behind the counter.

The small town of Salome, Arizona (pronounced "Sa-loam" by the locals), had been the site of a 1953 motion picture starring Rita Hayworth as the stepdaughter of King Herod. It was a desert fantasy that the residents still spoke of often since it was their only apparent claim to fame. Framed pictures of scenes from the movie lined the walls of the bar and the attached restaurant. Other assorted bits of memorabilia were hung behind the bar. On the menu under the name of the restaurant, which I have long since forgotten, was a picture of a veiled woman and the words, "Where she danced." I had never heard of the movie before I got to Salome, Arizona, and to this day I still haven't seen it.

Ted and I sat at the bar and ordered a couple of hamburgers with our beer, and we watched an overhead TV set that was reporting on the daily street riots and police clubbings that were occurring at the Democratic National Convention in Chicago. The Vietnam War was item number one on the nation's political agenda, and the brutal assault by undisciplined Chicago police on waves of young war protesters was now being broadcast for all the world to see. The twisted rhetoric of the American Establishment was being unmasked before our eyes while citizens who were rightfully petitioning their government to change a failed policy in some distant, abject country were being beaten by a domestic police force that was acting like thugs in any third-world dictatorship. The protesters chanted, "The whole world is watching!" and I thought I should probably be in Chicago for this important confrontation with the corrupt power structure of the nation instead of sitting in some forgotten desert bar.

"Fuckin' hippies!" a big guy growled at the other end of the bar. He was wearing jeans, a Caterpillar hat and a white T-shirt that couldn't quite cover his belly. "They oughta just shoot those bastards!"

He looked down the bar in my direction. My longish hair did not go unnoticed in this little desert town. The guy next to him nodded his approval, mumbled something I didn't catch, and finished the last of his beer. I turned back to the TV set and kept my mouth shut. It seemed like a smart thing to do in a redneck bar full of self-destructive dumbasses. These guys are pretty brave when they have you outnumbered. Still, I couldn't understand why he was so quick to support a regime that was sending a lot of guys like him to a tropical hell somewhere overseas to do the dirty work of the privileged classes.

Ted, who'd had his nose rearranged a few times in various barroom battles, was probably hoping that Mr. Fat Bigmouth down the bar would push the issue.

But soon the TV returned to some inane comedy show and the rednecks settled down into stupid laughter. We finished our beers and left as the cooling veil of night fell across the parched land, and we headed back out into the desert. We pulled the truck behind Elmer and Joe's old shack just off the Parker highway and tossed our bedrolls on the ground. I lay there for awhile on top of my bedroll in the cool quiet of the night and stared upward through the clear dry air into the brilliant depths of the Milky Way. I felt like I could almost touch those distant worlds, and wondered if people who might be living out there had somehow managed to transcend the boundaries of their own stupidity. Unlike us. Very soon, Ted was snoring in the background and for a while that was the only sound in the night.

Ted and I were a strange sight in these parts, and people would usually study us briefly whenever we showed up in town. I was 23 years old and felt the best I ever had in my young life. I had finally gotten out of the Marine Reserves after five long years of wasted weekends and another two weeks every summer, and I felt the most incredible glow of freedom that I had ever known. Bartenders were no longer checking my ID and the women my age were finally taking a serious interest in me. My shabby apartment by the freeway only cost me $60 a month, and that included utilities. I didn't have a special girlfriend to disappoint or to complicate my life, so I had the freedom to go off prospecting in the desert with Ted, this funny old character who was snoring on his bedroll about ten feet away.

Ted was a case. He was about sixty years old, short and wiry, and he had a ruddy, tanned complexion because he spent about half of his life outdoors. According to the stories he told, Ted had done more dumb things in his life than most people can imagine, much less be willing to admit to. The stories were endless and they were not so incredible that you ever completely doubted the truth of it all. Ted was eccentric but he was a straight shooter in his daily dealings, so I just assumed that most of this continual narrative of his life was true. After all, at his age, he really had been around long enough to do a lot of dumb things. Still, I was always surprised whenever he told another one of his stories.

Ted had the energy of a bantam rooster, and when he got a little drunk, he had all the sense of one, too. He reminded me of Popeye, usually getting into scrapes with someone a lot bigger than he was. But unlike Popeye he often got pounded by the bigger guy, although once in a while he did come out on the winning side. On those occasions when he won the battle, he considered the other guy a coward, a contemptible loser, a failure. It was only when he got his ass kicked good that the other guy was a worthy human being, a worthy opponent. Still, at least Ted was honest enough to blame this peculiar characteristic on his own Napoleonic complex. He was the short guy always trying to measure up to the big guys. Those other guys. The ones who got most of the glory in life. The ones who always got the girl.

I lay there for a while in the cooling darkness thinking random thoughts about my strange prospecting partner and my own nicely irresponsible lifestyle. And I studied the sky in the breathless quiet of the night. High overhead, that giant star cloud burned with the roar of a hundred million fires, and then somewhere in the distance a coyote called.

When I awoke in the cool slanting light of early morning Ted was lying on his bedroll with a pair of reading glasses and he was holding a copy of Julius Caesar's *Commentarii de Bello Gaullico,* about the Gaulic Wars. The library was another place Ted spent a lot of his time when he wasn't carrying on down at the local coffee shop or bar, or working someplace as a computer programmer.

"Listen to this," he said quietly in the cool stillness of the morning. "Caesar laid siege to this town and the other Gauls in the rest of the country formed a huge army and laid siege to Caesar's forces. He was completely trapped with the enemy on both sides and outnumbered about ten to one. So he built trenches entirely around the town and then he fought the enemy on both sides to a standstill. Then he concentrated on conquering the town, and finally he conquered the other army."

"Hm. Pretty amazing," I mumbled in my half-sleep.

"C'mon," he said. "Let's make some breakfast."

I dressed and stumbled off to pee behind a big bush. Then I joined Ted inside where he had put coffee water on to boil. We checked the fridge and then we started cooking bacon, toast, and scrambled eggs for Elmer and Joe. Since they let us use their kitchen in the mornings, we were delegated to cook breakfast for them. Everybody benefited since I could dish up a decent plate of scrambled eggs, and Elmer and Joe were both pretty sick of their own cooking.

I don't really remember much about where these two old guys came from and why they were living out here in a shack in the desert beside a minor two-lane highway about twenty miles from the nearest small town. They just seemed to hang around inside all day watching TV and hiding from the intense heat of the summer desert sun. About once a month they'd go cash their Social Security checks in town, if they needed anything. And they were both hard of hearing. The only way to carry on a conversation with Elmer and Joe after the TV came on, about 8 o'clock in the morning, was to speak loudly and very clearly. By mid-morning the burning heat of summer had penetrated the old uninsulated walls of the house and the rattling beat of an ancient, rusty swamp cooler added to the din of the TV set in their tiny, crowded living room.

But Elmer and Joe thought we were the eccentric ones. Nobody in their right mind wanders around in the southern Arizona desert in August. In the early morning the heat wasn't intolerable yet, but rattlesnakes were still out there crawling around those rocky hills in the relatively cool air. Anybody with any sense would naturally just spend most of the day inside someplace by an air conditioner. It was obvious to the locals that we didn't fit into the category of "anybody with any sense."

Come to think of it, I don't really remember any more why we decided to head down into the desert in August. I guess Ted had to take his vacation time when the boss allowed it, and I wasn't steadily employed at the time. Besides, I didn't see any real difference between working on a construction job in 100 degree heat and grubbing around in the low desert at 105 degrees. At least down in the desert, if it got too hot at midday, we could hang out at that air-conditioned bar in town until it started to cool down in the late afternoon.

Ted probably could have gotten some vacation time in the spring or fall but he also had a self-destructive quality that governed most of his decisions. Subconsciously, the desert heat of summer was probably a kind of penance for all the failures of his life so far. And while we're on the subject of self-destructive qualities, Ted was always at war with whichever "plutocrat" or "self-important bastard" he happened to be working for at the time. Ted's main goal in life was to strike it rich somehow, get on a good drunk, go up to the boss's office and tell the son of a bitch just exactly what he thought of him. I could picture the scene. Ted would have his chest puffed out and be sort of dancing around on the floor while he stabbed the poor bastard in the chest with his right index finger and threatened to kick his ass right there in front of the whole office staff. He would finally be on center stage, The Guy In Charge, The King Of The World.

Of course, a couple of big security guys would grab him by the throat and whack him a few times with their billy clubs. He'd wake up in jail, hung over and looking like hell. And later, the lawyers' fees would take most of his new fortune and he'd be back out in the desert looking for another jackpot. It was the classic male fantasy. The stuff of cheap books and second-rate movies. The only difference was that Ted never seemed to learn not to take it seriously.

Like the time at a party when he had way too much to drink and started picking a fight with the biggest guy standing in the kitchen. The guy reached over and grabbed a skillet off the stove, and whacked Ted with it. Ted woke up the next day with a bigger hangover than usual. And he told me the story later with a laugh.

Ted also had a broad streak of paranoia. Maybe it was due to his essentially libertarian outlook on life, but he never really trusted anyone for very long. He would trot out government conspiracy theories on a regular basis, and then he would laugh at himself if he thought it all sounded a little too bizarre for the listener. I detested many of the same corrupt people he did, and I also thought of them as venal, arrogant, self-serving bastards preying on an incredibly gullible, and also-guilty, electorate. But unlike Ted I never considered them bright enough to put together such a broad and overarching conspiracy.

In Ted's world the average person was also suspect. He never really trusted anyone very much, or for very long. And after a while I knew that he never really trusted me, either.

After a lot of time spent trekking around a bewildering number of similar looking, rock covered, sun-baked hills I realized the only rational way to ever exploit whatever riches might lie below the surface was to plot the whole thing out on topographic maps and look for patterns, anticlines, veins of mineralization. A few college geology classes had given me at least a sense of the possibilities that lurk beneath the earth and maybe a way to find them.

When I brought up this bright idea one morning over breakfast Ted said, "Don't worry about it. I've got it all right here." and he pointed to his reddish, sun-baked head. His bleached, Irish red-blond hair glowed with the morning light slanting low through the kitchen window. "Let's go." he said and turned away, "It's time to get moving before the sun gets too hot."

I let it pass. I figured I'd bring it up again sometime later. He couldn't really be serious. How could you ever prove your claim without a map of it? How would you ever get any financial backing if you never shared any information with the people who had the money? They weren't going to just hand us a bunch of money without any proof that we had something worth bankrolling. And he and I sure didn't have the money to start a mining operation. I would just bring it up later.

Meanwhile there was plenty of work to do gathering samples, covering our diggings so nobody else could find them, and generally killing enough time and piddling away enough money to comply with a law that requires lunatics like us to spend a certain yearly dollar amount "improving" each claim. But by the time we had finished messing around with the claims we were running low on cash and we no longer had enough for gas to get back to Albuquerque.

Ted suggested we head over to Parker, on the Colorado River, to see if we could find some work. A lot of Californians had vacation homes on the river and we could probably find something to do there. And since it was ungodly hot in August, it was pretty likely there wouldn't be any competition for whatever construction jobs might exist in Parker.

The next morning we thanked Elmer for his hospitality, but Joe had left early for Yuma in an effort to get out of jury duty. He planned to tell the judge that at his age he just couldn't hold his water any more, and so it would be impossible for him to sit completely through a trial. Elmer wished us luck, and we headed down the road to another adventure like some cut-rate version of those guys, Todd and Buzz, in the old "Route 66" TV show. Or maybe more like the Beverly Hillbillies.

Ted's ancient, ratty-red International pickup truck labored down that long highway in the blistering desert heat. We had painted the roof of the truck with some aluminum paint to reflect the sun before we left Albuquerque. It didn't seem to help at all as far as reflecting the heat, but it sure made the truck look even worse than it had before we came up with that particular idea. The roar of wind through the open windows kept most conversation to a minimum as we ate up the miles of highway which also happened to be visible through a large rusted-out hole in the floorboard. The blast of engine heat funneling upward through that open hole added to the general oven-like conditions inside the old truck and we were happy to pull into a roadside diner when we finally reached the outskirts of the winding, river-hugging community of Parker. We managed to nurse our burgers and ice-cold Cokes in the air-conditioned diner until late afternoon.

That night we threw our bedrolls on a cleared patch of riverbank and slept in the cool night air to the deep and quiet mumbling of the river. An old bulldozer mechanic named Jimmy slept in a tent with his dog at the other end of the clearing beside his D-9 Cat. He was leveling this area and a few other riverside lots for Californians to build their dream homes on. Jimmy was glad when we showed up. He looked pretty lonely and he was happy to let us stay there for a while, and let us warm our canned beans over his campfire.

In the evenings as the sun disappeared over the ragged rim of the canyon, temperatures began to drop ever so slightly. And then, in the dim twilight, several million moths came out of the stream-side bushes to fly around and run into anything and anybody near that cooling layer of air over the river. They would end up in your eyes, your mouth, your dinner pan full of warm beans. After a while I discovered they wouldn't bother me if I laid down on my bedroll. When I was no longer vertical, they would swarm around the large bushes that hugged the river's edge.

So I lay there, under the moths, staring at a narrow band of stars visible between the high canyon walls, and thinking of Janie, and even Marilyn. That damn Marilyn. Took off with that flashy bastard, whatsisname. Marilyn was truly a beautiful woman, but I guess I never really stood a chance with her. Janie would be around when I got back, but it wouldn't work with Janie. She was too strange for a longtime relationship, with all those cats she had. And I was allergic to cats, anyway. I lay there awash in fantasies that it would be great to live with Marilyn, maybe go on a lifelong adventure together, maybe see the world.

But that would never happen now. Ah, damn it, forget it. It's over. Hell, it never even got started, really.

Later in the night I awoke as a moist, cool breeze began to sweep downstream and I pulled myself into the sleeping bag that I had started out lying on top of. The rich sounds of a restless river murmured in the background.

Ted and I found a job building some concrete block yard walls for a guy with a contracting business in Los Angeles. He was in Arizona for the month and hadn't expected that none of the locals would work again until probably mid September, after the heat had backed off a little. But we were out of choices. We needed the money and we couldn't afford to wait until the temperature got reasonable again. We would start work in the morning.

Because of the moth infestation, we usually got to bed around sunset every night and we woke up when the sun first began to paint the eastern sky. After a refreshing swim in the river each morning before dawn, we got together some breakfast and then we were off to work long before the blistering heat of midday. Every hour or so during the day we'd run down to the dock at the end of the street and dive into the cool, swirling waters of the river still wearing everything but our shoes. Then we crawled out of the river, walked back up the street and worked till our clothing dried out and it was time for another cooling dive.

I was getting the best tan of my life since I never took a hot shower with chlorinated water to dry the skin. And because of all this frequent bathing in the river, I smelled better than usual. Or at least, I thought so. It was too bad there weren't many young women around to test this theory on, and the ones we met didn't seem very impressed by our general appearance. Or by Ted's loud mouth. And they couldn't figure out what we were doing hanging out together in the desert. Were we gay? Was he some kind of weird "father figure" for me?

The whole thing must have looked pretty strange and the women we ran into clearly didn't want to get into it. But that was probably for the better. It was a whole lot simpler this way, just working hard all day and living for free on the riverbank. I spent a lot of time swimming first thing in the morning, last thing at night, and a whole lot in between, and reading some good books before the light completely faded each night. This could go on for a long time as far as I was concerned.

The next few weeks passed quickly as we worked all day under the blistering sun, and we finally ended up with a little money in our pockets. After work, we often stopped for a burger and a beer at one of the local bars before heading back to our camp on the riverbank. Other times we would pick up a few groceries to share over a fire with Jimmie back at the riverbank. Ted was a passable block layer and I kept busy mixing mortar and carrying concrete blocks to the next work place along the wall. By the time we got back to the campsite each night we were usually dog-tired and ready for the bedroll. But Jimmy the bulldozer operator was always ready for a gam, so we'd sit around his little campfire and talk for a while. And bat at the moths. A campfire was pretty much superfluous in the lingering heat of a desert evening, but the softly glowing embers answered some deeper spiritual need for the comfort of a lighted hearth in the blackness of night.

So I'd hunker down and poke at the fire and just listen while Jimmy and Ted traded incredible tales of past successes, and many failures. It seemed that the boundaries of both their lives had been demarcated mostly by the latter and rarely by the former. There was a good-natured, self-effacing tone to the stories that downplayed their few accomplishments, but beneath it all lay the hard bedrock of truth. They were both getting old and neither of them had a hell of a lot to show for it yet except their stories, oft-repeated and finely-tuned around other campfires, or in coffee shops and bars.

One evening after a few banalities—call it male foreplay—something reminded Ted of a time he drove to Florida with some lady he happened to be married to at the time. They were passing through a small town in Georgia and stopped at a garage to have something adjusted on the car. They decided to have a bite at a little diner across the street and were seated at the long lunch counter talking to the waitress as she refilled their cups. Then she stopped pouring, looked across the street, and quietly said, "Oh no. There he goes again."

It was said in such a calm and matter-of-fact way that Ted and his wife turned slowly on their stools to see what was going on. The mechanic had taken out a long, heavy crowbar and was smashing in their windshield. Ted dropped his coffee and ran across the street. By the time he got to the car a couple of other guys were holding onto the crowbar-wielding mechanic and trying to calm him down. Ted was jumping up and down in his characteristic way, poking his finger at the air, hurling abuse and accusations. His wife was crying. Someone flagged down a passing police car and the officer spent some time figuring out what had happened, and why one of the hometown boys had flown off the handle again. Then he turned to Ted and said, "If I were you, fella, I'd just get in my car and head on out of town. And don't come back."

It's how small towns protect their own. It was a kind of pre-federal, country-style welfare system in which the local community shares the burden of dealing with their own basket cases. Sometimes it worked, sometimes it didn't. That's just the way it was. Kind of like the system we have today.

So Ted left town and drove onward, cursing profusely, to the next large town and paid out a lot of money for a new windshield and other repairs to the car. He'd been the victim again. His wife was in tears, again. This sort of thing always seemed to happen to Ted. At least he could laugh about it now, here in the desert, about two thousand miles and who knows how many years away.

Jimmy appeared to be a far less complicated person than Ted and he seemed to have found a kind of peace with his role as a permanent member of the lower middle-class working population. He mostly talked about how to fix bulldozers and trucks, and about other jobs where maybe he'd been stiffed by some developer who hadn't paid his people, the ones who did the actual work.

I was still young but I knew someday, the way things were going, I would probably be repeating these same stories, and some of my own, over a beer someplace. But I sure hoped that by the time I reached Ted's and Jimmy's age I would have something more to show for it than they did.

After a couple of weeks we finished up the block walls and got paid the rest of the money, and about then I guess I'd had enough of Ted, and his stories. Or maybe I just needed some quiet time. I had earlier come to the conclusion that Ted's paranoid and secretive ways were never going to result in any mining bonanza in the desert for him, or for me. Many of Ted's stories concerned some "bastard" he had been financially involved with, or partnered with, in the past, so I also knew it was only a matter of time before all this paranoia would be directed at me, and I really wasn't prepared to deal with it gracefully. So I figured I'd just cut my losses before I got in any deeper. It was time for me to leave.

I awoke early on my last morning in the cool, canyon shade that stretched along the riverbank, and I sat quietly on the river's edge, and watched the dark water—deep, swirling, and mysterious—lap the shore at my feet. As I studied the river, I saw there was a strong inshore current, then a large, circling eddy filled with water weed below an island at about the two thirds point across the water. And on the other side was California. Ted and Jimmy were still sacked out in their bedrolls, and I was alone with my thoughts on the bank. I considered just how beautiful the whole scene was, and quiet, in the shadow of tall canyon walls. Only the call of a distant bird broke the still murmur of the water in the cool morning air. But the quiet beauty of the moment only underscored a profound loneliness I began to feel in my heart. I had this special moment all to myself, undiminished, uninterrupted, and there was nobody special that I could share it all with. I shook it off and looked back into the river's depths, and then I stood up.

I took a long, deep breath, and dove into the swift tug of the current. As I surfaced, I began to stroke hard for the other side while the strong current swept me along past the island and I pulled hard for the swirling waters of the eddy. I pulled myself into and through the eddy, kicking myself free of the long, grasping fingers of river weed, and I readied myself for the next stretch of current. Soon I would be across the Colorado River, standing in the shallow water on the California side. Or maybe I would be dead.

Maybe I would drown in this rarest of desert rivers. The fates alone would decide.

My feet finally touched the hard rocky shallows, and I walked carefully between the rocks up from the river and into an unchanging landscape of desert scrub and sand. The first rays of morning sun had cleared the canyon rim and kissed the cool soil beneath my feet as water streamed from my body and I stood gazing into the sun-baked emptiness of distant California hills. Somewhere nearby, in one of those summer cabins, someone was already awake and listening to "Light My Fire," the long version, by The Doors. The throbbing intensity of music, faintly heard in quiet early-morning air, matched the heavy beating of my heart. I felt the warmth of my work-hardened muscles pulsing with life in the brilliant rays of the morning sun, and I began to work my way upstream along a rocky shore for the plunge back into the deep enfolding coolness of the river.

Once again I stood quietly by the shore and watched the beckoning, tempting, and treacherous swirls of life-giving—and life-demanding—water as it passed before me. Pausing thoughtfully at the very cusp, the very edge between a life that is past and the rich possibilities of a life to be, I looked for a moment into the rocky depths. Then I dove into the sweeping, pulling current of the river.

I pulled hard and was swept downstream and back through the eddy, as the main current caught me and I stroked for the other side. But the current was stronger than I had remembered and it swept me down farther along the bank, and into a dense growth of river weed that wrapped around my arms and legs and tugged me downward in a heavy embrace. The river was ready at last to claim its own. To claim its callow and prodigal lover. I gasped for air as I pulled against the power of destiny. Then

I broke one arm free and pulled again at the swirling surface. My other arm came ripping free with a hard tug and I kicked my legs loose as the current tugged against me. Then I pulled myself, coughing up swallowed water, toward a steep, gravely bank and out of the water's grip. I sat and rested for a while on the rocky shore at the river's edge, trying hard to catch my breath, and I studied the water. And then I turned away from the eternal flow, away from the beckoning lover's voice, and I walked back toward the campsite for my last breakfast with Ted.

We split up amicably, although Ted didn't really understand why I didn't want to ride back to Albuquerque with him. He finally just figured I was quirky and that it was my problem and not his. And probably he was right.

I took enough of our joint bankroll to buy some food, and maybe a bus ticket if I needed it, on the way home. I left Ted with most of the money so he could buy enough gas to get the old truck home. Besides, I knew he would probably have to repair a few more things along the way. It wasn't my problem anymore. I had other adventures to think about, the ones that still lay ahead on the open road.

September 1968

I hadn't been standing long beside the old two-lane highway leading out of Parker, Arizona, probably not more than fifteen minutes, when a late-model sedan pulled over and I quickly grabbed my backpack and bedroll and ran along the gravel shoulder toward it. The driver found a place in the trunk for my gear, and then we were off down the road.

It was a family—a husband, a wife, and two kids about eight and ten years old, and I have no idea why they picked me up. Families rarely pick up hitchhikers. Families and single women, that is. You can never really know who that person is standing beside the road. Could be a nicely-dressed serial killer, and how would you know before he got into the car.

And hitchhikers get killed, too. Hitchhiking is a completely anonymous and dangerous way to travel. They might not figure out who you were until several years later, or maybe never, after they found your bleached bones dumped somewhere in the desert. People go missing all the time. I thought about that a lot whenever I decided to hit the road. But a friend or even a relative could bump you off back home and dump you in the desert just as easily.

I knew this ride wouldn't last too long. They were a nice family from San Diego, and they had driven over to spend a week hanging out on the river. I must have looked like a college student when they decided to pick me up. That's a little more acceptable than a guy who's been living out in the desert looking at rocks, doing pick-up construction work, and eating beans for the last month or so. They were nice enough to take me to the Wickenburg junction where I stood a better chance of getting a longer ride and I thanked them for it as they wished me luck and left me standing by the highway in a slight, warm, late-morning breeze. At least I was out of the Colorado River canyon and there was a bit of air flow. The two kids watched me from the rear window as they pulled away and I disappeared from view, another small adventure in their summer vacation.

Simply standing beside a seldom-used highway in the middle of the desert has a liberating aspect to it. There was a glorious emptiness to the land that stretched away in every direction, and it felt as if a person could just heft his backpack, turn away from the road, and walk away into the heart of all that emptiness. And maybe disappear for a while. Or maybe stay out there for a very long time. Maybe even forever. Far away from all the social games of humanity. Immersed, instead, in the important and unnoticed daily events of the little lives around us. The lives of the lizards, ants, prairie dogs, and birds engaged in the serious ballet of daily life in the desert.

I read once about some guy who had gone wild in the early part of the twentieth century and lived like an animal somewhere out in the mountains of southern New Mexico. A rancher spotted him one day, clothed in animal skins and eating a rabbit he had killed. The rancher called to him and he stared back like a startled coyote, then he ran off to somewhere further back in the hills. Over a period of years, the rancher would see him occasionally running across a distant clearing, or disappearing into a copse of scrub oak. Then, the rancher didn't see him for a number of years. One day he found a human skeleton in a draw far out on the ranch. What was left of him was still clothed in animal skins but the scavengers of the desert had cleaned most of the flesh from his bones, and life in the hills went on without him. Nobody ever knew who the guy was or how he got there.

For a little while, standing there looking out beyond the edge of the highway and into the heart of the endless desert, the possibilities before me seemed more important than the trivialities of human life. I wasn't sure I was ready to return to the city.

Then a pickup truck pulled over and the ripping sound of braking wheels on a gravel shoulder forced me out of my reverie. Or was it madness? I had felt a strong pull toward the endless desert. A siren's call beckoning me to join her, and tempting me with promises of peace. Yet I had only stood there, fearful and entranced, and listened. I knew I might never return if I took the first step.

"Where ya goin'?" asked Hal as we drove onward in the direction of Wickenburg.

"Albuquerque," I said.

"Not goin' that far, but the road forks just this side of Wickenburg and you can get a ride to Flagstaff there."

"Thanks," I said. "I really appreciate the help."

Hal didn't say much else as we rode along and I didn't push it. I thanked him for the ride when he dropped me off at the Flagstaff highway just outside of Wickenburg and I waited for a ride that never came. At least the air was cooler than it had been down at Parker, but after several hours of waiting I figured I'd have to make a decision soon. Finally, I shouldered my pack and walked to the bus station in town, and there I bought a ticket to Flagstaff. I thought I'd have a lot more luck catching a ride on Interstate 40 than at this quiet crossroad in the high desert.

The bus pulled into Flagstaff after dark, and I walked in a light rain through moist, cool, mountain air to a nearby cafe for a sandwich and a beer. I sat at the counter nursing my beer and looking into a large mirror behind the counter, watching people pass behind me as they came into the diner. Locals stopped in for coffee and conversation. Most of the other travelers like me ate quietly, looking up from their food occasionally to see what was happening around them. But truckers are something of an exception. Truckers are locals wherever they are and, after a lot of lonely miles, the truckers who came through the door were ready to talk to somebody, usually the waitress. Their loud voices and explosive laughter cut across the sounds of dinnerware and the tunes from the corner jukebox. They were having a good time and generally entertaining everybody in the place.

The waitress behind the counter was young and friendly, and about my age, and we talked briefly about nothing in particular, as momentary companions do. She was a student at the local college, and I imagine she was glad to see someone of her own generation sitting quietly at the counter, nursing his money, with his backpack and bedroll sitting by his stool on the floor. For all I know I might have been her private vision of the magic and the mystery of the young traveler-adventurer. Maybe I was the personification of all her escape fantasies. Or maybe she was just being nice to a guy she knew didn't have much money on a rainy night in Flagstaff.

There was a hand-lettered scrap of paper in capital letters taped to the lower corner of the mirror. It read "YCHJCYAQFTJ."

I asked her what it meant, and she answered, "Your curiosity has just cost you a quarter for the jukebox."

I smiled and started to leave my stool for the trek to the jukebox in the corner at the end of the counter when she said, "Oh, you don't have to do that!"

"It's OK," I said. I dropped a quarter in the slot and decided to play "The Fugitive" by Merle Haggard. It seemed like an appropriate song for the moment, if maybe a little overly dramatic for my situation. I really wasn't being chased by the law or anything nearly that romantic. I was only on the road to kill a little more time on my way back from prospecting in the desert with that old codger, Ted. I wondered what Ted was up to now. He was probably in some bar down there in the desert enjoying himself telling lies to whoever would listen. Ted was good at that bar scene stuff. He was a lot better at it than I was.

I was happy to be on the road and having myself a good-time adventure while I was still young and I could still shirk the inevitable responsibilities of getting older. That part of life would come soon enough. Still, sometimes I wondered why I couldn't be honest enough about it to tell people that's what I was doing when they ragged me about not having a serious career yet. There were always certain people who were able to guilt-trip me easily. Maybe I would never have what most of them considered a "serious" career. And maybe that would be alright. At least I wouldn't end up sitting around in a nursing home later wishing I'd been willing to take a few chances while I was young and still able to do so. At least when I got old I would be able to look back on it all and be satisfied that I'd done it when I could. At least that's what I told myself, anyway. This all had to count for something.

After finishing my dinner I pulled on my faded Levi jacket, said goodbye to the waitress, and stepped through the front door to a dark, wet sidewalk. She wished me luck just before I left, and I thanked her for being concerned. I really appreciated her thoughtfulness toward a stranger in a strange town.

The rain had stopped and the air was cool and it felt refreshing after my long sojourn in the desert. I shouldered my backpack and walked eastward along the main street with a steady stride. I walked past the darkened doorways of small businesses that were closed for the night and some that were closed forever. Along the other side of the street there was nothing but railroad tracks and empty fields. That's how it is along the old main street in

Flagstaff. It makes the town look kind of lopsided.

After I'd walked several blocks, a young college student fell into stride beside me. He was filled with questions about my travels, my destination, my life on the road. We walked on and talked about "The Movement," that unifying force of commonality and comradeship which had lately swept through our generation. There were some exciting antiwar activities and other events planned on campus, and he wanted me to stay a few days. I could crash at the place he shared with a few buddies.

I saw the glow of some kind of hero worship in his eyes, like maybe a True Believer looking for a personal savior. I guess I had appeared like a vision out of a cold, misty night in my faded denim jacket, backpack, and bedroll, and I felt a deep strain of cynicism quickly rising to the occasion. I was a little older than he was. I had more experience with life, and maybe I was a little wiser— and then again, maybe I wasn't. But I was On The Road. Like Kerouac. Like Cassidy. And that must have carried some sort of cachet all by itself. It was heady stuff alright, but from this point on I knew it could only be downhill as he got to know me better and I failed to live up to whatever fantasies he might have concocted on this dark night. Sometimes, familiarity really only breeds contempt. Better to leave him with his dreams and just move on.

Then a cop car pulled up beside us, its red lights slashing through the dark, scattering like shattered glass ricocheting off every wet and rainy surface to create a phantasmagorical scene filled with brilliant blood-red explosions of light. He asked to see our identification. We pulled out our wallets and we continued talking about the issues of the day while the officer satisfied himself that there were no outstanding warrants for either of us.

After a while, the cop pulled away and we were alone again and walking past an area where the road curled tightly around a cutoff hill that was about twenty feet high. I paused and when there were no cars in view, I said, "Come on!" and we quickly scrambled to the top and out of sight of the police and anyone else who might be interested. We walked away from the edge and into a stand of young pine trees. I had intended to drop my bedroll under a tree and hope that the rain would stop or stay as only a light drizzle through the rest of the night. But there in front of us was an old rusted hulk of a car, lying long-abandoned in the woods. We scrambled inside and sat on the empty floor just as the rain returned and pelted the rooftop. We were hippie Hardy Boys, dodging the cops, talking subversion in an old wrecked car in the rainy woods.

Eventually, I declined his offers to visit the campus. I had to get back and pay my rent, and take care of a few other things. And besides, every other time I've been thrust into the position of guru by someone younger, I've been a tremendous disappointment. Some people cultivate the role of leader and they often end up with a gullible following, the kind of people I really don't want to hang out with. Some of us are occasionally introduced as "experts" on a subject by a well-meaning person. But soon after we open our mouths we're exposed as pompous assholes. I was sure his vivid descriptions of me were going to be more impressive to his friends than the reality.

We talked well into the night, and eventually the rain let up and he left through the damp darkness of the woods. I rolled out my bedroll and slept soundly to the occasional drumming of new waves of rain on an old rusty car roof.

The morning skies were clear and blue and the air was clean, and after an early breakfast of whatever was in my pack I climbed down to the road and put out my thumb again, and I got lucky. She was young and beautiful and she was on her way to Durango. The morning sun nuzzled into the brown softness of her hair. She was very friendly and went by the name of E.T., but she wouldn't say much more about herself. I could understand that. She really didn't know anything at all about me.

I was immediately infatuated with this young woman who was adventurous enough to pick up a hitchhiker on the Interstate. Not many women will do that. Mostly, it's the blue-collar, working-class guy who pulls his car or truck over to the side of the road and asks, "Where ya goin' buddy?"

But it was a bright, sunny morning and I was looking reasonably presentable. She had a long way to go and she probably wanted some conversation to pass the time. And it's just as likely she felt a bit guilty driving a big, empty American sedan a few hundred miles across the desert, and she didn't want to leave some poor, unfortunate guy standing in the dirt a long way from home. I don't know but I was very glad she stopped, and I told her so.

I managed to find out that she was headed back to college after a summer at home in California. She said she had never been to Albuquerque, so I tried to describe some of the good things that were happening at the university, some of the very interesting and unique architecture of the area, and that multicultural mix of peoples who inhabit the Rio Grande Valley from Taos south to Las Cruces. I was painting a romantic picture of life under the robust cottonwood trees that line the ancient, history-laden banks of the river. I was, of course, hoping I'd convince her to come home with me and we'd live in glorious happiness forever. We could build a little adobe house under towering trees down by the *acequia*, grow our own food, and raise a beautiful family. I imagined her riding beside me in my old bug-eyed Austin Healey Sprite that was parked and waiting back in Albuquerque.

She listened politely to my glowing descriptions and laughed easily at my jokes, but it was clear she had other things on her mind. She was probably thinking about the boyfriend she hadn't seen all summer. It was just as well, anyway. What was I going to tell her when she saw the one-room hovel I lived in? The one I paid $60 a month for, utilities included, with a couple of dirty motorcycle engines lying in pieces and covering the tiny floor of the living room/kitchen/bedroom. With the old outhouse nailed on the back wall. I hadn't even cleaned the place up before I left.

E.T. pulled her car over on the outskirts of Winslow and stopped to pick up another bearded young hitchhiker who was also wearing denim and carrying a backpack with a bedroll lashed on top, and that was the end of any private conversation we might have had. His name was Matt. He sat in the back seat and we talked for a while, then I read a book as the miles passed beneath us. She probably picked him up as a way to isolate herself from me. At Gallup, E.T. dropped us both off at the edge of town since she was headed north to Durango. Matt had a surprised look on his face because he thought I was with her and I hadn't said anything to correct that impression since he got into the car. E.T. took a slip of paper that I had written my phone number on in case she ever got to Albuquerque, but I knew she would never call.

Matt and I waved goodbye as E.T. drove away and headed north to Durango, then we split up since it was unlikely that anyone would pick us both up at the same time. Soon I saw a car pull over down the road a ways and give Matt a ride, and within about an hour, I got lucky again too.

Or at least I caught another ride. Interesting might be a better word than lucky to describe the experience, but I was moving farther toward Albuquerque, and I was no longer just standing beside the road.

It was a faded orange-red 1957 Chevy Nomad station wagon that ambled slowly off the road just past where I was standing and came to a laborious, gravel-crunching stop like an overloaded cargo plane. I grabbed my stuff and ran to where the car was waiting. The area behind the front seat was completely full of boxes and bags that were overflowing with, I don't know, probably the driver's life possessions. The old guy at the wheel introduced himself as John. He wore a broad and simple smile as he cleared a space on the front seat for me and he waited as I struggled to find room in the back for my gear. He looked half Indian and half Spanish. I climbed in and closed the door and we sat there in the car several minutes while he studied the side- and rear-view mirrors, watery-eyed, until the highway was almost completely empty of traffic.

Then he pulled very carefully onto the highway so as not to spill the red-colored liquid he was carrying in a large old paper cup. It looked almost chemical-like—a lot like antifreeze, in fact—but I wasn't curious enough to ask him what it was. And I was afraid he might want to share some of it with me. Shortly we were rolling down the Interstate at, oh, 40-45 miles per hour while the commerce of the nation ripped past us at speeds up to twice what we were traveling. I just hoped everyone else was paying a lot more attention to their driving than John was, and that we wouldn't get rear-ended by a semi-truck from traveling so slowly on a major highway. But there wasn't a whole lot I could do about it short of getting out of the car and taking my chances with someone else. He wasn't driving recklessly, and despite whatever he was drinking he wasn't even weaving down the highway. He was just incredibly slow.

And talkative. He told stories that blended, one into the other. And I just listened politely and responded with an occasional "Uh huh." I never quite figured out exactly where he was from, or where he was going. It didn't actually sound like he was in the process of going anywhere in particular. And it just seemed that he carried all that stuff in the back of the car on the off chance that he might need something and he wouldn't have it. As far as I could tell, he was just out for a day-drive cross-country, and he certainly wasn't in any hurry to get anywhere.

Occasionally, John would notice that his drink was getting low and he would pull laboriously over onto the shoulder to refresh it. Going as slow as he was, it always seemed to take an incredibly long distance to stop the car. Whenever he stopped, he never pulled very far off the highway either. At each of his frequent stops I worried that both John and the driver's-side door would be caught by one of those heavy long-haul trucks and that he would become instant hamburger when he swung the door open and stepped out onto the pavement. More than once my ears rang with the blast of a heavy air horn as a large diesel truck came within inches of the car. Meanwhile, John calmly ambled to the rear of the car, opened the tailgate door and busied himself concocting another round of whatever he was drinking. He seemed completely unflappable and content, and nothing seemed to bother him much. Once safely back in the driver's seat, he would wait for another long break in the traffic before pulling slowly back onto the pavement. We also pulled into every rest stop along the way since he was putting away a lot of fluids and had a frequent need to relieve himself.

We traveled the 70 miles to Grants in about two and a half hours and John pulled over at the first exit because he wanted to visit some friends in a local bar. I guess a fellow can build up a powerful thirst traveling seventy miles and he just needed another drink. He also explained that, since I was kind of a hippie, he didn't want his friends to see me with him. I was astounded and amused by his honesty, and I gathered my gear from the back of the car to try my luck on the road again. I was only 75 miles from home and I was pretty sure I could get a ride the rest of the way. But before pulling away, John assured me that if I was still here after he had visited for a while he'd pick me up again.

I smiled and thanked him for his kindness, and I waved goodbye as the great red beast continued slowly down the exit and off toward the nearest bar. It had been an interesting ride and he was a nice guy, but I was relieved to see him go.

I was enjoying the warm, sunny afternoon and there was a nice little breeze blowing across the high desert, bending the tassels of grama grass and cooling the dry earth beneath. I stood there looking hopeful on the shoulder of the road with my thumb out and a broad grin plastered across my face as the traffic of the nation roared past just a couple of feet away. Large trucks with heavy-laden trailers, station wagons filled with vacationing families, pickup trucks carrying Navajo families or local ranchers, I watched them stream past in a mighty flood, each driver bent on his own destination. Each vehicle containing a story, even a saga of a life lived poorly or well. The commerce of life carried on as it always had through the ages. A hundred years ago, there might have been a guy like me standing right here at this same spot at the edge of Grants, New Mexico waiting for a wagon or a buckboard to catch a ride east. The only thing that had changed was the speed and comfort of the transportation.

The steady roar of traffic continued with only an occasional break, and I stood there with my backpack and bedroll waiting for the weak link in this roaring steel chain. Sooner or later someone would feel guilty about leaving me standing by the road. He'd pull over and give me a lift, and before long we'd be in Albuquerque. I was even close enough that I could probably walk there in a couple of days if I had a canteen to carry some water. And I had to admit the thought was mighty intriguing, the solitude was beckoning me again.

But the traffic screamed past in a solid and unyielding steel wall. There were no weak links in the chain. Nobody would even let me ride in the back of a pickup truck. I would have been happy with that; I only had 70-odd miles to go. It couldn't be all that bad. I figured at this rate I might well end up sleeping right here at the edge of Grants among the cactus under a star-filled desert night. My luck was usually better in the morning, anyway. And so I stood there by the highway for a couple more hours and planned where I'd camp out for the night, until I looked up and saw an old faded-reddish '57 Chevy wagon rolling very slowly down the on-ramp.

I nodded my head and smiled expectantly with my thumb in the roaring metal breeze, hoping John had not forgotten his offer while he was drinking with his buddies. The old red car pulled just past me onto the shoulder and rumbled slowly to a stop, and I grabbed my stuff again and ran after him. He opened the door, smiled his trademark liquor-befuddled grin, and greeted me like an old friend. I stowed my gear and we were off once again. Very slowly.

The next 70 miles was a repeat of the trip from Gallup. Frequent stops to refresh the ever-present drink and more stops for my highway angel to relieve himself. We inched our way to Albuquerque while John told me about his friends who inhabited various bars along the way and generally repeated the stories he had told on that first leg of our trip. My contribution was mostly limited to "Uh huh," "Imagine that," "And then what happened?" Although by then I usually already knew the answer to the last question. Still, it didn't cost me anything to be nice to the old guy, and we were getting to Albuquerque faster than when I was standing at the Grants on-ramp.

It was late in the afternoon when we finally crested the last hill and the city of Albuquerque lay before us straddling the Rio Grande Valley like some kind of evil smoke-belching octopus. We took the old Route 66/Central Avenue exit and rumbled on toward town. The city of cars and sprawling subdivisions lay before me once again under a burning desert sun. I was home.

Well, I was almost home. My well-lubricated friend pulled onto a gravel shoulder at the very edge of the city and let me out again, just in case any of his friends might be sober enough to see us together. We'd had a nice time, but I was still a hippie and he still had a reputation of sorts to maintain. And I was thankful that at least he never offered me a cup of whatever he was drinking. The idea never came up and I had to count myself lucky on that.

I was glad to be back, and I was grateful for the ride. It was probably another seven miles or so to my grubby little apartment but it was mostly downhill, and I was actually looking forward to a nice long walk after being cramped up in cars and a bus for the past two days. I thanked him again for the ride, and I waved goodbye with a feeling of great relief mingled with actual affection for the guy. There was also a touch of envy in my soul for John's simple, and maybe simplistic, outlook on life, and his willingness to trust everything to the fates, to God, to whatever. He rolled off slowly down Central Avenue, and far in the distance I saw him pull into the parking lot of a small West-side bar. When I walked past a few minutes later, John was safely inside the dark and windowless bar among friends. And I was striding down the sidewalk with a pack on my back and a broad smile on my desert-tanned face.

"How are you doing back there?" Mark's voice sounded like it was echoing inside a large steel drum. I looked up to see him smiling at me in the rear-view mirror, his face framed by his curly, reddish-tinged beard.

"Fine." I said. "Just, um, fine." I was still in a joint-fueled haze surrounded by the clouds bearing my thoughts and I felt insulated from the world. I sincerely hoped Mark was handling the dope better than I was since he was doing the driving. He looked away and back toward the road. Linda was staring absently into the desert ahead. The weed was just starting to lose its mellow forward edge, and I began to ease slowly out of my reverie. I thought of Annie, again.

To me, she was very pretty—in a non-glamorous, farm girl kind of way—and she was born in Montana, a true young woman of the West. She worked as a waitress at a local barbecue stand while she went to journalism school at the university. I first saw her when I stopped to get lunch one day, and I wanted to get to know her but I couldn't think of anything to say that would sound un-stupid. I smiled and she smiled back. She had a beautiful friendly smile and I wanted to get to know the person behind it.

I was so unsure of myself I didn't go back for a couple of weeks. When I finally returned, she surprised by treating me to a slice of the cook's famous apple pie. I shyly thanked her and paid the rest of the bill before walking across the parking lot to my old Ford pickup truck in a light fall drizzle. As I backed my truck away from the side of the building and pointed it toward the street, I could see Annie leaving as she got off work. She pulled a barrette out of her hair and ran through the rain to cross the street on her way home, her long, curly, brownish-blonde hair streamed behind her in the breeze. I pulled up beside her and asked if she wanted a ride so she wouldn't get all wet. She looked aside, briefly thoughtful, then opened the passenger side door and climbed in with a happy laugh. It was an early evening in the fall and we were warm and dry, and everything was suddenly wonderful, as we drove on through glistening and leaf-spattered side streets.

Annie shared a small older house with a young married couple named Barbara and Fred. We had hot tea and split a muffin while we talked about school, the recent demonstrations on campus, the latest books we had read. As I was leaving, I asked if she wanted to catch a movie on Thursday night, but she had late classes. Instead, she asked me to stop by after her last class.

When I arrived that night, the house was dark and it looked deserted. I thought I had misunderstood something about the time I was supposed to arrive and maybe I was early, or maybe it was the wrong night. But as I knocked on the door, I noticed a candle flickering in a red glass jar on a table faintly visible through lace curtains.

Annie slowly opened the door wearing only a simple blue nightgown. She smiled shyly, handed me a glass of wine and stuck a lighted joint between my lips as she started to unbutton my shirt.

"Barbara and Fred are in Denver for the rest of the week," she said quietly. And then she put her finger to my lips when I started to reply.

"So you finally found someone to put up with your bullshit," Fred later told Annie. She laughed when she told me about it. I didn't know what he meant at the time and I let it pass. There are times when it's best not to know everything. I don't want people to know everything about my own past, and maybe hold it against me, so I didn't ask Annie about it.

Within a month we had rented a house together in the South Valley and three months after that, in January of 1970, we were married. Annie was radiant in a simple, flowered dress with fresh cut flowers in her curly brownish hair. I wore broad-striped bell-bottom trousers, a red shirt, and a paisley vest. We had a simple ceremony, and Annie made sure the preacher deleted all that biblical reference to "woman being the lesser vessel." I was good with that because I wanted a partner and not a dependent, not a disciple. I pressed a dimestore rhinestone ring on her middle finger while the Fifth Dimension sang "This is the Dawning of the Age of Aquarius" on a scratchy LP and everyone danced at what felt like the beginning of a new age. It was a truly wonderful time to be alive and young and in love, leaving the strictures of the past behind.

Several months later I told her I was intrigued when I first saw her running through the chilly rain that night, and she laughed a little nervously. She had watched me getting into my truck and decided to leave work just a bit early. She had pulled the barrette from her hair and ran through the rain in wonderful abandon hoping that I would notice. The whole thing had been a ploy for me to stop and pick her up because it didn't seem like I was ever going to get up the nerve to ask her out. I didn't mind the ruse. I was glad that she was brave enough to break the ice, because I was not. Life had indeed been simple then.

The reality turned out to be far from simple. With Annie, I soon learned there was never anything, any feeling, any emotion I could actually rely on. One moment's enthusiasm could be the next moment's painful reversal. Every question always had many answers, every statement had many interpretations—and it seemed that my feelings and my assumptions were usually wrong. Our relationship had begun on a simple note but it soon became a challenge. And the challenge made her somehow compelling.

There had always been puzzles inside of questions when it came to Annie. It seemed there were never any real answers, only contradictions, and nothing was ever simple —although everything had appeared to be so simple when we met.

Somewhere our early relationship had become a marriage. Because, I guess that's what society expects of us and we were too young then to realize there might be options.

At some point on our journey together things began to deteriorate, and our relationship started to slide inexorably downward into a morass of recrimination. And then it finally became a brutal game, a mental battle to the finish from which neither of us could emerge victorious, or even whole. We began drawing each other downward in a terminal vortex, leaving nothing but an empty shell where there had once been a relationship based on youthful hope, trust, passion, and idealism. Finally, we were both exhausted by the conflicts that we had created and there was nothing to do but to end it.

Mark and Linda still had a caring and respectful relationship, a strong partnership, after more than a decade together. Theirs was more than just a marriage. My marriage to Annie had survived barely three years.

At the very last we agreed that if Annie typed out the divorce papers, I would pay the twenty-dollar court fee. And then it was finally, legally, over.

And I blame myself for it as much as I blame Annie.

Outside the rattling windows of Mark's old VW bus, cattle were grazing in the high-desert grasslands that lie to the west of Isleta Pueblo. The large volcanic mass of Wind Mesa stood black and timeless against the western sky, its eastern face illuminated in the remaining morning light.

In summer, the rich colors of sunset also linger here in the desert West and a crystalline light fills the air long after that roaring, burning globe has finally slid from the sky. Then the western horizon goes flat against a glowing curtain of reds hanging full across the heavens. The faces of the western mountains become featureless and the ragged edges of the peaks that rake like broken saw teeth across the sky begin to look like a vast unframed composition of torn paper mountains in vibrant layers of browns and purples and maroons.

3   DRIVING

Onward and southward we roared as fast as a rattling old VW bus can go, down an almost-empty freeway toward the desert lands of southern New Mexico. We crossed over the river bridge just north of Isleta Pueblo where the muddy-brown flow gives life to an ancient cottonwood bosque and now we were almost past the irrigated fields of the Isleta people that lie along the western edge of this broad valley. Early bands of hunter-gatherers came into this fertile valley about ten thousand years ago, and left traces in nearby mountain caves. And maybe some people were tilling crops here two thousand years ago. I remembered reading somewhere that it is generally believed the Pueblo of Isleta was established around 1300 A.D. by Tiwa peoples who left their homes in the western mountains during a period of terrible droughts in the late 1200s. And fewer than 500 years ago the Spanish arrived with their strange gods, demanding submission from the Pueblo peoples living here and farther north.

During the Pueblo Revolt of 1680, the northern Pueblos of Towa-, Tiwa-, Tewa-, Tano-, and Keres-speaking peoples united with nomadic Comanches and Apaches in a religious war of their own to drive out the Spanish oppressors and their hated new religion. More than eighty years of Spanish domination had finally unified the tribes in a common cause. The ancient gods would be restored throughout the entire region.

The rebellion broke out at Taos Pueblo in the far northern valley as armed tribesmen killed priests and settlers at outlying communities before marching on the capital. When they arrived at Santa Fe hundreds of warriors were killed by the superior weapons of the Spanish, but ultimately the greater numbers of the unified tribes prevailed and Governor Otermín ordered a retreat down the small Santa Fe River to its intersection with the Rio Grande and onward along the valley to distant El Paso del Norte, the original gateway to the unknown lands of New Mexico for many of the early Spanish conquerors.

With memories of the bloody Revolt still fresh in their minds, many of the settlers wanted to continue on to safety in Chihuahua, but Otermín ordered a halt. They would stay at El Paso and wait until times were favorable for their return to New Mexico. Both Otermín and his successor would make attempts to reconquer New Mexico over the next decade without success.

But during that period, the great southwestern native confederacy would dissolve in bitter infighting and ancient rivalries. Ultimately this intertribal warfare severely weakened the alliance until, in 1692, the Spanish reentered New Mexico with a band of soldiers in a bloodless *Reconquista* under the command of Captain General Diego de Vargas Zapata Lujan Ponce de Leon y Contreras. These days, we just call him Don Diego de Vargas.

During the retreat, the Southern Tiwa peoples at Isleta had given shelter to the fleeing Spaniards and many joined the Spanish retreat southward. They would establish a new pueblo named *Isleta del Sur* near present-day El Paso. After the reconquest, other Isletas who had fled west to the Hopi lands returned to rebuild their homes and fields at Isleta;

but many of those who fled with the Spanish still remain today, far to the south, at the pueblo of Isleta del Sur.

All this history marks another part of the endless ebb and flow of human occupation here in the valley. It remains a rich history that lies open upon the ground—I could see it passing by just out the window. It's an indelible history of which even I am now a part.

"Why did you two ever get married in the first place?"

Linda's question brought me back to the present and I turned toward her. Her blue eyes were so beautiful that morning in the slanting light of the desert sun. Her long blonde hair was flowing in a warm breeze that poured like water through the open windows. I found myself wishing I knew someone just like her to share my life and adventures, that we could go away together, deep into the heart and deep into the mysteries of Mexico. She wanted to know more about me this morning, about my feelings, my hopes, my dreams. Women are like that.

Guys want to know what kind of truck you drive, how much it can haul, how big the engine is, what gas mileage it gets. It's guy code, words and phrases about trucks, tools, possessions. It's how they know you, or at least as much as they really want to know you. I've always been more comfortable talking about my truck than about my feelings.

"I'm still not really sure why we got married," I said. I needed more time to think about the question that I had been thinking about constantly for months now and still didn't have an answer to. There was the undeniable sexual attraction, of course, although that wasn't enough to get married over. She once said that I was her best and her worst lover. I thought that Annie and I had actually gotten married because we really did feel a strong commonality with each other. But I think we each also hoped it would repair some jagged holes in our personal lives before we met, and that we had tried to ignore. But how do you honestly explain something like that to another person, a third person? It implies there was something very wrong in each of us to begin with, doesn't it? That each of us was an incomplete person and we each had a very important part missing. The fantasy remains that marriage is supposed to cure those problems. Isn't that the way it's supposed to work?

"It was really just the thing that seemed to be right for us to do at the time." I felt myself mumbling something to fill the embarrassing silence. What kind of phony answer was that supposed to be? Why couldn't I have stumbled into something better, maybe even something brilliant?

Linda could tell I was dodging it, that I was not willing or able to confront the truth of my time with Annie. She knew I was hiding in my dark den of confusion. I was a fearful and bleeding animal behind a flimsy screen of borrowed words and worn phrases. There was really nothing of substance left. Nothing more inside a painful and empty shell.

Mark looked into the rear-view mirror and saw me staring into the loving embrace of Linda's eyes.

"How well is the urban communal thing working, anyway?" I changed the subject.

I really was interested in the workings of their commune, although I wasn't sure that it could ever work for me. Not since my own communal experience during a winter in Taos about seven years earlier.

September 1967

We were supposed to become a "working commune," whatever that meant, when a group of us settled into a large old adobe house on Ledoux Street about a block or two west of the Plaza in Taos. Some of us started a gallery, some ran a bakery, we had a woodworking shop, and a few others had jobs around town. What a "working commune" really meant for us was that some of the people involved did a lot of extra work—as a good example perhaps, or maybe they were just driven to work harder— and others spent their time hanging around the kitchen table talking about the glories of communal life without producing much at all. I would place myself somewhere in the middle of this group—I was not one of the driven ones, but I felt too guilty to just hang out all day as another "kitchen-table philosopher."

I spent my days working with a guy named Christofer making wooden toy-like objects to teach simple math skills at a Montessori school in Santa Fe. One of this size would equal two of that size, or three of the next size, or four of this other size, and so on. One of the problems was that Christofer was a former college English teacher; he was smart and diligent, but he wasn't much of a woodworker. He and I were relegated to the cold and dusty garage while others sat around a big table in the warm kitchen enjoying the latest products of the communal oven.

I don't know if "Christofer" was his original name or not, I mean with the "f" instead of the "ph," or even if he had some entirely different name that he wanted to forget, like Elmer or Oscar, maybe. A lot of people were reinventing themselves and their entire life histories in those days of youthful rebellion, and it was hard to figure out who was legitimate and who was phony with a completely fabricated background. And most of the time it really didn't matter, as long as the dope held out and the stories were good. Other people were looking for a guru to give meaning to their lives and spent little time working on getting their own act together. And with people casting each other into one category or another, I had trouble keeping track of who I was supposed to be at least part of the time.

"Christofer," or whatever his name really was, had been a writer of occasional fallacious feature articles for *The National Eye*, a cheap scurrilous supermarket rag. He could fabricate a completely phony story, take blurry pictures of his friends or his girlfriend to go with it and sell it to this rag that was run by some guy he knew. His story about gays on Venice Beach, with himself and a buddy in the fuzzy pictures, made it to the centerfold of the *Eye*. Christofer got three hundred dollars for that centerfold piece, enough to live on for a month or two. Another story had a photo of a young boy standing at the edge of a cliff in some National Park. His right arm was extended and he had a broad smile on his face. That story was about how he'd just pushed his sister off the cliff just as his horrified mother snapped the photo. There was something really sick about Christofer, though I enjoyed having a witty fellow inmate to share the dungeon-garage and the toy-making project as fall gradually gave way to a cold winter in the mountains of northern New Mexico. We spent a lot of time laughing, but our work got sloppier as the days progressed.

One day Christofer and I decided to take a break and go check out what was happening among some of the other semi-enlightened young people who had migrated to Taos over the past few years. It was a warm sunny day, so we stopped at the Presbyterian Church to recruit two other guys who'd come to town recently as part of a thespian group and the four of us went out to see how things were going a little north of town at a commune called New Buffalo.

Harold and Ed were both from New York City and they weren't actually Presbyterians, or any other kind of religion either. They had signed on to this thespian gig as a meal ticket for a few months and as a way to see some of the country. Before they got the job, neither of them had actually been very far out of the City, so this was all a big adventure for them. They were decent actors who had gotten tired of waiting for the call around stage doors off-Broadway and thought they might as well hit the road for a while. Their thespian group would get bookings wherever they could, usually at small colleges or progressive churches. They would put on a series of plays over two or three nights, then they would have a few days off to look around before they got back on the bus and drove to the next gig. They were glad to tag along for the afternoon with Christofer and me.

There was a lot of interesting stuff happening in Taos then, in the late 1960s. Somehow the word had gotten around that we were a kind of nexus for polar energies, if I got the logic straight. I think we were supposed to be on the exact other side of the world from Tibet, a place with strong psychic powers, although I couldn't figure out how that was true since we were both in the northern hemisphere. But hey, this was the 60s and magic was in the air, and who was keeping track anyway? Most of us felt that as long as it somehow led to peace and harmony in the world, why bother with the details?

One of the interesting things going on around Taos at the time was the commune at New Buffalo just north of town, so the four of us went out to take a look. In the fall of 1967, the community house was still under construction and we thought we could lend a hand hoisting a few beams or helping out in some other way. We drove north and turned off the highway onto a narrow dirt road which we followed until we saw the unmarked gate we were told to look for, and we stopped at the driveway.

One of the things I remember most vividly about every "alternative" building project I ever saw in those days was the mud. The gods must have been trying to tell us something because I never was associated with a single one of those projects that didn't include massive quantities of mud. It stuck to your boots and clothing and it was slippery. As if the process of adobe and beam construction wasn't difficult enough already, try strapping an extra ten pounds onto each of your feet before starting and then grease the soles of your boots for good measure.

We took one look at the deep muddy morass of the driveway and parked our borrowed car along the narrow dirt road, leaving just enough room for other cars to squeeze by. And then we tromped our way through a stand of tall grass beside the muddy driveway that led toward New Buffalo. As we drew closer a young, blonde, and very beautiful woman bounded down the hill to meet us and welcome us. She was wearing a pair of wonderfully well-fitted jeans...and nothing else. Now, Christofer and I had gotten somewhat used to the freedom of the alternative lifestyle around Taos and we were appreciative of this warm welcome. As we all stood around her trying to ask relevant questions and not be seen as leering morons, I noticed that Harold and Ed each seemed to have gone into some sort of altered state. Their jaws were hanging and they were having difficulty being coherent. I got the impression they had each just become seriously interested in joining whatever Movement she may have represented.

As for me, I was trying hard not to let my eyes wander far from the topics of world peace and brotherhood, but I noticed that whenever she turned to look at me, Christofer's eyes wandered as far as they wanted. For the four of us, and especially for Harold and Ed, it was a singular experience and not one soon to be forgotten.

Everything that happened after that initial encounter was anticlimactic. The rest of the tour was interesting in a philosophical way, but our minds had been seriously detoured and we really weren't into absorbing the details of communal life. Despite our best efforts it was impossible to focus on the larger picture of community, partnership, and peace and to ignore the sheer sexual pleasure suggested, but not offered, by this beautiful, bare-breasted young woman who accompanied us through the entire project and took ample time to answer all our questions. There really wasn't much else going on the day we stopped in anyway and there weren't many other people about. Just one guy who probably had carnal aspirations of his own and who just seemed to wish we'd leave. Some outlying buildings were under construction but sitting idle and we offered to come back to help when we could, but that never actually happened. Our own communal experience was in serious trouble and we had our hands full at the time.

During the autumn months we managed to patch our communal life together for a while and produce just enough to pay our bills. Then we reached something of a high point with the traditional festivities of Thanksgiving and we celebrated outdoors with a gathering of friends in a small canyon tucked deep in the mountains east of town. A grey sky, heavy with snow, hung low overhead and a pungent layer of piñon wood smoke drifted from the fire and settled among the trees. Red-brown oak leaves mingled with yellow aspen leaves in a scattered carpet upon the ground. Several of us had gone to the site a day early to dig a pit for roasting the young goat, a *cabrito*, we bought from a local farmer. And now the rocks were still warm as we pulled back a layer of protecting soil and opened the pit to release the savory smells of well-cooked meat. We sat on logs and patches of grass enjoying the tenderest of meat, with hearty mashed potatoes, vegetables, and several kinds of pie as a light snow began to fall. It was a welcome break from our communal life and we laughed easily with each other for the last time before returning to our group endeavors. The snow began to fall more heavily as we sat by the fire with hands cupped around hot drinks. Too soon the moment was over and we packed up everything for the journey back to town, through slick winding mountain roads. Bits of strained conversation tested the air, then yielded to empty silence as we followed two narrowing tracks of wet-black pavement in the darkness through the gathering snow.

Our sloppy production in the workshop couldn't last. We became cynical at being exiled from the group and spent more of our time in guilty laughter at Christofer's endless supply of jokes and stories. The output from the workshop became an embarrassment and our contract was soon canceled. The gallery and the bakery didn't make any money either since they had nothing of particular interest or quality to offer; and those who had outside jobs grew tired of turning over their paychecks to feed a large, hungry, and unproductive household. The whole communal thing disintegrated after six months in hard feelings and animosity. We somehow survived past the Christmas season, and during the cold and icy reality of a January day we ended our communal experience. It was hardly the "peace and love generation" at its best.

As far as I could tell, the main reason for our spectacular failure was that each member was an equal partner and nobody could make any decisions without endless meetings and attempts at consensus. And everyone involved was too independent to work well together. Accusations—some justified, others not—were leveled at various members during our after-dinner joint meetings, but the purpose seemed to be as much about deflecting justifiable criticism as about improving the commune. The most verbally adept among us seemed to come out best in the process, even if they really had little ability to formulate a reasonable plan for our salvation. I did a lot of soul-searching over the months after I left the commune and I tried to come to a resolution with myself over it. I'm not sure my ideas were the best for everyone either, but I came away from the experience thinking that smaller and less-complicated arrangements were probably better for me personally.

Honestly, there was really no way around it. I had failed as a commune member. But I had never been a good communal person at any time in the past, so there wasn't a good reason to think that I was cut out for it, anyway. That's just the way things were. I have usually preferred to do things on my own, and it seemed there was always something that needed doing that didn't require the approval of a governing body of my peers. It was time to move forward with some of the neglected aspects of my life.

I moved back to Albuquerque, got a job on a construction crew, and rented a small cheap apartment that gave me the freedom to pursue things. I was ready for some other kind of adventure.

June 1968

Janice settled into the driver's seat of my old bug-eyed Sprite and smiled at the thought of having it to drive for the next several weeks. She looked up and blew me a perfunctory kiss, then she punched the gearshift into first and made a u-turn across the highway to the median during a break in traffic. The morning desert wind ruffled her short blondish hair as she turned into a westbound traffic lane, picked up speed, and left me standing by the road out in Tijeras Canyon east of town, with my battered red backpack and sleeping bag sitting on the ground beside me. I listened for a moment as the mellow rumble of that four-cylinder Austin-Healey engine receded into the distance. She didn't seem to have any trouble with that balky second gear that I had warned her about. A couple of years ago, someone had used a can of bright red spray paint to spell L-O-V-E in large letters across the rear of the car over the old faded light-blue factory finish while it was parked outside a local coffee shop. It had seemed like a good idea back in the summer of 1966, so I just left it that way, and my friends called it The Lovemobile. Soon this spectacle faded from view and I was left standing alone on the shoulder of Interstate 40 watching the commerce of the nation roll by at high speed.

My relationship with Janice had always been casual. It was like we were both killing time and waiting for something more interesting to come along. As she cruised back down the highway toward town, I knew that she was actually glad I was leaving town for awhile and letting her use my car. I was pretty sure she was going to look up Brian while I was gone, and I really couldn't blame her. There wasn't much going on in our relationship, anyway, and I was actually kind of hoping she would just go ahead and pull the plug. Or maybe I should do it. Either way, we'd both be better off.

The roar of heavy traffic draining into the countryside from the heart of the city brought me back to the reason I was standing on the graveled shoulder of one of the main cross-country highways of the nation. I had ten bucks in my pocket, plus a loaf of bread, two bananas, and some small tins of cheap meat spread in my duffle. And I had tossed in a few small cans of chopped green chiles because I figured I'd be heading east into a green-chile desert. I brushed back my longish hair in an effort to look more-or-less non-threatening and semi-civilized, and then I stuck out my thumb. It was a long way to Washington DC, and I had a promise to keep.

Jimmy, my first ride, was an affable rancher who was only going about 40 miles east before he turned south to his ranch on the high plains near Vaughn. He was a quiet man and slender as a rail, and he smoked continuously. It was a hot summer day, and the noise of the wind blowing through the open windows of his old faded-green Ford pickup truck generally kept our conversation to a minimum, but Jimmy wanted to tell me about his ranch anyway.

"There's a lot of pretty grassland down there 'round t' place. But the winters are a bitch." He smiled at the thought through crooked, yellow-stained teeth. There was a round tin of Skoal in his left shirt pocket. I smiled and nodded and tried to think of something to say.

"How big is your ranch?" I asked and waited for the answer. There were long pauses between sentences. We had lots of time.

"Got a couple hunderd acres an' a two-bedroom house with electricity an' a well," he continued, "but it's real hard to make a livin' these days ranchin'."

"How many cows you run out there at your place?" It seemed like a safe question to ask, considering I didn't know a damn thing about ranching. Still, I did know that cowboys "run" cows out on ranches.

"Depends on th' year," Jimmy went on slowly and paused again while we edged down the highway in his old truck. Big heavy rigs blasted by us in the passing lane, and Jimmy's beat-up, dirty, straw Stetson managed to stay rigidly connected to his scalp in the buffeting breeze as if glued there by decades of Brylcreem.

"Some years you get a lot of rain early and th' grass is good." He picked up the conversation again. We had plenty of time. "Other years, there's no rain at all."

"Well, on average, about how many cows would you have?" I tried again.

"Not much way a knowin'," Jimmy said, " Sometimes th' summer rains come jist in time 'n ya don't have t' sell off yer stock 'til they're fat in the fall."

I wasn't really sure if Jimmy even knew exactly how many cows he had on the ranch anyway and I was becoming aware that it probably didn't even matter. He appeared to lead a seamless and uncomplicated lifestyle where he just took whatever cards he was dealt and made the most of them. I got the impression that if he needed some money for another sack of beans or cornmeal, he would just go sell a cow to pay for it. He didn't seem to have any larger plan, and as far as I could tell he was happy with that.

We made our way slowly down the Interstate with scraps of conversation floating in the air between us waiting for some kind of appropriate reply. Eventually Jimmie pulled his old Ford onto the broad shoulder as we came to the off-ramp for US Highway 285, a narrow asphalt ribbon that winds southeasterly across the deserted and open eastern grassland plains toward Vaughn, Roswell, Artesia, and Carlsbad. I had been down that road once several years ago. It was a spooky two-lane road through lonely country full of sinkholes from eroded and collapsed limestone caverns deep in the earth below. Whenever I had driven that road, it always felt as if cows, horses, people, whatever, could be swallowed by one of those festering caverns we all knew were down there struggling toward the surface as if they were desperate to breathe the clean free air above. As I drove along on that warm summer day years ago, I wondered who would disappear next. Maybe the highway would just open up beneath the weight of my wheels and the next victim would be me. My life would end as a minor footnote in the continuing evolution of the earth.

I thanked Jimmie for the ride as I stepped down onto the gravel shoulder and grabbed my pack and sleeping bag from the worn bed of a pickup truck that was more accustomed to hauling cattle and hay. A light morning breeze bent the lush full seed heads of the grama grass that filled the roadside. It had been a good spring so far, and the gentle hills had a greenish hue to them. Jimmie paused for a moment while I walked around to the driver's window.

"Just wanted to wish you luck on your adventure," he said and reached out to shake my hand. "Washington's a long way's off, an' I bet yur gonna have a few adventures along th' way. I ain't never been t' Washington myself. I bet it's real interestin'."

He was suddenly talkative, now that our common pathway had come to an end. I was probably the very first hippie hitchhiker he'd ever picked up, and I hadn't even bit him, or anything. There was a look of sincerity in his deep-blue eyes, mingled with a little envy and even respect, as he held my hand a little longer and a little tighter than he probably did normally. I thanked him again and I agreed there were probably many adventures on the road ahead, but I was still young and I didn't have much responsibility in the world just yet. It was a good time to be on the road. His eyes said he understood why I was going and why it was too late for him. He had land and he had cows that depended on his safe return to the ranch every few days to check on the water supply, the salt blocks, and all the other stuff on that endless list that people call "responsibility."

Jimmie regained his composure; the brief moment of unaccustomed male intimacy had passed. "If ya ever get down to Vaughn stop by out to th' ranch. Jist ask anybody 'round Vaughn where Jimmie Reed's place is. They'll tell ya. You git out to th' middle of nowhere an' it's about twenty-five miles past that. But it's real pretty there, an' real quiet too."

I watched as Jimmie looked away. He put the old truck in gear, pulled slowly onto the southbound asphalt, and finally disappeared beyond a distant hill, the only vehicle on a lonely highway. He and I both knew the moment was over. I would never stop for a visit at the old Reed Ranch. We both knew that, too. And I was alone again beside this small chunk of the endless mother road, the unbroken web of asphalt and concrete that connects every part of the nation. I looked down that asphalt ribbon toward the eastern horizon and imagined that I could almost see the tall buildings of Oklahoma City, Memphis, Chicago, Washington, DC, and every other city that lay far to the east of where I now stood. It must have been the same longing, the same curiosity, that has drawn every other explorer over the next hill, or across the next body of water. The least fortunate of these wanderers might be found later by other travelers, their bones in disarray, their origins unknown, the circumstances of their deaths unclear. Many others simply never returned and their bodies were never found by anyone. They just ran out of luck out there along the trail, and every trace of their being disappeared somewhere into the geological record perhaps to be rediscovered someday by an archeologist.

A few years ago there was a skeleton found at a construction site in the Rio Grande valley. He was a tall man and he was found in an undisturbed layer of sand about two feet down. There was no evidence that a grave had been dug. The Rio Grande used to run through the area and had deposited that sand where the bones were found, long before a network of earthen dikes was built in the early part of the century to contain the wild river. The police investigators and an archaeologist figured he must have been swept away in a spring flood sometime before the river was tamed and channelized a couple of miles further to the West. He had disappeared probably a century ago and he was never found. And now nobody knew who he was or where he was from. There was no memory of him at all. I knew something like that could happen to me out here on the road just as easily as it had happened to him and to many others through the years, but I knew I was never going to see much of life if I stayed home and never took any chances.

The roar of traffic and the buffeting winds created by a constant stream of heavy trucks brought me back to the present. I stuck out my thumb in the time-honored tradition of the road wanderer and I waited for another ride. Far to the north and high above the distant Sangre de

Cristo Mountains a line of puffy white clouds had been building since early morning, and now they were growing heavier and darker.

After a couple of hours waiting for my next ride, the afternoon thunderclouds had grown closer and more ominous and I knew it was only a matter of time until icy cold downdrafts swept across the open plains and I would be drenched with that super-chilled rain that is characteristic of the dry desert west. I had approached this whole trip pretty casually and I hadn't really bothered to think a whole lot about how I might deal with a cold, torrential summer thunderstorm on my way East. I had a cheap plastic poncho stuffed somewhere in my pack and I hoped it would give protection from the storm. I was traveling light and I had been running mostly on idealism and the romance of the open road when I threw a pile of clothes into my old pack and locked the apartment behind me. I was still standing near that little-used overpass bridge where Jimmy Reed had dropped me off in the late morning. I could duck under the bridge for cover if I needed to but for now I stayed in the open where I might have a better chance of getting a ride. I reasoned that anyone who might be inclined to pick up a stranger out here on the high plains might appreciate getting a decent look at him first to see if he looked like trouble. I stood in the open air and I waited with my thumb out as heavy clouds slowly filled the sky and blanketed the sun, and soon cold downdrafts chilled the air and I could feel the early droplets of a coming storm.

Then a large late-model Oldsmobile sedan rumbled onto the shoulder, and I was rescued from the immediate consequences of some of my rashest decisions. The driver was a big fellow who glanced at the coming rainstorm and frowned as he stepped out of his car into the rain to open the trunk. We wasted no time pitching my gear beside his small suitcase before we hurried to the front seat and slammed the doors behind us. He looked over his left shoulder and studied the wall of heavy trucks roaring past on their way to distant points before he picked an open spot and pulled quickly and smoothly onto the pavement. He looked into the rear-view mirror and carefully watched the long-haul truckers who streamed by us at high speed and he seemed to anticipate their moves until we finally reached cruising speed and fell into the rhythm of the Interstate. Then he visibly relaxed, took a deep breath, and turned to me. As he put out his large, calloused hand, he introduced himself as Bert.

I thought how funny it was that both my rides so far had been with guys whom I would have described at a glance as red-necks—hard-working, middle-class, middle-aged White men I'd have pegged as die-hard conservative Nixon Republicans. A quick glance at me should have provided enough clues to the high-speed traveler—my jeans, my windblown, longish hair and beard—that I might not be a suitable visitor at one of their family reunions. Still, I wasn't sure what I expected when I first stuck out my thumb back there at the edge of Albuquerque. Maybe a busload of hippies traveling cross-country and stopping to pick up one of their shaggy brethren along the way. But the fact was I hadn't seen one hippie yet on this trip. Out here on the plains, away from the university and away from a few other alternative enclaves, I just wasn't in hippie country anymore.

In a way, I was tired of hanging around with hippies, anyway, and I wanted to get out to where people didn't make a virtue out of being complicated. I had decided not to register for the fall semester because I just couldn't see where an English Literature degree was going to get me. I had switched my major from Philosophy the year before. And while I enjoyed literature and poetry, I sure didn't want to be a teacher putting up with a bunch of surly students like me. And I didn't want to spend my life stuck in some kind of office. I was in my early twenties, with a major urge to bum around for a while longer, get out and see the country, meet some different people, maybe even surprise myself. The flimsy premise for this trip was all I needed to leave town.

Both the guys who'd given me rides so far had been cordial and friendly, if not particularly talkative, and I realized they were mostly looking for a little company on the broad stretches of open country that characterize the West. They both seemed to have a long streak of loner buried somewhere in the eroded spaces of their personalities, and avowed loners often turn out to be the most loquacious characters you'll ever meet, once they feel comfortable with your company. And they probably even valued the eccentric experience of picking up someone who looked like me.

Bert was wearing a light plaid short-sleeve shirt and sans-a-belt slacks. His polished black loafers had little tassels on them. He would have looked very much at home at any suburban shopping center or any city-owned golf course. He was on his way back to St. Louis after visiting his sister and her kids in California.

"Time," he said.

I looked up and saw Time painted in large letters on the side of a passing semi truck.

"I drove for Time for six years," he continued. "Mostly

up and down the West Coast. Good company, Time. They kept us real busy. I made a lot of money working for Time. Got to see a lot of the US and start to understand what made this country great."

Two other Time trucks rumbled past as he told me about his travels and all the country he'd seen in his years of hauling the nation's freight. I noticed there were a lot of Time trucks on the Interstate.

"Why'd you leave Time?" He'd left the invitation lying there on the table. I was supposed to ask that question, but I dodged all that patriotic stuff. That's how the game of male conversation is played. Bert drops a hint on the table. My question gives him the opportunity to settle back for a good jawing session. Tell a few stories to the young kid. Maybe even sound a little philosophical. Later he could tell his buddies back home about the positive influence he'd had on this young hippie guy and about all the important advice he'd given—and which had been eagerly accepted. Probably even changed the kid's life. The young guy would later get together with friends over a glass of cheap wine and munchies or maybe share a joint in the darkened living room of some rented house and he'd tell colorful stories about the many "authentic" people like Bert that he'd encountered traveling through the broad heartland of America as the others marveled at the sheer adventure of it all. In the end, the way the deck was cut and the hands were dealt, both sides came out ahead of the game.

"Well," Bert paused for effect and took a deep breath before he continued. That's also a part of the Script. That's the way the Script is written, with a deep breath for effect. "I finally left Time and went to ICX because I wanted to spend more of my own time around th' wife and kids in St. Louis. I got a regular route to Chicago and back. Spent a lot of years hauling freight through the industrial heartland of America. That way I could spend every other night at home. 'Course that was before th' wife and I got divorced."

He looked out the left side window at the darkening sky and the increasing rain to let that last part sink in. He probably wanted to talk about the divorce, but I left that part of the conversation untouched and it hung there in the air until one of us could figure a way to change the subject. Heavy rain was now pouring onto the windshield and strong gusts of wind buffeted the car. The traffic slowed ever so slightly.

"Guess I picked you up just in time!"

Bert got there first with a new subject and we each said a few predictable things about how the weather was getting worse and it might not let up all night. The weather is always safe ground in a conversation. The subject that was left undiscussed was what he was going to do with me now that he had rescued me from the storm. I didn't really expect him to take me all the way to St. Louis. That's a long time to spend with some guy he didn't even know, but I decided it was in my best interest to avoid the subject and just keep riding in his nice comfortable car as long as it was possible.

"Where're you goin' anyway?" Bert finally asked.

He actually looked a little startled as he asked the question. We had been riding together for about an hour and Bert suddenly realized he didn't know a thing about this bearded young passenger who was sharing a segment of his life and enjoying his hospitality. For my own part, I had been wondering what I was going to say when the question came up.

I didn't know how to figure Bert. With his buzz-cut hair and conservative attire he could even have been the poster child for the American right wing. Still, he could see I was a shaggy hippie kid before he stopped to give me a ride. I wasn't trying to fool anybody. Could I tell him where I was heading and hope he was open-minded enough to understand why I was thumbing my way across the continent to help a bunch of poor people—who were mostly Black, by the way—protest the economic conditions that fostered what appeared to be a permanent American underclass? I wondered if that would sound a little too "Communistic" for a guy who was probably a regular at the American Legion Club, who'd probably worked all his life, raised a family in a lower-middle-class neighborhood, and eaten a lot of beans with some cheap hamburger meat stirred in. How would he take it? I glanced out the window at the raging storm and framed my answer in such a way as to avoid getting tossed out into the rain.

"I have relatives in Louisville." I dodged the question. "I haven't seen them in a long time."

"Louisville?" said Bert, "Haven't been there in years myself. Used to go through there once in a while on the way to Atlanta. Nice town. Right on the banks of the Ohio."

It was true that I had a lot of relatives in Louisville and that I hadn't seen them in many years. I was planning to stop in Louisville on the way home, but that wasn't the main reason I was on the road. And if this whole trip to Washington was just an excuse to leave town for awhile then exactly why the hell was I "On The Road" anyway? What was I hoping to accomplish? I thought maybe I should work a little more on clarifying that point. For myself at least.

For Kerouac and Cassady, The Road was a rolling party with friends, wild times and a whole lot of wanton generational rebellion. For Steinbeck's Jobe Family, it was an escape from the disaster of generations of poor farming techniques that resulted in the Dust Bowl. It was a way to make a new start in the "Golden West" of California. For Billy the Kid, it was a way to escape the hands of The Law back east and start on a whole new adventure. For Daniel Boone, Hernán Cortez, and Marco Polo, it was a powerful curiosity and a chance to risk everything for fabled riches lying just beyond the horizon in an unknown land. We Americans seem to have this notion of "hitting the road" as a rite of passage, a badge of honor. A burly truck driver with a deep voice will end up with a sizable audience— mostly young men—in any cafe when he starts to tell stories about the open road, and there's always at least one song about truck driving on every juke box in the country.

For me, the whole reason to hit the road had at least something to do with idealism. Actually it was probably half about idealism. Well, maybe less than half. Maybe even a lot less. I had to admit there was also a thirst for adventure involved in the decision. There were a lot of things, cities, places, people I had never seen. Hitchhiking cross-country seemed to be a way to experience all of that on someone else's nickel, if I didn't mind listening to their stories for hours on end. It seemed like a small price to pay, at the time.

But the actual catalyst for this particular trip was a guy from Los Angeles named Eric. A guy I'd only met once briefly. I hardly even knew him.

"S'good to go visit the relatives once in a while," Bert said quietly as he watched the traffic carefully through the heavy and constant rain that was washing across the windshield. It was so heavy the wipers had trouble keeping up with it. "They won't always be around and there's stuff you'll wish youda said to 'em after they're gone. By the way, I'm gonna turn off up ahead and go north through Dalhart 'n pick up th' Kansas Turnpike at Wichita. That OK with you?"

"Sounds good to me," I said. "I've never seen Dalhart."

I was surprised at his asking if the detour would be okay with me—as if it might disrupt my careful plans, or something. So far my plans just included ending up in Washington DC sometime in the next week or two. Bert seemed to be taking a paternalistic interest in my welfare and he appeared a bit relieved that I had family I was interested in seeing, that he hadn't picked up some homeless drifter who was maybe even a murderer. Some drug-crazed hippie murderer. I smiled at the thought and watched the rain stream across the side window as it caught the glare from the headlights of a truck behind us. Night had fallen and the high-desert grasslands of New Mexico faded quickly into the blackness. I probably wouldn't see a thing on my only trip ever through Dalhart, Texas.

The heavy rains stayed with us as we drove northeastward on an almost-deserted two-lane highway across the Texas Panhandle. When we arrived at Dalhart Bert stopped at a roadside diner and we each ordered something to eat. As he sat eating his ribeye steak and watching me eat a cheap hamburger, Bert looked outside at the gently easing rain and the reflection of the cafe sign in the mud puddles of the parking lot. There was a winking neon motel sign across the street, but he could sense that I didn't really have enough money for a motel room.

I was more or less mentally prepared to look for an old shed or an overpass to sleep under. I thought maybe I'd just find a big piece of plastic to wrap around my bedroll so I could sleep through the rain. There would be plenty of time to dry out in the morning sun.

"Tell you what," Bert turned back to look at his newest dependent. "It's gettin' late and I'm tired of driving. I been drivin' since Flagstaff. I'm gonna get a room at that motel back over there acrost the road, 'n you can sleep on the floor, if that's OK with you."

As a matter of fact, that sounded great to me. And despite my halfhearted protestations of "Gee, that's really nice of you, but you don't have to do that. I figured I would just...," Bert shrugged and took one last sip of coffee.

"You done eatin'?" he asked as he stood up from the table. "We better go get a room. We're gonna hafta leave at sparrow poop in the morning."

Bert woke early as the first rays of morning cast a grayish light across the room. I heard him roll out of bed and head for the bathroom. The flush of the toilet was followed by the sound of shower water hitting the thin wall and running down a cheap plastic curtain. I could just imagine sparrows lined up outside on the power line waiting their turn like I was waiting my turn as I lay in my sleeping bag on the floor. Bert had a way with down-home homilies and expressions. Soon he emerged from the bathroom. It felt good to get up from that hard linoleum floor, and my bladder was screaming for relief. After a quick shower we headed back across the highway for breakfast, and shortly after that we hit the road again.

Soon we were through the section of red-earth country that fills the Oklahoma Panhandle and into the greenness of Kansas. The astounding and overwhelming greenness of Kansas. Suddenly it covered everything in an endless, treeless, green-wet patina. Abandoned buildings, old cars, railroad sidings, fallen signs—they were all covered with the stuff. Anything left untended longer than a week or so was fringed in foliage. Anything left longer than a season would be almost completely devoured by it. Gazing upon this scene I could imagine "the horror" of an engulfing jungle described by Conrad in *The Heart of Darkness* as Kurtz slips deeper and deeper into madness. At least here I could see a horizon, although featureless, endless, and somehow sinister to a Westerner who's used to seeing mountains. There was nothing visible in any direction, except that every twenty miles or so a tall grain elevator would emerge from the misty horizon like something hidden and then forgotten, like the jeweled tower of a forgotten golden city. But when we finally got to each new grain elevator it was only surrounded by abandoned rotting houses and empty buildings surrendering to the relentless green—just like the previous elevator we saw, and the next one we'd see in about twenty miles or so. The windows of the homes were open and broken and the doors were hanging off the vine-covered hinges, like dead fish tangled in seaweed. I hadn't been out of the West in many years and I was surprised to see once again just how green and flat and empty, in a different kind of way, it really was here on the margins of the East.

After a couple of hours on the road, I noticed that Bert was starting to look around in an agitated manner. I was hoping it wasn't something I had said or done that seemed to put him into this mood.

"I gotta take a leak if it constipates th' Guvner," he finally muttered.

I was relieved that it wasn't my fault and I was also ready to stop since the coffee I drank at breakfast had finally worked its way to the bottom. Problem was, everything was flat for as far as either of us could see. There were no trees, bushes, not much of anything on the road-ward side of an endless barbed wire fence that had been strung up to keep the corn from escaping, I guess. Finally, Bert saw a big road sign advertising a motel about ten miles up ahead and he wheeled the car onto a bare spot just in front of it. A few other desperate travelers had probably stopped here over the years and that explained the convenient parking spot. A couple of cars went by as we stood there behind the sign united in a "male moment." The wet air was filled with the sound of insects flying, buzzing, calling to each other. It was a very different world from the quiet desert I was used to.

We resumed our travel northeastward through this verdant landscape, and eventually we came to the Kansas Turnpike and more of those endless fields of tall corn that line both sides of the highway. World hunger seemed like a remote possibility during the hours we spent among the corn fields while traveling at seventy miles per hour. Small white puffy clouds hung in the distance, but it appeared we had finally driven out from under the stormy weather that engulfed the Southwest.

We pulled into the outskirts of St. Louis as the sun set on that distant horizon far behind us. But a bank of rain clouds had somehow appeared overhead again.

"I'm gonna turn North from here." It was Bert's way of saying that his part of getting me to the East had come to an end.

"Tell you what. I'll drop you off at the YMCA downtown. You can get a cheap bed there for the night. Probably only cost you a coupla dollars."

I thanked Bert for his consideration and I told him that sounded like a good idea. I had never really seen downtown St. Louis before and I wanted to take a look around before I headed on to Washington. But I had less than ten dollars left on me and I wasn't about to spend a bunch of it on renting a bed. I decided not to tell Bert about the ten dollars. I didn't want to look like I was begging for money, and I didn't want him to feel any more responsibility for me. He had been a really nice guy and he'd gotten me maybe a thousand miles closer to my destination. Enough was enough. I thought I could probably find some safe and hidden place to throw out my bedroll in all that expanse of greenery we had driven into about ten or twelve hours ago. I stepped out of the car onto the sidewalk in front of the YMCA and I thanked Bert again for the ride and for everything else he'd done for me. And as soon as he rounded the corner at the first intersection I shouldered my pack and started walking.

I have always had a fascination with what I can only call "faded glory," and St. Louis, like most eastern cities, is just full of it. Old buildings with ornate, gray, crumbling Greek and Roman classical features were everywhere as I walked through the dark evening streets. And there were a lot of other building styles I couldn't begin to identify. I thought maybe someday I'd take a class in architectural history so I would know what I was looking at when I happened to be in a city with some of its history left.

Being a Westerner probably had a lot to do with my fascination for classical architecture. Most western cities have bulldozed their tiny historical areas in an attempt to project a pathetic kind of modern image. And what they built to take the place of their history was mostly a gaggle of cheap and charmless structures that are utterly devoid of character and will never stand the test of time. Nobody, I imagined, can ever actually love most of these new buildings and nobody will mourn when they are finally demolished. It's a sad epitaph for an architect, surely, that nobody will even care when his life's work is destroyed. In fact, most people will likely rejoice when the worst of these modern buildings are removed from the face of America's cities.

I stood for a while near a pay phone and watched people walking through the night in a light rain that seemed to be a natural part of this city. I tried to call a guy I knew long ago who was from St. Louis, but he wasn't in the phone book and the operator had no listing for him. So I stood there for a moment under a nearby streetlamp to consider my next move as various people walked up to use the phone, then wandered away into the night. Soon, a young Black man about my own age came up to use the phone. He looked down at my few possessions and nodded to me as he passed. He glanced over at me a time or two while he spoke into the receiver. After finishing his call, he walked over and asked me where I was from. It was obvious I wasn't one of the locals, standing there on a street corner in a very Black section of downtown St. Louis with my pack and sleeping bag at my feet. As we talked I could tell that we probably had more than a few things in common, so I told him what I was doing and where I was going. It all sounded like a grand adventure to him and something worth doing. After a while he suggested it might be dangerous hanging around downtown St. Louis at night and I should go get a cot at the YMCA for the night. I had only walked a few blocks after Bert had dropped me off in front of the Y, but I told him I was just planning to keep on going and try to find a field to sleep in somewhere on the way to Chicago. And besides, I really didn't have the money to spend for a night on a cot. He listened to me with concern and then he looked away thoughtfully before pulling out his wallet and handing me a dollar bill.

I was stunned. It wasn't supposed to work this way. I was the White guy here. I was supposed to be the one with the money. I was supposed to help Black people, not the other way around. I was the guy who was headed to Washington to join up with the Poor People's Campaign because politicians were more likely to listen if there happened to be a few white faces in the crowd.

He pressed the greenback into my hand and I was at a complete loss for words. He wished me luck and said he would love to be able to do what I was doing. And then he walked away into the darkness. I stood there for a moment with an amazed and stupid smile upon my face, holding the money in my hand as I watched him leave. I thought about the freedom I had to take off cross-country just because I was young and White. Hitchhiking was dangerous enough for me, but for him it had a far higher potential to be deadly—if he even got a ride in the first place. My benefactor in the night hadn't expanded on this simple gesture, but it hit me as a moment of truth, a moment to savor and remember, and to be thankful for. I pushed the money deep into my pocket and then I walked onward into the night.

I trekked on through dark and wet urban streets, and eventually I made my way to some railroad tracks where I thought I might find a hidden spot to lay up for the night. There's something romantic about the rails and I spent some time looking for a dry place under a forgotten trestle or down an abandoned side track, or maybe under an old neglected boxcar. But wherever I looked there always seemed to be some guy or two wandering in the darkness and I couldn't find anyplace where I knew I'd be left alone. I was in some kind of switching yard, as far as I could tell, with multiple tracks and an occasional heavy switch engine grumbling along assembling the trains that would be leaving sometime in the night or in the morning, and I even toyed with the idea of catching a ride in one of those dark, empty boxcars. But I had absolutely no idea where any of them were going.

I let it pass and I kept walking through a maze of rainy night streets through industrial St. Louis toward the nearest bridge across the Mississippi River that would lead me on toward the distant east coast. Huge steel bridge girders rose high into a drizzling sky and faded into the dark misty distance toward a necklace of lights along the far shore as I began walking a mile or so of ancient bridge arching the immenseness of the Mississippi River from Missouri to the Illinois side. The bridge boomed and creaked with the hollow sounds of trucks and buses speeding over steel decking as I trudged onward and upward to the center of the span. Tugboats pushed long strings of barges through the night on the gray, restless, swirling expanse of river that lay far below. I was crossing one of the greatest of natural barriers, drawn upon the earth down the emotional center of the country. This was the demarcational boundary to the eastern world. The Rubicon of the nation.

At the top of the arching span I paused to look back for a few moments at the glowing city of St. Louis, and then I walked onward down the long incline and onto the dark wet streets of East St. Louis.

This poor cousin on the "wrong side" of the river, appeared to be almost completely deserted. There were no cars on the streets and no people walking the sidewalks at this late hour. But up ahead I saw the lights of a small cafe a couple of blocks away. As I grew near, I reached for the old brass doorknob and looked through the glass panel of the door. There were about half a dozen Black men sitting at the counter and a few more at a couple of tables. There wasn't a white face in the cafe. There was no way I was going to slip inside this place and look inconspicuous. I had grown up in the southwest and this was a new experience. Sure, there were a few Black people in New Mexico, but there weren't very many and they were mostly a curiosity among the dominant Anglo, Spanish and Native American cultures. I had a Black friend in high school and a few more later in college but I had never actually spent any time in Black culture, any place where Black people outnumbered folks who looked like me. This could be a test of my White liberal ideals and credentials. I had no idea what to expect but I figured they were probably just as decent as anybody else. I hesitated for a moment to consider the worst thing that could happen, but I decided not to dwell too long on it before I figured "What the hell." and opened the door.

There was a very large guy in a dirty white apron standing behind the counter talking to several husky guys sitting on stools. They all turned to watch as I closed the door and walked past them. I wrestled my backpack to the floor and sat on one of the empty stools near the far end of the counter. Silence filled the place and I thought I could read "Whiteboy, you must be one crazy bastard!" written on their faces. I settled in and looked through the menu as they returned to their conversation and tried to ignore the long-haired lunatic that had just emerged from the mists.

After I finished a piece of pie and a hot cup of coffee, I saw that the drizzling rain had finally stopped. I paid my bill and stepped back out into the night. The other diners had mostly just ignored me, with only an occasional curious glance in my direction. I wasn't the first White guy they'd ever seen, but they probably didn't get too many shaggy White hippies dropping in to their favorite cafe for a cup of coffee after midnight, either. Now that the rain had stopped I figured I should find the nearest freeway on-ramp and try to catch a ride to Chicago. I shouldered my pack and started walking. With any luck maybe I'd be able to catch a little sleep in somebody's nice warm car. It was about one o'clock in the morning.

I walked about three more blocks through some very dark streets when I saw four big young Black guys headed my way. I took a deep breath but I realized I would feel the same fear if I was walking the streets of my own neighborhood and I saw four big White guys coming toward me in the dark. As they drew closer I pulled a road map from my pocket.

"Can you tell me where the freeway is to Chicago?" I asked. I figured I might as well break the ice. Maybe if I was friendly, they wouldn't kill me.

They looked very surprised, then three of them turned to point up the block and told me to take a left at the next corner. The on-ramp was about three more blocks from there. The fourth guy just stood and stared, and studied me. I tried to stop fidgeting, to appear unnervous, and just keep smiling. As they walked away and resumed their talking I thought I caught the phrase "...that's one dumb White bastard..." left hanging in the cool night air. I think it came from the guy who'd stared at me, and I had to agree that he was right.

There were few cars on the freeway as it approached two in the morning, but soon a rough-looking older Chevy pulled onto the shoulder. The small middle-aged Black man who was driving reached over and opened the door.

"Hope you don't mind ridin' with a preacher!" he said with a wide grin. A row of brilliant white teeth shone in the nighttime.

"I don't mind at all!" I said gratefully and laughed.

He was a friendly guy who almost looked like he could have been an uncle of mine, except he was Black. And at 2:00a.m. I wasn't going to be choosy, anyway. I was just glad to be on my way again.

His name was Elmer and he was very talkative for such a late hour. He seemed to want somebody, maybe anybody, along for the ride to tell his story to. He was headed for Chicago. Or more accurately, he was just leaving St. Louis. For good. He was fed up. He'd just had enough of it. He wasn't going to put up with that crap from Martha, his damned girlfriend, anymore. Ever. There were a lot of other places to be in life. And there sure as hell were a lot of other women to be there with. He just didn't need to put up with any more of that kind of crap. Not now. Not never.

I quickly had my doubts that Elmer was actually a preacher and I realized it was his way of saying "I hope you don't mind riding with a Black man." I really wouldn't have cared at all about that—even if I was in a position to be choosy. He didn't seem to be at all concerned about White-Black oppression and other larger political issues. He was an interesting character with problems I could understand. His love life was enough trouble without getting into all that other stuff. I enjoyed riding with him through the night and listening to his story. But like most guys looking for someone to talk to, he had a tendency to repeat himself. A lot. And I knew I wasn't going to get any sleep on this leg of the trip.

"A fella shouldn't have to put up with that kind of crap," Elmer said. "Y'know what I mean?"

"Uhuh."

"Jist ain't right to have to deal with it. No way!"

"Um."

"A man's got to have himself some dignity. He can't just go on lettin' people push him around like that, y'know?"

"Yeah, that's right."

"I'm leavin' this damn town right now, right this minute, an' I ain't never comin' back, y'hear? I'm goin' to Chicago an' startin' me a new life. I'm gettin' away from that woman. I got friends in Chicago. She'll never even know where I am. That's it! That's all! Good riddance, I say. Y'hear? There're a hell of a lot of other women in th' world an' I shore don' need t' put up with that one! Y'know what ah'm talkin' 'bout?"

"Yeah."

I never did actually find out what Martha had done to Elmer to send him speeding off to Chicago and picking up disreputable-looking hitchhikers along the way. In fact, I didn't really want to know what had happened and it wasn't even very important to the conversation, anyway. I had heard stories like this from other guys in bars, and on construction crews. More than likely, Martha had been so unreasonable as to scream at Elmer just for coming in drunk and late without calling. After midnight. Again.

I could understand Elmer's side completely. I had heard this line many times before, and I understood exactly where he was coming from. A fella just shouldn't be expected to put up with that kind of abuse. A fella shouldn't have to be accountable for his actions. Nosiree.

After she threw him out, he said something like, "You can't throw me out 'cause I'm leavin' this damn place. Right now! An' I ain't comin' back, neither."

That's how the Script is written. Martha's scream of "Good riddance!" was almost lost, but not quite, although he'd slammed the screen door hard in hopes of drowning her out. Still, Elmer could claim he hadn't heard it and had left of his own free will, dammit! And he was never going back! No way! That's it! I've had it! The commotion woke up Martha's kids—they were from a previous marriage— and they watched the whole thing from just behind the barely-open bedroom door.

I was glad there were almost no other cars on the road in the blackness of early morning as we drove north through darkened cornfields, since Elmer was very animated and he devoted a lot more time pleading his case to me than to watching the road.

But after we'd been traveling a couple of hours, we both noticed that something was wrong with the way the car was handling, so Elmer pulled over to the side of the road to take a look at it. There was an all-night service station surrounded by tall light poles right across the pavement from where we stopped to check out the situation and I wondered why he hadn't pulled in over there. The right rear tire had blown and Elmer had no spare. He stood for a moment and thought about the situation then we both got back in and he drove the car, flopping tire and all, across four divided lanes of deserted country highway and into the light for a better look.

At a glance, I could see there was no tread at all left on the tire and it had simply worn a hole through the exposed fabric. I was fascinated at how long the tire had lasted and I ran my hand over the smooth surface interrupted by the protruding grain of the fabric. Then I walked around the car and I could see that all the other tires looked about the same. We were just lucky one of the front tires hadn't blown instead and sent us careening into a ditch or into oncoming traffic.

Elmer walked into the service station to negotiate with the middle-aged White guy on night-duty to somehow get his tire fixed enough so's he could maybe get back to St. Louis where his friends could help him out, and the guy just laughed. A little patch on the front of his faded and stained gas station uniform said his name was Chuck.

"You can't fix that tire!" he said with a hoot and a look of incredulity. His mouth was hanging open. "There's not enough left of it to fix! It's completely worn through! It's shot! A patch won't hold because the tire's way too thin. You're just gonna need a new tire. You're lucky you got this far on that thing!"

Elmer listened carefully while Chuck explained the problem. It was the first time he'd been quiet since he picked me up back in East St. Louis. It was a strange and welcome interlude, although I felt real sorry for him.

"Well, how much is a new tire?" Elmer finally asked, in a quiet voice. He looked worried.

"I got this one here for nineteen ninety five. Plus th' tube, mounting an' tax." Chuck added it all up on a scrap of paper. "Lessee, it'll cost ya twenny six eighty seven, all together."

Elmer looked into his wallet and all he saw was a five-dollar bill. I was broke, by American standards, but still I had a couple bucks more in my pocket than he did.

"You got any used tires?" Elmer looked around the garage hopefully.

Chuck took a deep breath and looked over his shoulder. "Well, I think I got one over here that's not too bad." He pulled a tire out of a stack leaning against the wall. "This one'll fit your car. And it's still got some tread left on it."

This used tire—someone else's reject—looked a lot better than the other three tires Elmer had left on the car. A sign on the wall said used tires were seven fifty plus tax, mounting, and all that other stuff, but Chuck agreed to do it all for five bucks. He really didn't have any choice if he wanted to get us out of his station and down the road. I bought a couple of cold sodas for Elmer and me. I was grateful Elmer had gotten me this far down the highway, but he was looking very thoughtful as I handed him the bottle. I could see that he was seriously considering his options.

After the tire was mounted and the car was running, we both thanked Chuck for helping us out with fixing the tire. Then Elmer turned to me and explained the next problem. He was now completely broke and sure didn't have enough money for gas to get to Chicago. He just needed to turn around and go home, back where he belonged, back to St. Louis. Back to Martha.

I could understand what he was going through. Pride's a mighty big thing to have to swallow, and I hate it every time I have to do that myself. I told him I really appreciated the ride he'd given me and I wished him the very best of luck on his way home. He waved goodbye as he pulled back onto the highway and headed south. Back to St. Louis. A faint tinge of daylight silhouetted a tall smokestack somewhere far to the east beyond the cornfields as Elmer's taillights disappeared in the distance. In the calm and humid morning air, a column of black smoke rose high from the stack and then turned to lay flat across the sky in a long line pointing to the south. It struck me as an incongruous sight in the middle of rural America. I stood there beside the road in the cool quiet air and watched the sun paint a fine yellow glaze over the cornfields as I waited for my next ride.

He was a salesman, White, young, well-scrubbed, with a wife and a couple of kids waiting at a nice little home in Oak Park. He wore a suit and tie and he drove a brand-new Buick. I told him that I'd been up all night and I told him all about my ride with Elmer, so he didn't mind when I slouched by the passenger door a couple of hours later and caught up on a little sleep. He seemed like a decent enough guy, but later in the day he showed me the pistol he keeps in a holster between his seat and the door just in case there should be any trouble, maybe with some guy like me. After I saw the pistol, I was a lot less relaxed and I wished I was still riding in Elmer's decrepit but comfortable old car. Soon we were at the outskirts of Chicago and I was glad to say goodbye. He was headed north and I was headed east.

Throughout the afternoon I caught a couple of other rides across Indiana and onward into Ohio. It was dark as we pulled into Columbus; my last ride left me along a suburban roadway, and I walked on toward the east looking for some place to settle for the night in the midst of hundreds of suburban homes and neon-lit strip malls. The occasional street light cast an illuminated circle on the sidewalk. Some teenagers in a car drove past and they seemed to spend a lot of time looking back in my direction. I decided I wasn't interested in whatever they might be thinking about doing.

I had been walking past a rare piece of fallow and undeveloped pastureland just visible in the darkness on the other side of the road. Cars moved along in clumps regulated by widely-spaced traffic lights. I kept walking until the latest knot of traffic passed by and I found myself in a dark spot between street lamps. Then I glanced over my shoulder once more down that dark highway before taking a sharp left across the road. I hopped the fence and jogged toward the middle of the field and dropped into the waist-high grass as a distant light changed and the next wave of traffic came by. One car was driving slower than the rest as if looking for something. Or maybe for somebody. As far as those cruising schoolboys were concerned, I had just disappeared somewhere in the night. It's a big world out there after the sun goes down and I could have been just about anywhere. They drove slowly onward. I sat there for a while behind the wall of grass and watched to see if anyone else even cared about where I'd gone, then I flattened out a spot and spread my bedroll beneath the stars.

I was alone in the gentle embrace of a warm clear night in a lush meadow somewhere in the green heart of the great eastern landscape, and I lay awake for a while on the soft grass looking upward into the endless sky before shucking down to my underwear. Then, I slipped beneath a light sheet I had stuffed into my bedroll and fell into a deep sleep as gentle night winds brushed through the grasses around me. It would be the best night's rest I'd had so far on this trip.

Before dawn, streaks of light grayed the sky, filtered through layers of heavy humid eastern air, and I heard the first comforting stirring and buzzing of the millions of birds and insects that make their homes in the fertile lands of the east. I recalled these sounds from days of youthful summers visiting relatives and cousins at homes and farms in and around Louisville. I rolled over and I let the grand natural chorus of the east lull me back into a deep sleep. In another hour or so I stirred back to consciousness to the welcoming and embracing sounds of an eastern summer. The song of light breeze through tall and gently clattering stems of grasses, the call of locusts, bluebirds, and crickets were symphony in my ears. And in the background there was yet another of the comforting and familiar sounds of long-remembered summer mornings, but in my groggy state I just couldn't place it right away. It seemed to be drawing closer, but I let it blend and crescendo into the powerful song of youthful joys remembered, and I drifted back into a restful somnolence. Then suddenly I recalled that sound and sprang to my feet in panic. I looked over the tall stems of grass.

About thirty feet away, I saw a plump young farmer wearing a DeKalb seed hat sitting on a farm tractor towing one of those wide multiple-mowing machines you see cutting grass along highways across the country. He was traveling parallel to my ad hoc campsite and about one mower-width away. His bored expression changed to one of surprise at the sight of a naked hippie leaping to his feet in the tall grass. He sat there bouncing along with a startled look frozen upon his face, his jaw hanging loose, eyes shaded under his faded cap, his enormous butt engulfing the tiny jiggling tractor seat. And he stared at me as he passed. I caught my breath, rolled my eyes, and smiled broadly in relief. Then I stretched luxuriously, and waved to him as I began to dress and collect my gear. He waved back feebly and cast a lopsided stare over his shoulder in my direction as he kept on mowing the field. I had never had an alarm clock in my life that worked so effectively as that guy on his tractor mower. I wished that my wakeup call had been more gentle, but I was still alive and unmangled by the machinery, and it was time I was up and moving again anyway.

I hefted my pack and hiked back in the direction of the nearest freeway and then I waited. And I waited. Maybe things had been a little too easy so far on this trip. Or maybe suburban Ohioans weren't sufficiently fascinated by this new hairy generation to want to give them a lift. But by midday I finally scored a ride—in a big, flashy, late-model Oldsmobile convertible with custom pipes—and we pulled away from the curb on the last leg to Washington, DC. His name was Stan and he liked riding through the heavy air with the top down. Because of all the wind noise we could hardly speak to each other, but that was fine with me. After a while, most road conversations tend to sound the same.

In the late afternoon, we stopped to put up the top as rain started pouring down from another heavy gray cloud cover. We were soaked by the time we got back into the car. As night fell we were speeding across a long black steel bridge over the broad Ohio River into Wheeling, West Virginia, and the windshield wipers pushed hard against the pounding rain. In the distance, on the West Virginia shore, a huge neon sign flashed "Marsh Wheeling Stogies" into the darkness. Bursts of neon light splintered like broken glass across the black wet bridge deck and onto the dark surface of the powerful Ohio River far below. Near Pittsburgh we rumbled onto the rough and pitted surface of the Pennsylvania Turnpike, along with what seemed like tens of thousands of heavy trucks carrying the nation's commerce onward through the night.

We stopped for coffee at a late-night truck stop. We were both exhausted and neither of us had much energy for conversation as we sat in the booth and drank our coffee while a couple of truckers negotiated with a pair of prostitutes.

Then we walked back to the car through the heavy chuffing sounds and smoke of a dozen or so large diesel trucks in the gravel parking lot. We were ready for our final push to the Potomac. Stan had to get back to his job in Alexandria, Virginia, first thing in the morning, so he planned to drive all night. He would be happy to drop me off at the bridge over the Potomac, but he'd be cutting it close and didn't have time to get me into the city. I was content just to get what was offered, and I was glad to stay inside his warm dry car for the night and not have to find some other place to hide from the rain. Still, I figured I needed to stay as alert as possible and keep a conversation going to help keep him awake. My fate was in his hands. And actually, after all the coffee we'd just drunk, I was up for the rest of the night anyway. And what else would I do with my time? It's not like I had any pressing engagements at the moment.

We reached Alexandria at dawn. Stan looked remarkably alert for having had no sleep. He shook my hand and wished me luck as I stepped onto the sidewalk at the bridge and hoisted my pack. I thanked him for the ride and watched him leave the freedom of the road to disappear among the hordes of early morning wage-slaves being sucked into the gaping maw of American Industry. I thought of the recent movie, *A Thousand Clowns*, where Murray gets his nephew up early to show him the worst sight in the world: "People going to work." After the freedom of a long week-end Stan was a slave once again, but for now at least, I was free.

Traffic was backed up on the bridge as I walked, jaunty, smiling, and content, past expensive cars filled with scowling military brass and faceless, suited bureaucrats. I had no idea where I was going, but figured I'd find it somehow. It was somewhere near the Washington Monument, and I could even see the Washington Monument far off to my right in the misty distance. As I strode past each shiny and sealed air-conditioned car, heads swiveled in my direction. Faces turned angry and conversations began behind the sealed safety of closed windows. I could imagine their envy—and I could feel their hatred—of my youthful freedom, and their fear of my very real potential to cause each of them some kind of serious trouble in the years ahead. But it wasn't only me they had to fear; it was the potential of an entire awakening generation. My generation knew it, we could feel it in our bones, and we were reveling in the sheer power of it all.

But now I was finally here, if a bit groggy, standing at the nation's doorstep and headed for Resurrection City. It was time to start looking for that guy Eric.

The morning light had caught my eye and held me transfixed as it lay there deeply ensnared in those tiny curls at the back of Mark's head. Each curl held a complete genetic code within its perfect arc. They were entwined, each around every other one, in an eternal embrace. Each was interconnected to the whole and they were the essence of everything that Mark represented.

I remembered the tender way that soft fingers of morning light caressed the folds of Annie's golden-brown hair each morning at our breakfast table.

Mark was staring intently at the road ahead as if he had the wheel of a giant Greyhound bus within his grasp and he was on a cross-country journey that would take at least until forever. He felt the texture of the road as it telegraphed each tiny ridge and pebble upward through the steering column, and he studied the graceful sweep of this perfect roadway that sliced its way through the magical landscape of these high-desert lands.

I saw myself in the rearview mirror, a distant look in my eyes. I turned away to watch the stark and arid scenery that passed by outside just beyond my window.

I stood at the mossy, pebbly edge of an old weathered sidewalk in the gathering early heat of day with my pack and bedroll over my shoulder and looked out over hundreds—maybe thousands—of people drifting across a broad sea of grass that washed up to the distant base of the Washington Monument, and I wondered where I was supposed to go next, now that I'd finally gotten here, to the bustling encampment of the Poor People's Campaign. And I wondered how in the world I was going to find Eric. Hell, I realized I didn't even know his last name. He was just one more face in a very large crowd.

Eric and I had only spoken briefly. We had shaken hands only once, and that was more than a month ago. That's when I told him I'd be here, somehow, at the encampment on the Mall.

I realized I hadn't even thought about Janice since she dropped me off at the side of the road about two thousand miles ago, and I decided it was time to end our relationship when I got back. There must have been something between us in the beginning, something besides good sex. But neither of us seemed to remember that part anymore. And now we no longer had a compelling reason to be together, not the way it had been going lately. I was sure Janice would agree, or at least she'd get over it soon enough—if she hadn't already. I'd had a lot of time to avoid thinking about it while hitchhiking across the entire country and now the picture was finally clear, even to me. A lot had happened since I left Albuquerque almost a week ago.

Janice and I had attended this big rally at the Civic Auditorium back in the spring when the Poor People's Campaign came to town. She and a guy named Bob were assigned to write stories about the rally for the student paper as part of a journalism class. I thought it would be interesting to be a bit player in this historic moment and I was happy to go along and watch.

After we arrived at the Civic a line of buses pulled up to the curb outside. A bunch of cops stayed busy directing traffic and making sure the poor folks didn't try anything funny like crimes against property or some other direct form of wealth redistribution. The arrival of these buses was a big event, as they contained probably more Black people than the city had ever seen in its history. Now that the poor people were getting organized, the ruling class feared they were finally getting wise to the ways that bankers and developers had been taking them for a ride all these years and that they might just decide, right here in Albuquerque, to do something about it.

The buses were filled mostly with elderly grandmothers, young kids, and very few young adults, who were the ones capable of making trouble. Several days earlier these buses had pulled out of Los Angeles and made their way to Albuquerque after stopping for rallies at other towns and cities along the way. They had arrived in town early in the day and stopped briefly at a motel somewhere to allow the passengers to clean up a little before making their grand entry at the Civic. Most of the passengers looked a little tired and they really didn't look like much of a threat, but the Black population of Albuquerque had probably more than tripled when this caravan of buses rolled into town. For a mostly Hispanic and White town raised on lurid stories about all the bad things that happen in the Black ghettos of big cities, this fact alone was cause for concern among the citizenry. And the Albuquerque Police Department was there to watch over things, just in case.

Janice and Bob and I entered the auditorium and found seats in the crowd down in front by the stage. Speakers, politicos, and dignitaries were waiting behind the podium to deliver their prepared speeches, some words of support for the campaign, and the usual variety of political promises. Soon, Reyes Tijerina came to the front of the stage and grabbed the edges of the podium with both hands as he welcomed this crowd of people who had arrived in support of a better life for all Americans. His rousing words played well to this audience and he conducted the proceedings like an old-fashioned and well-tuned gospel preacher who knew the words and gestures that would move the masses. Tonight, he was the fearless social reformer willing to stand against the cruel capitalist masters. He was the lonely matador taunting the bull, gracefully sidestepping its deadly charge. He was fascinating to watch and the crowd roared with approval.

Janice and Bob were taking notes in a sort of 'journalist script' that looked like hieroglyphics to me. It was a hot summer night and the ventilation system wasn't keeping up with all the people who were still packing into the building. Everyone in the place was sweating heavily. We three college-age White kids stuck out in this sea of mostly dark people like flecks of bleached paper tossed onto a plowed field of rich virgin earth. Janice and Bob each had a look of nervous discomfort as the crowd milled around looking for any place to sit. People steadily poured into the building and stood around the stage until we couldn't see anything that was going on. I gave my seat to an older Black woman who looked like she was about to collapse, and I wandered over to the stairway leading up to the stage. Janice saw me go and quickly followed. Bob looked to his right at the very large Black man who had taken Janice's seat, smiled weakly, and glanced in our direction before deciding to stay put. Our departure was beginning to look like bad manners, so Bob stayed behind, a single white face frozen in the crowd. Someone was yelling for everyone to try to find a seat somewhere and keep the aisles clear. I started up the stairway to get a better look at the speakers, but Janice grabbed my arm.

"You can't go up there!" she said with a look of panic in her eyes. She glanced back at Bob. Bob was watching us.

"Why not?" I grinned, "Everybody else is up on stage. It just seems like the friendly thing to do."

I joined the crowd that had edged its way onto the stage, and we created a kind of multiracial human halo around the local politicos who smiled and tried to act as if all this "democracy" was a normal part of public gatherings in Albuquerque. Another scheduled speaker was now addressing the crowd, and Reyes was trying to maintain some order and keep an aisle open to the side door so the dignitaries could leave as they finished their speeches, but there was no way they'd avoid brushing their suit jackets against the common clothing of the proletariat.

Reyes was concerned that the Fire Marshall would order the building evacuated, but I got the impression he was also enjoying the shear anarchy of it all. The Fire Marshall and several of his staff were standing at the back of the hall watching the evening unfold. He was talking nervously with reporters and appeared to be considering the political feasibility of his options in the face of this yet unknown popular force. It was clear there was a new political movement afoot in the land, and things would never be quite the same again. Janice kept a firm grip on the sleeve of my blue JC Penney work shirt as I moved to a good vantage point where I could see over the crowd. I was loving every bit of the show. She looked terrified.

After each speaker, Reyes reminded us that the main event was still to come. Marlon Brando had just landed, and he was on his way from the airport to address the crowd. Brando had been advertised on flyers and handbills as the main speaker of the evening, and his arrival was the moment we were all waiting for; he was the main draw. He was a well-known supporter of popular causes like this one and this audience was ready to hear what he had to say. A few minutes later the great man himself swept in through the side door with his entourage and advanced across the stage smiling, and he waved to the crowd. The fellow who happened to be speaking at the podium was drowned in the roar as the crowd rose from their seats and screamed their welcome. Reyes introduced Brando while the previous speaker gathered his papers and attempted to retreat gracefully from center stage.

Brando stepped to the podium and spoke eloquently about the very real plight of Native Americans who spend their lives in unimaginable poverty right here in the heart of the wealthiest nation in the world. This was a subject of particular importance to him. He said it was time to make the American dream a reality for all its people and not just those fortunate enough to be part of the privileged class. It was time to build a new and more equitable America on the broken promises of the past. It was time for this great nation to open its heart and to craft a new and better future for all her people.

They were inspiring words and the crowd stayed on its feet throughout Brando's address. Their deafening roars of approval echoed from the cold brick and concrete walls of the Civic Auditorium as probably no others ever had. He spoke powerfully for about fifteen minutes of the need for fundamental change in the American way of life and then, too soon, it was time for Brando to go. There was a plane on the runway waiting to take him to another city, another rally, another appreciative crowd. He was a man who was deeply committed to a cause and his presence and his words were an inspiration to us all. He stepped back from the podium and waved to the applauding crowd. Then he turned to leave.

But first, Reyes had a few words of praise for this remarkable man, and Brando returned to a place by the podium next to Tijerina. The crowd roared at Tijerina's remarks and Brando smiled and waved. It was time to go.

Then Tijerina went on to further extol the virtues of one so selfless and willing to share his good fortune and his abilities with the many who were far less fortunate. More applause. Brando waved again and tried to leave, but Reyes was just hitting his stride and he carried on for several more minutes as Brando shuffled his feet nervously. His aides were pointing at their watches and he nodded in agreement. Reyes reached another crescendo. There was more applause. Brando stepped to the microphone and said a few more words of heartfelt thanks and encouragement to the crowd. Then he shook Reyes hand once again, waved to the applauding crowd and headed for the side door, gracefully acknowledging all the people who lined his path while several aides led the way. He glanced at me and smiled as he hurried past and I smiled back. I had become more than just an observer of this powerful moment, and I was happy and proud to be there with everyone else in the place.

Several other speakers tried to fill the enormous gap in the program when Brando left the stage but he was, as they say, a tough act to follow. After listening briefly to the next speaker, Janice turned and headed for the lobby with Bob and me close behind. We stopped in the lobby and leaned against a white-tiled wall as we watched a swirling sea of humanity dressed in varieties of brightly-colored clothing. I asked Janice and Bob if they were going to interview anyone, but the idea seemed to make them uncomfortable.

Next to us, sitting on the cool vinyl-tile floor, were a couple of elderly and overweight Black women fanning themselves with folded newspapers. They were minding several young children, grandchildren I assumed, who came and went in the crowd like small explorers in a strange new world, returning to home base often for reassurance. I squatted down and leaned back against the wall, and then I asked if they had come in on the buses.

"Oh lordy, yes!" they said almost simultaneously. "An' it was hot too, all the way from LA across the desert without hardly no stops at all! I never seen the likes of it b'fore! There ain't nothin' out there but sand an' cactus!"

It took only a simple question to get them talking. From then on, my end of the conversation mostly consisted of "Uh huh." "I see." and other assurances that I was still listening and hadn't left or fallen asleep or something. Janice and Bob were watching and listening over my shoulder.

"When we got to El Paso," they continued, "th' Poh-leese wouldn't even let us off th' buses for about two hours! We was all hot an' sticky! Them buses are˝ jis' like big tin cans in th' summer! Th' kids was cryin' and carryin' on like you never seen! Then we came up here acrost even more desert! How's come you ain't got no trees here? This's the driest place on God's green earth! I never seen nothin' like it!"

They reminded me of my own grandmother on my father's side. They spoke simple, unschooled, and true, like she always had, and with that same middle-southern accent. And, like Grandma, these women were both on the hefty side. I could picture them in their kitchens back home urging another helping of pancakes on the grandkids. And I could imagine the grandkids giggling and struggling to escape their sudden, engulfing kisses, like I always did when I was their age.

Their voices blended like two sisters who've lived together all their lives and one always picked up the narrative where the other left off. My eyes were drawn from one to the other as the story shifted between them. I nodded my head as I tried to follow their adventures. Regarding their question about why there were no trees here, it was actually more a statement than a question and they weren't really interested in the "rain shadow" created by the mountains of the high Sierras far to the west and the seasonal spotty rainfall patterns of the Southwest which led directly to our high desert environ-ment. And of course, they never paused for an answer.

A slender young man walked up to check on the two grandmothers and I stood up to make room. He was about my height and build, and I guessed he was within a year or two of my age, with beautiful olive-colored skin and an engaging smile. He'd also gotten on the bus in LA and he had taken these elderly women under his care, helping them on and off the bus, taking them to their hotel room, making sure they had cold drinking water. They treated him very affectionately, like just another of their many grandsons.

We began to talk, he and I, in that language of the socially-committed segment of our generation, and I sensed that we shared many interests. We talked about the issues facing the poor of America, about where the bus caravan was headed next, about what they'd do when they arrived in Washington. And we talked about "The Movement," the idealistic force that seemed to bind our generation in a common purpose, in what would be our defining moment.

Then he asked, "Why don't you come with us?" He saw my hesitation and he went on before I could think of any way to reply. "You could just get on the bus in the morning and come along. We need people to show their commitment and to help out with the cause. Just being there is important."

I was stunned at the invitation. It sounded like a wonderful idea. Just get a change of clothing together and get on the bus in the morning. Be a part of some important things that were going on. Do something personally to help force the changes we all knew the nation needed in order to make things right and fair for everyone. See the country from a completely different perspective. I would be off on an adventure and I'd actually do some good at the same time. At the moment, I was just working for a living and I wasn't really headed anywhere in particular. And this relationship with Janice sure wasn't going anywhere either. My emotional batteries were low and I could use a good dose of adventure and idealism.

But there was a problem. There's always a problem with any plan as simple as this. The problem was, I had a job. I needed that job to pay the rent on my shabby apartment and to buy food. It wouldn't be any big deal to just quit the job; I could get another one when I returned, but I needed to collect a couple more paychecks to pay the rent a month ahead and to have a little traveling money. I needed to stay here just a little longer to make it all work.

He saw my hesitation. "Come on," he offered again. "We're leaving in the morning. We have room. Just get on the bus and come with us. We need everybody to help out with this if we're going to make it happen."

He had me there. I paused just briefly and took a breath. Just how badly did I really want to change things, anyway? Or was it too much trouble? Was it maybe a little too inconvenient to really get involved, to make Martin Luther King's vision a reality now that he was gone?

"Tell you what," I finally said. "I can't leave tomorrow."

There was disappointment on his face. I was starting to look like just another White liberal who wouldn't take a stand. As Saul Alinsky, the fiery organizer would say, "A liberal is the guy who leaves the room when an argument turns into a fight." Clearly, he was right.

"But I'll see you there," I continued with a serious and steady gaze. "I'll see you there. I'll get to Washington and I'll see you there."

He looked me in the eye. Then he smiled and shook my hand.

"My name's Eric." he said, "I'll see you in Washington!"

And so, a brief conversation, a handshake, a promise made a month and two thousand miles ago, and here I was standing at the edge of a weathered sidewalk in Washington DC wondering what to do next. As I looked out across this vast crowd of people, that guy Eric was nowhere to be seen.

Several people pointed me toward the "check-in tent" and I made my way past families with children, a bunch of college-aged kids tossing a football, lovers sitting and talking on the grass—the brilliant green grass that seems to go on forever in all directions, another small piece of The Great Eastern Lawn that binds all those on the east side of the Mississippi River in a common purpose and a common destiny: the endless summer ritual of mowing, trimming, and fertilizing all this grass. Their reward, after the work is done, will be quiet moments under puffy white clouds upon this soft and richly-covered land. And, ultimately, the silent repose of eternity awaits them all beneath its lush green surface.

But where I stood the grass had been worn through like cheap carpeting by these new thousands who had come to petition their government and make their camp on the nation's lawn. And just beyond were the "No Swimming" signs that stand like pickets at the edge of the long reflecting pool that spans the gulf between the Washington Monument and the Lincoln Memorial. That's where people were wading and splashing in the shallow water, seeking relief from a humid and oppressive eastern summer. It looked like a very good idea and I would join them later, after I got settled in.

There was a great deal of activity around the check-in tent. It was a large tent with the sides rolled up for ventilation and it provided some welcome shade. Three people sat behind a long folding table and tried to answer questions while children ran through playing tag. There was a carnival atmosphere to the entire encampment. People had questions about the upcoming march to the Capital Building, about the arrival time of Ralph Abernathy, about the location of the nearest toilets. The people at the table were calm and reassuring and none of them seemed hassled by the general noise and confusion. I worked my way to the front of the line. A heavy-set man with a curly graying beard and a beaded African hat listened to my request for a place where I could stash my belongings and camp out for the duration. He had kind brown eyes and he was very patient, like an uncle. He told me to just go over toward the left side of the grass and find one of those empty lean-tos. No, they didn't really actually sign people in or anything like that. People just took care of themselves and looked out for each other. No, he didn't know anybody named Eric. There were thousands of people in the encampment and there wasn't any way they could keep track of everyone. Maybe if I just asked around somebody would know who he was. He thought there were some other people from California over by those empty lean-tos, and maybe they knew who Eric was.

I stepped back outside and saw the empty lean-tos in the distance, so I knew I had a dry place to crash for a few days. But I realized I'd probably never find Eric. It really didn't matter much, anyway. I was just glad to be here. Still, it would have been nice to let him know I'd made good on my promise.

Just to the right of the check-in tent, smoke was curling into the morning air from an old wood stove and a group of long-haired White people dressed in embroidered clothing and beads were tapping freshly-made whole-wheat bread out of coffee cans onto cutting boards in front of a hungry crowd lined up at the other side of a long table. The rich smell of fresh bread mingled with drifting wood smoke and filled the air. Large open cans of USDA commodity margarine, peanut butter, and strawberry jam sat on the table with plastic knives sticking out. As each of the small cylindrical loaves was cut, the hot slices were quickly claimed, buttered, spread with jam, and eaten on the spot. I ate several slices myself as I talked to a heavily-bearded fellow who stayed busy slicing a fresh loaf of bread while others kneaded dough and refilled the shiny cans for another round. Several rows of filled cans sat on another long table awaiting the magical action of the yeast before being placed in the oven.

These colorful "bread people" were members of a commune from Berkeley, and they had boarded a bus that ended up going through Denver on its way east. Here at the encampment, they baked bread every day using commodity flour and yeast and they loved giving the stuff away. Later in the summer, they would return to Berkeley and the house where they lived together and where they made unique varieties of bread to sell to local bakeries and natural food restaurants. I recalled my own communal experiences a year earlier in Taos and I knew it wasn't a lifestyle that suited everyone. Still, I could appreciate their warmth and their generous approach to life.

I drifted away with a fresh slice of buttered bread and found an empty lean-to under some trees. I flung my pack inside and laid my bedroll out onto the plywood floor. A midday nap seemed like a good idea since I hadn't slept at all during that last long overnight ride, and I was exhausted.

My new home was a clever wooden pup tent, like many others scattered here across the nation's lawn. It was made of two sheets of plywood nailed at the top to a 2x2 and then nailed along the bottom edge to a raised plywood floor on a structure made of 2x4s. It was open at both ends for ventilation whenever a rare breeze chanced to blow through the area, and it didn't leak during the frequent afternoon rains. A windblown rain could sweep in one end and run across the floor unless you rigged a piece of canvas or plastic over the doorway, but there were only a few light showers while I was there. I lay on my bedroll for a moment quietly looking upward at the wooden ceiling and retracing the long pathway I'd taken to get to the encampment. Outside these thin walls the low rumble of humanity filled the morning air. My eyes lazily followed the design of tree rings scribed in the plywood, and I felt lucky just to be here and a part of all this. And then I drifted off to sleep.

I awoke several hours later in the oppressive heat of a humid afternoon to the sound of voices just outside my lean-to. Two guys were looking for volunteers to go to the USDA warehouse and help load more commodity food onto a truck for delivery to the large mess tent near the center of the compound. It sounded like a good way to see a little of the city. As a bonus we'd stop at Howard University on the way back for a quick shower in one of the dorms. Because of all my time on the road I hadn't actually bathed in several days, and I was reluctant to get to know my neighbors until I cleaned up a bit. I quickly volunteered for duty.

There were seven of us on the work crew, all young and fit and ready to load the truck. And everyone on the crew was Black—except me. We joked easily as we climbed into the back of a big US Government troop truck and sat leaning against the sidewalls while we sped away into a busy maze of streets to a warehouse somewhere miles away. We could only see whatever was visible through the large open rear door and the whole scene played like a movie in reverse. As we watched the crowded streets of the city go by, there was nervous joking about how maybe this was a trick by the FBI and we were being taken to some concentration camp. The truck might dump us in the middle of a guarded compound and go back for another load of "volunteers" until the camp was empty and the Poor People problem was "solved."

But soon we arrived at a big warehouse and set to work carting boxes of canned tomatoes, vegetable soup, some kind of Velveeta-looking cheese, some Spam-looking cans of meat, and a bunch of other items. I suggested we just hide the Spam-looking meat somewhere at the far end of the warehouse, but some of the other guys raised objections. I think they were actually looking forward to eating the stuff. And to tell the truth, I even got used to it during my stay. By the time those magicians in the food tent were done with it, the Spam-stuff we ate almost every day had been so expertly blended with spices and vegetables that it was quite delicious and almost unrecognizable.

We finished loading the truck and climbed aboard between the boxes for a short trip over to Howard University. Along the way we passed through the heart of Black neighborhoods whose business districts had been looted and burned in one of the recent riots that were common in America's large cities that summer. The week before my arrival, it was Washington's turn to burn. We passed several blocks of destroyed storefronts and burned-out buildings and saw people picking through the ruins of what had been their livelihoods. At one looted store, busted TV sets and broken appliances poured out of a smashed display window and were piled onto the dirty sidewalk in front. All the good stuff had been taken and now the pile was only a glass and plastic cornucopia of worthless garbage spilling from a broken storefront window, sparkling in the afternoon sun and stretching outward into the street. The guys sitting with me in the back of the truck laughed and grinned self-consciously at each other at the first sight of all this destruction, a backlash against the economic oppression of the nation's wealthy establishment. But that quickly faded and they grew somber as they realized it was only the Black neighborhoods that had been trashed. Soon it was clear that this outbreak of urban anger had accomplished nothing good for the Black people of Washington. It only meant that soon most of the remaining merchants would leave the neighborhood as well. This was no way to accomplish anything meaningful and positive and long-lasting. It was a memorable scene that made for nightly TV footage, but it was no effective way to strike back at The Man. We rode onward in silence through the streets of shattered neighborhoods.

After hot and soapy showers in the dorm at Howard, we arrived back at the encampment to unload at the mess tent and were instantly sweaty again. But it was honest sweat and now, at least, we were clean and we smelled a little better. And the people we worked with at the mess tent seemed to appreciate the change.

That night I met five young guys who were camped out near my lean-to, and I had an almost complete lack of ability to understand their heavily urban Black dialogue. These guys were resourceful. They had rigged a bare bulb to hang from a nail in the roof of an empty lean-to with an extension cord that disappeared somewhere into the darkness. With one single light bulb, the place became a recreation center and hideout, devoted mostly to beer drinking, gambling, and raucous laughter. It was a guy thing and none of the girls in camp appeared to have any interest in stopping by to check out the action.

One of these guys was from Memphis and the rest were from south Chicago, and they spoke a very fast sort of urban patois which I found impenetrable. I'd been raised on that midwestern English spoken by the major networks and pronounced so clearly by Edward R. Murrow and Walter Cronkite. But these young Black men understood each other quite well and, with only one White guy in the place, there wasn't much incentive to speak the language of White America. After futile attempts to communicate, they mostly ignored me, and I sat back against a sloping wall to watch this nightly spectacle, a modern ballet of well-muscled young Black men on their knees in a circle throwing dice beneath a single glaring bulb. Shadows danced across the plywood surface. We were all shirtless in the intense wet summer heat, and the harsh burning light flashed off their finely-chiseled, sweaty-dark muscles as they performed an ancient rite of young male passage to the crash and rattle of dice on a bare wood floor. Primal shouts and laughs rang with each throw of small white cubes that caromed off a wall and danced and settled in the middle. Each young man acted out his role. The myth, the fantasy, was accepted by the others and rarely challenged, unless that role was taken by someone larger, or stronger, or maybe more threatening. And adjustments were made for new actors in this timeless drama. I could picture young Roman soldiers, Arabic sailors, or Apache warriors killing time around campfires in this same way, somewhere far away and long ago.

These guys had no idea what to make of the tall, longish-haired, and puny-looking albino who was propped against a back wall, and so I was happily ignored and I watched, fascinated with the visual beauty of the scene until the game finally broke up sometime late in the night. We all went back to our huts to get a few hours of rest in the still-shimmering heat of the night and to await the welcome cooling breezes that usually arrived from the Potomac River just before dawn. Tomorrow was the day we'd march to the Justice Department to demand fair and equitable treatment for America's minorities. It was time to get some sleep.

At breakfast I struck up a conversation with a young Black woman. She was tall and pretty, and we lingered over coffee until it was time to clean things up and leave. We agreed to meet again when the march got organized in an hour or so. Her name was Mary and she was from Chicago, but she didn't know any of the guys I'd watched gambling the night before. Chicago's a big place.

Mary came to Washington with her church group on several buses after an inspirational service on a recent Sunday morning. After the service the entire congregation gathered outside the church to send them off; everyone prayed and wished them the best of luck. This trip was important to their congregation and to their community and they carried a sense of responsibility with them on the journey.

Mary had never been out of Chicago, and a visit to the nation's capital was high adventure for her. She was quiet and shy and she never went anywhere without her good friend, Shondra, so the three of us walked the streets of Washington with several thousand others in the hot morning sun, and I tried to make clever conversation while the two of them laughed together in that urban tongue that remained an effective wall between us. They would say something that I barely understood and then they'd laugh at my fumbled reply. I also thought the whole thing was hilarious and we laughed as we walked the tree-lined morning streets.

There was an attraction between us. Between Mary and me. I could feel it, and see it in her sparkling brown eyes. We were ethnic polar opposites perhaps, but something drew us closer. We usually ran into each other at the food tent over breakfast. And sometimes we snuck away from Shondra and went out walking together, exploring the marble canyons and the streams of humanity that are the essence of this city. In the afternoons we walked together through parks covered in lush Washington summer grass. She walked with an easy gait and a bit of girlish gawkiness. Her slender body flowed lightly like a spirit upon the ground. I felt awkward with her, like that picture of Bob Dylan, unkempt and with his hands in his pockets, on the cover of his "Freewheelin'" album. At least that's where I thought I remembered it from.

After breakfast Mary and Shondra and I joined a large crowd gathered in a nearby cordoned-off street, and waited to march to the Justice Department. We were to present petitions demanding a fair and race-blind judicial system for all Americans, rich and poor. A leafy canopy gave some shade to the large group that was strung out well ahead of us and that stretched far behind. Despite the serious nature of the moment, we still felt the carnival atmosphere that pervaded much of what occurred in the encampment. We were marching through the morning streets of Washington D.C. because marches for justice were what we had come here for. It was an uplifting experience, but I was young and callow and tried to act as cool as the other guys, implying this was just another day's activity. Still, I was surprised that the average local resident seemed to ignore us as we passed, or simply looked down the street to see how long this latest demonstration was going to be blocking traffic. For most of them, we were just another of the daily hassles of living in the District of Columbia and the sooner we left town, the better. Looking back, I shouldn't have been surprised. We weren't really marching for them. We were marching for the news media and for some guy who might be watching the evening news in Peoria.

When we arrived at the base of the Justice Department Building, I was tapped for "security" duty along with most of the other large young guys. We stood in a line about three steps up from the ground, looking out across a crowd of mostly elderly people and women with young kids. Ostensibly, we were there to protect the speakers behind us at the podium, and the building itself, from attempts by these grandmothers to storm the hallowed halls of the United States Department of Justice. In reality, they just picked all the young guys who looked like they might cause trouble and put us in charge of security so we'd have something to keep us occupied. It was an effective way to keep us out of trouble and avoid a lot of bad press for the Poor People's Campaign. The guys on each side of me were huskier and a whole lot tougher-looking than I was, and I knew they would exert a chilling influence on any irate mom in the crowd who might want to start trouble or throw bombs at the government.

And so we stood shoulder to shoulder in the heat of a morning sun and looked serious with our arms crossed as speaker after speaker laid out the case for helping The Poor. Then someone from the Justice Department accepted the petition we had come to deliver, and he said a few words about all the good things the bureaucracy was doing for the people, and which none of us had actually noticed in our lives so far. I exchanged a glance and a grin with the big guy to my right who rolled his eyes at the official description of how good his life was, and I smiled at Mary who was standing in the crowd below. She looked beautiful as hot summer sunlight sparkled from the folds of her pure black hair reflecting hues of purple, and I lost track of the droning official speaking at the podium behind me. But soon the words returned and I wished the speakers would wrap it up so I could find a shady spot under a tree to catch a cooling breeze in the heavy air.

Local and national TV crews gathered footage for the evening news as those of us on the security line tried to look reasonably noble for the cause. My bright white face among a throng of Black and Brown America seemed to interest them. It might make good news film and add multiracial solidarity to the message that we meant to convey to the nation. While I had come from a middle-class background and could not really be counted as a basic member of the chronically poor, I had, in fact, made myself a legitimate member of the recent poor. As a sometimes-employed carpenter, I wasn't making much money at the time and, like many of the people I was now marching with and living with, I was living on a diet of mostly beans, tortillas, and potatoes. I felt that I could understand at least some of the uncertainty and the striving for something better that drove many of the others who were here today at the Justice Department. Maybe I was White and maybe my prospects were better than theirs, but in a way I was also one of them and I supported their efforts to gain a better life and a decent slice of the economic pie for their families, their children and their elderly in this richest of all nations.

I was giving a lot of thought to these questions at the time. Questions about what was truly right and what was clearly wrong. And whether I was poor because I had decided to be, so I could wander the world as I pleased—a luxury few of my companions had. I had plenty of time to mull over these thoughts as I stood there on the steps to the Justice Department in that summer of '68.

There's a basic truth that a nation's strength is not only measured in the simplistic calculus of military hardware, but in the degree of equity felt by its people. After all, a nation's inherent social and economic strength is what pays the bills for that military stockpile. And without equity for all citizens, there is no reason for them to fight their nation's wars. Machiavelli said that long ago. Powerful regimes have collapsed when the people became disillusioned enough to walk away and leave the arrogant aristocracy to their fate. When it happened in France, the King was guillotined. It also happened in Russia and Turkey and Cuba and any number of other modern countries. It happened in ancient Sparta and in Rome. And it could just as easily happen here if the people's real and immediate needs were ignored, and that huge gap continued to broaden between the wealthy and the growing poor and lower-middle classes. There was a need for change in America and it had finally become apparent. The alternative to inclusion and equity led only to increasing restrictions on American liberty. And judging by history, possibly to a heavily-armed American Praetorian Guard who would elect and manipulate despotic Emperors for their own benefit. It had happened before in human history and undoubtedly, it would happen again. And just as it led to the destruction of the Roman Republic 20 centuries ago, it could very well lead to the end of the Great American Experiment. If we let it. It was our choice, as a people, which way the country would go.

From the hot and steamy streets of Washington in the volatile summer of 1968, the Poor People's Campaign seemed the best opportunity in a long time to steer this country back in the direction it was supposed to be heading long ago when the Founding Fathers penned noble phrases about justice and equality for all. The Declaration of Independence and the Constitution were not factual statements of the condition of America in those days of slavery two hundred years in the misty past. Rather, each document was an expression of hope for the future, a set of guidelines we could follow toward a truly fair and equitable society. And I hoped that maybe my standing shoulder to shoulder with Black and Hispanic Americans on the steps of the Justice Department could help in some way to make it so. Eric was right. It was up to us to make it happen.

The morning wore on, the sun got hotter, and the speeches seemed endless. But eventually it was over and we began that long walk back to the grassy Mall and the shade of our lean-tos. I walked with Mary and Shondra and hundreds of others, and we talked about being here at the center of the movement and even getting our pictures taken by the national press. There were no TV sets at the camp for us to watch, so we really didn't know if they ever used any of the footage. But there was plenty of coverage of the whole campaign whenever we caught a glimpse of a TV set in a downtown store window. There was always footage of Ralph Abernathy and Hosea Williams and the other leaders whenever there was a speech or a press conference. And those of us who lived in the lean-tos saw Hosea Williams just about every day, in that brightly-colored jumpsuit he wore, managing the daily affairs of the encampment. He was a very accessible guy and people took their problems and concerns directly to him. Whenever I saw him, he was always surrounded by lots of people and a swarm of adoring children.

Every day in the compound, a flowing tapestry of colorful humanity swept across its green and fertile palette. The clothing, the language, the people from all corners of America painted a moving and changing portrait of the nation for all to see. I often joined in the human sea as they moved across the verdant landscape, just to be a part of it.

One day I saw someone I recognized in this ocean of humanity. He was a sort of new national celebrity that I remembered from a TV show, or maybe a movie somewhere. He passed us with a tall beautiful blonde woman who was probably another star, but not someone I recognized. I recalled that he was a budding comedian that I thought was named Richard Pryor, and I pointed him out to Mary and Shondra. They knew who he was but they weren't sure of his name, either. He saw us staring and he smiled. We smiled back shyly, then turned away, uncertain what to say that wouldn't sound stupid to a celebrity. They were not part of our normal experience. We walked on through the crowd with a few backward glances, until the celebrity disappeared into a dense thicket of the common people.

And then one day I saw Eric in the crowd, and I made my way toward him. Yes, he remembered me and our brief conversation that now seemed so long ago and he was surprised that I had actually made it to Washington. That I'd even hitchhiked all the way just to get here. We talked for a while about marches, gatherings, speeches, newspaper accounts and so on, and then we shook hands and parted. I watched him fade into the ever-flowing crowd. And I never saw him again.

After a week in the encampment, and several more marches, it was time to be heading home again. On my last evening I went to an impromptu free concert by Johnny Rivers on the steps of the Lincoln Memorial. Word had gone out earlier that he'd be entertaining the people, and I wanted to see one of the waning stars of early sixties rock 'n roll in person. I walked alone at dusk by the edge of the long beautiful Reflecting Pool past the poor people of America lounging in the evening on the cooling grass. Lovers sat on the limestone edge of the pool, with their feet in its cooling water.

And soon I was at the towering shrine where the finely-chiseled statue of the Great Emancipator is seated between majestic stone columns, and there was a small group of people waiting to hear Johnny Rivers. Mary was not among them.

It had been an intense week for both of us, well beyond the political reasons for our individual journeys to Washington. Earlier in the day we had managed to evade Shondra and we spent some time talking about our prospects. Despite our common interest in civil rights and other causes of our generation, Mary and I each realized there was a gulf of background and experience between us. Neither of us could really fully understand the other, our different histories, the problems we each faced and were destined to wrestle forever. What would she do with me in the foreign environment of Black south Chicago? She was at rest in urban Black culture. As a westerner who needed mountains and wide desert vistas, I would have plenty of trouble adapting to her urban world. And I didn't think she'd ever understand the appeal of the stark and lonely West. We had fallen in love with a national moment that we had shared with each other, but for only a brief time.

We each knew we'd never be together again after we left the encampment and returned to our distant homes. We were bound by our cultural limitations and unable to continue a long-distance relationship. In the end we held hands for a moment, my white hands, lightly tanned and brilliant in the sun upon her smooth and velvety black skin. Then I kissed her and we parted quietly. I watched her walk away and disappear into the crowd, and that evening I went to the concert alone.

Fifty or so people were gathered at the ancient base of the Lincoln Memorial as Johnny Rivers sat down on an upper step and began to softly strum his guitar. Between songs, he spoke with us about the importance of what we were doing here in Washington bringing these problems to the attention of Congress and the public, and the significance of what we had accomplished so far. He had come to be a part of it and to help the cause, in his own way. It was good to see him with a small group of poor people in the open air of a waning summer evening. He didn't have to be here and we appreciated his support. The last faint rays of light etched a golden halo across a misty horizon as the night unfolded and for the next hour or so his songs spread through the air. Then he ended with his most famous and most appropriate piece, a simple, acoustic version of "The Poor Side of Town." Fine notes drifted from the heavy limestone steps with a light evening breeze off the Potomac. That song still mingles with my recollections of the Mall and those thousands of committed people, and it remains one of my favorites to this day.

I listened to the last of the music as the first hazy distant stars appeared in the sky. Then I walked away through the slowly cooling night to my lean-to, and knew it was a good thing to come here and be part of something that was meaningful. We were the next generation. It was our turn to take responsibility for some of the problems we saw around us and to craft a better solution, to make things better than they had been. It was good to be part of it all.

But there were important things to do back home, like figure out how to pay the rent next month. I was running low on traveling money, too. I hadn't started out with much in the first place and hadn't managed to acquire much along the way. I would be going home by way of Louisville to visit some relatives I hadn't seen in years. Many years might pass before I'd see them again. Some were getting old and it was possible they might not be around the next time I was back this way. I had done what I came to do—whatever those original intentions had been. Hardly anything ever turns out the way you think it will, and my time in Washington was different from whatever notions I had when I hit the road several weeks back. It seems like it always happens that way.

The road was calling me again, its sweet song rising above the speeches and proclamations, its call drifting over the voices of the people I'd met and the restless sounds of this powerful city. The road is a jealous lover who won't let the wanderer rest for long in someone else's warm and loving arms. There would be more adventures on my way back to brilliant and fiery sunsets among the dry and rugged mountains of the West.

In the morning I tied up my bedroll, hefted my well-worn pack, and took my last walk across the Resurrection City. There were new arrivals at the check-in tent and now there would be another empty lean-to for them to claim. The day's marches and events were posted on a bulletin board and these new people would carry on the effort. People still sat along the rugged edge of the Reflecting Pool and swirled their feet through its cooling waters as I walked onward into the crowded streets of Washington DC.

I caught a ride with a delivery truck driver to a good spot on the Beltway. He was curious about how things were going on the Mall and seemed to realize that it was also about him and his future in America. I did my best to explain what was happening in the short time we were together, but where to start the story? And where to end it? As he stopped the truck I stepped to the ground and I thanked him for the help, and he wished me luck. Then he disappeared into a steady stream of workday traffic as I set my pack at the graveled edge of the pavement.

There was a clear morning sky overhead, with a few small white clouds scattered across what little I could see of the horizon beyond the trees. The roadside grass stood tall between gusts of traffic wind. The daily heat of summer was starting to build, and between the guttural roar from passing cars and trucks a song of crickets and locusts filled the air. This small slice of roadside nature and the adjacent stream of traffic were part of the endless flowing fresco of American life, and it would still be here if I ever returned.

There was still a five-dollar bill in my pocket and some fruit I had stashed off the breakfast table. I faced the traffic and stuck my thumb into the morning's heavy, humid air. Next stop, Louisville, Kentucky.

4

A CONVERSATION

We were still driving south toward Mexico and I drifted back to the conversation in the VW Microbus. It was a conversation hindered by the wind from the open windows, and thanks to the lingering effects of the joint that Mark had passed around when we started this trip, it had taken a long pause as we each drifted away on our own stream of thoughts.

After my experience in the Taos commune debacle, I was interested in the workings of Mark's and Linda's urban commune experiment, although I remained suspicious of utopian schemes in general. But I had a lot of questions that Mark seemed happy to answer.

"Actually, the commune thing works pretty well for us," Mark said. Something in the dope had started to make him more talkative.

"With six people and two dogs involved we've had a few problems, but we've been able to work them out by staying focused on our original goal of creating a viable sense of sharing and community." Mark was always positive and idealistic about the possibilities for a communal and socialist world order. He and Linda and the others felt it was the only political form that had the potential to distribute the world's assets equitably. I agreed that capitalism wasn't likely to do it anytime soon, but the real question was whether the people who controlled most of the wealth were going to allow anything like that to happen on a meaningful scale.

"So it's working out alright for the six of you," I asked, "but how do you see your group efforts relating to the larger world? That is to say, how do you see it translating to a broader context?" I knew there were utopian communities established in parts of this country long ago. Wasn't there a New Harmony, Indiana? What about the Amana Communities in, I think, Kansas or Iowa? But I didn't know enough about them to even ask the right questions.

Mark loved a question of broad magnitude. In the rear-view mirror I saw his eyes glow at the prospect of an intellectual exchange. And I was focused on the way he expanded his wonderful ideals.

"It's working well for us now and the bonding mechanism we've created has given us each a richer and better life than we could've had individually. With this little experiment of ours having been so successful, I would hope that we can lead by example," he continued. "The world is clearly looking for a better way to ensure a decent life for all. Americans are a relatively wealthy people. We're the ones who can afford to experiment. We can afford to try new things, to learn the lessons of community and then bring them to reality. When other nations of the world see the potential for positive change, they'll demand their rights and I hope then we can all work together to build a better system."

Mark was confident in the inherent intelligence and good will of the peoples of the world and he personally found the communal life to be rewarding. In my own limited experience with communal life, I had found the process to be difficult and challenging. I wondered if others would be willing to work harder than I had been at making it happen. Maybe the commitment and honesty it required was just too much for me. And I wondered whether the vast majority of the world's population—the ones with little or nothing of value—could ever get organized enough to demand what might be their rightful share of the wealth, the wealth they had in fact created for someone else through their own hard work. They seemed to spend much of their time worrying that some guy just down the street was getting something over on them and never seemed to notice the fancy cars and lavish mansions their bosses owned. And clever politicians supported by the rich recruit the young and the strong from this lower-economic group to join private armies and turn their guns on their own countrymen, their parents and their brothers, to protect the holdings of the rich.

I had been having this conversation with Mark for years now. He'd become less of a radical bomb-thrower since he'd been busted for scrawling "Kick the ass of the Ruling Class" on a wall at the university a few years back. But he was still action-oriented. And I probably spent too much time thinking about things, and not getting much done in the process.

For me there has always been the question of how we can strike a balance between the two extremes that have traditionally defined this debate: the traditional libertarian capitalist view of the sanctity of private property and complete personal freedom on the one hand, and the socialist ideal of communal strength through collective ownership, joint decision making, and collective responsibility. Were there really absolute answers to these questions?

"It's the old Hobbes versus Locke discussion if I remember my philosophy classes correctly." I could see by the glint in Mark's eye that I had scored with that gambit, using a classical source to support my argument. But he was waiting to see if I could pull it off. "Hobbes, I recall, had the idea that all powers were held by society, through the government or whatever, and the individual could freely exercise only those rights which had been granted to him or her, although come to think of it I don't recall that women were mentioned often in his thoughts."

Linda glanced at me and I continued, "Locke said the individual held all the power and was only required to grant portions of that power to society in order to achieve some kind of workable social contract that would enable us all to live together in relative peace. As far as I can tell, Americans seem to follow some extreme Lockeian model that allows them to do whatever they want and anybody who says otherwise can go to hell, at least until they get into trouble. Then they want the government to bail them out. Big business especially likes bailouts."

It sounded good to me so far, and neither Mark nor Linda seemed to remember enough about two old English philosophers to challenge it. I seemed to have established an early beachhead in the discussion. Now I sat back and waited for Mark to demolish it. He usually nailed me when he quoted some obscure contemporary leftist philosopher I'd never heard of. I always preferred obscure classics myself and so, for a brief moment at least, I had him on the ropes. It was a rare occasion in our many discussions over the years and I cherished it while I could.

"It seems to me that neither pure capitalism nor pure socialism really works all that well." I stayed with the initiative before he had a chance to respond. Mark had a grin on his face. I was clearly enjoying this round of our endless intellectual grappling. And he was too. Linda laughed as she watched from a ringside seat, her eyes shifting from one combatant to the other. She was content for now to let us play the intellectual fools, the court jesters, in our own segment of a never-ending conversation that had engaged many others who were far more intelligent throughout the ages.

"In fact," I continued, "neither of these systems, in their extreme incarnations, actually exists in the real world

Neither of them has a chance in hell of actually working in anything other than a theoretical and artificial academic environment." I was trying to find the right words, "*les mots juste*" that Hemingway and Pound used to debate about, but by now I was pretty far out on a limb and Mark was patiently waiting to sever it.

Mark smiled again at my assault on his layers of academic credentials. He always considered me to be something of a "noble but ignorant proletarian savage," I suppose, with hammer and sickle in hand, doing daily battle with the construction foremen of my life, the "running dogs of capitalism" who keep the whole system working for the corporate bosses. Yet, since I spent my days out on the front lines of the class struggle, my lower economic and social position in the capitalist world gave me something of a portfolio to his world of lettered and learned academic leftist discourse, and my early classwork in philosophy had even provided me a tenuous anchor to his own academic world. Mark seemed to view me as a touchstone between the intellectual and the practical sides of this never-ending discussion.

"As far as I can tell," I rambled onward with my latest unified theory of political science, (Mark and Linda were now laughing in the front seat as I held forth on the subject.) "in real life these systems have all been highly bastardized in order to cobble together some kind of actual, workable system. They're held together by a mythology of rhetorical fantasy with intentionally vague boundaries to allow for adjustment to the requirements of the real world. It's politically impossible for any American politician to admit that this country actually works reasonably well because of the obvious quasi-socialist system that exists today. They'd be thrown out of office in the next election if they weren't assassinated first!"

I thought I'd put it together pretty well. Mark was looking into the rear-view mirror again, but this time with arched eyebrows, feigning a recoil from my rapid assault. His black beret was tilted forward toward his right eyebrow. Linda was laughing at both of us.

Mark is a bright guy with a master's degree in Latin American Studies, and he's very politically active, but he'd grown tired of the endless academic cycle of discussion that never seemed to result in any form of meaningful action. He made the decision several years ago to leave all that behind and to forge a new life, one in which he made an honest living with his hands while working more directly to implement a new world order. He'd managed to put together a decent set of woodworking tools and skills, and began making a reasonable living as a furniture craftsman. And he still enjoyed rousing debates as he attempted to bring socialism and the concept of shared wealth and responsibility out of the university and into the workplace.

Linda was a respected educator and author of several books on early child care. She ran the married student childcare cooperative at the university. It was her turn to join the discourse.

"I agree that American 'super-patriots' have always represented our system as solely capitalistic," she began. "They portray it as a system based on the foundations of unfettered free enterprise with a so-called democratic veneer. And yes, during economic boom times they demand an end to governmental intrusion so that they can make fabulous profits, but when times are bad they want a quick bailout at someone else's expense. They're such hypocrites, and never willing to assume their share of the real risks of their beloved and selfish system! They want all the benefits and none of the inherent responsibilities. And I think you're right that the American political system really functions as a republic wherein an economic elite makes laws to govern the majority so they can more easily transfer the assets of the poor into the pockets of the rich. Only lip service is paid to the concept of democracy! We never really have a meaningful voice in the workings of our own government or our own economic system."

I rejoined the fray, rambling off in a new direction, "But is there realistically a way every citizen can have a voice in the daily workings of government when there are millions of us?" I've been interested in this question of the workability of a pure democracy versus a pure republic. Plato did not believe it was possible; he preferred the idealistic and impractical utopia of a benevolent dictatorship. "Very likely, nothing would get done if we all had a voice in every decision. While I prefer the concept of democracy, I have to admit the reality of the American system is that we have constructed a mild form of democratic-republican socialism wherein the victims of the capitalistic system—the elderly, the young, the less competent—are at least somewhat protected from starvation, and from freezing to death in the cold of winter. A lot of so-called patriots scream about our alleged 'drift into socialism,' but very few of them are willing to return their own Social Security checks or are willing to fight against government intervention to aid some large company when their own jobs are really at stake. Some countries do a better job of this socialism bit than we do but many others do nothing for the poor. Very few of us really want to see the elderly at our front door begging for food and shelter after we've actually succeeded in ending the so-called 'welfare state.' Sure, some people have figured out how to make out a lot better than others in this system, but I'm not sure I want to trust my own future to the alleged good intentions of a so-called revolutionary mob."

I'd managed to wander far into dangerous new territory now. In the late 1960s many of us had been longing for "The Revolution," but I eventually lost confidence in a complete overthrow of the present system. I came to realize it's not a perfect system we have inherited, but it works, mostly, as long as we make constant adjustments and improvements to attain greater equity for all. From what I'd been able to learn of past human experience with various alternatives, I was fearful of those other outcomes. While our frustrating system of socialist capitalism seemed to work just well enough, it showed no inclination to work any better than that.

We were young and we knew little about the horrors that followed the French Revolution and other popular upheavals of the past. And the extreme anti-communist propaganda of the Cold War had done nothing to clarify the real lessons of history. During the days of our youthful rebellion, we were blissful in our ignorance. Hard lessons of the distant past are largely forgotten by a culture that places little value on world history, that seems to value only the present. We Americans have long valued our isolation, and have tended to set ourselves apart and aloof from the rest of the world. This has made it easy for us to maintain a comfortable ignorance of the tragic lessons of world history, to keep those lessons of the past safely imprisoned in dusty historical reference works. Shortly after the initial euphoria following the triumph of common people over the rule of kings, the French Revolution was stolen by gangs of thugs who butchered and terrorized their way into the power vacuum that had been created. Later, after the betrayal of the Revolution and the rise of the new Emperor Napoleon, the poor were swept up again into brutal wars of conquest. Those who survived this period of upheaval may well have been far worse off than they were before the Revolution even began. Was Carlisle right? Was Dickens right about the French Revolution in *A Tale of Two Cities*?

At the same time, I have never had patience for the willful ignorance of "America, Love it or Leave it!" crap. A static and rigid system is an even greater threat to a fair and equitable world than the endless process of incremental change. By allowing none of the essential changes to occur, demagogues create untenable pressures that ultimately doom their so-called beloved nation to failure. Rigid economic and political systems never prevail in the long run and they are always subject in the end to catastrophic change and even violent bloody upheaval.

"But don't you think a pure socialist system is fundamental to the human condition?" Mark was back in the discussion, pulling me back from my mental wanderings.

"What do you mean?" I asked warily. I sensed tremors beneath my fragile ideological house of cards.

"Isn't the family actually the most communistic unit in the world?" Mark asked. "I mean, in a healthy functioning family, isn't each member expected to contribute according to their ability and receive according to their needs? Not many people charge their little kids for room and board, do they? And can't this obviously basic tenet to the very fact of human existence be extended to our workings with each other on a larger scale?"

Dammit! I thought to myself, there he goes again with that Socratic Inquiry stuff that he's so good at. I didn't have a quick answer for him and I considered the possibility that maybe he's even right. Maybe all that stuff I just said was basically stupid. Why can't I think a little faster than this and take a real stand on issues of importance? Why do I always end up sounding so damn vapid and undereducated at times like this, when it comes to basic philosophical discussions? I turned to look out my window at the high desert grasslands stretching far to the west. I needed time to think about this.

Mark and Linda were talking in the front seat. I envied their erudite observations. They lived their adult lives as committed idealists, attempting to fashion a real-world and personal version of communal life. They had managed to craft a workable living situation with two other couples in a large old rundown Victorian home that Mark and Linda had bought on Arno Street several blocks southeast of downtown. Each member of the commune had a career outside the home, and they shared the chores of everyday life according to a schedule that was adjusted weekly at their Thursday night communal meeting.

The main chore, to which each person was assigned one evening each week, consisted of assembling a dinner that cost no more than 50 cents per person. There was no formal vow of poverty among the household membership, but they wanted to make a group political statement. Several commune members had been in the Peace Corps, and all had traveled to many poorer countries than our own. It only seemed just and right that they should live within a modest and rational food regime. Still, even in the early 1970s, it wasn't always easy to come up with palatable dinners that were cheap enough to meet the group's criteria.

I'd stopped by one day several months ago to talk to John, one of the other members of the Arno Street commune. John was a tall and thoughtful man who maintained a nearby independent VW repair garage, and he mentioned having trouble coming up with an idea for something to cook for the group dinner that evening. As a joke, I mentioned the cheap fried-baloney sandwiches on white bread with Miracle Whip that my mother fed us when she had to deal with a houseful of hungry kids and Dad wasn't bringing home much money. We were just kids at the time and we didn't know that fried-baloney sandwiches were considered to be relatively disgusting by people of good taste. They tasted pretty good to us.

I laughed at the memory, but I noticed that John looked thoughtful and wasn't sharing the humor. Then he said, quietly and almost to himself, "Say, that's a good idea." John was always sincere and analytical, valuable traits to have when dealing with old Volkswagen engines. He was also guileless. I was still laughing when I realized he was actually serious. And then I realized that Mark was going to blame me for the culinary surprise he was about to endure at dinner.

"Yeah." John had turned away and he was staring for a minute at the wall where an assortment of wrenches hung from a row of nails as he went through the calculations. Then he continued quietly and intently, "Yeah, fried-baloney sandwiches wouldn't cost much at all."

He did the calculations in his head: so much per slice of bread, so much for a piece of baloney, a dab of mayonnaise or mustard, etc. The commune members had worked out these basic costs long ago. John was lost in deliberation, and I decided to leave the area before Mark showed up and found out about it.

Mark confronted me later and asked me to keep any further dinner suggestions to myself. John was now in enough hot water with the other commune members to last a long time without any more help from me.

Over several years our relationship, Mark's and mine, had evolved into a closeness that became closer after Annie left. And we had any number of adventures together, including an unfinished workshop we started at the back of the lot behind the old adobe house that I bought after the divorce and was still trying to renovate.

It seemed like a good idea at the time. We would build a workshop out of "liberated materials" in my back yard. The materials would be "wrestled from the evil clutches of the ruling class," and would be "placed into the service of the people." To put it another way, we were going to steal some stuff and build ourselves a cheap workshop. I suppose it played as well to our inherent young-male anger as the rhetoric of the radical right played to our opposites who wrapped themselves in the flag of cheap patriotism.

No, that makes it sound worse than it actually was. Albuquerque, like many American cities, was going through an unconscionably wasteful period at the time. It was a process officially called Urban Renewal, and in large eastern cities it was known as "negro removal," but often it actually amounted to little more than federally-funded vandalism. A large number of buildings—some beautiful, others not—were being destroyed all through the older sections of cities across the country. A front-end loader and a dump truck would show up one morning, and soon a nice older home or small building would be reduced to a pile of splintered wood, crushed brick and shattered glass. It would all be scooped into the back of the dump truck and hauled away to a landfill. There was no effort made to salvage any of this reusable material. It seemed like a lousy thing to do to our built heritage and to our natural resources.

Mark and I decided to intervene. We took adobes out of the crumbling walls of abandoned homes. We pulled old planks from the roofs of half-demolished buildings. We picked up truckloads of used cinder block. And shortly we had a pile of reusable materials for our building project.

Then we dug a 16-inch deep foundation trench. We carefully placed the cinder blocks on a 12-inch deep bed of large, fist-sized, rocks—just like we'd seen under some of the oldest adobe walls around town. Concrete foundations were overrated, in our liberated world view.

We banked the sides of the concrete blocks with dirt as a stable base to carry the adobes and keep them from wicking moisture from the earth. Soon, the adobe walls were up and we built a roof on our quaint little workshop. We were just starting to mud-plaster the walls and give thought to where we might find some glass for the old salvaged wooden window frames when a bright red "Stop Work" tag appeared one day from the City Building Department. It was sticking out of the front door jamb when we returned from one of our salvaging forays. After a few days of hassling with various officials, we came to realize that we were finished with our project. The inspector wouldn't pass the gravel foundation we had read about in an old book written by Frank Lloyd Wright, and the roof timbers were insufficient for the span. It had felt a little spongy when we laid the tar paper down, but we figured it would probably be OK. We tried one last time to talk the inspector into approving it.

"Yeah, sure!" the inspector laughed when he stopped by after a couple of days to check up on us, "Just have Frank Lloyd Wright go down to the office and approve your plans, OK?"

We stood there watching as he drove off, still laughing.

Mark and I managed to have quite a few of those kinds of adventures together, and I thought at the time that they had to be the best part of my life so far. I don't remember why we happened to be driving north on Carlisle Boulevard on one particular afternoon—it's been a while now and I just don't remember the details. Most likely we were on our way to "collect" some more "orphaned materials" we had spotted somewhere in our travels.

We were sitting in traffic on Carlisle Boulevard in Mark's ratty old VW bus waiting for the light to change at Menaul, and we were staring at the elephantine rear end of a huge Winnebago—the tin-and-plastic symbol of American excess and irresponsibility that we detested. A temporary dealer's plate was hanging by a rubber strap protruding from under the trunk latch. A salesman was probably taking a prospective buyer out for a drive around the block. Or maybe they had just taken it out onto the freeway and were headed back to the car lot. I was staring dumbly ahead at the wall of painted sheet metal when I heard Mark's fiendish laugh roll across from the passenger seat.

"Quick, pull up closer!" he said, with a menacing giggle.

I could hardly wait to see what he had in mind as I eased closer to the great barn-like beast. Mark was digging for the big folding Buck knife he kept in his pocket. He had this devious smile plastered across his face.

Now, I don't know of another vehicle in the country that we could have used for what came next. You can pull the average VW bus close enough to another vehicle to reach out and touch it—if you could just open the windshield. But Mark's bus was not a standard US-type VW Microbus. It was a model that was sold in the tropics, and it was the only one of its kind that I've ever seen. Mark and Linda had brought it back from their days in the hot and steamy jungles of Puerto Rico, where flow-through ventilation was a big advantage.

This bus had a split windshield, with each side hinged at the top and dogged down at the bottom. With our front bumper almost touching the Winnebago, Mark leaned forward and unlatched the windshield. He swung it outward and upward and locked it into position. Then he leaned out of the front of the bus and sliced the two ends of the rubber strap with his razor-sharp Buck knife. With a vicious giggle, he pulled the dealer's plate into the bus and flipped it over his shoulder onto the pile of perennial clutter we were always hauling around with us.

Then, we both howled with laughter as the light changed and we watched that obese symbol of the indolent rich waddle away from us. I unlatched my half of the windshield and locked it upward and we rode onward with the winds of liberation caressing our faces and tossing our hair. The roar of a mighty 36hp VW engine filled our ears as we watched the Winnebago accelerate and quickly leave us far behind in a petrochemical cloud. We could only imagine the scene later when a smarmy salesman tried to explain to his boss how he'd managed to lose one of their Goddamn Coveted Dealer Plates.

"Honest, boss." We could imagine the conversation. "We never even stopped anyplace! The damn strap was almost new! It couldn't have broken! Take a look at this end here! It looks like some bastard cut it, or something! I'm damned if I know how they did it! I swear we never even stopped!"

We later included that dealers' plate—another piece of material liberated from the grasping clutches of the corporate oppressors—into one of the adobe walls as we built our brand new, and doomed, workshop.

Those were great times that occupied my days and evenings after Annie left. Recalling them now helped to dull the pain of her leaving.

Another friend named Jack came by the house one day with a brand-new Ford construction tractor he had just bought. He wanted a place to practice with it, and it just happened that I was interested in having a root cellar dug behind the house. I'm not sure exactly what I was going to do with a root cellar but it seemed like a good idea to have one in those back-to-the-land organic days. Jack pointed its wide front blade at the ground and within a couple of hours I had a large hole in the yard measuring about six feet deep and eight feet across. I never did get around to building the root cellar, but for some reason that I don't remember now another old VW bus with a blown engine ended up being rolled down into the hole. The neighbors always had this bizarre image of a VW bus having been buried in the backyard of the house where some hippies lived and where a lot of other strange things always seemed to happen. Those were funny times and there was something wonderfully carefree about them.

Things like that happened in the days just after our divorce. Back in those early days before the depression really set in.

From my seat in the rear of the bus I studied Mark's face again in the rear-view mirror, the way the slanting morning sun caressed his rich, curly beard and the way it glowed a dirty brownish-red in the intense sunlight. Something about the marijuana had made the colors far more vivid than usual. I realized at that point I really loved him and that I appreciated his gruff concern for me. And I knew I could never tell him so.

To his right sat Linda, his wife of fourteen years, his partner in life. She was strong, beautiful, intelligent with her own career and intellectual pursuits. Somehow, they made room in their lives for each other. It seemed they were always on a common quest to create a better world. They had the kind of partnership that Annie and I had never attained, competing as we did with each other.

For some reason Annie and I just couldn't seem to grow together in dignity. Hell, we couldn't even just allow each other to grow at all; neither of us let the other become a complete individual, a whole person, without making crippling comments. What were we afraid of? Was it the fact she had finished her college degree and I had not? I had given up early and hadn't even come close to finishing mine. It seemed there was always another distraction, something else begging my attention and I never went back to school. Was I resentful of her success?

And did she resent my ability to get a good-paying job whenever I wanted, without any academic papers? She had done well in school and had gotten her degree in journalism, but she could never break into the field. Was she destined to be nothing more in life than a waitress? Why weren't we able to rise above these problems together and help each other through this period? What made us so weak? I didn't know the answers to these questions then, and I still don't know the answers now. I could never really figure out what was happening between us. Mark and Linda had been partners in an exciting and fulfilling life for fourteen years. Our marriage had always been a struggle and it had lasted barely three!

I turned away to look out again through the dirty side windows of Mark's van and across the broad and verdant valley of the Rio Grande.

We had shared our winter evenings, just Annie and me, by our little corner fireplace made of adobe and we read our books. As long as the logs stood vertical in the back corner of the fireplace the piñon smoke would exit through the chimney, leaving a trace of its special aroma, and the magic of firelight shining in Annie's eyes made those winter evenings into a special time for me.

And we took long summer walks in the forests of the Rio Grande Valley under towering cottonwoods, the rugged sculptures of winter, the majestic giants of summer. I remember Annie lying on a patch of grass in the leaf-dappled sunlight and wearing a light summer dress. Her long golden-brown hair lay across the grass and there was a bright yellow dandelion playfully stuck behind one ear. She was a sundress kind of girl. A jeans kind of girl with little interest in fashion. I thought of Debussy's "Girl with the Flaxen Hair."

We rolled onward to the south, past huge cottonwood trees standing by ageless little adobe homes at the edge of broad fertile fields. These were lands that had been cultivated for a thousand years and provided food and shelter for the unknown generations of people who had lived here. Their lives under the sculptural beauty of rough and massive cottonwood trees were a natural contrast to that unlovely city, and that broken life, that I was now leaving far behind me.

5

ONWARD

January 1971

"You don't own me, you know! You think just because we're married that I belong to you! I don't belong to you or to anyone else! I'll do whatever I want to do with my life whether you like it or not!"

There was something almost sophomoric about Annie's outburst, like she'd copied the words to that old Leslie Gore song. But I didn't dare say so. I never knew where Annie got this stuff, and it always surprised me to hear it. I don't think that I had ever made any gestures or demands that might suggest I intended to be her boss or the undisputed head of household. I had always been more attracted to independent women, to a partnership with a woman who'd want to share my life. I never wanted to dictate to a subservient and dependent woman, and that was one of the reasons I was attracted to Annie in the first place. She was strong-willed and curious about the world. Yet she seemed to need to cast me in the role of enemy.

We were on our way home from a party and the atmosphere in the truck had been tense when Annie finally broke the silence. She had run into Allen and she spent a lot of time dancing with him. And it seemed important to her to ignore me as I sat there nursing my beer.

"I didn't say I owned you. I just said it was embarrassing that you spent so much time dancing with him like that. Everybody else could see it, and they tried to ignore it. But they glanced in my direction when they thought I wasn't looking."

"He's just a friend of mine and I don't have to please everybody. They can mind their own damn business. Whatever I do is my own business, not theirs."

"And not yours," she might have added but she didn't. I was relieved when she stopped short of actually saying it.

"I thought you were just going to take off and leave the place with him."

"Well what if I did? What if I decided to do that?"

I was stunned. Did I have to explain the fundamentals of a relationship to her? There was no way I was not going to look real stupid if I even started down that road. You can't always fight illogic with logic—especially on the roller coaster that our marriage had become. I often found myself grabbing for the safety rail and trying to hold on until it came to a stop.

"What if I had done the same? What if I'd decided to take off with some other woman I'd met at the party? And what if I spent the night with her? How would you feel if I did that?"

"I'd hope you would have a nice time together and that she would treat you well." she said as she watched the road ahead without looking at me, "It wouldn't bother me at all. I'd want you to be happy."

I sat there numb behind the wheel of my truck and stared down the headlights into the night, and I knew what she just said wasn't true. I always felt stupid whenever we got into one of these arguments. I could never think of anything intelligent to say at this point in the discussion. There was really nothing else I could say. I knew she would be anything but happy if I spent the night with another woman, but there was no point in saying so. We'd be right back into another circular argument.

I drove onward through the night toward the little house we still lived in together. Tomorrow she would be a different person. She was always a different person on the day following one of these blowups. And there seemed to be no escape from my pathetic obsession with Annie.

January 1972

"It's someone named Misty. I think that's what she said her name was."

Annie eyed me warily as she handed me the phone. The unspoken question was written in her eyes. Why was I getting phone calls from someone named "Misty?"

Misty was a friend from Truchas. I don't even think that was her real name. She had been living there for several years now, in a little adobe home in the high mountains on that back road to Taos. She was part of a community of free spirits who lived along the various muddy roads of Truchas and other mountain villages, and they spent a lot of time with each other. Misty was just a friend now and I hadn't seen her in several years. She was calling with bad news.

"Martin is dead."

It took me a second to recover. I could hear the tears in her voice.

"Dead? Martin's dead? Are you sure?"

"He was out riding his old BSA 650 on the highway last night with no lights on. You know how he loved to ride free in the night with the cold mountain wind in his hair. He was on the road heading north out of town and a car ran into him. They never even saw him until it was too late. He just suddenly appeared out of the night with no warning. They couldn't help it."

It was some kind of accident of the universe, Misty explained in a way that fit her mystical vision of the world. It was just Martin's turn, she said. He was part of the greater sphere now, a part of the greater energy for good that eventually requires the sacrifice of us all. There was something vaguely even Christian in her atheistic view of the meaning of life.

I was stunned. There was nothing I could say and I just listened as Misty tried to rationalize this terrible event to herself, to the universe, and to me.

"I've been staying here in town at Franco and Marge's house for the last two weeks for some medical tests and I just got the call about an hour ago. Larry's old lady, Oxygen, called and told me what happened and then I called you. You're the only other person I still know here in town."

"Oh my god. I can't imagine Martin's gone. I was gonna head up there to see him this summer when I got a chance. I wanted to help him with some of the work on that old house he bought. I don't know what to say."

"Can I meet you someplace for a drink? You're the only person here who really knew him. I really need to talk about it. Would that be ok?"

I could feel Annie listening from where she sat on the couch just across the room. She was scanning through the pages of a magazine but I knew she was aware of everything I said. She hadn't known Martin very well, or of my involvement with Misty long ago. It was all over with Misty years before I met Annie. I wasn't trying to hide anything. There was nothing to hide.

"I'll meet you at Randy's Lounge on Central in an hour." I knew as soon as I said it that it was a mistake. I hung up the phone and turned to Annie.

"Who's Misty?" she asked. She was still looking at her magazine as she thumbed through the pages.

"Martin was killed in a motorcycle accident last night. I can't believe he's gone. She's just a friend I haven't seen in years since she moved to the mountains. She wants to talk about Martin. I won't be out late. I wish I didn't even have to go. Martin was a very good friend of mine. And hers. She just needs to talk."

I wasn't doing a very good job of explaining things and I knew it. It just didn't seem like there was any way I could explain it all to Annie. My own thoughts were scattered and confused by the news and I felt strangely disconnected from everything. Annie looked at me and then back down at her magazine.

I grabbed my coat and I kissed her on the forehead as I left. She didn't look up.

The first time I ever saw Martin he was riding into Placitas on an old oily motorcycle that he managed to keep running. It was an Ariel 650 twin. Those English bikes had a tendency to be oily and need a lot of repairs. It was part of their charm.

Martin had long hair and a full curly beard and he wore a dirty Levi jacket. There was a raven sitting on Martin's knee when he pulled up in front of the half-completed dome-house where I was talking to some friends. It was a memorable sight to behold. Martin had nursed the bird back to health after he found it with a broken wing. He wanted to release it but the damage was so severe that it could never fly again, so Martin and the big black bird become friends. Interesting things like that always happened to Martin.

Misty talked about the life that she and Martin and the others in their loose community had forged in the mountains, and I thought about Martin and the years we had known each other. We had been very close before he moved to the mountains.

He was always picking up dependents of one species or another. His friend Marlon—his buddies called him "Brando"—was a big bear of a guy who slept on a mattress for a while on the floor of a back room in Martin's house. He shared it with Martin's collection of spare motorcycle parts, but Brando was a member of the Cabrones Motorcycle Club and it suited him well.

One day I noticed Brando had been gone for a week or so and I asked Martin about it. Brando had run into a member of a rival Club in a bar and the guy had tried to drink him under the table. The other guy was smaller than Brando—most people are—and with a lot less capacity for booze. Soon he got tremendously drunk and searched through his addled brain for an ace card. Suddenly he pulled a gun, pointed it at the barkeep, and slurred out the words, "This is a stickup! Gimme all yer goddam money!"

That left Brando with only one choice to avoid losing status in the biker community. He said, "Yeah! This is a stickup!"

It didn't take the cops long to find them and their motorcycles about five miles down the road. Brando and the other guy were leaned against a tree, sitting in a pile of money that was blowing loosely in the wind, and finishing off the last of a couple of bottles of whiskey they had grabbed on their way out of the bar. A couple of minutes of stupidity got them each ten years in the State Pen.

Martin visited the State Pen whenever he got the chance. He was probably one of Brando's few real friends. And now Brando was going to miss him a lot.

The stories I could share with Misty were almost endless. I remembered that nice little old Hillman sedan his mother had given him to get around in. As soon as she left his driveway, he'd taken a cutting torch and hacked out the entire trunk area and turned it into the most half-assed looking pickup truck I'd ever seen. He even cut out a set of sheet metal "teeth" that he screwed to the top bar of the front grill. They kind of vibrated in the breeze and rattled against the remains of the grill as he drove around town before he moved to the mountains, and you always knew when Martin was in the neighborhood. You could hear him coming.

There wasn't anything Martin couldn't do with machinery, but it usually didn't turn out to be pretty when he got finished with it. I knew I would miss him forever as I slowly drank my beer and shared stories with Misty.

Martin had told me about that trip he took a few summers back, when he decided to drive from New York City to San Francisco. We were sitting at his kitchen table having a beer and sharing a joint as he told of leaving New York in a faded-blue 1958 Plymouth station wagon headed across the northern states to the West Coast. It had an odd push-button transmission panel on the dashboard, and the last-most bench seat faced backward, with a view out the rear window. The car looked ratty, but it was in more or less workable mechanical condition, and it was the same car he'd left Albuquerque in to drive to New York in the first place, so he was familiar with it. The condition of the car didn't bother Martin because he could fix just about anything. In fact, cars always ran better but seemed to look a lot rattier shortly after Martin got hold of them. He was actually thinking about being a full-time mechanic because it was a lot more honest than his previous life of torturing animals as a biology grad student.

By the time he was ready to head west, the car was looking a lot worse after a summer of bouncing through the potholes of New York City, and the salt air where he lived along the coast had started rusting several of the body panels. The old Plymouth V-8 had also developed a slight knocking sound from a bad rod bearing in the engine, but Martin tossed some hand tools, a case of cheap motor oil and a few other belongings into the back and headed west anyway.

Martin's long flowing hair and full curly beard, along with his grubby ragged jeans and an old shirt, meant he'd be dressed for the occasion if he needed to crawl under the car to fix anything. He surely cut a memorable figure crossing the heartland of the nation in the battered Plymouth with the wind in his hair and its rattling engine sounding through the woods and meadows while streaming a blue smoke trail of burning oil.

But by the time he got to somewhere near the center of Ohio, the knocking got so bad he knew the engine was going to blow to pieces at any moment, so he pulled over to the side of the road. First, he removed the oil pan to gain access to the crankshaft. Then he disassembled the bad connector rod and removed the entire piston assembly from the engine before reattaching everything and pouring in a few more quarts of cheap oil.

As he stood up to brush most of this newest layer of dirt off his clothes, he paused just a moment to savor a deep breath of clean country air and the call of a distant meadowlark. Then he reached down to pick up the piston, connecting rod, and rod bearing from the pavement, and with a mighty heave, he sent the whole mess sailing far out into an adjacent cornfield. It was a bright sunny summer day and just a great day to be heading West.

Martin pulled onto the road and got the Plymouth back up to speed as that two-lane road carried him westward through the cornfields of the nation. He was surprised by just how much the entire car shook now that the engine was so far out of balance, but at least the engine itself sounded better, except for that now-misfiring cylinder. After a little experimentation, he found that the car shook the least at about 63 miles per hour, so he kept it there as much as possible for the next couple of days. Martin could sense, in the back of his mind, that the engine wasn't going to last forever with an entire piston missing but it was a V-8 engine and he still had seven left, and so far, everything seemed to be working out more or less alright.

But two days later something important gave way about halfway through Montana just as he got to the top of a high mountain pass after a long uphill grade. The rattling and shaking had gotten progressively worse over the course of the previous thousand miles or so. Ominous sounds had been emanating from under the hood, and this long uphill stretch had put a lot of strain on the engine. Suddenly there was a loud bang as something vital and metallic finally sheared off deep inside the engine and the car quickly started losing speed. Martin put the transmission into neutral and started looking for a clear spot to steer the Plymouth onto the shoulder. Just then he saw there just happened to be a junk yard up ahead on the right side of the road. The momentum of the heavy car carried him onto a mud and gravel driveway and the rusted hulk shuddered to its last stop just outside the front door.

The middle-aged owner of the junkyard set his tools aside and wiped an accumulation of grit and oil from his hands as he looked out the garage door at this latest arrival. After a few moments of conversation, Martin offered to trade him the car for a ride into the next town, and soon the office door was locked and they were on their way.

"By the way, what's wrong with the car?" the garage man asked.

It was a valid question, of course, and another of those many questions guys have about cars, a subject that two men can always find room to talk about for a while. Even if one of them is a hippie and the other one is a redneck. It's how they get to know each other, and forge a bond of male camaraderie.

"Oh, there's a rod out of it." Martin replied in his relaxed and friendly manner, and they went on to discuss Plymouths for a while. They talked about this particular car and others that each of them had known over long years of working under the hood.

Now, in male shorthand, "...there's a rod out of it" generally translates to mean that one of the rod bearings has gone bad and needs replacement. It means that there might be scoring on the main shaft that requires disassembling the engine to do a complete rebuild. It usually means the engine is rebuildable, and reusable. It is not generally assumed to mean that the entire connecting rod and piston assembly is lying somewhere in a cornfield back in Ohio, but Martin didn't think of that at the time. It really didn't matter much anyway because the interior of the engine had probably been fairly well destroyed when one of the other parts had sheared and fragments of metal were thrown about as the engine spun at something like 5000 RPM. Likely there really wasn't anything usable left in the engine block anyway.

In town, Martin saw a railroad yard and thanked the junk yard owner for the ride. He got the idea to look around for a freight train that might be headed to California. This is more difficult than it sounds because they don't actually post signs on freight trains to let passing hobos know which train is headed in which direction, and how long the trip might be. And there weren't any open boxcars sitting around, either. Everything seemed to be full and everything was locked. He stood there beside one of the longer trains, deciding what to do, when he noticed an official-looking individual checking over things farther down the tracks and walking his way. Rather than leave, Martin decided to wait and see if he could talk to the guy. Martin was a very personable fellow and people generally took a liking to him. His slight British accent didn't hurt the process too much either.

"Hi!" Martin started the conversation just as the other fellow pulled up beside him. A broad, innocent-looking smile broke through his heavy beard.

"H'lo." The railroad man wore a broad-brimmed Stetson that slanted down over his eyes. He didn't smile as he paused to study Martin briefly, then he glanced up and down the tracks checking the equipment.

"Do you get a lot of trains through here?" Martin hadn't been run off yet, or arrested, so he decided to continue the conversation, such as it was.

"Some." The railroad man looked off down the tracks again.

There are a lot of people in the West who just don't talk all that much. They seem to lose the ability to communicate somewhere out in those broad open spaces that separate human settlements in the mountain West. It was occurring to Martin that this railroad guy might well be one of those people.

"Do you get many trains headed for California?" Martin figured what the hell, just go ahead and ask the question.

"A few."

The answers hadn't gotten significantly longer but there seemed to be nuggets of valuable information buried deep within. Martin nodded his head toward the flatbed railcar beside him. It was carrying a full load of large-diameter steel pipe lashed down with heavy chain.

"This one?" he asked hopefully.

"Yup," said the railroad man, and he walked off down the tracks to check on the other cars in the train. He never looked back.

Martin knew this was a gift and it might be his only opportunity, so he took a quick glance down the tracks toward the distant engine, tossed his rucksack aboard, and climbed up after it. The pipes were coated with oil and grit, but Martin happened to be wearing some of his oldest and dirtiest clothes. He figured it would only be a day or so from here to wherever the train ended up in California. He would thumb a ride the rest of the way to an ex-girlfriend's house in San Francisco. Meanwhile, he tried to make himself comfortable inside the round interior of one of the pipes. This was not an easy task because there was no flat place to sit or lie down and he hadn't thought to bring along any kind of padding on the off-chance he'd catch a ride inside a carload of oily pipe. Sitting outside on the end of the flatcar was also not a possibility as there was no place to hang on when the train got up to speed. So, he settled in as best he could, leaning on his rucksack, and waited, passing his time by reading a tattered copy of *Steppenwolf* he had been given by a different girlfriend back in New York City.

Several hours later, there were engine sounds and a long series of heavy metallic crashes as the engine finally began to pull away and the hitch on each train car engaged the one behind it. Slowly the train gathered speed and they were off in a southwesterly direction. Given the reluctant tone of his rail yard acquaintance, Martin hadn't bothered to ask where in California this particular train was headed. That might have been pushing things a bit too much. Kind of like a hobo trying to book a reservation or maybe even complaining about the accommodations. But at least he was now moving generally in the right direction.

The train rolled on southwesterly and soon left the Montana mountains behind for the open Great Basin country. Eventually the grassy plains became more arid, and finally they entered the desert as long shadows of afternoon inched their way across barren hills. The train pulled steadily forward at high speed down the tracks, and the wind howled through the long open piece of pipe that Martin had wedged himself into. Somewhere, they rolled through a dust storm and another layer of airborne grit settled onto the pipes, onto Martin's belongings, and onto Martin. As he rolled onward and southward under a blazing afternoon sun, the hot desert breath gave him the impression of being slowly roasted in oil. In very dirty oil.

Well, it can't get much worse than this, Martin thought wryly, as he managed a somewhat crooked smile. That fabled romantic notion of catching a free ride on a railroad car had never included most of what he was now experiencing, but at least much of it would wash off when he got to wherever this train was going.

Eventually darkness fell, and the train rolled onward into the unrelenting heated air of a desert night. The hypnotic sounds of the train eventually took effect, and Martin fell asleep inside his round and grimy steel cell as huge steel wheels beneath him screamed their cadence into the slowly cooling night air. Then sometime late in the night, Martin woke as the train began to slow down. He stuck his head out the end of the pipe and he could see no lights piercing the deep blackness of the desert night.

"The engineer needs to take a whiz," Martin mumbled to himself over the train noise as a crooked smile creased his parched lips. Gallows humor is always a comfort against the unknown, even if no one else is around to appreciate it.

The train finally slowed to a complete stop and the intense quiet of a desert night rushed in to fill the void suddenly left by the abrupt absence of searing wind and the pounding sounds of steel wheels making heavy love to steel rails. In its place, a buttery soft and hot desert breeze caressed the night.

There were voices in the darkness as two men with flashlights walked past the flatcar and stopped somewhere far down the tracks. Shortly, there was another long series of crashes as the train backed onto a siding that was hidden in the blackness of the desert. Then there were distant shouts and uncoupling sounds followed by the heavy diesel purr of the engine as it pulled away and disappeared into the black void of night. Martin's car, and several others, sat silent in the dark.

The night was still and empty and Martin was alone on a siding somewhere in the Great American Desert. He was exhausted from the buffeting of the wind and the constant noise, and soon he drifted quietly off to sleep. There wasn't much he could do out here in the middle of the desert. The fates had decreed his presence here and Martin thought he might as well just relax about it. A couple of hours later, a faint rosy light from the coming dawn slowly illuminated a far horizon and began to reheat his oily home in the pipe. Martin awoke and crawled from his messy nest to stretch his legs. It was good to touch solid ground again. There was nothing around but a broad expanse of desert and distant ranges of dry jagged mountains.

"Hm," Martin said to nobody in particular as he scratched his curly beard and pushed back his long hair with a dirty hand while he surveyed the scene of his latest adventure. He had not even remotely considered this possibility. In his wallet he had a couple of hundred dollars from saving his money over the summer. In his rucksack, cushioned by a layer of spare clothing, were three small peaches he'd bought in a store in the Dakotas. He had no other food with him. He also had no water.

It was just like Martin to cast his fate to the universe when he boarded the train. But until now the universe had always been kind to him.

In the desert the daily installment of intense summer heat is dropped like money into a savings account and is added to the remains of the previous day. Heat builds on heat. Barren rocks and sand hold their heat through the night and passively await the fiery light of another dawn.

Martin took a walk and enjoyed the clean coolness of early morning air, but he knew it wouldn't last long. As he reached the end of what was left of the train, Martin stared down a shining pair of tracks in the direction of that long-departed engine. He could almost imagine a vision of Los Angeles somewhere out there in an early shimmering haze as the sun rose above the eastern horizon behind him. Maybe, if he looked hard enough at that western horizon, he might even catch a glimpse of the beach at Santa Monica. He was so close he could even imagine faint sounds of surf in the distance. A dip in the ocean would feel wonderful right now and it would be a good way to wash off some of the grime he'd collected in the last day or so. But he was somewhere in the desert and he still might even be a couple of hundred miles from the coast.

He turned and walked back to the pipe-loaded flatcar. There would be time for fantasy later. He realized he needed to lay low during the increasing heat of the day and hope for the best. He had gotten very little restful sleep in his windblown "pipe berth" during the night, so he pulled himself into the shade under the flatcar and got as comfortable as he could. And very soon he was fast asleep again.

A lizard or two and maybe a few small bugs might have wandered through the shade as Martin slept, but he was unaware of them. He awoke several hours later when a passenger train roared past on the adjacent tracks headed east. As Martin looked up toward the tall glistening side of that speeding silver train he saw paying passengers in air-conditioned comfort staring out of large windows at the stark and cruel beauty of the American desert on their way to distant destinations. And then they were gone, and the desert was quiet again. Later, in the piercing heat of the afternoon, Martin ate one of his warm peaches while a freight train passed by headed west.

It was a blistering day, but eventually the blessed cool kiss of evening fell upon the land. Martin took a walk in the desert as the sun drifted slowly downward behind distant mountains, and he savored the cooling air. As the sky grew intensely dark once more he lay beside the pair of cold steel tracks on the warm earth and watched a million stars appear in the moonless blackness, magnified by the crystalline clarity of desert air. Each star was larger than he'd ever seen before and the nuclear fire that kindled each one seemed to roar through the universe. The sound, real or imagined, had a frightening edge of madness to it now and Martin found himself drawn to its hypnotic and comforting warmth and the escape it offered.

There was a sound somewhere in the distant desert that broke the spell and he pulled his eyes away to a faint black horizon where an outline of barren mountains sliced into the exposed belly of the starlit sky. An animal had moved somewhere out there, unseen in the night. A hot gentle breeze covered him like a blanket and he realized he was still sweating long after the sun had gone.

After years as a biology student, and a couple of pre-med classes, Martin knew there was a well-defined limit to how long he could last in the desert without water. He considered walking down the tracks in the night toward the west, toward some kind of civilization. He had checked all the boxcars earlier, but they were secured with heavy locks, and there was no other possibility of water in any direction, as far as he could see.

When night fell again, there were no lights visible in the distance. Nor was there even the faintest telltale loom of city lights against the sky anywhere on the horizon. Trying to walk out of the desert was a risky option. He decided to wait where he was. Somebody was paying to ship all the stuff in these railcars somewhere. They weren't just going to leave it all sitting here in the desert. Sometime in the night, he ate the second of his three peaches while another west-bound freight train roared by. The peach did nothing to ease his hunger and little to soothe his rasping dry throat.

Martin waited beneath the flatcar through most of the next day lying in a sweaty bath from the reflected red-orange desert heat as he tried to conserve the water that remained in his body. He had long finished reading his worn copy of *Steppenwolf* and had idly considered rereading it to try to maintain some contact with the human experience, and to keep from going entirely mad as an afternoon sun shone upon the desert with frightening intensity. But *Steppenwolf* was depressing, and he felt it would add to his problems if he dwelt on it. The last peach had been a sort of dinner long ago, and now he found himself staring dull and listless across a baking desert as he sat in a small patch of shade leaning against one of the heavy steel wheels of the flatcar. His flat gaze was fixed on the empty tortured volcanic redness of a distant mountain range. His thick tongue filled his blistering dry mouth. He had drifted quietly into the kind of drug-addled stupor given by the body as a courtesy to those in pain.

A million or so years of evolution had provided for this moment at the end of a person's life when there is nothing more to be done. Various bodily systems begin to shut down to conserve the last margins of life as long as possible. Martin had drifted into a gentle and comforting embrace, and he was quietly awaiting the end. In the distance there were some vague railroad sounds, but he was no longer listening. It was just another train headed east. Or maybe it was headed west. It didn't really matter anymore. They wouldn't stop for him.

Then there was the rolling crash of one railcar against another, and the wheel that Martin was propped against rolled a few inches backwards down the track. He fell sideways with the wheel and found himself lying on the ends of a pair of weathered oak ties sticking out from beneath the rails.

Shouts and other sounds mingled in the air as Martin's clotted brain began to register what was happening. He rolled to his knees and crouched to look into the distance toward the head of the train where two men were checking the connections on each car. Martin crawled out of sight behind the flatcar as he realized this train might be going somewhere after all. He wrestled his pack out from under the car and stuffed it back into his berth in the oily pipe oven, and then he crawled in after it. He was breathing heavily from weakness and exhaustion as the men walked by. The two crewmen finished checking the connections and headed back toward the engine. One of them glanced up to see Martin hunkered in the pipe and covered with layers of dirt and oil. After several days alone in the desert, he had a hard and dirty look of madness about him. The railroad man paused briefly and glanced over at his partner who had walked on further up the track. Then he slowly shook his head and gave Martin a "You poor bastard" kind of look. Then he pulled his cap down and proceeded on toward the engine.

Martin closed his eyes and breathed slowly and deeply for a moment. Soon, he heard the welcome sound of serial crashes as each railcar engaged, and the engine began pulling through a scorching afternoon breeze toward Los Angeles.

A couple of hours later he was sitting in an air-conditioned diner near a rail yard in the middle of Los

Angeles sucking down several tall cokes and a large cheeseburger with fries. With extra salt. And he sat there for a few more quiet minutes marveling at the tenuous link we have with existence when we stray very far from the elaborate network of human systems we've developed. He considered for a moment the web of biological dependency we have crafted and the stunning helplessness of the individual isolated human being in this modern world. It was just like Martin to go scientific and philosophical at such a moment.

But Martin was still heading to San Francisco, so he dragged his pack to the curb and caught a bus to the airport. There was plenty of room on the seat for his stuff since nobody had any interest in sitting next to him. He arrived at the airport with a few minutes to spare before the next plane was to leave. As he ran to the ticket counter, the agent looked at his ragged, filthy clothing and dirty pack and his mouth fell open in disgust.

"I'm not going to sell you a plane ticket!" he said emphatically. His eyes were open in amazement at the spectacle before him.

Martin stood there for a moment, surprised at this latest turn of events, and stared at the agent.

"I mean, would you want to sit next to somebody that looked like you?" the agent asked in an impatient voice.

Martin looked down at his oily, dirt-covered clothing and realized the guy probably had a point.

"Can you hold the plane while I run into the john and clean up?" Martin asked quietly as he looked again at the posted departure time.

The agent looked surprised. His mouth was hanging open. He couldn't imagine that Martin could scrape all the crud off and look presentable in anything less than an hour.

"Please? I'll only take a moment," Martin added. He was always polite.

The agent exhaled through his nose, and his face had grown redder than normal. He turned sideways and cast an annoyed look down the counter while he slowly shook his head at this request. "Well, hurry!" He spat it out and watched doubtfully as Martin ran for the Men's Room. "I can't hold the plane very long!" he called with an audible sound of disgust at the entire hippie generation. It echoed off the hard surfaces of the building and followed Martin as he loped up the concourse.

In the men's room, Martin stripped off his shoes, shirt and pants and dunked his head under a stream of hot water and hand soap to get the worst off. Several of the other patrons stopped washing their hands and stepped back to watch this half-naked hippie sloshing water everywhere at the sink and performing whatever ritual he seemed to be involved in.

Martin quickly washed his neck, forearms, and ankles with a wad of damp paper towels so that whatever was showing would at least look clean. Then he wiped the worst of the mess off the only pair of shoes he had and rummaged through his pack for the cleanest change of wrinkled clothing he could find, then he ran back to the ticket counter. He was careful not to stand too close to the agent who rolled his eyes dramatically before giving him the ticket. With a tremendous sigh of relief he walked down the gangway, leaving the ticket agent to deal with shoving his filthy pack through the luggage door behind the counter.

Now, finally, he was on the last leg of his journey across the country. He was on his way to San Francisco. To the Haight- Ashbury District. To the unofficial gathering place for a new tribe assembling itself in that glorious summer of 1967. What a great time to be young and alive and in San Francisco!

We drove south through dry desert grasslands paralleling the river and I kept being drawn back into the past, back to Annie. It was a beautiful morning and I wished I could forget about Annie, but my mind kept replaying scenes from a life that was now gone but impossible to leave behind. I turned instead toward the river valley and considered its eternal essence.

A slight upstream breeze sent the broad leaves of towering cottonwoods quaking and the rays of late morning sunlight flashed a brilliant green from the shiny surface of each leaf. The clatter of windblown cottonwood leaves in the middle of summer always sounds like rainfall to me, the song of "cottonwood rain." I've been told the Rio Grande Valley contains the largest continuous cottonwood forest in the world stretching, as it does, from Colorado to the Gulf of Mexico. At least that was its historical range. This marvelous valley used to contain a continuous linear forest before the river was dammed and channelized and the ancient connection was broken into so many small areas. Today there are long stretches of the former river bottom—mostly in the southernmost valley that divides Texas and Mexico—that are dry much of the year because all the water is drained off into irrigation ditches. And other areas are now completely under deep water from the large invasive dams that have drowned the ancient river course. Today we have strange bodies of deep water lapping the feet of cactus, mesquite, and creosote bush that line the shores of these improbable desert lakes.

Early people in the Valley dug networks of small ditches and temporary dams to water their fields. These simple structures, of earth and rock and wood, were often swept away in the spring floods and then rebuilt for the next planting season. It was a natural part of life itself, as natural as the floods of spring and the new small lakes and ponds that formed each year in the endless cotton-wood forest.

The federal government began a program of channelizing and damming early in the 20th Century to finally control the river's replenishing spring floods and to drain a lot of swampy areas that were seen as unproductive. This dam building initiative pushed back the ancient wild and natural processes of the Rio Grande Valley and it made these fertile lands more livable for settlers—a lot of them from the dust bowl areas of Oklahoma, Kansas, and Nebraska—but it marked the end of a vigorous, young, and unpredictable river, the end of an essential piece of the old west.

When my own family arrived in the Rio Grande Valley, where it meanders in a green ribbon through the stark beautiful high desert lands of central New Mexico, there was still an aura of wildness to the place. A person could get lost out there in the open mesas and canyon lands and wander for days until he died of thirst, and it was likely that nobody would even find the body for a long time. If ever. Now that was all in the distant past of a romantic childhood memory. Now there were people everywhere. People I didn't know, or maybe even want to know. And the wild land itself had been finally tamed. There was no place left in this part of the country to escape to. Very few of us could, or would, really have escaped to the ultimate freedom of those wild lands in the past. But the point is that today there is no wilderness left for the imagination. There is no place left for the mind to escape to.

But there was still Mexico. My buddies and I nourished a lot of dreams about Mexico, through high school and into college and beyond. And the Mexico of our fertile imaginations still existed somewhere far to the south. In our rich fantasies there were still exciting things to do, hidden places a fellow could escape if he really had to, a refuge somewhere "south of the border." We needed it to still be there. And now, all these years later, those adventures were waiting deep in the mysterious heart of a land called Mexico, somewhere beyond the pitted windshield of Mark's old VW bus.

Mexico I

The morning sun burned fine and hard through a dusty haze hanging over the ancient stone streets of Chihuahua. I stopped for a long, unhurried breakfast of *huevos revueltos con tocino y café* and practiced my minimal Spanish by picking slowly through the morning paper with a Spanish-English dictionary by my elbow. A feature story, with pictures, documented the presence of *jipis* right here in the capital city of the State of Chihuahua. I smiled at the phonetic Spanish spelling for "hippies."

The photos clearly showed these people, described as *greñudos* (unkempt) and *melenudos* (disheveled), walking the streets *a largo*. The pictures were taken several days earlier, and since I had arrived yesterday on the bus from Juarez, they didn't show me wandering these dusty streets. The good people of the quiet provincial city of Chihuahua had enough to worry about without the threat of another *gringo jipi* wandering their city at large.

I finished my breakfast and stepped outside into a blinding mid-morning Mexican sun. It was going to be another hot dry June day and already a dusty mist of dirt and diesel fumes hung upon the air like a soiled and faded linen curtain. Each passing truck or bus painted another dusty layer across the hazy horizon. I turned and walked toward the Cathedral.

The huge and ancient front doors stood ajar, and inside, a reservoir of cool air hung silent in lofty space giving relief from the gathering heat of the day. On this weekday, as on any other day, the *abuelitos* were kneeling and praying for divine assistance, for small measures of relief from their wretched lives of poverty. Decades of struggle were written in their leathery faces. I sat quietly in an old wooden pew and studied the handworked stone of the walls, the massive columns, and the high, distant ceiling. Small particles of dust hung silently in shafts of sunshine streaming down from clerestory windows overhead, washing a strip of floor and wall in a golden light. A murmur of shuffling feet and muffled prayer filled the space. It was a quiet time to sit upon ancient wooden pews for a moment of peace and reflection before moving on.

I left the Cathedral and walked several more blocks down a narrow, shady street toward the Pancho Villa museum. Thick walls of old adobe homes crowded the hewn-stone sidewalks on each side of the street. A front door opened to a private courtyard filled with flowers. Women were cleaning and doing laundry. A bird cage hung from a beam under a long portal, with a pair of brilliant yellow canaries happily greeting the morning.

I passed the Bar Impala at a corner just before the museum, and I thought how good a cold beer would taste. But it was still early in the day and a beer could wait until later.

The museum was privately run by Luz Corral, one of the ex-wives of Pancho Villa. As I understood it, she was the last of about fourteen of them. She had managed to collect a number of paintings, photos, guns, clothing, and other Pancho Villa memorabilia through the years after his death, and now she was making a modest living showing them in her home, mostly to American tourist types like myself.

Displays were arranged under a courtyard portal and even included the car that carried Villa when he was finally ambushed and killed in Parral, a town in the hills southwest of the city of Chihuahua. Jagged holes were visible along the side where bullets had slashed through the old hulk, now rusty from years of neglect. On a wall behind the car hung a picture of Señora Villa posing with the car, her hands on the bullet-riddled door, a broad smile upon her face.

I had been slowly following a chubby, middle-aged Anglo couple through the displays, and had successfully avoided contact with them as they tried to make sense of the accumulation around them. They wore that classic 1960s American tourist costume that was a caricature of the era. He sported blue madras shorts, a Ban-lon shirt that failed to cover his large belly, and a small straw hat with a loudly-colored cloth band. An expensive camera hung around his neck. His wife wore a plaid shirt and white stretch pants that struggled to contain her enormous rear. A pair of sunglasses with pointy corners hung at her neck from a beaded necklace. They were both having a lot of trouble with the display labels, which were all in Spanish, and I stayed just far enough away to be of no help to them.

I had not come here, to the heart of northern Mexico, to spend time with gringos. I had hoped to leave the US far behind and seriously work on my Spanish. And after the divorce I really needed the space to think, to look at my life in a different way. Maybe I should even live in Mexico. The thought crowded its way into my cluttered mind. Growing up in the southwestern US, the idea of living in Mexico always had a certain allure. As teenagers, my friends and I spoke often of heading for the border to escape trouble, but what we would actually do there after we arrived, we had no idea. Like most teenage schemes, it was poorly thought out. Kind of like joining the Marines to get away from the oppression of living at home with your parents.

As I watched the heavyset American tourist couple struggling through the museum displays, I was sure that, politically speaking, we were polar opposites. I had lived an alternative lifestyle, so far. I had written some bad poetry. I had lived in a commune. I had smoked my share of dope. They looked like a pair of Nixon Republicans. I couldn't imagine anything good could possibly come from our acquaintance. Still, I grudgingly respected whatever curiosity had brought them to this small museum in a back street of the northern Mexican town of Chihuahua. There weren't a lot of tourist attractions here, and they may not have been aware of that before they arrived. On the other hand, after this one trip they'd probably have collected enough stories to amaze their friends for years to come.

We finished our tour of the dusty remains of the life of Francisco "Pancho" Villa and moved toward the exit. We passed Señora Villa seated in a rocking chair, and she began to tell us about her life and the exploits of her infamous husband. She began her monologue slowly, in a dead-weary voice of heavily-accented English with an occasional Spanish word thrown in. I could only imagine how many times she had given this talk to groups of tourists like us. As she progressed with her tale, she began talking faster and Spanish soon replaced the English entirely. The "Republican" couple leaned forward trying to hear and decipher the story as she moved at an increasing pace. Then she stopped and stuck out her hand, palm up. She'd finished the story. It was time to pay up and move on. The Republican guy and I each fumbled with our wallets and soon we all found ourselves standing on the sidewalk out front—the Republicans mumbling to each other, me laughing softly to myself at the whole ridiculous scene. We may have had little in common north of the border, but in Mexico we were equal-opportunity suckers. I realized that now I really was thirsty, and I walked back down that hot, dusty street toward the Bar Impala, slowly shaking my head and smiling wryly.

The cool air inside the dark little one-room bar greeted me like a lover's welcome as I walked through the open doorway. When I stepped inside, six pairs of eyes turned in my direction. Two guys were sitting at a small table in the corner, three more were sitting at the bar, and the barkeep was leaning on the counter. I looked around the room, nodded hello, and took an empty stool at the bar. The place went silent as they all tried to digest the vision of a lone gringo suddenly appearing in their midst.

I broke the silence and asked for *"Una cerveza, por favor."*

One of the men, the only one wearing a suit, motioned to the bartender to put it on his tab, and I nodded *"Gracias"* in his direction. He smiled and nodded back, and for a while yet, the bar remained silent. Soon, the man in the suit introduced himself and the other two men at the bar in Spanish, and I introduced myself in English. He handed me his card, and on it was the word *Abogado*. He was a lawyer. We tried a few more sentences, but it was obvious my Spanish was not up to the task. Still, they got a few laughs from my inept efforts.

The very large fellow sitting beside me, his name was Victor, pulled out a leather *cubieta* cup containing five dice with face cards printed on each surface, and soon we were shaking it in the air and slamming it to the bar to see who would buy the next drink. I won the first round with a full-house, everyone laughed, and another beer was placed on the bar in front of me. I quickly drained my first beer and started on the second, trying to keep up with my new drinking buddies. On a wall behind the bar, little plastic bags of small dried and salted fish called *charales* were stapled to a cardboard display. I bought a couple from the bartender and passed them around.

After somehow winning a few more beers at a game which required no more than dumb luck, I asked for the *baño*, and the bartender pointed to a ragged old curtain hanging across a doorway in a back corner of the bar. The space behind the curtain was completely dark, and I guessed it to be about three feet square. It had a slippery-wet sloping floor, and I felt in vain for a light switch. The acrid smell of stale urine coated the air and stung my nostrils. As my eyes adjusted to the darkness, I looked down to where a small shaft of daylight entered from a hole in the corner at the base of the wall. I remembered a visit many years before to the men's room at the bus station in Tijuana where the floor sloped to the wall, men peed against the wall, and a water pipe along the wall dripped into the sloping trough which drained somewhere outside. This was about the same, but with no water pipe and no light to see what was going on. From the smell of things, I decided it was probably just as well I didn't see what was going on. I was careful with my aim since there were no wash-up facilities either, and I watched yellow, beer-laden liquid pour into the light and down the hole into an adjacent alley.

When I returned to my stool, one of the men sitting at the table staggered over to the bar and challenged me to an arm-wrestling contest. He was short, probably in his late twenties, heavily muscled, and there was an unexplainable anger in his eyes. I had noticed him glaring at me through beer-sodden eyes when I walked into the bar, and I had immediately headed for a stool where the people looked a lot friendlier. I knew at a glance that he would like nothing better than to kick some tall gringo butt, and he had been sitting there all afternoon with another guy, studying me and building his liquor-fueled courage. Up to this point I had done a decent job of avoiding eye contact with him. I was in fairly good shape since I had worked for years as a carpenter, and I was bigger than he was. But he looked like some kind of weightlifter or prizefighter, and I was sure he was considerably tougher than I was.

I knew this wasn't going to be much of a contest, and I wished I could figure some way out of it. The others sat quietly cradling their beers and wondering how this game was going to play.

The weightlifter wasn't interested in my efforts to laugh it off, and shortly we were engaged in arm-to-arm combat at an empty table. I struggled to stay in the bout but ended up losing two rounds in short order. I tried to take it good-naturedly and just laugh at the outcome, but this only pissed him off even more. Somehow, in the derelict remains of his feeble mind, he portrayed the whole episode as an insult; and now he wanted to fight in the street outside the bar. The arm-wrestling part had been a test, a kind of foreplay, and now he wanted blood. He glared hatred at me with dull and mindless eyes.

About this time Victor, who happened to be the biggest guy in the place, stepped between us and talked the guy into cooling off. I don't think any of the more intelligent people in the bar wanted a nasty incident to develop, and they all looked relieved when my antagonist finally backed down and returned, cursing, to his table where he sat and waited until I was ready to leave. Victor wouldn't be around to help me on that long walk back to the bus station, and this guy knew it. I knew it too. And I kept drinking and ignoring him, hoping he would leave first.

Before too much longer I had several more beers sitting in front of me getting warm. Somehow, I had been winning more than my share of rounds in a game I had never played before, and I was starting to feel bloated and alcohol sick, as well as considerably drunk. And with all my winning, I could sense that I was starting to wear out my welcome anyway. So, I told the guys I needed to walk back to the station to catch the late afternoon bus headed south to Torreón. Victor glanced over his shoulder at my drunken and sullen arm-wrestling opponent and offered me a lift which I gladly accepted.

At the station I thanked him for the ride, and he gave me his card. It read, *"Victor Coria H., Mecánico en Refrigración."* I still have his card today.

Linda looked over her shoulder in my direction. I had been quiet for a while and thinking about the possibilities that awaited me on the trip ahead, but her glance pulled me back to the present. Linda turned again to the asphalt stretching before us, and I turned to stare out the window at the passing landscape.

We passed the Los Lunas exit and it reminded me of a guerrilla theatrical group that my friends Robert and Patsy were involved with. They called themselves the Los Lunatic Players, even though none of them actually lived in Los Lunas. It was a group of lawyers, construction hands, nurses, waiters, and pre-med students who rewrote Shakespeare's plays in contemporary language and added a lot of relevant political commentary along the way. They put together ingenious costumes and minimal props to go along with their altered story lines, and if it all looked a little tacky, so much the better.

These plays were just another part of the joke our generation created often for our own amusement. Hunter Thompson called it "the cosmic giggle," or maybe it was Ram Dass, and it seemed to sum up the times. Many creative juices were flowing during this period, and something interesting was always going on. Each performance was held only once, in somebody's large borrowed house, and admission was by personal invitation only. Guests were expected to bring their own good humor, and their own booze.

I was reminded by the Los Lunas exit sign that I hadn't seen Robert and Patsy in a while. It's good to have creative friends like them, and I promised myself I'd call when I got back. I thought for awhile about the surprising number of friends I had here in this valley. Sometimes when you feel like hell you forget important things, important people. Sometimes you spend too much time alone in your misery, and alone in the world. But it can be a good thing to get away from it all for a while. To find a way to balance it all, somehow, somewhere.

The old red-and-black VW bus rolled onward through layers of dry dusty morning air. Mark and Linda were talking about seeing *Blowup* by Antonioni the other night, and they were discussing the mime scene at the end where he tosses back the imaginary ball.

"It's the same in *King of Hearts*," Mark was saying, "where Alan Bates realizes he's just a small part of a larger and insane machine during the butchery of the First World

War, and the only sane ones around are the asylum inmates. It's the same kind of crap that's going on in Vietnam today, and it never seems to end. The lunatics and the profiteers are in charge of this one, too. The profiteers are glad to support the lunatic fringe, as long as they don't have to do any of the fighting. They only leave their mansions now and then to lead the next round of flag-waving as the young on both sides march off again to kill each other. It never seems to end.

"By the way, how long were you in the Marines, anyway? You must have been sweating that damned war."

Mark had veered the conversation in my direction. He was looking at me in the rear-view mirror. I tried to gather my thoughts and search for an answer. He wore that black beret tilted jauntily down toward his right eyebrow, and he had a Che Guevara button pinned to his leather vest. He was tall, broad-shouldered and husky and he had a commanding air of self-assurance. On some days it got tiresome, but today it was reassuring to have someone else making the decisions about how much gas we'd need to make it to Juarez. And where we'd stop for lunch. And how we'd divvy up the expenses for the trip. In a way, I supposed that Mark and Linda had almost become my surrogate parental figures since the divorce. I think they needed to play out the role as much as I needed the help.

When we first met, before they formed their urban commune, Mark and Linda were renting a house in a poor section of the valley and they had a Viet Cong flag hanging over the front door. Inside, leftist political posters adorned the walls, and political tracts lay on the coffee table. Someone—probably Mark—had written "Property is Robbery!" on one wall with a large black marker. When we first met, Mark had seemed too intense for the two of us ever to be friends. But a kind of common fascination kept drawing us together.

I actually agreed with much of what Mark said about the visible corruption of society, and the hypocrisy of the corporate war machinery, but he was far more driven than I could ever imagine myself being. We were so very different. He had his master's degree in Latin American Studies, whatever that was, and he seemed to spend much of his free time in intense political discussions with professors and teaching assistants at the university. I had dropped out of college after a couple of semesters in Philosophy and Old English Lit and had become more enamored of the non-cerebral process of adobe construction. It was almost funny that we had ultimately managed to become such good friends.

"A lot longer than I wanted," I joked, getting back to Mark's question. "Probably a lot longer than the Marines wanted, too."

Something told me that Mark and I needed this long stretch of time together on this empty freeway to discuss our individual thoughts regarding the military. I had never really been Marine Corps material, but I was just a kid at the time and there was a lot I didn't know when I signed the enlistment papers. A lot had happened to change the entire world since those days when childhood delusions led me to join the Marines.

Mark was waiting for something more than a simple answer to his question, and I would spend the next twenty minutes or so sharing Marine Corps memories with Mark and Linda while the pebbly texture of asphalt roared beneath our tires.

May 1963

I had wondered about the so-called "IQ" part of the test and questionnaire I had just completed, but when I asked the Marine Recruiter if I had done okay, he said, "What? Oh, yeah, yeah. It's fine. Don't worry about it," and stuffed the whole thing into a file folder with my name or it. Then he hurriedly rummaged in his desk for an enlistment form before I had a change of heart. He was probably surprised that I could read the forms without help, and without moving my lips. I later realized I was probably one of the brighter ones he'd seen lately, and he didn't want me to get away.

When I got to Boot Camp in San Diego, it was clear that I would be spending a lot of time with some guys who were a lot dumber, less educated, and a lot less privileged than I was as a middle-class kid. Some of these guys had never had three square meals a day or had ever taken a hot water shower with soap, and they saw the Marines as a step up in life. And then there were a few others who were a lot smarter than I was—college grads, mostly, looking for a way to get past the draft and get on with their lives, marriages, and careers.

At that time, in the very early sixties, none of us knew much at all about some distant place called Vietnam. We didn't join to get out of being drafted to fight in "Nam," and we sure didn't join up out of a deep sense of patriotism to go over there and fight in some hell-ridden jungle. In early 1963, the Vietnam War hadn't even started yet, and we didn't know anything about the place.

For the great majority of us—even the non-college types—patriotism was about the farthest thing from our minds, although later in life most of us would revise our stories so we'd appear more heroic for posterity. The fact is, almost all of us freely admitted to each other that we had signed the enlistment papers to get away from the "old man" who was hassling us to get out and get a job and rent an apartment somewhere now that high school was behind us. Most of our fathers were real tired of paying our bills and having us around the house. And most of us were sick of school and didn't want to go on to college just yet—or maybe ever. But we weren't ready to enter the work force either. There were adventures to be had out in the world beyond our neighborhood, and if we joined up, someone else was going to foot the bill for food and lodging and we could put off having to grow up for a while longer. The Marines were another meal ticket, a mother figure to take care of us. I imagine the military has played that role in societies through the ages. And the restless young are a ready source of armed guards to protect the assets of the wealthy. None of us had yet heard of General Smedley Butler, one of the most highly decorated Marines in history, who testified before Congress back in the 1930s that, "War is a racket."

There was one guy who said he joined the Marines because it was his patriotic duty. He came from a military family, and the examples of his old man and older brother had set a bizarre tone for his entire life. The rest of us honestly just thought he was ridiculous, and probably even mentally disabled by his family background.

"I've decided to join the Marines," I told my Dad one Saturday morning as I was nearing graduation from high school, "so I don't have to take orders from you anymore, and so I can go do what I want."

I thought he was going to choke on his coffee as he let out a hoot and leaned forward in his easy chair. He had been quietly reading the morning paper when I entered the room and peered over the top of the Editorial section to make my announcement.

"Wait, wait a minute!" he coughed as he tried to regain his composure amid all the laughter while the newspaper crashed into his lap. "Let me get this straight! You're going to join the Marines so you don't have to take orders from me anymore?"

His mouth was hanging open in disbelief. He was laughing so hard that a tear was running down his face. He dabbed his eyes with a handkerchief and peered back at me with an incredulous look.

"Wull, yeah," I said and looked away at the floor.

He had me this time. What I had just said was amazingly stupid and I knew it instantly. But it was the same kind of stupid thing all my buddies were saying to each other and to their own parents at that time in their lives. We knew nothing of bullying sergeants and incompetent lieutenants, and the horrible reality of war. We only shared a Saturday-morning cartoon fantasy about war and bravery. We weren't smart enough yet to figure out that John Wayne and other phony celluloid heroes had been draft-dodgers during the Second World War. That's why they had the time to make cheap propaganda movies in the safety of sunny California instead of going overseas to join the real battle. They'd hung out around Hollywood creating a fantasy world of heroism while other guys went off to fight and die by the thousands in that sordid meat grinder called modern warfare. It was the most venal form of self-promotion directed at the young, the simple, and the naive. And I had fallen for it just as other young guys had long ago.

But now that I had made the announcement it was too late to reconsider. I had already told my buddies that I was going off to the Marines. I couldn't back down now without losing face and looking like an idiot. I had to go through with it even though it was starting to look more and more like a big mistake. What is it about this damned male pride business, anyway? Why do we do this to ourselves?

Mark listened silently and studied my face in the mirror as we rolled onward toward Juarez. I wondered what he was thinking.

6   **FURTHER**

Mark's old bus crested a sandy, windblown hill and we dropped into a broad fertile valley of farmland embraced by an ancient oxbow at the town of San Acacia. The river has long been channelized here along the eastern side of the valley below where it passes through a natural cut in the dark volcanic mesas. It no longer floods the old oxbow which is now planted with orchards and alfalfa. A few years ago, a friend of mine caught an eel somewhere in the river along here. An eel, for god's sake! I never even knew there were eels in the Rio Grande. The idea of eels in this river seems so ancient now in an age of dams and channels and industrial farming.

When Don Juan de Oñate led the first band of Spanish settlers northward up this river into New Mexico in 1580, they reported finding previously-unknown kinds of fish and seeing an amazing abundance of waterfowl in the many oxbow lakes and backwater sloughs that were reshaped and recreated each year by the spring floods. Their written descriptions weren't scientifically accurate, so we don't even know what those fish actually looked like. But they were doomed when modern engineers straightened and tamed this vibrant river. Many of the unique species that had lived here since time began are gone now. Because of human progress—because of us—we'll never know what managed to survive here for millions of years only to be obliterated by human activity. And they still lived in this river only a hundred years ago.

"So how tough was it in the Marines, really?"

We'd been riding along feeling mellow for awhile, looking out the window and thinking our own thoughts as the landscape passed when Mark broke the silence and steered the conversation back to my military days. He seemed to hate it when things got too mellow. He'd throw out a comment or a question—a challenge, really—to shake things up, to get people engaged again. At times he seemed to have too much energy.

And he had an interest in the so-called "military experience." He'd been safely in college during the worst of the Vietnam War but was a vocal part of the anti-draft movement, and I respected him for that. He'd missed out on the draft and the opportunity to have some dumbass drill sergeant scream orders in his ear. It was a basic rite of male passage, of male bonding at the most primal, most animal level, that he and others had intelligently avoided during a period when the political leaders of the nation decided that the Gross National Product and the profits of Boeing, Dow Chemical, and Bell Helicopter were more important than the lives of the nation's young. Given the lucrative political payoffs, they quickly abdicated their responsibility to guide and protect a younger generation. And they never even considered the lives of a million or more Vietnamese who would be killed during the War.

Most draftees were minority kids and their parents had no political power, so the Congress and the President really didn't give a damn about them anyway. I opposed the draft myself at the time, and not because it affected me personally. I had already joined the Marines out of high school. But the draft was a too-convenient way to supply fresh young bodies for an immoral war. Those who opposed the war and the draft were dealt with harshly by the professional war bureaucracy. People who spoke out against the madness and the corruption were accused of sedition—essentially, of being traitors to America for speaking freely. It was a time for real patriots to question the architects of this crime. But there were few in Congress or in our parents' generation who were brave enough to do so at that important point in our nation's history.

I was once threatened with court martial for discussing the issue with other Marines, and also for passing out a few copies of an antiwar rag with an article of mine condemning the bombing of Cambodia. I was called into the colonel's office early one morning, and I stood at attention as he accused me of gross ignorance of the historical facts regarding the nation of Vietnam and its relationship to the larger strategic picture of Southeast Asia and China. He had a simplistic answer to everything.

I happened to know that he was working on a master's degree in history at the time and that his basic thesis in support of the discredited "domino theory" of US involvement in the war had been poorly received in the History Department. A friend of mine in the department told me he was not going to be getting his master's degree at this university any time soon as he had demonstrated a fatal inability to synthesize original thought and to separate propaganda from reality. In short, he was prime Marine Corps material.

The colonel had a willful ignorance of the facts regarding the ancient conflict between the Chinese and the people who occupied the lowlands of Southeast Asia. A unified Vietnam under Ho Chi Minh would prevent his dreaded domino effect from ever becoming reality. So now he was lashing me with his hare-brained theories. I was the unwilling subordinate who was forced to stand at attention and endure them. He had a copy of my article laying open on his desk, printed in a rag called *The Burning World Review*. What could be the problem with that?

I soon lost the flow of the colonel's confused diatribe and was distracted by the morning sun sparkling across the array of golden insignia, good conduct medals, and the other cheap ornaments, the "fruit salad," that hung from his starched and pressed uniform. As he slogged through his rhetorical mire, I figured this guy was probably a "terminal colonel." A guy who lacked enough intellectual horsepower to ever make the rank of General. I was still naive enough then to assume that the higher-ups expected someone to be able to think clearly when he made that last hallowed rank. And I thought how primitive we still were as a people when this pompous red-faced fool in a military costume could have such real power of life and death over me and so many other young men just like me. Why had society granted him and his kind this level of power in the first place? Where are the responsible voices when the nation needs them? What's happened to our Wise Ones, our Sachems?

After some futile attempts to reason with this colonel I knew the smartest thing was to shut up until he ran out of vitriol. After the tirade he dismissed me from his sight with a contemptuous wave of his hand. And I heard no more idle threats of courts martial or other attacks on my First Amendment rights—which, by the way, are not sacred in the courts of military justice.

We drove by a pile of broken beer bottles sparkling on the shoulder of the road in the morning sun, and I thought about another rite of passage in our society. In young male culture being an irresponsible asshole is one of the more acceptable routes to manhood. At a certain age, peer pressure seems to demand it.

"Jesus Christ!" Mark spat out as he switched off the radio in the middle of some barely audible Led Zeppelin song. The static had increased to the point of being a major annoyance as we pulled farther away from town. "That's enough of that racket!" he said, putting the world of AM radio behind us. The sudden advent of blessed quiet was broken only by the constant drum of tires on pavement.

"Hey, tell us about your heroic frogman days," Mark continued. "What the hell, we've still got a few hours to kill."

He flashed his impish grin in the rear-view mirror. At the speed we were going, we had about four or five more hours on the road. He wanted to know what it was like to train in the deep waters of the cold Pacific Ocean in January at night off the California coastline. He'd asked me about it before, but he was always a little uneasy bringing up the subject, and we'd never had this much time to really talk about it. It seemed easier to ask the question now, with Linda here.

Mark was fascinated with the idea of swimming through the night and crawling like a primitive life form onto a remote and deserted beach. I think it was even titillating for him, a kind of naughty thrill for a hardcore Leftist who would never experience it for himself.

And he'd gotten me distracted again, for which I was grateful. I was no longer festering over Annie—at least for a while.

September – December 1963

The first stop in my not-illustrious military career was boot camp at the Marine Corps Recruit Depot, MCRD, San Diego. There was another Marine boot camp on the east coast at Parris Island in South Carolina, but I never saw it. After sixteen weeks of hard physical training, riflery, and military indoctrination, they trucked us north, up the coast for four more weeks of Advanced Infantry Training at Camp Pendleton. We spent a lot of time marching along dirt roads in long dusty columns, and practicing infantry maneuvers in the golden grassy hills of Southern California. We lived in the dust and the dirt, we ate in it, and each night we made camp, and we sat around a fire in the dirt cooking our meals until we crawled into little green tents to sleep on the hard ground. One night I had the clearest dream that in the morning when I awoke all the other Marines and all the noise and all the dirt were gone, and everything was quiet and clean. The rising sun had rinsed the land with a cleansing light and I was alone.

But my most stunning memory at Camp Pendleton came just a few days after our arrival. The sergeants and lieutenants in charge marched us to the chapel, as is customary for new troops, to hear a talk by the chaplain. We filed into the plain wooden building, filled rows of hard-backed pews, and sat down facing a simple, nondenominational altar. We listened to the standard chaplain's welcome containing futile exhortations about maintaining the purity of thought and language here in the Marines that our parents would find acceptable when we got back home. Without the sergeants and lieutenants standing along each wall and watching over this sea of cocky teenaged energy, there would have been a lot of rib-poking and guffawing in the audience. But we maintained a respectful silence while the chaplain droned on.

Then someone hurried in from a side door and whispered urgently into the chaplain's ear. He was clearly shocked by the message and turned toward the messenger to exchange a few more words. His brow was knit with concern. We sat there, alert now, our backs straight against the hard wooden pews, wondering what was going on. The sergeants exchanged glances and watched the lieutenants. Then the chaplain turned toward us and cleared his throat.

"We have just gotten word that..."

He stopped and looked down at the podium where his notes lay, now irrelevant in light of the news he had for us. As we sat in the pews, we still had no idea what was happening. We glanced at each other.

The chaplain swallowed hard and then he continued, "...that the President has been assassinated." His voice was breaking as he told us the President of the United States had just been murdered, and the Vice President had been sworn into office. He stopped again and stared back down at the podium. We could see he was badly shaken by the news.

We glanced at each other in shock. It couldn't be. Not an American President. The officers and sergeants were speaking in hushed tones. The last president that was assassinated was…Garfield, or somebody? And wasn't that about a century ago? This kind of thing wasn't even a possibility at this time in our history. Kennedy was one of the brightest, youngest, and most inspiring presidents we'd ever had. He just couldn't be gone already.

The chaplain cleared his throat and led us in a prayer for the nation and for the Kennedy family. His voice was failing and he stopped repeatedly to regain his composure. With the rank of Captain, he was the highest-ranking officer in the building for what was supposed to be nothing more than a routine, pro forma talk to the troops that was required whenever a new group of young kids like us arrived on base. He struggled to maintain his dignity as the prayer came to a close, then he instructed those in charge to return us to the barracks and to await further orders. As we filed out of the building in close formation, he hurried to a side door with a handkerchief at his eyes. I was struck by his essential humanity, here in a place where it was important to hide those kinds of feelings.

We didn't know what it meant, the assassination of an American president, and later, as we watched the news on TV in the barracks, the rest of the country was as confused as we were. Over the next few days there were rumors that we might invade Cuba for some reason. Or maybe we'd soon be at war with the Soviet Union. Speculation and rumors spread quickly through the camp. It was hard to put it all together.

A couple of days later we resumed training, and the sergeants gave us plenty of other things to worry about while the nation tried to sort through this stunning event and decide just what it all meant. In the end we were left with an aching suspicion that there was much more to the strange assassination of John F. Kennedy than we'd ever know. It was a farewell to an entire nation's childish innocence.

After four weeks at Camp Pendleton, in January of 1964, some of us were transferred back down the coast to the Naval Amphibious Base located at Coronado Island, across the bay from San Diego. For the next six weeks I would spend a lot of time in the ocean. For a desert boy like me, there was something captivating, and even magical, in the real danger and the terrible beauty of the sea.

January 1964

Even now I remember clearly how the night lay hard and black on the rolling surface of the water as it lapped against the hull of the ship. A moonless night was important for what we were about to do. Through the darkness, an occasional flash of light glinted like fire from the steely edge of a passing wave—the reflected light from a star, a light on a distant ship, or even from a building or a car far away on the dark Southern California shoreline. The heavy engines of the destroyer had finally stopped, and we were lying a-hull about a mile offshore as the ship lifted and settled in the endless embrace of the restless Pacific Ocean. We braced ourselves against heavy gray steel gunwales enclosing the gently heaving deck as we awaited our orders. There were four of us, dressed in heavy black wetsuits. Our faces were smeared with oily camouflage paint—a kind of pancake makeup for the late-night show. At our feet was a pile of carefully-packed waterproof bags containing all our food, clothing, weapons, and everything else we would need for the next two or three days.

When the order came down, we slipped over the side and climbed partly down the heavy rope cargo netting with our swim fins in one hand, then we dropped into the dark water below. The stunning cold of the water along the Southern California coastline always caught me by surprise, and it took my breath away this time again as it squeezed downward into my wetsuit and chilled me to the bone. It was the same last time and the time before that, when that first jet of icy water shot through the neck opening in the torn wetsuit that had been used by countless trainees in the past, and poured down my back. My bony young ribs clattered in agony and screamed, "Why are we doing this?" I muttered, "I'll get used to this pretty soon and it won't be so painful the next time." But I never got used to it.

I pulled my swim fins onto my feet over a pair of heavy cotton socks that I wore as a cushion against blisters. I started stroking against the water to build up body heat while a couple of sailors dropped our dry-bags overboard. I wondered why we weren't issued rubber booties like real frogmen instead of cotton socks, but this was a low-budget production and we had to make do with what we got.

When everyone had his gear, we started pushing for shore, the engines came back to life, and the huge dark hulk of the destroyer slowly pulled away and back out to sea. She would return tomorrow night and wait for us at this same location. Tonight, it was up to us to get ashore in the darkness without being seen, hike a couple of miles inland to measure an open area for helicopter landing sites, and get back tomorrow night without being caught or "killed" by the "enemy."

On the following night this same destroyer would flash a coded signal with a red light at midnight. We would reply with our own signal and then leave the beach for the long swim back out. The ship would wait on station for about two hours before she pulled away again. If we didn't make it, we were on our own for the night. She would try again the following night, but we didn't have a lot of extra food with us, so it was best if we made it back the first time. Besides, if we didn't make it, we had a lot of explaining to do to the sergeant and the lieutenant in charge. It wouldn't be a pretty scene.

If this were the real thing, they would figure we were dead after the second night. They wouldn't try a third time. I was glad it was just another drill and we were only "invading" Camp Pendleton. If worse came to worst and we were desperate, we could walk about ten miles down the shoreline to beg for a hamburger at a beachside food stand in Oceanside. Maybe we'd talk to a few of the cute girls who hang out there. Maybe even have a little wine and read a little poetry in the warm sunshine while gulls wheel and call overhead and surf caresses the shore. That would be my kind of war. Refined. Civilized. Nobody gets hurt.

But now we were in the cold Pacific Ocean, facing a

long slog for a dark and distant shore. We rolled onto our backs and began the process of heavy stroking as our leg muscles pushed against the rolling water and we moved slowly toward the coastline, each of us dragging his waterproof bag on a tether behind him.

The destroyer was quickly lost among the distant lights of coastal shipping moving well offshore and we were alone in the darkness, each of us an independent entity responsible for getting himself to our destination. We drifted apart to find clear areas to swim, and my wetsuit began filling with the warm

water of exertion—broken by an occasional cold wave down the back of my neck. It caught my breath again each time and I had to concentrate to resume a rhythmic pattern of breathing in time with the long strokes of my legs and the rolling motion of my body.

There's a quiet unrelieved monotony to swimming in the open ocean and it yields grudgingly. Soon my legs began to ache with muscle pain. I looked over my shoulder at the dark shoreline and the jagged hills beyond slicing across a star-filled sky. There was a long way to go. After an hour or so of heavy swimming, we were still at least half a mile offshore. Because there are no real markers to gauge against, ocean swimming seems to take forever to get anywhere. It was going to be a very long night.

I settled into my thoughts and tried to ignore the pain burning through my throbbing leg muscles. I was looking forward to the surf zone where breaking waves would give us a welcome push toward shore. It's exhilarating to have a large curling wave break over your head if you're ready for it; the rush of thundering water grips your body and shoots you forward above a receding layer of water just below. You ride encased in foaming surf like a piece of ocean debris and grind to a stop on the sand. Then you pick yourself up, no longer weightless, and waddle clumsily up the beach as waves try to knock your feet out from under you. Once your feet have touched the ground, you've reached the point where your graceful ballet with the relentless sea is over, and you're land-bound again. As you desert your jealous lover, she makes it difficult for you every awkward step of the way.

But I still had a long way to go to reach the shoreline. It was best not to think too much about it. It was better to concentrate my thoughts on what was happening at the moment.

One of the most striking revelations of ocean swimming at night is the phosphorescence of algae in the water. It paints the crest of each breaking wave with a soft and eerie glow, creating a halo of light around anything that stirs the water. As I stroked along across the vast surface of the dark Pacific Ocean, I was surrounded by a glowing cloud of my own making. I could imagine that we might even be visible from an aircraft above us. And to large animals lurking in the ocean far below as we made slow progress across the star-speckled surface of the sea. I thought of the times I had been fly fishing, and I recalled the way the fly settles onto the surface and drifts quietly with the current, enticing the trout below until the trout takes it and disappears in a splash and a flurry of bubbles. But I was now the bait. And there wasn't much I could do about it except to keep swimming and hope for the best. I knew there were a few shark attacks every year along the California coast, and I couldn't help thinking about it as I stroked, with renewed enthusiasm, for the distant shore.

I had settled into a deep rolling rhythm and into an almost trance-like state when I was suddenly jolted back to reality. I hit something in the black emptiness of the water and found myself lying on a large and spongy and strange looking mass floating in the dark. I turned to look forward and was relieved that I had only run up onto a kelp "island," part of a dense kelp forest stretching along the coast just outside the surf zone. I had been stroking hard, making headway toward the beach, when suddenly I ran high aground onto this large soft mound of floating plant matter rising, falling, swaying, and undulating with the sea. I rolled onto my belly and pushed down to lift myself enough to slide back into the sea, but each time I pushed on the kelp it sank beneath my hands and I was still stranded among the clinging fingers of the plant. I felt long anchoring ropes of kelp in the water below wrapping around my dangling feet, fouling my swim fins, and tangling me in their embrace.

I kicked hard and fought to free my legs until I was clear of the underwater part of the problem and my legs were floating free again on the surface. But I was still lying on a soft, rubbery mass of kelp leaves and branches that broke off in my hands whenever I tried to grab something to pull or push myself off. I was breathing hard from the swimming and struggling, and each time I did anything to extract myself, a loose branch or two of rubbery, slimy leaves would slap across my face and at least some of it would end up in my mouth. I spit out the salty slime and stopped for a moment to think about the situation.

I realized the only way I was going to get out of this mess was to roll over and over sideways like a log to the edge of this floating kelp island until I fell off into clear water again. It was a shorter distance rolling to my right, and I could see a channel through the kelp toward the shore, so I pressed my arms against my sides and started kicking my feet in a rotating motion. By the time I had rolled twice, I slipped back into the cold dark water of the Pacific Ocean and began swimming on my side, looking forward and steering for clear water as I threaded my way through an archipelago of kelp islands. Every so often, far beneath the surface, I caught the flash of a large shape as it bolted through deep phosphorescence in the kelp below me. I was in the ocean jungle where the struggle between prey and predator plays itself out every day. And every night.

I threaded my way through the remainder of the kelp until I was clear of it, and I could feel the waves building as I neared the back edge of the surf zone. I was just outside the surf zone and the foaming edge of a breaking wave was visible just ahead. I stopped and surveyed the beach from the safety of the water to see if there was any "enemy" activity. If there was a sighting, like maybe a bunch of other Marines having a beer party on the beach, we'd have to swim along the coast until we found a better place to come ashore. Or we'd have to stay offshore until they left the area. That could take a while, depending on how much beer was left and how the party was going.

But this time the beach was clear, at least as far as we could tell. It was pitch dark and there was no way we could have seen anybody waiting in ambush behind the first line of dunes or in the line of scrub just beyond the edge of the sand. I was glad that on this night we were only playacting. Finally, we signaled each other with the all-clear and started swimming toward the beach.

There was a roar of heavy water just over my shoulder and I turned to my left to see a thin curl of foam topping a large breaking wave just behind me. Then I felt the powerful lift and acceleration of tons of water as I rode up the front of a curling wave, engulfed by the foaming crest as it roared down a steep face of water and swept me onward in its grip. I had gotten a welcome ride from a large coast-wise breaker and I glided effortlessly with the force until I settled into ebbing waters in the middle of the surf zone. Then, smaller inshore breakers pushed me to the shore and I was grounded in about a foot and a half of shifting, sandy water.

We looked around again for signs of activity before rising from the ocean. The fact was, at this point if there was anybody out there with a gun, we were all screwed. We didn't have scuba gear, and the buoyancy of our wetsuits wouldn't allow us to dive below the surface of the water, anyway. And there was no way we could swim back out through the surf fast enough to avoid being killed. We'd be silhouetted against a wall of brightly glowing phosphorescence in the turbulence of the surf zone. If this were a real war, we'd be sitting, or swimming, ducks.

If this were the real thing, our only hope would be a bored, sleeping soldier who'd wasted many other nights guarding this same empty expanse of beach. Our only hope was that enemy soldiers were no more efficient than we were, and I hadn't really thought of us as a "crack" force of invaders. We were in pretty good shape, and we were doing what we needed to do, but we weren't exactly "lifers" and we weren't completely dedicated to it. The fact is, we were a bunch of kids just out of high school looking for an adventure. If this were the real thing, we'd all be cut down by machine gun fire before we got out of the surf or halfway across the open ground, and that would be the end of it, the end of our life stories. We were nameless and wouldn't rate a footnote in a history book. As if we'd even care at that point.

Most of us didn't really look much like those hulking, iron-jawed guys on the recruitment posters that snared us into the Marines in the first place. When I checked the mirror, or watched the other guys going through this wetsuit and rubber boat training, I saw anxious young kids trying to get through a kind of manhood ritual. At some point I guessed I would burst full-blown into manhood. Black hairs would curl from my chest and I'd grow muscles of steel. But although I had put on some solid weight, I was just another boyish face in the crowd. I was another teenager, fresh out of boot camp with a weird haircut and wandering the streets of San Diego whenever I snagged a weekend pass.

That was all somewhere far away. At the moment I was still lying in a couple of feet of swirling salt water on a southern California beach in the middle of a moonless night, trying to hide as the water surged past and foamed upward onto the beach. I knew that any minute now the rubber was going to hit the road. Our team leader, Jensen, would yell, "Let's go!" Then we'd jump to our feet and struggle through the remaining water with our bulky waterproof bags, and cross the broad stretch of completely exposed beach to find cover, some place to hide and regroup for our march inland. And after that we still had a busy night ahead of us.

Jensen waved his right arm forward and we all scrambled to our feet and started running and splashing through the surf, trying to look inconspicuous under the circumstances.

Everybody but Chabot, that is.

A loud whoop and a scream of "Geronimo!" shattered the night behind me as Chabot ran whooping, hollering, and laughing through the surf and up the beach. There was something about all this playacting that he never managed to take seriously.

"Chabot, you bastard!" yelled Jensen over the incessant roar of the surf. "Cut that shit out!" Jensen and the rest of us ran up the beach following Chabot's maniacal outburst. He must have practiced that laugh in his spare time. I never could replicate it, myself.

By the time the rest of us ducked behind the dune where Chabot was sitting, he had already wrestled off his wetsuit and was digging into his waterproof bag for his only dry set of clothes.

"Chabot, goddammit, we're supposed to take this seriously!" Jensen was sounding like a top sergeant or something. He came from one of those southern families, from Alabama as I recall, where his older brother, his Daddy, and his Gran'daddy had all been in the Marines. Worse yet, the older two had each fought in a war somewhere, and his brother was probably headed for a new war that was just starting in Vietnam. The family made a big deal out of this Marine Corps bit, and Jensen had to prove himself because he had a lot of family pressure to deal with.

The other two of us thought the whole thing was funny, but Jensen was trying to jump on Chabot's case and Chabot was mostly ignoring him.

"Aw shit, Jensen, don't sweat it! There's nobody out here but us four assholes freezing our butts like a bunch of idiots! God-dammit my clothes are wet! Just look at this shit!"

Chabot always did everything in a kind of hurried, half-assed way, and I wasn't at all surprised that his clothes were wet. Hell, I'd packed mine carefully and part of my stuff was also wet. We had a long way to go tonight and Chabot was going to be miserable until his clothes dried out—probably sometime tomorrow while we laid up during the day and waited for the cover of darkness to hike back down here to the shore.

"Shit! My socks are wet, too!" Then he laughed maniacally again. Sometimes the strangest things were funny to him.

I was glad that at least my socks were dry. Socks are serious tools when you have a lot of hiking to do. Chabot was going to have a championship set of blisters on his feet by morning.

"Damn! My crotch is raw from swimming in that fuckin' wetsuit!" More maniacal laughter. "My balls are gonna be hamburger by the time we get back! What am I going to tell the girls in Tijuana this weekend?" He had a lewd grin plastered across his face.

"Chabot, can you hold it down?" yelled Jensen. "Besides, you know the base commander declared Tijuana off limits. It'll be your ass if they catch you down there!"

"Aw, fuck the base commander!" laughed Chabot. "You worry too much, Jensen. You're gonna die of ulcers if you don't lighten up. I'm cold, let's get going!"

The rest of us looked furtively over our shoulders to see if the lieutenant or somebody else important was lurking in the dunes listening to Chabot's reference to the base commander. We were all still only about half dressed. We hurried to get the rest of our gear on and catch up with Chabot who was disappearing into the darkness.

Jensen leapt to his feet in pursuit, still stuffing things into his backpack and stopping to grab a few things that had fallen out. Traynor and I grabbed our stuff and tried to catch up.

Ahead, just beyond a line of tall bushes at the edge of the sand, I heard a loud "Boo!" followed immediately by a scream of fright from Jensen, and then Chabot's crazy laughter.

"Goddammit, Chabot! You stupid bastard!" yelled Jensen, "Cut that shit out!"

Jensen was always falling into one of Chabot's stupid pranks. Traynor and I usually managed to stay back far enough to avoid getting caught in anything but the laughter. I could hear Chabot's ridiculous laugh somewhere up ahead as we started shagging our gear inland into the trackless hostile wastes of Camp Pendleton.

Well, it wasn't exactly "trackless" since we were not the first poor bastards to go through this whole exercise. In fact, there was kind of a trail that we could just follow— unless we thought there might be a few sergeants and other Marine lifer types out there just lying for us. That's where the hostile part came in, if we got ambushed by those guys.

First, they'd take turns running our asses ragged for the rest of the night. They would probably take all our food and warm clothing and make sure we missed our rendezvous with the ship so we'd have to wait another night shivering in the dark with no blanket and nothing to eat. Plus, they'd probably harass us all day to keep us awake when we were supposed to be sleeping up for the long hike back to the beach. They'd be real bastards about the whole thing, and they'd enjoy every minute of it. But they wouldn't just kill us like a real enemy would. Anyway, we hoped they wouldn't.

After I remembered this possibility and reminded Traynor, we ran to catch up with that idiot Chabot who was somewhere far ahead of us, making enough noise to wake the moon. I heard Jensen behind me yell "Fuck!" and hit the ground as he tripped over a tree root that Traynor and I had managed to avoid. We were already making a lot of noise trying to catch up with Chabot, but when Jensen hit the ground wearing his pack stuffed with a couple of day's supplies, it sounded like a kitchen cabinet had just fallen off the wall. Traynor and I finally grabbed Chabot, wrestled him down, and shut him up while we waited for Jensen to catch up.

After he got a look at just how pissed off the other three of us were, Chabot agreed to cut back on the bullshit. He might be a world-class wiseass, but he wasn't dumb enough to want to go through a couple of days of constant harassment anymore than we were. We'd all had enough of that crap in boot camp. We also decided to take a less obvious route to our destination. We would climb out of the easy ravine we had been following and make our traverse through a line of bushes that ran just below the ridge line so the enemy couldn't see us silhouetted against the skyline. It was a moonless night, but a guy with good eyes might see us against the stars. There was no sense in making it easy for those bastards.

We were at a disadvantage already. A big disadvantage. Those guys knew this country, and we didn't. They knew where we were going. They also knew the only route we could reasonably take to get to our destination before dawn and have enough time left to make our reconnaissance before we'd have to lay up for the day. The only advantage we had was that they didn't know exactly when we'd be coming through. Maybe they'd get bored and give up on us, or maybe they'd fall asleep by the time we passed their position. Maybe they'd get tired of laying around in the dirt in the dark and head back to the Noncom Club for another beer or two and another drunken night with a bunch of other lifers. Maybe it wasn't likely, but it could happen.

To those of us who were in this for the short haul, the word "lifer" meant "loser." We liked to think that lifers were too dumb to make it in the real world back home, and that they stayed in the military where they had someone to take care of them, feed them, and tell them what to do. They'd never make it on their own outside the Corps. At least, that's what we liked to tell ourselves.

To the lifers, "short-timers" were one step above pond scum, one step away from being "slimy civilians" once again. They knew that soon we'd be gone and we'd be civilians again, and they only had a limited amount of time to take a big bite out of our scummy young asses. That was the best thing about my choice of joining the reserves. I had planned to join the regular Marine Corps, but my dad said, "Knowing how little you like taking orders, you might try the reserves first." I had to admit it was good advice.

Honestly, there probably wasn't one among us short-timers who didn't give some thought to the idea of staying in, of re-upping, when our tour was over. There would be none of those hassles about having to make the rent each month, buy food, and deal with the uncertainties of real life. It would be easy to put your brain on hold and roll out of the bunk each morning in time to make the chow line. Then you'd wander to an office somewhere on base to kill another day of your life and wait for retirement. When you're seventeen or eighteen years old, fresh out of high school, the uncertain world beyond your parent's house can hold a lot of terror. What if I don't get a decent job? I don't have any skills at all, and I'm sure as hell not getting any out here wandering around in the dark, tripping over goddam roots and stuff.

If I stay in, a guy might think, I can retire with an income in twenty years—when I'm only thirty-eight. Then

I'll spend the next forty or fifty years knocking down a monthly check. I've already got almost six months logged in the Corps. I only need another nineteen and a half more years of this crap and I can retire. But I was only eighteen years old, and the thought of wasting another whole lifetime like this was too terrible to contemplate seriously. I would never make it without getting into some kind of trouble. Hell, they'd probably throw me out anyway long before my twenty years was up, and I'd have nothing to show for all that wasted time. Not a damn thing.

I stopped fantasizing early in my short military career about something so improbable and unrealistic as staying in the Marine Corps any longer than I had to, and I got back to the serious business of just trying to survive the experience.

It might have been a game that we were playing in the coastal barrancas of Southern California, but we had already hiked a couple of miles inland after our long swim to shore and we were getting tired. We trudged silently onward into the hills, and the sound of pounding surf receded behind us in the darkness.

By three AM, we reached the edge of our destination, the Helicopter Landing Zone—the HLZ—a large open grassy area at the top of a gently sloping hill. We spread out quietly into the fringing bushes to watch, and to listen, in case there was an ambush planned. We waited and watched for about half an hour, but we were just going to have to risk moving onto the open ground to scout the site and take our measurements. In about another hour and a half, the sky would start to lighten at the approach of dawn, and we had to be done in time to camouflage ourselves for the day. We couldn't wait any longer to start our work.

It was Jensen's call. He was in charge of this patrol. He would have to decide when to move forward into the open. If this were the real thing, the first ones out there would be easy targets, reduced to a mass of quivering tissue by a murderous rain of liquid fire. But in our case, if the noncoms were watching and taking notes, and if we screwed the whole thing up, we'd all just get reamed by the lieutenant when we got back—especially Jensen, for being a poor leader. We couldn't even just hang out under cover and fake our report when we got back, because they knew what the place looked like. They'd been here before and they had the measurements on file. They knew where the large rocks, trees, and bushes were that might cause problems with landing a chopper. They would know in a minute if we faked the whole thing. But of course, the thought did occur to us. Except, probably, Jensen.

Jensen waved to me and Chabot to ease into the open and scout the perimeter for enemy activity and then report back. Of course, in a real situation, they'd know by the sound of gunfire and our dying screams if we had encountered the enemy. Reporting it back to Jensen and Traynor would be academic if this were the real thing.

I took the low side, and Chabot went high. I could see Chabot now and then against the stars of a black night sky as he scouted the upper edge of the clearing. Occasionally I could hear him over the soft moan of a cool coastal night breeze combing through the bushes and the waving tops of the grasses. I was dodging from bush to bush along the lower edge, wondering just what a hail of bullets actually felt like. It's hard to get that sort of thing out of your head when you're playing at war games, and my muscles twitched each time a twig snapped. We reached the end of the long clearing alive and doubled back to join Traynor and Jensen to start measuring the place and taking notes.

I paced off the length of the field, noting the location of a group of bushes near the center while Traynor tried to draw a diagram in the dark. Chabot and Jensen paced off the width in several places and guessed the height of nearby trees that might interfere with a landing chopper. Eventually we came up with a very rough sketch that we all more or less agreed on.

The sky began to lighten ever so slightly in the east, and it was time to leave. We had as much information as we were going to get, so we moved out to find cover as far away from the field as we could. It was an obvious place to land helicopters, and in a real life situation it would be watched regularly. It was a good idea to put some distance between us and the landing site before dawn broke.

We climbed over a nearby ridge line that angled generally back toward the coast and moved about halfway down the slope into some brush where we scattered to find hiding places for the day. A golden sun dawned over the chilly, damp coastal hills as each of us found a place under the brush to spend the day lying on the rocks, roots, and twigs that covered the hillside. We were traveling light, without tents, sleeping bags, and all that. We made the best of our situation and got some sleep for our night hike back to the coast and that long cold swim out to the destroyer that would be waiting for us in the dark water about a mile or so offshore.

I watched from a thicket as the sun rose slowly and melted back a curtain of dew that covered the golden grassy hills. There was a silken sheen to everything. Rolls of grassy hills and bushy valleys receded into the distance. A dense web of leaves and branches just above my head filtered the morning's light and scattered it onto the ground, and I watched a few ants begin their daily toil near where I lay. Slowly the chill of a long night left my bones and I fell into a deep and welcome sleep.

My story came to an end, and Linda studied my face as the old Microbus pulled onward through the high desert and brought us closer to Socorro. I wondered if she caught a glimpse of a trained young killer still lurking somewhere in my eyes.

So far, my life had been a collection of interesting experiences but had not really amounted to much of anything. And was that the way of life? Wasn't there more to it than this? The young spend far too much time mired in trivial personal problems when there are people out there who have it a lot worse. I was still young and the notion of reflecting back on my life seemed absurd, especially since I had not yet accomplished much of value. A final assessment would be the work of an old man, and I still had to earn that privilege.

Ranges of stark dry desert mountains loomed far to the southwest of us. Mark was quiet as he concentrated on the road. And I felt that he might be lost in his own private thoughts about the strange rites of male passage.

7

INSIDE

The highway crested the last of a series of small rocky hills and settled into a stretch of flat valley lands just a little north of Socorro. Small and modest adobe homes, and an occasional old adobe barn, lined the edges of the highway. A large collapsed adobe farm building appeared on the left side of the road, a victim of neglect and the recent rains.

When Don Juan de Oñate and his band of settlers finally got to this fertile section of the Rio Grande Valley they were exhausted from their long northward trek across the dry lands of the *Jornada del Muerto*, the Journey of the Dead. Rough and rocky terrain carves the lands along the river south of here, and most travelers in those days left the only water source in the area to strike out across the dangerous flat shortcut through the Jornada. Depending on the whims of weather, and the time of year, it could be a good way for travelers to bypass rugged sections of the trail cut by deep canyons and ravines. The Jornada is a gentle route across a high plain to flat valley lands once again. But it could be a deadly route if they weren't well prepared and didn't carry enough water—or if they were just unlucky. If they didn't travel in the heat of summer, if they didn't waste time, and if the horses and cattle kept plodding along, they could cross the Jornada in a few days. Sometimes a rainstorm would leave short-lived watering holes scattered in small natural depressions. However, it wasn't something that travelers through the Jornada could count on. If they left the river and began that long walk through the forbidding lands ahead, priests and settlers alike prayed for divine salvation from the horrors of a slow death by dehydration under the relentless rays of the desert sun.

The Oñate expedition took that risky shortcut through the Jornada in the late springtime of 1580. It was a difficult passage and when they finally arrived at the river's edge in the Socorro area, they encountered several small adobe communities of Piro and Tompiro peoples who gave them food and provisions. Because of the help he'd received, Oñate named this area after *Nuestra Señora de Socorro*, Our Lady of Succor, or Sustenance.

The warm sun, the droning rhythm of the highway and the dope were still having a profound effect on me. I drifted back to a party maybe a year before I met Annie. It was sometime in the winter and there was a small fire crackling in the fireplace. I took a puff or two from a joint that was making its rounds and then I sat to watch the dance of flames with a glass of red wine cradled in my hands. Most of the others were in the kitchen and I heard their bursts of laughter. They sounded distant through the chemicals in my brain as I slumped in an old overstuffed chair and watched the tapestry of brilliant flame while it crackled and licked against the wood. More sounds. Wineglasses. More laughter. A door closing. A voice speaking through the mist to someone nearby, but I was transfixed by the fire. There was meaning in the fire, a meaning unnoticed in every fire before this one, and somehow I had missed it.

Another burst of laughter from the other room, and someone droning through the crackle of fire. More distant laughter as I studied the flames. Then I looked at Connelly sitting beside me, stoned, smiling, and I realized he was talking to me. Or talking at me, since I had been unaware of him sitting there and I hadn't heard a word of whatever he'd been saying.

Mark pulled off the highway at the Socorro exit to top up the gas tank and get some coffee. Driving stoned at high speed in a hippie van had finally seemed like a dumb idea. What was the matter with us, anyway? Were we trying to get busted? There are times just like this when "the collective wisdom" seems to fail. In our case, we'd probably get searched and arrested if the State Police pulled us over for any reason at all and got a whiff of that sweet smoky scent in our hair and clothing. It was the smell of rebellion that hung, heavy and ominous, in the air, the rejection of all the hypocrisies of modern society. It was a challenge to the guardians of a corrupt society. It was a red flag for the cops.

Traveling toward Mexico in a hippie van was provocation enough for the heat to pull us over. We didn't need to cause ourselves any extra trouble. We weren't any more self-destructive than the average thirty-year-old hippies in a van. We all had jobs, usually, and were reasonably well-educated. But we started out the day acting a lot dumber than we should have. Getting busted now would put Mexico on a distant back burner for all of us. We had defied the nation's latest moral crusade against its young, the demonizing of marijuana. But it was a battle we could only lose if we did it this way.

We looked around for a decent restaurant in this once-historic town that was now little more than a strip of gas stations, cheap motels, and greasy chow houses.

July 1971
Annie had been funny about dope. And about liquor too, for that matter. Neither of us ever smoked much dope at

parties, although we'd enjoy a toke or two when a joint was passed. But we never had it around the house. That was fine with me because I wasn't a real dopehead anyway, but Annie was always sure the FBI, or somebody, was going to single out the two of us, out of the millions of young people who enjoyed a little weed, find marijuana ashes under the couch, and send us both off to prison for life. And though she never actually said it in that way, this would all be my fault. I thought she was too worried about it but I didn't see any point in pushing the idea, so we never had the stuff around. There was plenty of dope at parties, so why bother having our own stash, anyway? Besides, I preferred to bring a bottle of red wine to pass around. It was my chemical of choice and it didn't damage the throat so badly.

But Annie didn't care much for wine or liquor either, although it was handy to get her into the mood for sex. I thought it was strange, considering the passionate way our relationship had begun. But I started to understand that Annie never really enjoyed sex all that much. I came to realize that she had a fear of desertion and that she regarded sex mostly as a reward system for companionship. And maybe that had something to do with her father disappearing for a while when she was a young girl.

Gladys, her mother, was more than a little shrill, and usually too busy talking to listen much to anyone else, especially her youngest daughter. It was painful to see Annie still needing the love and approval she was never going to get from her mother. Gladys mostly found something wrong with whatever she did and was stingy with praise when Annie did something well. Gladys came once for a three-day visit and I was relieved when she left. I mostly stood aside and watched the proceedings, having

made the early mistake of trying to say something I thought
might be meaningful. And then getting a cold "mind your
own damn business" stare from both of them. It was a
private fight with deep roots, and I was not welcome in it.

Annie's father, Oscar, was a miner in the open-pit
copper mines when they lived in Butte, Montana. He had
been part of early unionizing efforts at the mines and did
his share of fighting with the goons that management hired
to get rid of troublemakers like him. He was a big man and
I imagine he gave as good as he got in the battles for
equity and decent pay, although he didn't talk much about
it. Being married to Gladys, he never talked much about
anything. I got the impression that Annie never really got
to know her father when she still lived at home and now
she wanted to make up for lost time. I could understand
that. I never felt that I knew my father well either, but as I
spent more time dealing with the demands of working life I
began to understand why he needed some peace and quiet
when he got home. And I was glad I didn't have a bunch
of surly kids to bother me at night when I got home. Not
like he had to deal with.

Times were tough for Annie's father in the mines in those
early days. And when things got too shrill at home, Oscar
would spend his evenings at Charlie's New Deal Bar or the
Helsinki Bar and Steambath with the Finns and Cornishmen
who made up the mining crews. They'd share a meat-filled
pasty and a beer or two before walking home in the icy
darkness past the brothels down on Mercury Street.

He was about the age of 35 when he left Gladys and
the four screaming kids and caught a ride in an empty
freight car leaving Butte, Montana, and heading east.
About five years later, when little Annie answered a knock
at the door one morning, there was a man she didn't know

standing on the porch wearing a battered fedora and some old clothes. He asked to see Gladys.

A hot cup of coffee felt good going down, and the morning's fog began to lift from my brain. Refortified, and with a full tank of gas, we headed further down the freeway and left Socorro behind us. Trying to talk above the road noise and the whistle of wind through open windows had taken a toll on our conversation. We rode quietly for a while, each of us lost in our thoughts as an endless desert landscape lined the highway around us.

My mind drifted back to the early happy days I'd spent with Annie, and I sifted distant memories for the answers I knew would never come. Yet it still seemed important.

November 1969

Annie and I rented an old adobe house in the rural south valley just off Isleta Boulevard. The home had not been rented in a while, the floors were dirty, and there was a coating of dust on everything. But at $80 a month it was affordable. We had a lot of work ahead of us to make it livable, but Annie saw a charming little home beneath the dirt. We scrubbed and painted, and she bought some inexpensive cotton lace curtains for the windows and a red and white checkerboard tablecloth that reminded her of happy times she'd spent at her grandmother's house in Nebraska.

In the early mornings we often saw three roadrunners searching together for food in the open fields around our new home. And on quiet summer evenings after work we sat in a pair of old chairs under a light on the side porch and watched as a large toad hopped toward us to collect a nightly feast of June bugs that buzzed and crashed against the house to lie on their backs on the warm sidewalk, struggling to right themselves. It seemed, at the time, that it was almost too beautiful to last.

At Christmas, we bought a small tree and hung it with trinkets, chains of popcorn, handmade Mexican decorations, and things we made ourselves. There was an elegance to the non-electrified tree in our small living room and a simple beauty to our uncluttered lifestyle.

Annie could be especially thoughtful and generous. Besides taking great joy in decorating our own little tree, she felt we should also get one for a very poor family who lived nearby. They seemed uneasy when we offered it to them and we helped set it up in their living room all ready for decoration. We stopped by their house a few days after Christmas and the tree was lying in the front yard as if it had been tossed out the front door. It had never been decorated. We asked Elsa the youngest daughter what happened and she told us, "It was ugly, so we threw it out," before running off to play with her friends. I laughed at Elsa's youthful honesty but Annie looked deeply hurt.

We set up a small darkroom and work area for Annie in the back bathroom, and we hung her best photographs on blank walls throughout our little home. Annie had become a talented photographer with the rare ability to capture the essential humanity of her subjects. And she especially loved to photograph children. She was more at ease with children than she was with most adults, and they were at ease with her. It was one of the things I dearly loved about her, the innocence and generosity that she always showed to children. I hoped she would share that generosity, and that patience, with me.

I encouraged her photography. It was better and more insightful than her writing, but I never told her that was the reason. Still, I think she knew it, and I think she resented it.

She worked hard on her writing and it meant a lot to her, while she tended to devalue her photography. Looking back on it now, I never fully appreciated the fact that she wanted above all else to be a respected writer.

Just like her mother, her grandmother, and her sister had been before her.

October 1972

Annie said she had to get away for a few days. She felt suffocated by our relationship. She had to go visit her sister Audrey in Seattle for a week. On a warm fall morning I drove her to the airport. She looked out the window and watched the scenery go by, and said very little. I helped get her bags to the counter and tried to kiss her goodbye. She absently returned my kiss and then disappeared down that long walkway to the plane. I watched her disappear into the doorway of the plane but she didn't look back, and I was alone with my thoughts again.

Two nights later she called, crying, and asked me to please come to Seattle and be with her. She really missed me and she wanted us to share some time together in the beauty of the Pacific Northwest. We talked quietly and I borrowed enough money for a ticket. I had been missing Annie, too—a lot more than I thought I would. I missed her warm embrace after work, and I missed the sound of her in the house. I missed being with her and thought that a few days in the romantic rain of Seattle might rekindle something between us. It seemed we had crossed an important bridge in our conversation over the phone, a bridge back to that magical space we had started from. I was looking forward to hugging her when we met in the airport, and starting our life over together again.

When I arrived, Annie was waiting with Audrey. I walked up to embrace her and she said, "Let's go," and turned toward the exit. I was expecting a warmer welcome, but Audrey and I turned our frozen smiles toward each other and made small talk as we both tried to keep up with Annie who was striding to the door. The ghostly sentinels of tall pines in the great Pacific Northwest forest passed in the misty, rainy night outside our car windows as we drove away from the airport.

Later, things changed—I don't know why—and we had a romantic couple of days walking in the rain and watching the Bremerton Ferry depart from the dock as we enjoyed hot bowls of clam chowder and schooners of Oly at the Olympia Cafe. We held each other at night and we made wonderful love in the spare bedroom Audrey had arranged for us. And we awoke each morning to hot coffee, bagels and cream cheese, scones and jam from a little bakery on the corner.

On our plane ride home Annie sat quietly and thumbed her way through a magazine. I sat looking out my window at dense cloud banks far below and imagined the green landscape beneath them. I felt that we had crossed a barrier in Seattle, some kind of frontier in our relationship. Maybe we could count on a normal relationship now and even think of having kids. We'd talked about it at times but our relationship had never been stable enough to bring kids into it. Maybe we had reached a point where it finally made sense. Outside my window the sun was shining brilliantly down onto the broad backs of the clouds.

Annie turned to me and said, "I have to tell you something." I turned to look into her beautiful green eyes as she continued. "I spent last Wednesday night with a guy

I knew a long time ago when I lived here in Seattle. I told you about him once."

I remembered that she had mentioned him. His name was Quentin, or something. I had tried to forget it.

"He just got out of jail and now he's moved back to the reservation." She continued, "It was nothing planned or anything, it just happened. I called him up to see how he was doing. We were very close friends, and I've been worried about him. Don't look at me that way. You must have known this might happen when we got married. Look, this sort of thing can just happen, you know?"

She looked into my eyes as she gauged my reaction. She had called me in tears just last Thursday night. Had she called out of remorse? Out of regret, confusion, about a bad decision made too quickly? Out of what? Maybe things hadn't turned out to be quite as wonderful in Quentin's arms, or whatever his name was, as she had thought they'd be. I had no way of knowing.

She studied my speechless reaction, then looked away for awhile before turning back to me.

"I don't owe you any apologies, and you don't owe me anything either. We can just end it now, if you want," she said and looked away, trying to look like she was concentrating on an article in her magazine.

I sat for a moment staring at the beautiful brownish curls of hair that brushed her cheek and wondered if the concept of fair play was ever going to have a role in our marriage. The whiplash of our life was never-ending. Maybe now it really was over. I couldn't even think straight about it. But what about those wonderful days we'd just spent taking ferry rides across Puget Sound and gathering raspberries as feeble rays of sunlight peeked through the soft Pacific rain? What was that all about?

I turned to look out my window at brilliant sunlight on the dense layer of Oregon clouds that were hugging the earth below. Through a hole in the clouds I saw tree-covered mountainsides and sparkling hidden lakes, a paradise hidden in the clouds.

What was I supposed to do now? Was I supposed to say, "That's OK, dear. I understand." I didn't understand a damn thing about any of it, and I didn't know what to say, so I sat and stared out my window onto the rugged beauty of the mysterious mountain west with a lump in my throat that I just couldn't swallow.

I turned away from the whistling Microbus side window into Linda's question about why I was so quiet and what I had just been thinking about.

"I was thinking how remarkable the mountains are off to the west along this stretch of the valley." I knew it sounded artificial, but I hoped it would be sufficient.

"Oh, ever the artist!" she laughed and gave me a knowing grin. "I'm just sure you were thinking about the stunning mountains along this stretch of the valley."

I don't know how it works that one thought leads to another until you're right back where you didn't want to be in the first place. Recollections of stories that were better forgotten brought back more of my most deeply-hidden images of Annie. And they had just reawakened one of the most painful scenes of our relationship.

Linda knew Annie well enough and she knew something had been wrong between us for a long time. She'd watched the way Annie managed to keep me entangled in a web of pain and confusion. And she saw my inexplicable willingness to continue the relationship—my addiction to it, really—our renewed commitments always followed by another painful failure. Linda was an insightful and thoughtful person and she knew that our recent parting was inevitable, and that it was final this time. And she also knew it would be a good thing.

But I found it difficult to understand that all this pain was somehow good for me, and I turned away to look back outside the window. And to hide a tear. Why couldn't this damn VW Microbus go any faster? How long was it going to take us to get to Mexico anyway?

Mexico II

I enjoyed a good and inexpensive meal alone in the crowded restaurant at the Chihuahua bus station. I was glad to be a couple of miles away from the Bar Impala, and that homicidal drunk who was probably still sitting there with his drunken friend at their dirty little table. It was good to have that behind me.

The station was filled with travelers waiting for their buses to depart. Campesino families wearing torn and dirty clothing waited along with well-scrubbed businessmen in clean suits, and Indians wrapped in multicolored blankets —all of them waited on the hard benches or at small restaurant tables until their time came to leave. The entire colorful spectrum of Mexico was waiting in the Chihuahua bus station. After I finished my dessert I relaxed with a decent cigar I'd gotten from a corner shop before boarding the night bus for Torreón. The last evening rays of sun were coloring the sky as I stepped aboard.

I took the night bus so I could sleep and save on lodging costs and stretch my tiny budget to cover a few more days below the border. This was going to be a long ride and I settled into a seat at the window. Outside, the narrow streets of southern Chihuahua passed in the deepening evening. I was feeling mellow, thanks to all the beer I'd consumed at the Bar Impala over a long hot afternoon. When we boarded the bus it was comfortable and it was air-conditioned. I knew I wasn't going to have any trouble at all sleeping through the night while the bus rumbled southward. I was looking forward to watching the sunrise as we pulled into Torreón.

But we hadn't gotten far past the city limits of Chihuahua when the breath of cool air from the vents under my window began to blow warm. By the time we reached Delicias, there was a steady stream of warm air blowing through; and there was no way to open the sealed windows on this bus which had *"Aire-Acondicionado"* clearly painted outside by the door for passengers to see as they boarded. There must have been a leak somewhere in the system and all the freon had escaped. I would later realize this was a common situation on Mexican buses and I guess the mechanics would just add more freon at the next major city—in this case Torreón—to lure a new set of passengers to board the bus. In the smaller towns where we stopped they didn't bother with this formality, since they had a captive audience aboard.

And then, somewhere between Delicias and Ciudad Camargo, I started to develop a fever and to experience an intensifying nausea, probably from carelessly eating a salad back at the bus station in Chihuahua. Fever and nausea slowly built in my system and I wished I'd thought to bring along a water bottle and some kind of medicine, just in case this sort of thing happened. The sun had set long ago and now it was pitch-black outside. On the inside of the bus a few people were reading by the dim glow of overhead lights. I loosened my shirt and pulled off my boots and socks to cool down, but the summer heat of the Mexican desert burned into the cabin of the bus as we hurtled southward through the night.

The once pleasant rumble of the diesel exhaust gradually became an echoing roar in my fevered brain as the hours stretched on while we roared onward through an increasingly hot Mexican night, and I hoped I would be able to control my nausea until we reached the bus station at Ciudad Camargo. But it was not to be. Sweat was dripping from my forehead as the demon within clawed at my intestines.

Waves of fever and nausea roared through my body as I tried to keep my dinner down. Weakness and dizziness swept through my brain. Soon I realized I'd have to face the inevitable, and between waves of nausea I started to make my way to the restroom at the rear of the darkened bus, gripping seat backs on either side of the aisle for support as the bus lunged down the highway, dodging potholes and taking curves at high speed. As our bus passed heavily-laden trucks and other vehicles on this narrow and crumbling two-lane road, the twin beams of our headlights pierced and searched the darkness like the antennae of a great lumbering beast alone in the black of night. The reflected light of the roadway ahead cast a sinister glow back onto the faces of the other passengers as I slowly moved to the rear of the bus, pausing occasionally to breathe deeply and regain my strength.

I reached the door to the unlit restroom and moved to step inside but my foot kicked something that sounded loudly like a pile of metal trays. I felt around in the darkness but the toilet compartment seemed to be full of them. There was no way to squeeze through the door and find a moment of privacy. I reached for a light switch on the wall and I found none. My confusion turned to panic as I felt the other walls for a switch and ran my hand around the mirror and the light fixture over the sink, but metal trays covered the sink and the toilet and were piled several feet deep throughout the entire compartment. By this time the forces of nature were beyond my control and I tried to find a place beside where I thought the toilet was and where the resulting mess would not contaminate everything. As I crouched there on the dirty floor puking I could not imagine ever attaining a more wretched state of being. I hoped fervently this would be the lowest point of my life and that I would never plumb these depths again. The resonating rumble of a huge diesel engine just beneath the floorboards added an almost comforting tone to this hot and rolling, steel prison cell.

Afterward I stumbled weakly back to the front of the bus and paused to lean on the corner of my seat. As I glanced back in horror at the dimly-lighted rows of passengers, their pale greenish ghostly faces seemed to glare at me in the night in accusation of my crime, real and yet unimaginable. In the darkest recesses of my fevered brain they had taken on a sinister role and we were a busload of sinners on the way to our final landing at the Gates of Hell. I was certain that when we arrived the other passengers would stand witness against me to save their own filthy souls.

But by this point I was also beyond caring. The misery sweeping through my body made me wish for some kind of ending to this journey, no matter how terrible. I wedged myself against the slightly cooling surface of the window glass for the rest of our long trip into Torreón, and I slept fitfully as the bus jostled and jarred its way onward over the old broken pavement. I awoke briefly as the bus wound slowly through the narrow streets of Ciudad Camargo and we came to a stop under the weak glow of a street lamp beside a dusty bus station. The driver killed the engine and the night was quiet once again.

I stayed in the bus and watched as our driver checked the tickets of new passengers. Two large diesel engines lay on their sides covered with oil and dirt where they had been left by local mechanics after long-forgotten transplant operations. Moths and bats swarmed around the lone street lamp and moths flew through the open doorway to a single bulb hanging above the ticket counter. Two older women, wearing traditional brightly-colored shawls, boarded the bus and found seats toward the front. I drifted back into a fevered sleep, and the heavy diesel engine roared to life as we resumed our long passage south.

Sometime during the night we stopped in the dusty town of Jimenez to board a few more passengers and to begin the last leg of our journey to Torreón. I got off the bus and slowly made my way to a dirty restroom with a filthy toilet inside the building where I left the last of my dinner. There was fresh blood all over the sink as if it had been the scene of a recent crime, and I kept my hands away. In the lobby of the station I approached two policemen seated at a table.

"Hay mucha sangre en el baño," I said and pointed to the door. They both looked at me with steely and malevolent eyes as if to say that I'd better mind my own goddam business if I knew what was good for me. I looked from one hardened face to the other and swallowed hard, and then I mumbled *"Me desculpa, por favor,"* before backing away and leaving the building. I could feel their cruel eyes watching as I left to re-board the bus.

I slept poorly as we rumbled onward to our destination, and I awoke now and then to find a more comfortable position as the first light of dawn began to creep into the sky. A red and burning sun soon rose into a hazy sky and the ragged outline of the roadway was bathed in a dusty golden glow.

The bus finally slowed as we threaded our way through the narrow and busy morning streets of Torreón, and it came to a stop at the terminal. I pulled on my boots and gathered my things from the seat next to me, and I stuffed them sloppily into my suitcase as all the other passengers disembarked. Then I slowly rose in the empty bus and carefully made my way down the steps. The fever was raging through my body, and my head was aching as I paused to steady myself when I reached the ground beside the doorway. My legs were weak, so I leaned for a while against the cool skin of the bus to breathe deeply and to gain my balance. I surveyed the scene and planned my next move as waves of nausea gave way to chills in the hot morning and my dry throat begged for water.

There was a dripping faucet on the side of the building. I struggled over to it and sat on my suitcase, drinking from my cupped hands. The water surely contained any number of microbes and bacteria, and I wouldn't have dared to drink it under normal conditions. But I figured I was already about as sick as I could get and I needed something cold to settle my stomach and cool my forehead so I could regain enough strength to find the Hotel Galicia on the main plaza just a few blocks away. After resting for a minute or two, I began walking toward the Plaza, stopping every few feet to sit on my suitcase and rest in the shadow of a building.

I checked in at the front desk of the Hotel Galicia, and then climbed an old marble stairway to the second floor, pausing every few steps to gather my dwindling resources while holding the palms of my sweating hands full upon the cool railing. The hotel clerk watched me furtively until I reached the upper landing and disappeared from view. I found my room just down the corridor and opened the lock with an ancient skeleton key.

The Hotel Galicia probably dates from the 1920s and it was constructed when this desert valley was just starting to be developed by large agricultural interests producing winter vegetables for the *Norteamericano* market. It was built in a classical style and was probably elegant for the time, although there is also a larger and fancier hotel of the same era just across the plaza. But now the Galicia rests on faded glory and it's a cheap place to stay in the center of town. There was no air conditioning available when the hotel was built, so the interior walls of each room were made of wooden lath screens to provide some ventilation in the incredible summer heat of central Mexico. The lath screens were doubled for privacy, but the hollow sounds of footsteps echoing in the hallway drifted through my room with every breath of air. The wide dirty blades of a ceiling fan turned lazily overhead and kept the increasingly hot air circulating slowly throughout the room. An ancient toilet dripped water and the cold-water shower dribbled constantly, producing only a slightly larger stream when the faucet was on.

By the time I got to my room I had developed a bad case of diarrhea, so I dropped my suitcase on the floor and headed for the toilet. Afterwards I took a cold shower under the dribbling faucet before falling onto a hard bed under the slowly turning fan. The sound of dripping water in the background prevented any sleep, so I rose again to deal with it. I was able to quiet the toilet with a couple of hard turns on the water supply valve. And a washcloth on

a water-stained tile floor by the drain muffled the constant
dribbling of the shower. With a cold wet rag by the bed
and a couple of aspirins, I slept well into the increasing
heat of late afternoon.

When I awoke, I was weak and lying in a bed of sweat
from the fever, along with the heavy air and intense June
heat of the central Mexican desert. I sat upright carefully
and rested for a while on the edge of the bed. I knew I
should get some kind of food, but I was too weak to do
anything more than grope my way, half crawling, back to
the bathroom to deal with a new wave of vomiting and
diarrhea which continued to sweep through my fevered
body. Another cold shower and more aspirins helped me
sleep through the rest of a burning afternoon and on into
the night.

The view outside the dirty windows of Mark's bus had
changed dramatically again without my even noticing it as
I emerged from the thoughts in which I had been
immersed for most of this trip. We were passing through
deeply-fissured mountains and dry arroyos filled with the
pungent fragrance of creosote bush. The familiar sting of
creosote felt good on the nose.

8

OUTSIDE

In the late hours of morning the blistered landscape slowly evolved into an ever hotter and drier desert as we headed south. We rode along quietly, each of us consumed by our personal thoughts.

Along this section of the river, south of Socorro, I-25 departs the valley again and runs through gentle foothills sloping down from the eastern flank of the dry Chupadera Mountains that edge the western horizon. For me, the intriguing deserts of southern New Mexico begin somewhere along this stretch of highway. Rock-covered and rain-starved mountains just to the west of the highway, and those beyond the river to the east, are all part of the vast Pedro Armendaris Land Grant, embracing the verdant Rio Grande Valley. This is a hot and dry place and yet there is life everywhere. In this desolate land the creosote bushes, apache plume, and mesquite grow taller and fuller than the small grasses that cover the land further north, near Albuquerque. This is a harsh land with little rain but it doesn't freeze as hard this much further south and larger plant life abounds everywhere. And with a greater variety of leaves, twigs, and seeds, antelope and deer and small animals are common, despite the heat.

The dry and broken mountains that flank the valley create a variety of microclimates and life zones over a vast area. Countless canyons and ravines, after millions of years of erosion, run down these slopes to the valley and add layers of complexity to the land. The north-facing slopes sometimes shelter residual communities of ponderosa pine, piñon, and juniper, while a few hundred feet away, on the south-facing slopes, are cactus, yucca, creosote bush, and ocotillo. The varied plant communities harbor diversified animal communities—animals that have adapted to a wide range of habitats and food sources. These transitional life zones may be home to a broader range of animal life than the beautiful pine forests found in the high country.

A little south of the turnoff for the Bosque del Apache Wildlife Refuge we pass two old and dead volcanic spires, a pair of ancient geological sentinels with chunks of broken red stone spilling down their flanks, the relentless marks of time and erosion. The Rio Grande Valley follows an ancient fault line that bisects the state from north to south and creates the river valley itself. From a high hill or a mountain overlooking the Valley, there will usually be several old volcanic plugs visible along the valley floor marked by their red stone flanks, a reminder of the explosive fires of their birth, and their death.

Those two old volcanic remnants felt like a strange metaphor for my relationship with Annie. Once filled with the young fires of passion, we were now dead, burned out, and scarred with the wounds of time. Yet it seemed overdramatic and ridiculous. I was thinking too much about Annie again, and I turned toward the green life-giving valley of the river.

Below the rim of the highway lies the wildlife refuge where thousands of migratory birds winter over every season as they have for longer than anyone can know. In late afternoons in the winter, people gather at the northern end of the Bosque to watch probably 40,000 to 50,000 birds glide in from their daily feeding in the grain fields that lie several miles to the north. Massive flocks come in layers across the clear winter sky against a brilliant palette of sunset colors. It's an awesome sight to watch so many large birds glide onto the marshes as the sun sets. I came here alone on a Saturday after-noon in the last months of winter to watch them return, to witness this raucous annual ritual involving thousands of snow geese and sandhill cranes. It was something I could rely on.

We sped onward down a long and empty highway. On a weekday morning we only see an occasional truck and few cars on this remote stretch of desert Interstate.

"I bet something interesting happened around here, in the middle of nowhere. Where nobody in his right mind would spend any amount of time. It just looks like the kind of place where something important could have happened," Mark said and grinned at me in the rear-view mirror. He knew I spend too much time reading about that kind of stuff. He knew I had useless information available and he challenged me to concoct a story out of the nothingness that surrounds us. By the glint of his eyes he was betting that I couldn't. Then I saw the exit sign for San Marcial up ahead.

A neighbor of mine, a very old woman who lived just across the street from my little adobe home, had grown up in San Marcial and she told me her family escaped the flood that destroyed it. San Marcial was once a community of small farms along the banks of the River and it was named for the third century Saint Martial of Limoges, France. The town was originally established on the east side of the river in the 1850s and remained there until a flood in 1866 forced the residents to find higher ground on the opposite bank. The railroad tracks passed nearby in the 1880s and their small town prospered. There was every reason to believe that San Marcial had a bright future. Until the devastating flood of 1929.

That was the year when heavy rainstorms swept across the Rio Puerco drainage, far to the north and just west of Alburquerque. The lands of the Rio Puerco basin, denuded by years of overgrazing, were unable to absorb the sudden downfall. Waves of muddy water swept down the barren hillsides and scoured the Rio Puerco to where it enters the Rio Grande Valley north of Socorro. And then it swept downstream, destroying fields and homes and banks, and wiping out the community of San Marcial. My neighbor recalled standing on the high ground above their village with her family when she was just a small child and watching as their home and others were swept away by the rising muddy waters.

People living far upstream had created a disaster for the people of San Marcial. Entire families left the area with only the few possessions they were able to save and they moved to safer parts of the valley, places that were protected by high banks and levees. Today, only a few people remain in this remote area, protected by the dikes and levees that now isolate them from the river. But the memories, with frequent retelling, are as vivid as yesterday. History remains a continuum, a rich and unbroken thread, as long as the old ones are still with us.

Soon we were abreast of Black Mesa, a heavy, brooding landmark that hugs the eastern side of the Rio Grande just south of the scattered remains of San Marcial.

"See that large dark mesa over there?" I asked.

"Yeah." Mark grinned, "You have some kind of story about that place too, right?"

"Well actually I do," I replied. "I had to write a report about it once a long time ago."

"Why am I not surprised?" Mark said, and rolled his eyes.

Linda laughed at the game that Mark and I engaged in. Maybe she saw it as a sociological study, if she could find the time to waste on it. We still had a long way to travel, so I began to tell the story, or what I could remember of it.

Black Mesa is the spot where Oñate's party of Spanish settlers, back in 1580, first encountered the native Pueblo inhabitants of New Mexico living in a large earthen community that used to lie at the base of the ancient basalt-covered mesa. The pueblo no longer exists today, swept away long ago by spring floods probably caused by the overgrazing of livestock introduced by the Spanish to the fragile desert grasslands that lie far upstream.

Almost 300 years later Union and Confederate forces would fight an indecisive battle on the high ground near where the old pueblo had once stood. Depending on which account you read, the "Battle of Valverde" may have been more a comedy of errors than an event of any importance in the Civil War. It may have been little more than saber-rattling and chest-beating. As I watched the old mesa pass by in the distance, I thought that if there were more battles like this one the world would not be such a dangerous place to live.

Sergio Leone's epic film, *The Good, the Bad, and the Ugly*, had come out in the mid-1960s, with an adventure story that was loosely wrapped around these largely-forgotten events of the Civil War and now there was renewed interest in that part of New Mexico's long history.

In January of 1862, Confederate Brigadier General H. H. Sibley marched north from El Paso up the Rio Grande Valley in a strategic move to draw Union forces from the battlefields of the East. They planned to take Santa Fe in a move to gain access to the rich gold fields and ports of California, and to open a new front in the war. Colonel E.R.S. Canby was charged with strengthening the defenses at Fort Craig on the western bank of the River at the northern end of the Jornada del Muerto to defend the recently acquired Territory of New Mexico.

The Mexican-American War had ended about fifteen years before, in 1848, with the signing of the Treaty of Guadalupe Hidalgo and the cession of a huge tract of land to the US, comprised of what we think of today as The West. The large Territory of New Mexico had only recently become "American" when the United States itself was split into the Union and the Confederacy. The American Civil War suddenly became a factor in the lives of its newest, Spanish-speaking, citizens.

Canby had Army regulars under his command along with a small volunteer army recruited from among the local inhabitants. It's likely that Canby's local volunteers didn't understand, or even much care, about east-coast American politics, but they set to work reinforcing the earthen works of the old Fort against assaults by the larger force under Sibley's command. And they waited for the coming battle.

Sibley's forces reached the fort in late February and stopped briefly to engage Canby's Union troops in a skirmish or two on the eastern side of the river in the shadow of Black Mesa before Canby's outnumbered troops retired back across the river to the safety of the fort. After both sides had suffered enough casualties Sibley bypassed the fort and marched onward to the more important towns of Alburquerque and Santa Fe. Canby's local troops of mostly farmers were probably ready to return to the more important work still waiting back at their farms.

Meanwhile, the Colorado Volunteers, considered to be a more reliable force of recent immigrants from the east, proceeded to build Fort Union on the eastern plains of New Mexico to block the Confederates from a flanking maneuver directed east toward the Mississippi River. But the Confederates seemed content to stay in Santa Fe. When word came that the Union forces had left the fort in late

March and were heading toward Santa Fe, the Confederates marched out to meet them in the lower reaches of the Sangre de Cristo Mountains. The Union Army managed to capture the poorly-guarded Confederate supply train and Sibley's forces fell back to their headquarters in Santa Fe before continuing their retreat down the valley. On their way south through Alburquerque they buried several cannons that were later recovered, and they sit today on Old Town Plaza.

After Sibley's forces began their march into New Mexico, a group of California Volunteers was assembled under the command of General James H. Carleton. In the heat of summer, Carleton's Column began marching across a thousand miles of the most forbidding deserts of southern Arizona and New Mexico to cut off Sibley's retreat back into Texas. At the time, there were only two or three settlements in the entire area.

Sibley's army drew closer to Fort Craig as they continued their retreat, and this time Canby's forces stayed safely inside the fort. A few shots were fired and Sibley bypassed the fort again, on his way south. Carleton's Column continued marching to cut off their retreat but arrived shortly after Sibley and his men were safely back in Texas. The two states have had a fraught history of conflict, and New Mexico had been saved again from an army of Texans.

Mark grinned and watched the road ahead after my recollections from a high school term paper. It was so long ago that I probably didn't even have most of the details right anymore, but I hoped that didn't ruin a good story this far down the highway, and out of range of a decent radio station. As communal animals we avoid the ominous silence of our own thoughts, and most of us will put up with just about any kind of distraction.

I've lived in this valley most of my life, and it's become what I know. There are important historical events that happened in Boston and Savannah and in a lot of other places where I've never been, but the Rio Grande Valley is where I've lived and it's my experience. It's what I know. You spend enough time in one place and you're bound to hear stories about how things came to be. I always wanted to find out more about those place names on the highway, to fill in the details, to parse the pattern of tiny threads in that rich tapestry of the past. Even if it bored Annie.

And what is it that drives young guys—isn't it mostly the young guys?—to go fight people they don't even know. And maybe end up dead or maimed for life. Is it testosterone poisoning, the over aggression of the young male? Maybe it's nature's way of trimming back the number of young males and weeding out the dumb ones. By the time I figured this out I could only count myself lucky that I had not been among the Darwinian detritus hauled away after the carnage.

Mark asked again about my time in the military. Maybe I knew more about that than about the Civil War. He's such a sceptic. And I was such an unlikely ex-Marine that he wanted to get to the heart of what had driven me to that odd decision in the first place. It was a question I still wrestled with myself, but I never figured the answer would be all that interesting to someone else.

"You were even in the Airborne, weren't you?" he asked. "Why in hell would you want to do that, anyway? Were you just young and crazy or what? I can't imagine any reason I'd even consider jumping out of a perfectly good airplane."

He stared at me in the rear-view mirror with penetrating eyes. A smirk creased his lips. Linda turned to hear this next piece of the saga of my short life story. I had always thought their life was more interesting, living in Venezuela and Puerto Rico. But then, I hadn't lived their life and they hadn't lived mine.

It was hard to explain a decision made long ago as an ignorant teenager, and I wasn't even sure of the reasons myself. I remember I was curious about the supposed soul-freeing process of jumping out of an airplane into the all-embracing emptiness of a glorious blue sky. There was the shear physical beauty, the aesthetics of it all. But how to explain all that in only a word, or a phrase, as we rolled onward through the desert?

July 1964

The early Georgia morning was already hot as we stood in a long line that snaked across a concrete runway to the rear side door of a C-130 cargo plane. That's what one of the other guys said it was—a C-130. I could never keep it straight which plane had its door on the side, and which one had it at the rear. I wasn't sure I really cared a lot about which was which, so I took his word for it. I was more interested in the philosophical questions surrounding a bunch of sweaty young guys in green suits being hauled through the air in a heavy metal sarcophagus.

I had questions about even flying in one of these things. How do they really get that heavy metal thing to fly? If the plane loses power and crashes before we've gained much altitude, what are our chances of survival? If my chute doesn't open after I jump or if I end up with a streamer whipping in the air above me and tangling up my reserve chute, what then? It's happened before. I've heard of guys actually shitting their pants while they hurtle toward the earth crying, screaming, waiting to die as the useless chute whips the air above their heads. There are a lot of things that can go wrong. As we stood like so many cattle in the hot and humid morning, I had time to waste on questions like these. But I had largely made my peace with it long before I got this far.

A few nights ago one of the guys was sweating his first jump, talking about it in the barracks while he sat on his bunk with a couple of friends. He was almost at the point of panic and he was about to see if he couldn't quit and go home. He hadn't really thought it all out clearly in the first place. He and a couple of buddies had signed up for jump school because it was the manly thing to do. They joked about it and each had his fantasy of how it would play with the girls back home, and with the guys who stayed behind.

I had given it a lot of thought before I signed that paper the friendly sergeant laid on the desk in front of me. This could get me killed, I thought as I went about life for a couple of weeks while I decided whether to go or not. But they put a high premium on safety and preparation and the statistics showed that they only lost something like one in one million in jump school, or at least that's what they told us. I probably stood a better chance of getting killed driving to work each morning. And it was an opportunity for an adventure I was unlikely to see again—actually jumping out of an airplane and floating gently to a beckoning earth far below.

I decided that the odds of survival were good and I also decided not to worry about it. If I died it would be too bad but I didn't want to spend my life regretting I had passed up a chance at something like this. The other guy, sitting on the bunk discussing it with his friends, realized that his buddies at home would consider him a coward if he backed out now and it would be better if he just went ahead and got killed than to face those guys again. That, and the fear we all had of those large tough sergeants he would have to answer to.

I imagine that's what mostly motivated the poor young bastards who found themselves under Pickett's command when he ordered them to form up and march onward to a certain death against a line of entrenched riflemen in one of the most notorious screwups of the Civil War. And young Redcoats marched and died in stiff formations while farmboys shot at them from the bushes during the Revolutionary War. And those Australian kids who died when their commanders sent them into the machine guns at the Battle of Gallipoli. And all the other young men throughout history who have fought the battles of incompetent old men. Most of them died for nothing and nobody even remembers why.

That young soldier sitting on the bunk was terrified on the eve of his first jump. But we all survived with a few bruises and sprains, and now he joked with his buddies as we waited to board this shiny aluminum plane for our fourth jump. He was a veteran of this stuff now.

In the military, things are done "by the numbers." My number, taped in large characters across the front of my helmet, was 221. They lined us up alphabetically on our first day, and we counted off. Since my last name sits far down the alphabet, I ended up with a high number. It had no significance and I was usually near the end of the line for just about everything, although sometimes the military does things in reverse alphabetical order to keep it interesting.

When we boarded each plane I was usually near the door, and I could see a small sliver of what was going on outside. When we boarded the opposite way, I was back in the bowels of the plane rattling through the air, the engines roaring, the wind blasting the outside skin at hundreds of miles per hour. It was impossible to talk above the noise and there wasn't anything to look at except lines of rivets and struts inside the skin of the plane across the aisle just in front of me as we sat on a long bench that led to an open side door near the back. We sat there and waited. And waited. And stared at the wall. Then the guy to my right elbowed me in the ribs and pointed to the sergeant standing at the door as we neared the drop zone. I elbowed the guy next to me. We had been through all the hand signals before and we knew what to do next.

The sergeant motioned for us to stand. Then he lifted his right hand and we each raised the heavy clip we held in our right hands. It was attached to a long nylon strap that led to the top of a large green parachute tied down with cotton string in the pack we each carried on our back. He motioned for us to clip on, and we each tugged the heavy locking clip over a thick steel cable rigged overhead. Now that we were clipped on, the rest would be almost automatic. As we each left the door our chute would be pulled out of the pack by the heavy nylon strap and we'd find ourselves afloat in a humid blue sky high above the southern countryside.

But this time we were still standing there on the concrete, ready for our fourth jump and waiting in the hot sun for someone to give the order to board the damn plane. Most of my time in the military I waited for someone to decide the time was right to do something. We were all used to waiting. The long line of green soldiers finally began moving forward, and we started slowly loading into the open side door of the plane.

"221!" I heard the sergeant bark my number. I turned and leapt out of the line, and ran across the runway to where he was standing. What had I done wrong this time? They don't usually bark your number because they're lonely and want to talk. But I couldn't have done anything wrong yet. I was just standing there on the pavement waiting to board.

I snapped to attention about nine inches from the gleaming toes of a pair of spit-shined boots and shouted, "Yes Sergeant!"

"You're a Marine, aren't you?" He shouted back only inches from my face. Most communication in the military is held at a high volume. I could smell his coffee-laced bad breath hanging in the air.

"Yes Sergeant!" I shouted back.

"The Marines always go first, don't they?"

"Yes Sergeant!"

"You're going first! Get at the end of the line!"

"Yes Sergeant!" I shouted again.

My end of the conversation had remained unblemished by brilliant repartee, but I was secretly delighted with this turn of events. Finally, I would be able to look directly out the door of the plane and actually see what was going on. Until now each plane had been little more than a deafening tin cavern with a bunch of guys stuffed inside to be transported who knew where, and shat out upon the landscape as a pelican might dispose of the remains of a fish dinner. But this one time I was going to watch the whole thing unfold through the big open door at the end of that long bench.

The heavy C-130 taxied onto the runway and sat for a moment revving its engines. Then the pilot released the brake and we waddled down a long stretch of sun-baked concrete while a pair of broad wings stretched to grab the air. We gained speed and then we were off the concrete, floating above the ground, and over the trees standing like sentinels at the end of the runway. We climbed slowly to about 1200 feet above all that red Georgia clay while the roar of pistons and the turn of four large propellers added to the general din of air rushing over an aluminum skin and past a big open door.

I looked up from my seat on the bench to where the sergeant was standing beside the door with one hand gripping a grab rail. He wore a safety harness with a six-foot tether attached to a large ring that was bolted through the sidewall. The Army doesn't like it when their jump sergeants take an unexpected dive out the door without a chute, so they tether them to the plane. If he falls out, he can claw his way back in.

He was a big guy. Most of the jump sergeants were big guys, and the reason became obvious after our first jump earlier in the week. We had been trained to snap into position at the door and wait for the sergeant to signal us with a swat on the butt. Then we'd spring outward through the door and tuck ourselves tightly into "the position," legs together, with the body bent slightly at the waist so we could just see over the reserve chute to the first four eyelets on our boots. We had one hand grasping each end of the reserve chute strapped to our chest, with our right hand on a large steel pull-ring in case the main chute failed. This tight legs-together position would keep our legs from getting fouled in the overhead shrouds if we flipped end-over-end when we left the plane and hit the airstream outside.

But in actual practice, we would shuffle forward into our position at the door and the huge sergeant waiting there would grab each guy in line and heave him into the ether like a sack of flour. It was the sergeant's duty to get everybody into the air before we came to the end of the drop zone. If someone got out late and got injured in a tree or something, the sergeant's butt would be on the line. Once we boarded the plane we had run out of choices.

We were going to be airborne under a parachute in the buffeting roar of the outside air. We had to tuck in tight and hope for the best.

The sergeant sat beside the door and looked out at the green land far below. He glanced at me like I was some kind of worm and then he looked back out at the beautiful woodlands passing beneath us. He was a lifer. Probably been in the Army since high school. This was it. This is where his friends are. This is what he knows how to do. It's all he knows how to do. But someday he'll retire and he won't have to put up with a bunch of damn trainees anymore. He could buy a little farm down there somewhere in the piney woods and forget about this part of his life. Maybe he'd raise a little cotton, or tobacco, or something. Maybe live someplace where he wouldn't have to listen to the roar of planes every day. But the wife has gotten tired of moving every three years and now she's settled in. Her friends are here now. The base hospital and the commissary are here. The flower garden in back of the house is looking good. No, he'd probably live somewhere around here forever.

Outside that open door, just a few feet away, a new world opened up to me for the first time. We were close enough to the ground that everything in the open woods below looked like a miniature railroad set with an occasional old farmhouse nestled into the trees next to a couple of acres of vegetables. It looked like a gigantic toy set that you could reach out and touch. A two-lane highway cut through the trees and I saw a yellow 1955 Chevy sedan headed in our direction as we flew high over the pavement. In a few minutes we'd be out there in our soldier suits, under our big green nylon parachutes.

The sergeant rose and looked forward again out the door toward the looming drop field. The pilot had gotten us here and now it was the sergeant's job to gauge when to start throwing us out the door into a blanket of thick and humid southern air. Somewhere on the ground below us, an arbitrary line marked the end of Georgia and the beginning of Alabama. The fields and trees looked just like the ones we'd passed ten miles back. In fact, they looked just like those where my relatives lived in Tennessee and Kentucky. I couldn't really tell the difference.

The sergeant tapped me hard on the shoulder and made the "stand up" sign by raising the flattened palm of his hand. I elbowed the guy next to me and each guy sent the word down the line till we were all standing. The sergeant's heavy calloused hands maneuvered me to the door while our big lumbering plane droned slowly on toward the drop point.

He positioned me in the doorway with the toes of my boots hanging slightly outside the yawning door. I grabbed the door-frame with my hands, ready for the leap. A strong wind tore past me and my left eyeball felt like it was being blown out of the socket as I stood there waiting for the signal that we had crossed the fences and the edge of the woods below. I closed my left eye tightly and squinted with my right to watch the remaining moving tapestry of open fields below as we crossed the tree line.

Suddenly I felt a heavy whack on the butt and I was airborne. I could barely hear the fading sound of the sergeant screaming, "Go! Go! Go!" as each of those behind me arrived at the door to be flung into space.

Before our first jump, the instructors told us in class what to expect when we exited the plane. They explained the process clearly and in simple terms that everyone could understand so none of us would panic at the sudden unfamiliarity of it all. By the time they finished drilling it into our skulls even the dumbest among us could understand it. We practiced jumping out of mock-ups, landing and rolling in a sand pit only three feet below. Then we leapt out of a tower attached to a cable to simulate riding under a parachute. We ran mile after mile in the summer heat, so we were in top condition. And finally, in the third week, we were actually jumping out of large aircraft.

On our first jump there was so much going on all at once that it was almost impossible to sort it all out. The airplane noise, the buffeting of the rushing air, and the popping of each of those tiny tie-down strings as the chute deployed. On that first jump I held tightly to my reserve chute ring and counted to ten. If that big chute didn't pop open, I would have to pull the ring. I held my position, legs tightly together, body slightly bent, and watched the first four rows of eyelets on my boots as my body kicked upward into the sky. And I waited for the braking power of the huge main chute to stop my fall. Suddenly, there was a line in the sky that appeared from nowhere as if it were drawn across the sky itself, and it passed quickly downward past my boots and on behind me. I turned my head in surprise to see that it was the horizon, the dividing line between the green-brown earth and the clean clear blue of the sky. And it was now somewhere at my back. The earth now hung like a painted picture over my head, and my feet were thrust upward into the center of the intense blue sky. Then the parachute canopy opened fully and I swung back down in the direction of the earth once more as if I were on a wild carnival ride. It had all blended seamlessly into a cacophony of sensations that finally left me quietly swaying in space under the shade of a huge green nylon umbrella.

The deafening din of the plane, the noise of rushing air, and all the noise of the world disappeared as rapidly as if it had been sucked down a funnel. And I was left standing there quietly. In the air. Somehow standing on a brilliantly colored tapestry of distant summer meadow. It felt like… like I was standing on the air itself, or on some large blanket, or an endless beautifully painted quilt. Floating in the air, with the horizon fading away in all directions. It was an altered universe I had no way of understanding. We spend our lives earthbound with the dirt beneath our feet. We're simply not ready for this. It's an experience few of us will ever get unless we jump out of an airplane and hang in the air under a large parachute. I was no longer falling. I was just kind of standing there. In the air. On nothing.

I even pulled my feet up to see the soles of my boots before I could accept the fact that I wasn't really standing on anything at all. A slight morning breeze whistled quietly through the thin nylon risers attached to that huge khaki canopy high over my head. After the noise aboard the plane, after all those guys in the barracks, and after all the yelling from sergeants over the past two weeks, I couldn't help thinking this was one of the quietest places I'd ever been in my life. I had entered into a serene and magical place on a gigantic beautiful tapestry that spread as far as I could see. Fields and quiet woodlands stretched toward the horizon and disappeared into a misty haze like a scene in a storybook kingdom.

I was floating quietly above it all, away from endless lines waiting for vaccinations, chow, transportation. And sergeants. Always the sergeants. Herding us like cattle from one line to another. That was all gone now, left behind far below. Maybe in another life somewhere far away. I was hanging and drifting quietly above a green and endless earth. I wasn't going up and I wasn't coming down. I remember the most intense feelings of freedom during that first jump, like I could just stay there and keep drifting, drifting with the morning breeze. Maybe I would end up several states away, in Tennessee, or North Carolina, depending on the breeze. It all seemed too beautiful to last.

And then I saw the trees below slowly getting closer, the ground rising to embrace me, to take me back. And soon, somewhere, I heard sergeants yelling orders. At the edge of the drop field was a line of cattle trucks waiting to haul us back to base. I watched the landing zone come closer.

About thirty feet above the ground, I pulled into the landing position we were taught over the previous two weeks. It was drilled it into our heads so we'd do it automatically. So we wouldn't break our legs, our backs, our necks, whatever. If it all worked the right way, the energy of the fall was absorbed by the way we hit and rolled onto the ground. It was a sort of controlled collapse that distributed the impact from the balls of the feet, to the right side of the knee, to the right hip, and finally diagonally across the back. Landing under a parachute is roughly equivalent to jumping off the roof of a one-story house—about a ten-foot drop. It's a good idea to distribute the impact forces of a ten-foot drop. All that stuff made sense. But still, I hoped it would work out the way they said.

I hit on the balls of my feet and went through the entire collapse and roll sequence as my feet kicked through the air, and I was lying in the moist grass of an Alabama field. The buzzing and humming of a thousand insects filled the heavy summer air. The society of meadow life was mostly oblivious to this armed invasion from the air. The burning heat of a southern sun stirred the humid air into distorted layers against a misty sky. It was beautiful.

And then I heard a familiar sound.

"221!" yelled the sergeant. "Don't lay there on the ground smelling the posies! Get that damn chute gathered up, and get your sorry ass over to the trucks!"

"So I guess they didn't much appreciate your aesthetic take on the whole airborne bit." Linda's eyes sparkled when she laughed. She was amused at some of the things guys willingly put themselves through. Mark smiled but he was silent as he glanced at Linda and then turned back to watch the road. I wondered if he felt as if he'd missed something by not doing the military shuffle like so many of us. He was smart enough to know that it wasn't really a necessary part of manhood, but I guess I don't really know exactly how he felt about it.

I smiled back at Linda and looked out the window. To the southeast loomed the reddish peaks of the Fra Cristobal Range. It was a good time to be quiet for a while. There are so many rich stories about the mountains of New Mexico, and especially the Fra Cristobal Range, but I decided to keep it to myself. I wondered what combination of desperation and avarice might have driven those people in the Oñate party to make that treacherous journey northward through the Jornada del Muerto just on the other side of those mountains and away from the life-giving river. What drove them to come here and fight and die to take these arid lands away from other people who'd been hunting here for ten thousand years, and farming the land for maybe a thousand years? I quietly studied the scorched red summits.

Oñate's band of settlers passed through the open desert reaches of the Jornada del Muerto that lie just east of the

Fra Cristobal range. At some point, they were faced with a sudden violent lightning storm—the kind that occurs in the high desert during the hot afternoons of late summer. There was no place on the open Jornada to take shelter as the storm bore down on them.

Fra Cristobal, a monk who accompanied the expedition, led them in a prayer of deliverance. The storm subsided and everyone gave thanks for God's intervention on their behalf. In thanks to Fra Cristobal, Oñate named the rugged nearby mountain range in his honor.

More than two centuries later, the entire Fra Cristobal range became part of the huge Pedro Armendaris Land Grant. Armendaris was a special breed of man who had petitioned the King of Spain for this grant after years of loyal service in the colonies of New Spain. Armendaris had attained a degree of notoriety before Mexico gained its independence from Spain. In an interesting historical footnote, he was the officer in charge of the firing squad in 1811 that executed the rebellious priest, Father Hidalgo, who led the early battles of the movement that would soon throw off the yoke of Spanish rule. Pedro Armendaris had executed the priest who would later be known as the Father of Mexican Independence.

The description of these lands in Don Pedro's petition for a grant sounded like a modest request for a small piece of land after long years of loyal service to the King. But after it had been fully staked out, the Armendaris grant would cover more than half a million acres.

Through a notch carved by an arroyo I could see a portion of the lake that now fills the valley here. Late morning sunlight glistened off the breeze-rippled surface of Elephant Butte Lake where it lapped at the base of the Fra Cristobal Range. Much has changed in this valley since the days of Oñate and Pedro Armendaris. I thought back to a time embraced by the warm waters of the lake.

August 1970

Annie and I stood together between a pair of the old concrete lampposts that line the top of the dam at Elephant Butte. We leaned on the concrete railing and looked out across the improbable desert lake impounded behind the dam. In the far distance water lapped against the feet of jagged mountains. A sign said this charming old classical-style concrete dam was constructed in 1917. It was one of the early western water projects, and it still provides hydroelectric power to surrounding communities. Until they built Egypt's Aswan Dam in 1970, it was the largest irrigation dam in the world.

We spent a weekend, Annie and I, camping on the shores of this lake in the summer after we were married. She didn't particularly care for the sand and the heat of Southern New Mexico, and later in our short marriage we went north on summer weekends to escape the heat of the city. North into the cool piney mountains of the Jemez or into the Pecos.

I didn't know it at the time, but we had come here, far away to this southern desert lake, to get away from Allen.

Annie had run into Allen again recently. They'd had a short affair about a year earlier and Annie ended it when she met me. But Allen always seemed to pop up in Annie's life whenever it was convenient, for himself at least.

He was a perpetual student still working on his master's degree, and then planning to go for his doctorate in biology, cruising his way slowly through college to stay out of the draft. He told me once at a party that was his plan. He was one of the big party hounds around campus, always headed someplace to race his ratty old Triumph TR-3 or visit a winery in Cucamonga, California, to fill the back of a pickup truck with gallons of cheap zinfandel.

His father was a wealthy doctor in Santa Barbara who thought his son was a worthless piece of crap. As far as I could tell, his dad wasn't far from wrong. But Allen's mother secretly supplied him with money for school, clothes, a modest apartment, and all the other things he needed to avoid having to work. She would write to her son and tell him when his father would be leaving on one of his weeklong fishing trips for marlin on a charter boat out of Mazatlán. Allen would bundle up the bills he had accumulated over the past several months and mail them to mom while dad was out of town and she'd write the checks that bailed him out for a while longer. No one I knew could imagine Allen ever working for a living.

Annie had run into Allen after class at Bell's coffee house, an all-night place across from campus. He was going away to party in Santa Fe for the weekend on his motorcycle, a nice BMW 75 RS, and he would pick her up late Friday afternoon. I didn't know at the time why we needed to leave before noon on Friday for the lake, but Annie seemed to be nervous until we pulled away and headed for the freeway. But she was bright, beautiful, and relaxed after we reached the freeway and we'd finally passed the city limits sign.

In a couple of hours we arrived at the lake. We set up a small tent we had borrowed for the weekend and made love in the heat of the afternoon. Then we bathed in warm lake waters before cooking dinner over an open fire as the setting sun painted carnal crimson ribbons across the sky. We sat together quietly in the dark, sipping red wine and watching the dying red embers of the fire. The deep night enveloped the desert around us, and a million stars burned through clean desert air. The torn upper edges of dry distant mountains were just visible against a curtain of starlight that draped the sky beyond the lake. Annie turned and kissed me hard. I was surprised and I held her close while she clutched me tightly, almost desperately. The red-amber light of the dying fire shown faintly on her smooth soft cheeks and glistened in her eyes. She was trembling slightly and a look of fear seemed to glow in her eyes as if she were afraid I would leave her there, alone in the desert. Alone in the night. Then she told why we had to leave town early, and she told me about Allen.

"Hey, wake up back there!" Mark yelled over his shoulder. "You've been quiet for a while."

"Yeah," I said. I was startled by the sound of his voice, and even by my own. Linda smiled at me with a look of concern. I felt as though I'd just left the most wretched portions of my soul lying there in the open. And I smiled back weakly.

I had been doing well so far at holding up my end of the conversation. Yet all morning I kept drifting off into long consuming moments of silence, staring at the dry and dusty landscape that passed outside my window. And there was something terrible about the silence.

Malcolm Lowry described these terrifying moments of silence in his moving novel, *Under the Volcano*, about a dying British Consul in Cuernavaca. The silence might start like a dark and growing presence in part of a crowd sitting in a bullring somewhere deep in Mexico, and it would expand until it threatened to engulf the entire arena. But then someone would shout and others would respond like a primitive tribe beating drums to drive away the darkness of an eclipse. And the silence would be driven back. But as the noise subsided, the threatening wall of silence would move forward again to engulf the crowd. And if left unchallenged it might even engulf the world. That powerful image has given me pause when I find myself talking for no good reason.

"We'll stop in about an hour for lunch somewhere in Las Cruces, OK?" Mark was checking on me in the rearview mirror. The miles had begun to click off a little faster now as we drew closer to the border.

"Yeah," I said, "that'll be OK." The words had a hollow ring to them. I suddenly felt isolated from Mark and from Linda, as if a thick blanket had been pulled across the space between us.

9   **BEYOND**

January 1964

A small landing craft left the dock at the Naval
Amphibious Base on the Silver Strand in late afternoon and
headed across the harbor to San Diego. There were four of
us aboard this boxy little boat, not counting the boatswain
and the mate, as we plowed through the water on our way
to a bit of freedom. We were dressed in "civies" but the
two Navy guys knew we were Marines, and the
condescending look in their eyes said we didn't look so
tough to them. They'd been doing ferry duty for a while
and they'd seen plenty of us. We were four post-high
school kids with a weekend pass.

We docked at an industrial pier near downtown and
made our way to the bus station to catch the next
outbound to Los Angeles. Chabot knew a cheap hotel near
a couple of bars where some hookers hung out. They had a
floor show where the girls were young and they took off
almost everything. We had a weekend to kill, and it looked
endless from the perspective of a Friday afternoon. And
this might even be our lucky night.

Before long we were in a sleazy section of LA and
checked into a room at the hotel that Chabot had heard of.

It wasn't as bad as I imagined. The floors were clean and the threadbare towels smelled like they'd been washed. The four of us shared a room with two double beds because we couldn't afford anything else on our monthly salaries of $82.50. We left our overnight kits on the bed and locked the door behind us. It was time to find a drink someplace, and hope we didn't get carded.

But there was some gung-ho bastard checking IDs at the door of the bar that Chabot led us to. We were a bunch of fresh kids in the military, as you could tell by our silly haircuts that made us each look about fourteen years old. Chabot pulled out some phony ID and the guy waved him through, but the other three of us had nothing like that on us. We looked so young they never would have believed us anyway.

Chabot disappeared into the crowd and headed for the bar, and the three of us were left standing on the sidewalk trying to figure out what to do next. It was a typical Chabot kind of deal. He never glanced back to see if we were still behind him. We looked at each other and then left to find another way to spend our time.

"Let's get some coffee," I suggested. There was a neon Cafe sign down the street.

"Nah, the hell with that!" said Jensen. He'd been silent as he realized we'd all been shafted by Chabot again. "I didn't come all the way up here to 'go get some coffee!' I came here to go to this damn bar that Chabot made a big deal about! And now that bastard's gone and we're standing out here in the goddam dark! Dammit, he makes me so mad sometimes! Maybe there's another damn bar around here that'll let us in! That damn Chabot! He never looked over his shoulder to see if we were still with him! I sure as shit wouldn't wanna be in a firefight with that bastard!"

He'd been screwed by Chabot so many times. I was wondering if he would ever learn not to bank on things Chabot told him. Sometimes Jensen could be so naive. Actually, we were all naive most of the time. Chabot never spent much time worrying about whether anybody else was doing alright, unless there was some advantage in it for him. The difference between Jensen and the other two of us was that Jensen was actually surprised at this latest gambit.

Jensen always believed what he was told. He was made of gung-ho Marine stuff. I figured it was going to get him killed some day. Traynor and I had also been screwed but the wry look on Traynor's face said he'd expected it all along. I think he came along on this trip out of a perverse desire to watch Chabot pull something like this. And watch Jensen be surprised again.

"God damn it!" Jensen finally blew his cork. He actually jumped into the air and stamped both feet on the pavement. I had never seen him so animated before and I don't think I had ever heard him swear before either. It wasn't how they brought up kids in his patriotic southern family. Maybe this was his awakening. Maybe we'd witnessed the first major break with his rigid heritage, and the reason why he agreed to go on this trip into "sin city" with the rest of us. We had all done our best to corrupt him ever since we arrived at boot camp, and now I couldn't tell whether he was really all that mad at Chabot or not. Maybe he was just pissed off with himself for being so damn gullible, again. That he'd gotten taken, again. And that he was missing his biggest chance yet to break free from a sheltered life. He stared at the grimy sidewalk beneath the clumsy military shoes that he'd spit-shined just before we left the base. He was a captive of his past, even in his moment of wild rebellion.

"Ok! OK! Let's go get some damn coffee!" Jensen finally admitted defeat. He'd been whipsawed again and there was nothing to do but throw in the towel. Tonight was not going to be his lucky night, anymore than it was going to be ours. The only women who would have gone with the three of us dumbasses would be hagged-out and desperate. Jensen was going to have to lose his cherry some other way, some other night. And maybe he'd even have to get married first. He had changed over the past few weeks and now he seemed to concentrate on doing something dramatic that would surprise everybody in his small southern town. Especially his cute little former girlfriend, who had stopped writing to him a while back. But tonight would not bring liberation from a suffocating family. I wasn't sure he could handle the guilt, anyway.

We went to get some coffee. There wasn't much else to do. Later we wandered the dark streets from streetlamp to streetlamp, past the old crumbling buildings of this dying retail/warehouse district. The muted roar of a nearby freeway was a background track to a night in these deserted streets. Cars and trucks were going somewhere else now, somewhere far from here. I wondered why I had come along on this brainless trip to what must be the most soulless and least attractive city on the West Coast.

On another weekend I went to the bars and clubs of Tijuana, another disappointment. Much was promised and little delivered, but the wild stories that followed made me wonder if I had been on the same journey, in the same bar. The hype was everything and the reality mattered little. That seemed like a good job description for the human race as we wandered along dark streets in a shabby part of the city.

We passed the dry sad towns of Truth or Consequences and Williamsburg. Then the highway crossed the river and the fertile valley into the dry desert lands that flank the Rio Grande along its eastern side and soon become the broad southern end of the Jornada del Muerto. A trip that would have taken several brutal days for a caravan of settlers took us only about an hour. A hot desert wind began to blow across from the west and it whistled through the leaky side windows of Mark's Microbus. Eventually we saw a sprawl of cheap housing and scattered shopping centers with empty parking lots that smothered the desert. And an exit sign for Las Cruces, City of the Crosses.

The story goes that a small band of traders were driving their oxcarts down the long Chihuahua Trail as it followed the Rio Grande on their way from Santa Fe to the pass at present day El Paso. This branch of the trail ran beside the reliable water source of the river, but it was a dangerous route to travel, through cottonwood forest and thickets of brush. Somewhere near here the traders were ambushed by a band of Apaches and they were all massacred. In those days, in the lawless wastes of southern New Mexico, it could have been bandits who killed them for the valuables they carried. But the Apaches got the blame, for this crime and for others. The next group of traders found what was left of their bodies after several days of exposure to a merciless sun and various scavengers of the desert. Their remains were given a decent burial and simple wooden crosses marked their graves. When a village was established along the fertile banks of the Rio Grande near where several old weathered crosses still stood, it was named for those crosses.

Billy the Kid came through here in the 1870s. He spent time hanging around the plaza at nearby Mesilla before he rode off to become a major player in the Lincoln County Range War about a hundred miles east of here. He was arrested for a murder and after he broke out of the County Jail, he strutted around town over the course of a long afternoon, daring the terrified townsfolk to do anything about it. From Lincoln, the Kid went north to Fort Sumner where he was finally gunned down by Pat Garrett as he made his way through a darkened room at an old hacienda where he was staying. Garrett was crouched in one corner and stayed silent until he knew who it was. The Kid heard a sound and called out, "*¿Quien es? ¿Quien es?*" When Garrett pulled the trigger it ended one of the more colorful chapters in New Mexico's history.

Garrett himself was later killed on a lonely road by a friend who claimed it was an accident. But many who knew the irritable and abrasive Pat Garrett doubted that his death could have been an accident. Garrett and the Kid had both outlived their times, their brief shared historical moment, and they became relegated to the stuff of legends.

That was all long ago. Garrett and the Kid and the traveling bands of Apaches and the others who made this place legendary are gone now. Replaced by lawn sprinklers, fast-food joints, and asphalt, for crissakes.

"El Ranchito?" Linda asked. "Are you sure you remember where this place is? Wasn't it about ten years ago that you were in school down here? If I remember right, you were here only one semester?"

"I can find it." I winked. " No problem."

Linda laughed and rolled her eyes. Mark glanced into the rear view mirror. His black beret had that jaunty angle that he must have practiced in front of the mirror back home. He was sure we were on another long back-alley search for a nonexistent "enchilada nirvana." He'd been through this with me before. And so had Linda, but not as often.

El Ranchito was a family place specializing in good cheap Mexican food, and it was on a hidden back street not too far from New Mexico State University. I hadn't eaten there for maybe three or four years now. Not since the last time I stopped here with Annie, but I didn't want to bring that up now. So far, I had tried not to talk openly very much about Annie on this trip. I had managed to deflect the conversation in other directions because it started to sound like whining, although I had thought about her almost constantly since the trip began. And I wasn't sure I could muster an appetite for lunch.

After a number of seemingly random turns Mark and Linda looked at me in surprise when we rounded a corner on a shabby residential street and pulled into the restaurant's dirt parking lot. I shrugged my shoulders, and reached for the handle to the sliding side door.

Between bites in this air-conditioned refuge we began to talk about Mexico and about some of the adventures we each imagined were to come. But I was distracted by the surroundings. Mark was talking as I scanned the familiar decor that had not changed a bit since my last visit. I looked out through a window into a searing summer's afternoon in Las Cruces and the white-hot glare of the day burned deep, the burn of memory, and I didn't feel all that hungry anymore.

December 1969

It was a cold winter's afternoon, the day after Christmas. Annie and I had moved in together a couple of months before and now we were headed south looking for a break in the weather. We were late leaving town and drove through a heavy snowfall over slippery white pavement in a brand-new Ford pickup I'd had no business buying at the time. I'd grown tired of the old unreliable trucks I had always owned in the past. Or maybe I was trying to impress Annie, and myself. Within an hour we finally drove out of the thick and icy cloud cover.

Annie read a detective novel for most of the four hours it took us to get to Las Cruces. I never cared much for the cheap novels she disappeared into. I thought they were predictable, like a bad movie. She was quiet and seemed preoccupied, as she often did when she was reading. I had learned not to bother her. I listened to a local rock station until it faded out and the static grated like gravel. Annie turned off the annoying radio and we rode along in icy silence. The station had been playing something by Dos Snakes, a group that had a couple of minor hits in the local market. It was a band that might have done better but they always sounded a little out of time with each other, and the static did nothing to improve it. That discordant band reminded me of our relationship as I silently drove south. Annie and I had been living together only a short time, but sometimes we sounded a lot like that band.

I studied the road and hummed something to myself while the wind whistled at the side windows and the miles passed beneath our wheels. It was a frozen day and I concentrated on the driving as bits of pavement peeked black through a layer of dirty ice. We had planned to go to Mexico for a few days on a beach at Mazatlán. I hoped things would be warmer in Mexico.

We stopped at El Ranchito for an early dinner and Annie stared out the window at several badly-pruned and leafless trees around the muddy parking lot as she toyed with her food. The cold wind rattled against a loose piece of window glass resting in the old wooden sash beside me. People seated at the other tables were enjoying each other's company. Red and white checkered tablecloths gave a warm feeling to the place, like the one that Annie bought for our own table a few months ago, in the warm and lusty days of autumn.

As Mark talked, I stared through the old cracked and heavily-painted wooden window at the end of our table and into a hot afternoon, lost in my thoughts. Why did I suggest that we stop for lunch at El Ranchito? There are other good Mexican restaurants in Las Cruces. Was I hoping I'd see the ghost of a happier moment here with Annie? Or was I trying to obliterate a sordid memory? There were happy times in our life together, but we both should have realized the relationship was in trouble long before we bothered to get married. I'd even seen it sitting here at this same table by an old wooden window, looking out into a waning day. Did I need to relive the pain? Was I still addicted to Annie? I sat at the table, my food half-eaten, looking out the window at a scorching dust-blown day, and that's the only way I could explain it to myself.

Annie and I arrived well after dark in El Paso and decided to wait until morning to cross the border. We had little money and we drove around looking for an inconspicuous place to park for the night. We had planned to live in our camper shell on the beach at Mazatlán for a few days and find cheap hotel rooms in Mexico on the way down, but we hadn't planned to stay overnight on the US side of the border because of the cost. There was a double mattress, two sleeping bags, and some camping gear under the camper shell in the bed of the truck. We just needed a quiet place somewhere to spend the night.

There might be public campgrounds around but we didn't know where. And we were afraid that if we parked in front of someone's home, it would look suspicious and they might call the cops. So we drove through the streets of a city neither of us knew well, trying to find a safe place for the night. Then I saw a brightly-lit Ford dealership up ahead.

I drove past the dealership and stopped at a Seven/ Eleven store to buy the El Paso daily paper and a roll of masking tape. Annie questioned what I was planning to do while I tried to act confident and not appear too evasive. We kept an eye open for security guards as we pulled into the back of the Ford dealership and stopped in a parking space near the service department. I set the parking brake, and we ran to the back of the truck to climb over the tailgate and under the camper shell.

"This is crazy!" Annie said with a dubious smile that reminded me of our better days as I wrestled the wide camper door down and latched it shut behind us. "Are you sure we're not going to get into trouble for this?" She was often afraid we were going to get into some kind of trouble.

We taped newspaper over the windows as she waited for an answer. Annie got worried whenever I did something "creative." She'd imagine herself ending up in jail a couple of hundred miles from home. It was fine if I wanted to do that on my own, but she had no intention of going to jail with me.

"Well look, Dear. Can you think of a safer place to stay?" I avoided the question of whether we might actually get into trouble or not. She didn't know whether to snap at me or keep laughing, reluctantly, at the adventure of it all.

"Hey, we'll have a security guard watching over us all night long," I continued, "and if they wake us up to ask what we're doing here we'll just tell them we had some overheating problems and didn't want to risk driving any further 'cause it might hurt the engine. The truck's still under warranty. We're just waiting for the service department to open in the morning. The same guards won't be on duty in the morning. If they ask as we're ready to leave in the morning, we'll tell them we're going to get breakfast and we'll be right back. We actually will be going to get breakfast in the morning. But we'll get sidetracked after breakfast, drive across the bridge to Mexico, and forget to come back. They're not gonna send an escort with us to make sure we return. And besides, security guards are not being paid to hassle customers, like us."

I kept talking so she couldn't come up with valid reasons why this wasn't going to work out. And to convince myself that I'd figured most of the angles. During creative moments I tend to adjust the details as I go along. It's a process of successive approximation, of getting closer to a desired end result by dealing with the issues that might arise along the way. It's an inclusive way of coming to a joint action. But Annie suspected I was trying to confuse the issue and boondoggle her into going along with something she'd rather not be involved with in the first place. When we first met, she had a propensity to fall in love easily with anyone who seemed to have a plan. But over the few years of our involvement I had proven myself to be only human, and very capable of failure. She had stopped giving me points for trying something new.

Annie giggled nervously and taped sheets of newspaper to the windows while I held it to the glass. I hoped this gambit would remind her of some of our earlier and happier capers together. I knew that if this scam didn't work, she was taking no responsibility for it and I would never hear the end of it. But I was too tired to spend several hours driving to find the closest state park, and I was at the point where I really didn't care if she was happy about it or not. Annie had yet to come up with a better plan, a plan that we could afford. Still, I truly hoped she would enjoy this little adventure.

Our clandestine campout worked out fine and we slept well through the night. Nobody hassled us or seemed to be interested, and in the morning light we climbed into the cab of the truck and drove south toward the bridge that crosses the border. Probably we weren't the first people to spend a night in the Ford dealership parking lot in El Paso. Probably it wasn't an original idea after all.

In Juarez things didn't go well. The Mexican official in charge of granting us passage south shrugged his shoulders and decided we needed more paperwork. We had everything we were given by the Mexican Consulate in Albuquerque, but the man behind the desk, blocking the door to our southerly progress, politely insisted we needed more forms. We drove slowly back across the bridge to El Paso in a huge traffic jam filled with legions of poor people from Juarez going to their jobs as housekeepers and gardeners in affluent American suburbs that were visible on the high ground beyond the border.

At the El Paso Mexican Consulate we were told there were no additional forms required and that we should explain to the other official that we had everything we needed. He assured us he would even call ahead and discuss it with the other official, so we headed back over the bridge. In Juarez, they told us the Consulate was wrong and that we still needed several forms. After a couple of trips between El Paso and Juarez, the American border guards started to recognize us and ask us questions about our frequent trips. I guess we were starting to look like some kind of inept smuggling operation. We explained the runaround we were getting, and one of the younger guards finally mentioned the real problem wasn't in our paperwork. It was my longish hair and moderate beard.

By American standards I didn't really look all that radical, but we were dealing with the conservative society of Mexico. A lot of hippies had invaded their country over the past few years and some of them had outraged the local people with skimpy, shabby clothing, and bizarre behavior. For this and other reasons, people like us were no longer welcome. Modern Mexican society was forged in the terrible crucible of the Mexican Revolution and ten years of violence had touched every Mexican family. This sunny land to the south is still fragile and there lingers a fear of new and radical ideas.

I didn't feel like shaving, so we finally gave up, said to hell with the hassle, and headed for California to visit some friends. Annie and I would never see Mexico together.

After our divorce I realized it was just as well we didn't go onward into Mexico that time, or any other time. Traveling the roads of Mexico requires a degree of flexibility that I believe we were not capable of attaining. It requires a willingness to deal with the unexpected, with problems encountered in a very different culture. The experience would have been another addition to a collection of unfortunate memories.

"Excuse me for a minute." I stood up from the table at El Ranchito. I could barely manage a mumble as I turned away with my voice breaking. I couldn't bring myself to look directly at Mark or Linda.

Not much had changed since the last time I'd been in that tiny restaurant, sitting at the same table, looking through the same menu, probably ordering the same thing. There were the same faded copies of paintings on the walls, of a little adobe home under a cottonwood tree, some cactus in bloom, a flaming sunset over a mountain range. The same plastic bud vase sat beside the cash register with the same dusty plastic flowers in it.

I fiddled in my pocket and dropped a couple of dollars on the table beside my unfinished meal and then I turned toward the door, and away from Annie's memory. I walked across the parking lot and turned left down the street. I had a sudden need to be alone for a few minutes.

A miserable little brown dog barked from behind a short chainlink fence as I thought about just what I might have wanted or might have expected from this trip south into Mexico. Was I expecting something to reveal itself in that strange land south of the border and that I would be changed forever in some remarkable way? So far, I'd done little on this trip but think about Annie, even though I tried to stay distracted and think about anything else. Was there any reason to believe I would think about something else if I went on with this trip? What was the point of being a thousand miles south of the border if all I could think about was Annie? I had spent the morning sharing stories about my adventures and whatever history I could remember of these tortured desert lands. But always there in the background, like an apparition, had been the image of Annie. I had tried to talk her away, to obliterate her from my mind. But still she was there. Silent. Unshakable. Staring back from just beyond the boundaries of the moment.

I stopped walking and sat heavily on the dirty edge of a broken curb that lined this unpaved street past a stretch of vacant lots. I needed time to think.

February 1973

It was over. It was finally over and I was free, whether I really wanted to be free or not. The destructive years we spent together had come to an end. And the road ahead, for me at least, looked more like a precipice than a gateway to a bright new beginning. I thought, "So this is the first day of the rest of your miserable life." There's nothing quite like a cheap throwaway metaphor.

I watched Annie's car pull away from the restaurant where we had our final meeting. She merged into the lines of traffic and quickly disappeared, and I knew I might never see her again. Lonely tears streamed down my cheeks as I watched her drive away. With any luck we could each go on with our lives. With any luck, we'd finally leave each other alone. I wiped the tears on my sleeve and looked to see if anyone had been watching. It was time to go back to the little home I was living in now and act like nothing had happened.

Mark was going to drop by the house in about an hour and we were going to start taking adobes out of the walls of the old derelict ruin on the corner lot across the dirt road from my place—my shack, really. Annie had gotten tired of living in one half-finished project or another, in homes she had never wanted to own. Yet I don't really think she would have been much happier in a pretty little house with a garden. I think she was tired of being married, of the confinement, and she moved into an apartment near the university. And I was worn out by the whipsaw of the entire relationship. I wasn't really strong enough for this stuff.

As I drove back to my place, the late winter light glared through dry western air and burned into my reddened eyes. In the rear-view mirror I looked worse than I'd ever looked in my life. Jesus, what the hell was I going to tell Mark. What kind of excuse would hide this latest and last episode with Annie? Maybe a bad case of allergies or something. Mark would never know the difference, anyway. That lucky bastard never had allergies in his life. We had work to do, anyway, and we wouldn't be spending a lot of time talking about personal crap. I don't deal well with that stuff. I never have.

We attacked the old building with hammers and flat pry-bars, and we broke the bond of clay mortar and lifted the ancient adobes from the wall. The beams and boards of the roof structure had been taken long ago and were probably used to build one of the other houses nearby. Only thick adobe walls and a large concrete foundation remained. On the inside, the adobe walls had been plastered with mud and then painted. Years of exposure to the elements had peeled back layers of paint like the leaves of an old book. An old history book, in fact. We counted seven layers that began with a simple whitewash and moved through various pastel colors that became available over the years. Each room had its own history, its own story to tell of the people who once lived there.

The old place might have ended its days as a picturesque ruin except that a necklace of ragged stucco wire left sticking from the top of the wall had given it a tawdry industrial look. The sharp and jagged ends of wire raked disturbingly across the sky. There was a heavy layer of mud plaster beneath the stucco wire that indicated the stucco was added much later when the owners had a little more money and had gotten tired of re-mudding the outside walls every few years. That was a common pattern in the Rio Grande Valley as durable modern stucco replaced beautifully weathered adobe walls.

Several neighbors said the place had been a dancehall and saloon for a portion of its long life. We could imagine the sounds of music and dancing spilling through open windows and doorways on hot summer nights. The blackened walls in one corner of the building were evidence of a fire, and we guessed that it was so badly damaged that its useful life was over. The windows, doors and salvageable roof beams were stripped away and the adobe walls were left exposed to the summer rains and winter snow. I hated to destroy all this history and I wished I could rebuild the place. But I didn't have that kind of money. Mark and I needed the adobes for a workshop we planned to build, and they were just going to wash away if we didn't take them.

We pried each adobe out of the walls and sheared off remaining bits of dry mud mortar with a glancing blow from a large hand trowel before we stacked them into the bed of my 3/4-ton '65 Ford pickup for the trip to the back of my lot where we planned to build our workshop. I took a substantial loss when I sold that new red truck just six months after I bought it, but I needed one that was less pretty and a lot more suitable for heavy work.

A couple of the salvaged adobes had dog prints hardened into the surface from drying in the desert sun maybe a hundred years ago. The dog was long dead by now but his paw prints had been immortalized—a cut-rate version of the dinosaur prints that archaeologists find in layers of fossilized mud. That dog, like ancient dinosaurs, had made his impression on a future generation. On me, anyway.

I wondered if I would leave an impression on anybody after I was gone. Considering the shambles my life was in, some might be just as glad I was gone. They wouldn't have to deal with me and my stupid problems anymore.

I sat on the dusty curb under a ragged mesquite tree in a poor older section of Las Cruces with my boots on a dirt road that had never gotten itself paved. Behind me stood a row of ramshackle homes with derelict cars parked in every yard. I stared across a line of vacant lots filled with tumbleweeds and debris toward a distant group of simple working-class homes. The people who were making a modest life in those small homes might have little idea what I was mumbling about to myself. Or why I was sitting there in the dirt. They didn't have the luxury of grieving over a relationship that should never have happened in the first place. They spent their time working to support their families. They'd be justified in telling me to get over it and get on with my life.

A trip alone into Mexico, especially at this time of the year, wasn't going to solve anything or do anything to clarify my life. I needed to make my way back out to the freeway and catch a ride home. I had done some of my best thinking standing by roadsides in the vast south-western desert waiting for whoever happened along to give me a ride. That had worked for me in the past.

"Oh, goddammit!" I said as a rush of tears filled my eyes and I stared at the ground as the droplets landed between my feet.

Somewhere, in one of the little homes just behind me, a pot of red chili was simmering on a stove and I could smell its savory breath drifting out on the hot afternoon air. Home-made tortillas were toasting on a griddle. It was someone's lunchtime. Life goes on.

I heard Mark's VW Microbus turn a corner and rattle its way down the washboard rutted road to where I was sitting.

Mexico III

I awoke to the hard light of morning shining onto the riffling fronds of tall palm trees in the Plaza at Torreón, and the sounds of a city awakening just outside my hotel window. A cooling breeze drifted from the plaza and through the open sash. After a hot night of fevers, chills, and vomiting, this faint breath of cool air was welcome, although mixed with the nauseating smell of diesel fumes. Unmuffled heavy trucks and buses rumbled through the narrow streets of this desert city as the commerce of the day began.

On weakened and shaky legs, I slowly made my way to the balcony doors to gulp the soothing coolness of the air. Birds called from the tall palm trees shading the plaza as I leaned on the cold edge of an old dirty marble railing. As weak as I was, I felt as though a weight had been lifted from my body sometime during the night and I had finally expelled the malicious demons from my system.

Below my balcony and just across the street stood a long canopied juice stand with rows of large glass jars that resembled barrels and were filled with freshly-squeezed fruit juices. Large chunks of ice floated in the clear glass barrels as people in white aprons sliced and squeezed piles of ripe oranges, grapefruit, lemons, and other fruit from the abundant local groves, pouring their golden juice over the ice and then ladling it out into big frosty glasses.

I needed some kind of food. But in my weakened state I only craved ice-cold fruit juice. The nutrition would be good for my starving body, but I mostly needed the cooling effect it would have on my fever-ravaged system. It was the only thing I could imagine keeping on my tender stomach. I knew the quality of the water in the ice was suspect, but in my present state I was sure that it wouldn't matter.

I stepped away from the balcony and its cooling breeze and began the slow process of dressing and then packing my gear, stopping often to lie on the bed in exhaustion. I was still sweating and my head throbbed in pain. I blessed each cool morning breeze that rustled the palm trees along the plaza and lifted the curtains to flow through my open window and across the bed where I lay gathering strength for the next stage of packing.

When I was finally ready, I moved my two bags into the hallway where I sat on them for a while and waited for my strength to rebuild enough to take the next few steps. I made my way to the edge of the large marble stairway where I sat on my bags again and rested. Slowly I moved downstairs to the check-out desk, across the lobby, and out to the cool shade of the street.

Just beyond two lanes of parked cars and two busy lanes of traffic sat the juice stand with tall frosty glasses of orange juice, grapefruit juice, and lemonade. I rested my head between my hands with my elbows on my knees and sat staring across the street waiting for the strength to move on. Over the sounds of morning traffic, I heard the clink of large dippers plunging into deep barrels of cold juice, stirring up the fruit, and rattling chunks of ice against thick cold glass. After a few more minutes I stood with my bags and waited for a break in the traffic so I could make my way across the street. Then I sat again and waited for enough strength to approach the counter.

"Un vaso de jugo de naranja, por favor," I said weakly and carefully, and when a tall cold glass of orange juice arrived I drank it slowly and completely, its coldness soothing and feeding my body.

"Un otro, por favor. De toronja." I placed my tall empty glass on the counter and they refilled it with icy grapefruit juice. I finished it slowly to savor its cold richness and to feel it tumbling down the deserts of my dry throat.

I paid for the juice and looked around the Plaza while still grasping the cold glass to quench the fires burning in the palms of my hands, and I saw a *farmacia* just across the opposite street. With my strength partially restored by icy juice, I made my way slowly across the plaza to the store where a druggist who spoke little English handed me a product labeled *Entero-Vioformo*. I paid the cashier for the package and I went to a restaurant for some breakfast and more cold orange juice. I still felt queasy, but I hadn't eaten since I boarded the bus in Chihuahua a day and a half ago and I knew I needed food. I could only hope it would stay with me long enough to do some good.

Entero-Vioformo was a product I had never heard of, and I would only find out later about its terrible side effects that were then being reported in distant medical journals. But at the time I was trying to recover my health and enjoy a modest breakfast in a small cafe on a dusty plaza in the heart of the Mexican desert.

The libertarian spirit of Mexico makes products easily available that would require a doctor's prescription in the US. This might be a good thing or it could be a bad thing. New drugs that might save lives are often delayed by years of clinical testing, and the ones who die before it becomes available are the unlucky victims of a more deliberate approach to approval. For unproven products, the Mexican people may benefit by their early availability. Or they may be unwilling "guinea pigs" for large international drug companies. And those who die or are irreparably harmed by unproven drugs become a reminder to the rest of us that shortcuts can have consequences.

In my youthful ignorance, I had become one of society's guinea pigs, and I wouldn't know about it until later in my trip. I downed a dose of Entero-Vioformo with the orange juice and waited for relief.

After breakfast my clouded brain considered modifying my loose itinerary so that I would end up in a place that wasn't as hot as this dry desert town. It was going to take a while to recover from the fever and regain my ability to function. It would probably be easier to recover if I were someplace where the air was cooler and I could get a decent night's sleep instead of rolling in my sweat hour after hour until a breath of morning air drifted through my balcony door. I thought of cool sea breezes and a broad sandy beach and a cleansing ocean to bathe my burning body.

I caught the next bus to Zacatecas and then traveled onward through San Luis Potosí to the Gulf coast at Tampico.

ARRIVAL

January 1964

Traynor and Jensen and I walked back to our room in that cheap hotel because there wasn't anything else to do. Traynor had bought a newspaper and the three of us were propped up in our beds reading through different sections of it when we heard Chabot banging on the door.

"Lemme in, goddammit! I can't find my key!"

Jensen looked at me with a disgusted kind of grimace then leaned out of bed to open the door. I think he was fed up with his role as the perpetual fall guy for Chabot. He still had his hand wrapped around the doorknob when Chabot burst in, and the force pulled him half out of the bed.

"Jesus! A couple of bastards jumped me when I left the bar! Where were you guys, dammit? I could have used some help!" Chabot was short on detail, as usual, but somehow this was our fault.

"Good thing I had that Marine Corps training!" he said with his cynical laugh. "Had to kick both their asses and run for it before their buddies came out to help. At least I was in shape to outrun 'em! I'll thank Sergeant Gronsky for those five-mile runs when I get back to base! Saved my young butt this time. As long as I can outrun the Viet Cong, I'll be fine when we get to Vietnam!"

Being shipped out to fight a pointless war in Vietnam was something we all assumed was part of our immediate future and we enjoyed walking and running while we still could. Before our legs were blown off by a booby trap in the jungle over there. It was always on our minds and one of the reasons we went into a self-destructive frenzy each weekend. We were doomed to die young anyway.

Chabot laughed again, and kept talking. "Saw a couple a creeps out in the hallway when I came in. Looked like queers to me! I'm tired. I'm going to bed."

Up to this time none of us had said anything. There wasn't room for more words when Chabot was talking. He occupied all the available space, but we had gotten used to it. Chabot looked at Traynor and me lying in bed side by side, leaning against the headboard.

"What's this, the ladies knitting circle or what? You're sitting around reading the paper and playing with each other?" He laughed again. "Move over Jensen, I'm tired."

Chabot locked and bolted the door. Then he pulled off most of his clothes, threw them into a pile against the wall, and slid into bed. "And you keep your hands to yourself, Jensen. Both of 'em, you horny bastard. I'm watching you!" He laughed his maniacal laugh and flung his head into the pillow.

Jensen looked at us with his mouth open, stunned at the accusation. A homosexual act with Chabot had been the farthest thing from his mind. He rolled his eyes and sighed, then he reached over and picked up his newspaper from where it had fallen on the floor. It was best to ignore Chabot. He'd be sound asleep soon, anyway.

Chabot rose to his elbow and glared at Jensen, "And don't crinkle that damn newspaper all night! There are people trying to sleep here." He punched his pillow a couple of times until it had the shape he wanted, then dropped his head heavily on top of it.

There was giggling outside our thin door and the sound of feet scurrying away. Then a door slammed somewhere down the hallway. Chabot blinked his eyes and stared at the inside of our door as if he could see through it, and then he saw something on the floor. "What's this shit?" He rolled over and scooped up a small square of paper.

It was a single piece of toilet paper that had been carefully torn from the roll. There was a neatly lettered message on it:

"Marines, we'd love to spend the night with you. We'll do whatever you want."

There were two hearts drawn in the upper corners.

Chabot leaped from the bed, and fumbled with the locks and bolts while he muttered a string of obscenities. Then he threw open the door and leaped into the hallway. The door crashed against the bed frame where Jensen was reclined.

"I hate you fucking queers!" Chabot screamed into the empty hallway. He looked left and then right, at a line of closed doors. The hallway was empty and silent. He felt dirty and violated that he had actually touched that piece of toilet paper with its offensive message. Chabot never felt anything in moderation.

"Hey, Chabot," laughed Jensen, "take it as a compliment!" Someone had finally gotten the better of his old nemesis. "At least somebody thinks you're handsome!" he continued. "This might still be your lucky night!"

Chabot turned and glared at Jensen for a moment while he considered pounding him to a pulp. A crimson veneer spread over his bulging veins and he stood silent before he stepped back into the room.

"Jensen, you're a goddamn faggot, too!" he screamed and slammed the door. Then he locked the door behind him and jammed a chair under the doorknob. He glared again at Jensen, who was still holding his newspaper with an apprehensive look on his face.

"Fuck you, Jensen," Chabot said in a wounded voice, and got back into bed with a flourish of covers.

It would be a long night for all of us. We woke up every time the old building creaked or there was any noise outside our door. I thought about peaceful times I'd had by myself, in Balboa Park in the heart of San Diego. I doubted I would come along on any more adventures with these guys. We really had little in common, except our brief military connection. And I was wishing for something more intellectually stimulating for a change. I'd probably never see any of these guys after this gig, whether any of us survived a tour in Vietnam or not.

I stood up from the curb and turned for another private moment to look at the shabby yards of the little homes that lined this street, to take a deep breath, wipe my nose, and dab a handkerchief at my eyes. Mark and Linda sat in the Microbus with the engine idling and waited for me. I looked out toward the wind-carved and heat-tortured Organ Mountains that etched a jagged line across the distant eastern horizon and I couldn't think of a single damn story about those damned Organ Mountains. I laughed to myself when I thought how relieved Mark was going to be when he heard this good news.

In my preoccupation with Annie's memory I had forgotten that Linda had to catch the evening express bus to Mexico City. She was on a tighter schedule than mine. It was time to leave Las Cruces behind and get to Juarez. I wasn't going anywhere in particular and I could catch any bus leaving for Chihuahua. I opened the sliding side door and I climbed back in for the final leg of our trip.

Soon we crossed the Texas state line, leaving the deserts of southern New Mexico and heading into the ugly northern outskirts of El Paso. I thought of that Marty Robbins song where he's riding away from a gunfight in El Paso and "...out to the badlands of New Mexico."

The river flows through a narrow pass north of the city of El Paso. It was an important destination for Spanish settlers crossing the rugged deserts north of the village of Chihuahua.

Oñate came through this same pass with his band of settlers looking for land and treasure. There was decent land in the fertile river valleys to the north and the Spanish would find gold and silver and the other minerals that drove their conquest of this fabulous new world. But by and large, the greatest mineral treasures of New Mexico would remain hidden until the Anglos invaded from the east a couple of centuries later and large-scale drilling and mining commenced in the West.

The soot-blackened hulk of an old steel smelter dominates the ancient pass where the river cuts through the mountains. Just across the river, cardboard shacks and hovels dot a low range of dusty hills that mark the northern edge of Ciudad Juarez. There are more than a million people living on the Mexican side of the Rio Grande across from El Paso. That makes Ciudad Juarez one of the largest cities in all of Mexico. And most of its inhabitants are among the poorest people in the world. The contrast between "first-world" and "third-world" countries is nowhere sharper than here.

The freeway sliced its way in a narrow grungy corridor through the city to an off-ramp into the uninspiring streets that lead to the border. Soon we were over the international bridge and winding our way through the crowded and dusty streets of Ciudad Juarez. And I remembered Cynthia.

May 1965

Cynthia and I had come just once to the City of Juarez, about five years before I met Annie. It was a part of my life that I probably should have forgotten.

She was a year older than I was. We had been occasional lovers in my second year of college and it was agreed that we would make this trip to the border together.

At the main hospital in the eastern part of Juarez a kind young nurse spoke to us in halting English and gave us the name of a doctor located somewhere close to the center of town. It was a Doctor Joaquin Morales Abdul who had a small office on a quiet side street just off the *Avenida Dieciseis de Septiembre.*

The Doctor spoke to us in an exam room. Then I was sent away and told to come back in an hour and a half. I found a bar where I nursed a couple of beers and watched a wrestling match from Mexico City on a black and white TV set mounted on a shelf high in the corner.

Cynthia and I had enjoyed each other's company but neither of us really wanted anything more from the arrangement. Still it was strange to be sitting alone in a bar in Juarez, downing 25-cent beers and watching a mindless TV show in Spanish, as I waited for a doctor to finish the procedure.

Cynthia and I didn't talk much as we drove back to Albuquerque, and when we arrived at her apartment she suggested that we break off the relationship, such as it was. We never saw each other again. Now, years later, I don't even remember her last name. And she probably doesn't remember mine.

Mark navigated the noisy flow of Mexican traffic on our way to the main bus terminal. The old faded VW Microbus had acquitted itself well on our trip to the border and seemed to fit in with the shabby and dented cars of Juarez, the pot-holed streets, and a tapestry of tourist shops, restaurants, cheap hotels, and bulk liquor stores. The country of Mexico embraced us in a maze of brightly colored signs and displays. A savory aroma filled the air as we drove onward to the terminal.

Each pothole reminded me of Jimmie Romero, back in his little house in Albuquerque. I wished he were here to appreciate all this for himself, but I was also glad he decided not to come along. I needed to do this trip alone. I would tell Jimmie all about it when I returned.

I remembered a colorful episode in Jimmie's checkered past. After his sophomore year, he quit college for awhile and got into Chicano Power issues. There were demonstrations and other distractions during that period and he didn't have time for school anymore.

One Friday afternoon, he and Andy Lopez stopped for a few beers at a local bar. They were heading back to Andy's apartment when they saw an unattended City truck with a trailer carrying a compressor. There was a jackhammer with an air hose, and some traffic diversion signs, lying in the bed of the truck. Andy stopped his car and Jimmie jumped into the driver's seat of the truck. The keys were in the ignition, so they saw this as a sign from the cosmos that some *lambés* had left it for them to put this truck to work in "the service of the people."

They drove to the corner of Fourth and Menual, right outside Tito's Bar, and set up their traffic signs. Then they enjoyed themselves for most of the afternoon taking turns digging a big hole in the pavement before they walked away from the whole mess and rode off together in Andy's car to score another six-pack. They had struck another blow against the Empire. They had struck a blow for the common man, ¡por la gente!, by god! It was a small blow, but it was significant when you saw it in the larger scheme of things. After another beer or two.

But later they had misgivings about what they'd done because probably some Chicano work crew had caught hell for letting their equipment get hijacked like that. They realized that maybe some of their own people got blamed for their stupid prank. Next year they were both back at the university to finish their degrees and start making positive changes from inside the establishment. But Jimmie would have enjoyed the memory when he saw all these potholes, and he still would have thought it was funny.

I could also smile now that I was here at the threshold to this next phase of my own passage through life. With help from a few of my best friends, I had managed to get this far and soon I'd have a bus ticket in hand. The rest of the trip was up to me and to whatever events might take me further to the south. I was drawn onward into this strange and unique land like a modern- day Ambrose Bierce.

Linda looked at me, her mouth slightly parted. The word, "Who?" was on her face.

Mark glanced into the rear-view mirror. "Ambrose Bierce," he said. "A writer for the New York Post, I think it was. Disappeared somewhere in Mexico during the Revolution. He was their war correspondent and they never found a trace of him. He's part of the legend of Mexico now."

Linda was impressed that Mark knew about this guy. As long as they'd been together, they could still manage to impress one another.

I thought that it might not even be such a bad way to go, to do the Ambrose Bierce thing somewhere south of the border. No one might ever know if you had been killed like many others in the endless turmoil of class war and conflict, and your body might never be recovered. Or maybe you could change your name and walk away from a culture that you had decided to renounce. You might end up living in a quiet village on a deserted beach with a beautiful Mexican wife and some kids. And no matter how it happened, your disappearance somewhere in the fabled land of Mexico would play well to the romantic in almost everyone.

Mexico IV

The big shiny Estrella Blanca bus pulled away from the Torreón terminal, its heavy diesel engine purred as the gathering heat of another late morning seared the dusty streets of this desert town. We rumbled down a rutted two-lane highway stopping at smaller towns along the way to take on passengers and drop off packages that were carried in the belly of the bus. Slowly the landscape changed as we drew nearer to the flanks of the Sierra Madre Occidental, a jagged mountain range that rims the western edge of the broad central Mexican plateau. It's a barren land with a few small, fertile valleys and dirty towns of impoverished people trying to make a minimal living from virtually nothing. It's a land forested with tall cactus, their spines clawing anything that moves, even clawing the air. It was hard to imagine how people had populated the area, how they'd built the first trails and roads through this cactus forest. The land is so inhospitable that it was hard to imagine anyone would ever have wanted to.

Eventually our bus climbed out of the cactus desert and into the cooler mountain city of Zacatecas. The rain of a heavy evening thunderstorm dripped from the porch roof of the bus terminal as I stood with my baggage and watched traffic splash by in the swirling waters that filled the street. A policeman in a brown uniform shared the shelter of the porch with a few other people who were waiting for the rain to stop.

"*Me desculpa.*" I asked him, "*¿Donde esta un hotel barrato?*"

I needed to find a cheap hotel. He looked at me. He seemed surprised that I had addressed him. I had noticed that Mexican officials held themselves aloof from the population and demanded a measure of what they apparently regarded as respect. But the populace seemed to regard them with fear.

"*Allá.*" He pointed to the hotel across the street.

Across the street was a flickering neon sign. I had already checked out that hotel during an earlier break in the rain, and at six dollars a night it cost more than I could pay if I was going to stretch my disappearing money.

"*No,*" I said. "*Mas barrato, por favor.*"

The policeman looked at me in disbelief. I was a gringo with a piece of decent luggage in hand and I was wearing decent clothing. Everyone knew that gringos had money. Was I a beggar in disguise, a North American reject, who had sneaked across the border into Mexico?

He turned away and looked at the traffic moving slowly in the night rain. Headlights of cars, trucks, and buses ricocheted off the glistening street and the intersecting rivulets of water running down from a steep side street. He shrugged his shoulders and pointed dismissively to a dimly-lit doorway barely visible up a side alley. Then he wandered to the far end of the porch and continued to watch the traffic.

As the rain started to ease, I made my way back across the busy street and up a muddy alley toward a beckoning light. I entered the open doorway and down a short flight of crudely built, uneven, and slippery concrete steps with no handrail, trying to avoid brushing against the dirt-stained yellow walls as I balanced my way to the bottom. Every few steps I dodged water dripping from various places overhead. Maybe it was a roof leak or two, or maybe it was bad plumbing. I didn't want to find out, so I stepped around the slick puddles of dirty standing water on the stairs and on the floor. Two bare bulbs shed a weak and painful light over a shabby lobby whose walls and ceiling had a dirty yellow glow.

"*¿Donde esta el dueño?*" I asked one of the plump and scantily-clad women who were leaning over an upper railing. They had been silently watching since I first walked through the door. With a flick of her head, and a staccato of rapid Spanish, she indicated the door to the manager's quarters. Then she and the other women went back to talking, glancing occasionally in my direction.

I opened the door and saw a one-eyed Chinese man sitting on a dirty floor with several children gathered around him watching a very loud television program. The children wore scraps of filthy clothing and they were eating something from a shared bowl. The manager's office and living space were one small room in the basement of this "hotel." There was a small stove, a sink, and a refrigerator crammed into one corner, and there were no windows. The manager's wife stood beside the old filthy stove stirring a big pot and watching me with large sad eyes. When I looked in her direction, she turned away and busied herself with whatever was in the pot. I thought that she might have been pretty as a girl, in another time long ago. A young and dirty child stuck his head from behind a curtain-covered toilet room when he heard my heavily-accented Spanish.

"*¿Cuanto es un quarto?*" I asked, but I wasn't really sure I could spend a night in this place no matter how cheap the rooms were. I was hoping to come up with a graceful exit line. The air smelled of menudo mingled with damp mildew and the ever-present smell of sewer gas, very common in a country where few buildings have adequate ventilation and there are no p-traps under the sinks.

He had one room available for 8 pesos—about a dollar. There was another room, with two beds, for 14 pesos. He offered to show them to me, but I thought that probably wasn't necessary, so I thanked him for his time and walked quickly to the outside door.

One of the women leering at me over the upper railing said something with a wink and a smile but I didn't catch it, although I was pretty sure I knew what she wanted. I smiled and said, *"No, gracias."* And she and her girlfriends giggled as I hurried to the door.

I stepped onto the dark and rain-slicked streets of Zacatecas. Damp heavy air hung in a soggy curtain over the city. There were no other hotels in sight, so I went back to that six-dollar hotel and got myself a room. It was late, I was tired, and I was still sick after the long bus ride from Torreón. I would look for a cheaper hotel in the morning if I decided to stay here, and I'd have to figure out other ways to economize later in the trip. My head hit the pillow in the antiseptically clean hotel room and I was grateful for a warm bed on a rainy night. I leaned over and turned out the bedside lamp.

The flashing neon sign just outside my window lit the walls of the room in bursts of red, and the soft sounds of rainfall pattered against the window pane. I got up later in the night and took a couple of aspirins to help break the fever and to act as sleeping pills to escape from the palpable loneliness of the moment. I was no longer feeling queazy, so I decided to skip the Entero-Vioformo.

Sometime during the night the rain stopped, and brilliant morning sunlight greeted a clean and cloudless sky. The sickness and fever that raged through my body had subsided, but as I stepped toward the bathroom the weakness returned. Recovery was going to take more time, and the cool air of Zacatecas was having its effect.

I felt better after a simple breakfast and decided to go for a short walk upward through the steep and winding cobblestone streets of the city as a few clouds began to grow on the mountains nearby. I worked my way slowly upward, stopping often to rest, until I was standing on a hillside overlooking the intertwining street patterns of Zacatecas below. It had the appearance of a maze, a cipher, a puzzle—forever unsolvable. Like a Kafka novel in Spanish translation. Like the inscrutable nature of Mexico itself. And then the rain began to fall again. It was an early afternoon thunderstorm in the desert and it probably wouldn't last long. I ducked under an overhanging roof as heavy drops exploded into the dusty soil around me. The thirsty ground looked as if it hadn't rained at all just the night before. After a few minutes I was joined by a Mexican fellow about my own age, although much shorter, with neatly combed black hair. We stood there quietly looking out through a curtain of dripping water at the rooftops of Zacatecas, waiting for the rain to stop.

He was dressed in a clean sport shirt, black slacks, and a light jacket. I had seen him earlier carrying some kind of briefcase from door to door among the ramshackle houses scattered along the hilltops that overlooked the city. We nodded and smiled, and for a while longer we quietly watched raindrops falling on the thirsty ground.

"¿*Mucha lluvia, no?*" I finally broke the silence. A comment about the weather is always a safe gambit.

He looked at me, surprised that I spoke any Spanish at all, and replied, "¡*Sí, mucha!*" And we stared again at the rain as it continued to fall.

"What's with the briefcase?" I spoke in English since I was completely unable to ask the question in competent Spanish. His broken English was barely adequate to the task but he told me he sold graduation and catechism pictures on commission for a photographer who came by later to do the actual picture-taking. Digging into the briefcase, he pulled out samples of beautiful young Mexican girls floating breast-high in a sea of cloud-like material that looked like cotton. Each girl was radiantly posed with her eyes uplifted, an angelic look on her face. I wondered if the photographer ever actually showed up after this guy disappeared with the deposit money. Still, I had noticed that there were quite a few of these pictures hanging on the walls of homes in the area, visible through open doors as I walked through the maze of streets.

As we talked, the rain stopped and my new acquaintance asked if I'd had lunch yet. He was tired of trying to sell pictures and was looking for a good reason to goof off for a while. It hadn't been a fruitful morning and he hadn't sold anything, so he offered to show me around the town. That sounded good to me, and we headed downhill to a small restaurant that he said made "…the best and most cheap *tortas* in Zacatecas."

He introduced himself and handed me a simple business card with his name printed on it. As improbable as it seemed, his name was Ramón Limón, and he was from León. It said so on the card.

After a decent torta lunch, we spent the rest of the day touring the town. Unlike most Mexicans, Ramón was widely traveled. Few of the other people I've run into in Mexico have ever been far from their hometowns, but Ramón had been to Zacatecas several times and to many other cities as a traveling salesman. He was also knowledgeable about the highest-quality shoes and boots since his hometown of León was the shoe-making capital of Mexico. He pointed out the best brands and styles as we walked through an area of leather shops. I wasn't in the market for shoes, but it was interesting anyway.

Later into the afternoon he asked where I was staying and I told him about the six-dollar hotel. He was surprised I was staying at such an expensive place, a place for "*turistas,*" and he would help me find a cheaper hotel. In fact, I could spend the night for free in the room he was renting. It had two beds.

I was surprised by his kind offer, and I felt that maybe the karmic gods had taken notice of the many times I had stepped around ants on a busy sidewalk or had dropped a coin into a beggar's cup. This was the kind of break I needed to get my budget back on track.

We went back to my hotel and I quickly packed my bag before checking out at the front desk. Outside the door we took a left turn and walked up the sidewalk to the next alley where Ramón turned left once again and walked straight to the open door of that shabby little hotel run by the one-eyed Chinese man! Ramón kept up a constant banter while I tried to mask my horror. Was I really going to tell him the place where he always stayed in Zacatecas was too filthy and disgusting for his new gringo friend?

As we climbed down the steps past the same women leaning over the rail, he carried on a familiar banter with them. *"¿Ramón, quien es tú amigo nuevo?"* they asked and smiled at me. There was more rapid-fire conversation and a lot of laughter.

"Rita say she like you!" he told me as he smiled broadly and pointed toward a plump woman in her mid-twenties. Rita giggled and hid amongst her friends. "She only charge sixteen pesos!" he laughed as we reached the doorway to his room. "You have the room with her for a while if you like," he offered earnestly. "I go get coffee for a while and leave you have the room."

I told Ramón it was kind of him to offer the use of his room but it really wasn't necessary. We could stash my bag by one of the two double beds and go back out for another walk. Then we'd get dinner and a beer. The girls weren't very pretty and I also didn't think I wanted to take chances with whatever diseases might be rampant here in what was obviously one of the lower-class local brothels.

When we were safely inside the door, I took a quick look around at the accommodations. The room itself was actually clean, if drab and somewhat shabby, and there didn't even appear to be any recent leaks in the ceiling. We were on the top floor, so I wouldn't have to worry about someone's leaky plumbing over my head. And the rain had stopped earlier in the day, so there probably wouldn't be any other water dripping on me in the middle of the night. The sheets and a faded pink bedspread were tattered and threadbare, but they were clean. The room was well ventilated and a large window looked out over the tar and gravel rooftop of the building next door and on toward a horizon of gray and dusty hills beyond.

I had a great deal of gringo discomfort at the prospect of spending the night in this cut-rate brothel, especially when I noticed there was only a flimsy lock on the door. But I didn't see a graceful way out of the situation. Ramón had been kind to me, and I had taken a liking to him. He was bright and had a great sense of humor. I was also taken by his concern as he explained that the prostitutes in the hotel lobby needed to make a little money to pay their rent. He encouraged me again to hire one or two of them for the rest of the afternoon, but I declined. The whole scene, prostitutes and all, appeared to Ramón to be as natural as life itself and not a tawdry secret buried from polite society, like in a cheap novel, something that you'd keep hidden from the outside world. To him, the girls were people too. His people. People who worked hard for a minimal living, just like he did.

Or I could just walk. I could say something like, "Uh, hey man, I gotta take off. This isn't gonna work out too well. Hey, I'll look you up in the morning. We'll have breakfast together or something, but I've gotta find a better place than this to crash. Sorry, man. No hard feelings, OK?"

Yeah. And look like some gringo bastard who's too good to stay in a shithole hotel with the *pobres*, the poor folks. Yeah, that'd go over real well.

I looked around uneasily and wrestled with the decision I had to make. Or maybe not make, in my usual fashion. I finally decided it probably wouldn't kill me to spend a night among the poverty-ridden people who called this place home. At least I sure hoped it wouldn't. I also hoped I wouldn't catch a disease from the fleas, roaches, and bedbugs that were hiding in the crevices.

But regardless of all that, I didn't want to spend a second night in this hotel. So, over dinner I concocted a story about how I would need to leave on the early morning bus because I had to be in San Luis Potosí the next day. Afterwards, Ramón and I talked about his family in León and some more about his friends at the hotel.

I spent a fitful night, half sleeping, half listening through paper-thin walls to the laughter, the partying, the slamming doors, and the loud music of the women's nightly trade. Several times I looked over at Ramón in the other bed, sleeping peacefully through it all. It was probably two or three in the morning when things settled down, and I drifted into a deep sleep. But other than the noise, the night had not been disrupted. Nobody had tried the door.

A clean morning sun crested the hills and woke me as it fell across the bed. I showered under a dribbling trickle of cold water, then I packed my bag and dressed to catch the bus. Ramón had risen earlier and we had a quick breakfast in the room before I went to the station. We walked quietly down the rough concrete stairway to the first floor, our footsteps echoing in the ugly yellow concrete lobby now standing empty of all but the two of us.

At the station I gave Ramón my home address and phone number and told him I sincerely hoped to see him again someday. He assured me that he would travel north to visit me at some time in the near future but he didn't know exactly when it would be possible. The trip would be expensive for him even though I offered him a place to stay at my small house. I waved goodbye out my window as the bus pulled from the station into the morning traffic. Then we sped away and down from the mountains on the highway toward San Luis Potosí, leaving Ramón in the fading distance.

About a year later, I received a postcard with a picture of the statue of the *"Niños Héroes"* that stands at one of the major crossroads in Guadalajara. This famous statue commemorates the brave cadets who refused to surrender to American forces during the Mexican-American War and who died at the Battle of Chapultepec. The American victory over this small band of young cadets is commemorated today by that red stripe down the leg of the Marine Corps dress uniform. It hardly seems worthy of commemoration.

On the back of the postcard was a simple message. "You wait. Me very soon. Ramón." There was no return address, and I never saw Ramón Limón again.

I was ready for the next leg of the trip, to San Luis Potosí. We passed an area of fertile lands then entered the desert west of the Sierra Madre Oriental, the eastern edge of the great Mexican plateau. Forests of tall cactus up to 20 feet high again lined the roadway. Then the cactus gave way to short scrubby trees and finally to taller trees, green shrubs and grasses as we began a descent through low mountains on this leg of my long journey to sea level.

At a midday stop in a dusty town I bought some food from an old woman wearing a black shawl, with a brightly-colored basket over her shoulder. She pulled back the red and white cloth covering from her basket and handed me two warm *gorditas de carne* in a brown paper napkin. I bought an ice-cold Coke from a young man carrying a battered metal cooler and forced myself to eat despite the queasiness that had returned, drinking the Coke slowly to savor the cold liquid. The icy glass of the bottle felt good in my hand. Before our bus left, the young man came back to collect the valuable empty bottles and I had to chug down the last of it.

By mid afternoon, crystalline desert skies had given way to small, puffy clouds and then to a thick blanket of cooling thunderstorms as we drove slowly out of the high desert and into greener and wetter mountain valleys. The cool damp air permeated the bus and soothed my burning face and arms. I pulled my jacket around my shoulders and watched through the window as heavy rain cleansed the land outside, with the deep rumble of a throbbing diesel engine lulling my exhausted body into a deep sleep.

I awoke as the bus slowed somewhere in the darkness of a rainy night. There were no village lights along this empty stretch of road. A woman and a boy were standing beside the driver as he brought the bus to a stop. Pale green light from the dashboard illuminated the scene like a Medieval painting of the Madonna and Child asking for shelter at the inn. The woman was holding her young son's hand reassuringly, and the driver nodded slowly as she spoke, like a priest hearing a confession. Finally, he stood to explain that there was *"una emergencia"* and laughed with the rest of us as the woman smiled sheepishly and led her son into some bushes beside the road. Soon they were back aboard and we continued our passage into the night toward San Luis Potosí.

But I was unable to return to sleep and I sat quietly watching rivulets of rain streaming along my window and listening to the high-pitched song of large tires on wet pavement. Lights from an occasional farmhouse drifted past in the misty blackness of night, and finally the bus slowed as we entered the outskirts of San Luis Potosí. We found our way through a maze of narrowing streets as we drew near to the center of town and finally arrived at the depot.

The rain slowed to a misty drizzle. I stood with my bags at the doorway of the depot that led to the sidewalk and the street beyond, watching the flow of water as it drained into chiseled stone gutters. The weak light from a streetlamp in the next block lit my way toward the main plaza. I was feeling better than I had in Torreón but still stopping often to rest.

An emaciated beagle-cross dog limped along the shadowed street in the dripping rain looking for something to eat. His hair was missing in places, he was matted with dirt, and his right front paw was bent under where it had once been broken and had never healed correctly. He ignored me as I struggled with my baggage. The dog expected nothing from me, and he received nothing for I had nothing to give. He went slowly on his way, smelling the dirty pavement for morsels of food, and I went slowly my way—two cripples, accidental comrades alone together late at night on a wet, loveless, and deserted street.

Ahead, the dimly-lit, deserted lobby of an old hotel beckoned, and I checked in at the counter, leaning heavily on a cold ancient marble countertop while a sleepy night clerk rose from an overstuffed chair to fill out some forms and take the money from my hand. After a short pause I wrestled my bags to a second-floor room overlooking the plaza. The cold night air felt good and I fell heavily on the bed to sleep.

A faint misty haze softened the morning sky and I heard the sound of a light drizzle tapping quietly on loose panes of glass in the balcony doors. The sharp hollow ring of steel hammers and bars and other tools echoed through the fog in my brain as I stirred from the bed and made my way to the balcony door. Below, a group of men had begun their daily work on a project to rebuild and renovate the plaza. I stood on the balcony and leaned on the wet railing for a few minutes, watching. Then I closed my eyes and raised my head to the sky to let the cooling drizzle run down my forehead and over my dry lips, to soak into the collar of my bathrobe. The cold, pure water slowly pulled the fever from my brain and cleansed my face and neck as I stood listening to the workmen below.

In the blackness of night on my way to the hotel I had vaguely noticed there were barricades and some kind of work going on at the plaza but was too exhausted to think much about it. In the morning the incessant pinging of hammer upon chisel had awakened me early. At first, I rolled over with a pillow covering my head and drifted back into sleep. Now I was awake, still groggy and still addled by fever. The rhythmic pinging of steel tools continued in the plaza below as I made my way to the bathroom.

The diarrhea and vomiting were finally under control, and I had slept reasonably well, but the weakness remained as I reached for the shower faucet. A small stream of cold water dribbled out and fell onto a cold tile floor, regardless of whether I turned the white porcelain knob labeled *"C"* for *caliente* or the one labeled *"F"* for *frio*.

I had grown used to low-pressure, cold water showers in Mexico, but this shower would be especially refreshing on a chilly and rainy morning. I stood for a moment to watch the dribbling water bounce toward the drain, waiting for hot water that I knew would never come. I knew I'd feel better if I were clean, and I readied myself for another cold shower. I placed my towel, shampoo, and soap in the best location, took a deep breath, and stepped beneath the icy stream.

After I was clean and dressed, I stepped back onto the balcony to watch the workmen below in the drizzle as they laid out each new walkway and ran the leveling strings and side boards. I was more interested in their progress now that I was fully awake, and I could see the plaza was laid out in a formal, cruciform pattern with a sidewalk around the entire edge and a broad walkway from each of four surrounding streets to a new bandstand at the center. The paving stones were a standard size— about one foot wide and two feet long, hand-chiseled, and with a rippled non-skid surface. I had seen them in other plazas, in other towns. The bandstand was a classically ornate style in keeping with the architecture of the large formal government buildings that stood facing the plaza from across the adjacent streets.

The clean, fine ring of hammer and chisel continued as my eyes wandered the plaza looking for a stack of uniformly sized paving stones, but could see none. Finally, my gaze fell upon two workmen standing at a heavy table beside a large pile of rocks on the street below and just to the right of my balcony. As I watched, they took large stones from the pile of random rubble and shaped each paver by hand. When a stone was properly shaped, a workman would carry it off and nestle it carefully into a bed of fresh mortar. The stone cutter then chose another rough stone from the pile and began the shaping process again. I stood transfixed by the timeless beauty of the process and watched them work. It was an ancient and honorable skill, and I hoped to return someday to appreciate the completed work.

After a while I went downstairs to the street to get some breakfast and take a look around the city before catching the next bus that would carry me to the coast.

The cool rainy weather had helped cut the fever that still gripped my body, and I could think of nothing more pleasant than the cleansing waters of the sea. After a day or so here I would be ready to move on.

San Luis Potosí is a pleasant small city with an economy based on mining and agriculture. It was named long ago, during its boomtown days, for the fabulous Potosí mines of Bolivia, but today it is an unpretentious place of moderate aspirations.

In the late morning after a leisurely breakfast I found a Mexican government tourism office in a shopping area and stepped inside to look at the collection of brochures. I glanced through racks of literature and saw that they were all in Spanish, directed at the domestic traveler. I took several to help with my study of the language, then I asked the man behind a large desk for *"Una mapa de México, por favor."*

"¡No es una mapa de México!" he thundered as he glared at the tall gringo, *"¡Es un mapa de la República!"*

I stood there stunned, another fumbling gringo in paradise, guilty of violating some deeply-held convictions of this minor governmental official. And my Spanish ability was not good enough to engage him in a meaningful discussion about the subject. I swallowed hard and cleared my throat.

"Bueno," I said haltingly, *"un mapa de la República, por favor."*

"Mejor," he said, as he slid a map of the Republic of Mexico across his broad desk.

I thanked him and retreated into the anonymity of the streets, a casualty of a minor international skirmish not really worthy of mention. The rain had stopped and the sun began to change the day from a soothing chill to the glow of warmth and humidity. I again felt weakened by fever and nausea in the building heat. The call of cooling waters beckoned, and I returned to the hotel to check out for the final leg of my journey to Tampico.

Heavy darkness had fallen along the coast by the time we arrived and I checked into an older high-rise hotel not far from the bus terminal in downtown Tampico. I was given a little room with a small bath and a curtain hanging over a window on one wall. I felt weak and exhausted and went to sleep quickly without looking much around the room or out the window. That could wait until morning.

Many hours later I emerged from the soundest sleep I'd had in days, awakened by the sound of maids working and talking in the hallway. The room was pitch black except for a sliver of light that appeared beneath the door from lights shining in the hall. I thought it was strange they were cleaning in the middle of the night, but their voices disappeared into one of the other rooms and I rolled over and went back to sleep.

Shortly I was reawakened by the maids and I realized I no longer felt tired. I fumbled in blackness for the bedside light and reached for my watch. It was thirteen minutes after eight in the morning.

I rose from the bed and pulled back the curtain to look out at the city, wondering why the room was still so dark. But there was no window in the wall. Only a blank wall with a curtain hung over it! I stood there staring for a moment at this solid masonry wall and thinking about the implications. What if there had been a fire and I needed to get out through the window? That sort of thing happens now and then in these countries. Hell, it happens in the

US! I'd have died in a fire, just another family footnote, part of a short article buried in the back pages of the local newspaper: "American Traveler Among Those Dead in Mexican Hotel Fire." It would be quickly read and quickly forgotten. I decided I'd better pay closer attention to these things in the future. And I'd stay in rooms that were no higher than the second floor so I'd have a better chance of surviving a jump.

I dressed quickly and checked out, dragging my baggage through a drizzling morning rain to the nearest decent restaurant I could find, where I shoved my bags under the table and ordered breakfast. I lingered there with a second cup of hot coffee and watched people walking by under broad umbrellas in a light morning rain that was peppering the shining surface of the sidewalk and the puddles collecting in the street and draining into gutters on their way to the sea. Buses, trolleys, taxis, and trucks passed by with wipers slapping slowly at a liquid sky.

I turned from the window and fiddled with a piece of silverware as I drank my coffee and savored this quiet moment. *"Hecho en Mexico"* was stamped into the back of each knife, fork, and spoon that lay upon the table. It was on the back of silverware at every restaurant on this trip. I did not recall what was stamped on silverware back in the States, but I didn't think I had seen "Made in USA" on a fork or spoon lately.

A soft rain continued to cleanse the world outside, and small streams of water ran from sidewalks in silent cascades to the street. Buses and trolleys stopped at a *Parada* on the corner to load passengers waiting beneath a jostling cloud of brightly-colored umbrellas. An occasional trolley had *"Playa"* on its sign-board just over the windshield. After finishing my coffee, I swung my baggage onto a passing trolley and headed for the beach.

We rattled along in an ancient, crowded trolley car, hanging onto the handrail overhead as the unyielding steel wheels found every bump and swerve in the old tracks beneath us. Soon we left the rutted streets of downtown Tampico and clattered onward atop an eroded earthen roadbed through a dilapidated maze of settlements. A steady drizzle continued as we bounced and shook our way along stretches of badly undermined roadbed that threatened to pitch the entire train into one of the muddy ditches running along each side of the tracks.

Inside our rain-sheltered rolling cocoon, the passengers were smiling in communal resignation as we listened to a young man with a very old guitar singing *corridas*. We were unified in a fatalistic abandon that seemed to increase with each jolt of the trolley car, not knowing if we were going to survive this trip intact and uninjured, and knowing we were powerless to change anything about it. The bonding power of common circumstance had brought us together, and for a brief portion of our lives it made us one as we traveled onward to our destinations.

At each rainy stop, the trolley became less crowded as grateful survivors stepped onto solid wet pavement and disappeared under umbrellas down muddy streets into a tropical mist. Soon the rain eased, and the few of us left aboard arrived in the dripping remains of the morning at the end of the line.

I stood on a wet and sandy street with baggage in hand as the trolley made its loop and disappeared on its way back to town. I looked for clues as to which of the funky one-story hotels might offer the quiet solitude I was seeking, at a price I could afford with the few dollars remaining in my pocket. Soon, three young Anglo guys walked up with their luggage to wait for the next trolley into town. They were about my age and they looked like Americans, so I struck up a conversation.

They were medical students. They had come down from Houston for a week of fun before starting summer school and they told me about their hotel. It sounded nice but too expensive for my budget, so they pointed out a cheap and decent place they'd heard about nearby with rooms that opened directly onto the beach.

While we were talking, I asked about the stuff I was still taking occasionally for my dysentery. Since they were med students, I thought they'd know if there was something better I should be using. When I mentioned the name Entero-Vioformo, they exchanged glances and one of them asked the other, "Isn't that the stuff we were just reading about in one of the journals? The stuff that's been causing blindness in Japan?"

I laughed as one who is used to guys bullshitting each other, but I noticed they weren't laughing. They asked me where I'd gotten the stuff and how long I'd been taking it. They were clearly concerned. In the end they said it was my choice, but if it were them, they'd pitch that package into the closest trash can and get by with aspirin for the duration.

Shaken by the news, I thanked them and dragged my baggage to the cheap hotel, the one that opened directly onto the beach. I set my bags against a wall and closed the door. The sound of Entero-Vioformo landing in a bathroom trash can rang through the silence of the small and shabby room. I lay down to rest on a hard and simple bed and stared at the ceiling, thinking how lucky I was to run into some American med students on a beach near Tampico. I thought about it for a long time while I stared at a leak-stained ceiling and listened to the incessant roar of the sea.

February 1964

I spent the night on a cot at the YMCA in downtown San Diego and I was still a little stiff as I walked to a coffee shop nearby. The waitress was friendly to the locals and she was nice enough to me but it was obvious from my haircut that I was just another young kid in the military. There were lots of us in San Diego and we were all just temporary residents. I wouldn't be around long enough to become one of the locals. She knew it. I knew it. Everybody in the place knew it. There wasn't much point in pretending any different. I finished breakfast and then caught a bus to Balboa Park.

The park sits on high ground and I lingered at the overlook viewing the city and the shining bay below. I turned away and walked into the gardens toward a gathering of stately mission-style buildings. I sat on a bench painted with shade beneath a large tree and began to read a book of poetry by Wilfred Owen that I had bought in my wanderings through a small book store the night before.

Owen was a young officer in the British Army who wrote about the insanity and brutality of the First World War, the war that finally destroyed the myth of military gallantry and replaced it with the reality of efficient mass murder. He was killed in 1918, another casualty of the war, consumed like millions of others of his generation.

One poem especially, *"Dulce et decorum est,"* stands out as perhaps his most eloquent cry against what I realized now was the madness and avarice of war. I had recently become aware that there were others long before me who dared to speak out against this most basic form of criminality. And many of them had paid a heavy price for their honesty, inspired by the bitter irony of that empty phrase by Seneca which resounded in the Roman Senate some two thousand years ago to justify the brutality of some other pointless and long-forgotten war: *"Dulce et decorum est pro patria mori."* Sweet and proper it is to die for one's country.

I sat in the quiet green of Balboa Park and reflected that it was easy for Seneca to say such things while young men were slaughtered. Someone else took his place in distant battles while he was safe back in Rome. Wilfred Owen and others of his generation fought in the horrible trenches of Europe, and they died by the millions for trade, profits, and empire. I wondered how many other bright young people had been sacrificed in the wars of our era. I wondered if a similar wave of national hysteria might yet consume my own generation. I wondered if my parent's generation had read enough of history to try to stop it. And I wondered if my own young life would be, as Thomas Hobbes had starkly described medieval life, "nasty, brutish and short."

I stood and walked aimlessly through this vast parkland. A squirrel bounded across the grass, never far from the safety of a large tree. Overhead, a few small clouds had begun to gather in a deep blue sky and I thought it might rain sometime later in the afternoon.

I passed the Old Globe Theatre where a matinee crowd was just emerging for an intermission and I mingled with the crowd. I was in the company of people enjoying an afternoon in intellectual activity, a moment of community. For a brief time, I was one of them. There were some in this crowd, I was sure, who had read the words of Wilfred Owen, some who understood his message. Back at the Marine barracks on base such thoughts were seen as treason.

A light rain began to fall upon this broad and beautiful park. The theater-goers looked into a gray blanket that filled the sky, and they covered their heads with the afternoon's printed program.

A bell rang and the crowd filed back into the shelter of the theatre. I crossed the street and walked onward through an open gate and along a walkway that lead through a formal rose garden. A misty rain fell clean upon my face. A man walking ahead of me hunched his shoulders against the drizzle. He dropped a smoldering cigarette butt from his right hand and it lay where it landed near the edge of the walkway, the smoke curling upward like a vine, entwining itself into the rain. And then it was gone.

Mexico V

The refreshing breath of the sea blew all day through my open window and billowed the tattered white cotton curtains. I lay on the bed and read for several hours as a warming afternoon sun slowly cleared away the coastal fog. On a distant misty horizon freighters and fishing boats were heading up the coast in slow procession, or down the coast. The faint heavy thrum of their engines echoed over the water, carried in by the breeze. In the farthest distance several oil derricks were just visible through the remnants of a lingering haze.

In the warmth of afternoon, I pulled on my swim trunks and went to where the sea lapped the shore. Small oil clots dotted the dirty sand and a light oily sheen glowed rainbow colors on the face of each breaking wave. I found a spot in the sand to sit on my towel, and I studied the pattern of breaking waves while the sun warmed my back and the wind brushed my face. The lusty golden pirates of the Spanish Main were long gone now from this backwater port and the grimy oil pirates had taken their place in the broad Gulf of Mexico, leaving their dirty industrial footprints along the ancient shoreline.

Farther down the shore, families were playing in the water and enjoying a day at the beach and seemed mindless of the oily residue. But then, what are their choices? They can catch a cheap ride to the beach on a local trolley, or they can take a long road trip to a clean beach somewhere else—if they can find one, and if they can locate someone with a functioning car. Or they can try to confront the directors of that huge national oil company named Pemex and get them to clean up the mess they've created along the public beaches. But in the end, their only realistic option is to ignore the pollution and enjoy their day away from a small sweltering shack on a crowded and dirty side street in the city.

I quietly studied the throbbing sea, knowing the cool water would feel refreshing as it flowed across my fevered body, and I decided not to worry about the oil any more than the locals did. I'd wash off later under the dribbling cold-water shower back in the room. It was a decent little room and I didn't want to get back on a bus to look for a better spot somewhere along the coast. It wasn't likely I was going to find anyplace else nearby with a better beach.

I waded into the ocean and dove through a wall of cooling water at the front of a breaking wave and swam beneath the oily surface that hugged the coastline. I stroked hard and pulled myself onward through the frothing turbulence until I rose, out of breath, at a point where the water seemed cleaner. The salty taste of primal ocean painted my lips, a remembrance of that place that is the mother of us all. And I tried to ignore the terrible damage she had suffered.

I swam farther out to sea and then paralleled the beach, on that grand ebb and flow of ocean that caresses the sky above and the sandy ocean floor below. Around me were the beings of the water, and I felt a oneness with them as the fever drained from
my body into the cooling liquid. Things were beginning to get better for me.

After a cold shower I walked down the sandy street in front of the hotel to an open-air restaurant for a platter of *camarones al mojo de ajo* and an ice-cold beer. My improving appetite was starting to demand the food that I needed to rebuild my drained reserves, although my stomach was still uneasy. Nevertheless, the fever had broken, the cold sweats were gone, and I felt better than when I was tossing endlessly in the middle of a desert night back in Torreón. And I was glad to be taking only aspirin from a small bottle I had brought from the States.

That evening I read myself to sleep by the weak light of a bedside lamp, and outside the rising tide of a restless ocean touched and caressed the shore in its tender and eternal way.

PASSAGE

It's almost funny how scenes repeat themselves through life as a sort of theatrical fugue, as an endless and meaningless farce, or as a tragedy. I was sitting again on the edge of a dirty, broken curb and staring at another street. But this time I felt a kind of peace as I sat in front of the Ciudad Juarez bus station in my old jeans and an almost-clean white cotton shirt with my sleeves rolled up. I watched an endless line of old cars, city buses, and heavy trucks as they passed by on the Avenida de la Reforma. The smell of diesel fumes mingled with the aroma from a nearby taco stand and the ever-present odor of sewage that drifted from manhole covers. The sharp bark of a taxi horn pierced the roar of unmuffled trucks and city buses. Sleek and shiny Dina long-distance coaches emerged from the station driveway, with "*Estrella del Norte*" or "*Estrella Blanca*" or "*Chihuahuenses*" painted on their sides, muscling onto this busy street and into the distance toward a far destination, the mellow rumble of their big diesel engines fading into the din of the day. The polluted sky overhead glowed a curious dirty-white—almost yellow—under a relentless baking afternoon sun. I studied the deep brown faces of the people who walked past in the dusty street.

In the hazy distance the Franklin Mountains rose across the sky just north of El Paso and south of the New Mexico border. Americans, especially westerners, worship "the freedom of the open road" and the mobility of cars so most western cities sprawl mindlessly across the land.

The city of El Paso wanders aimlessly upward through dusty foothills like an uncontrollable fungus and it's not a lovely sight once you pass the few remaining older buildings that define the carcass of a small downtown. Most of the world's population seems to crave the mobility that Americans enjoy, but I was looking forward to a few weeks of freedom on public transit systems. And being rid of the sick-dependent relationship Americans have with cars.

Mark was in the bus terminal dealing with something, and I had time to myself. I had a bus ticket to Chihuahua in my pocket, and I sat on the curb contemplating the pattern of my life amid the ceaseless flow of my surroundings.

Oñate had been here, somewhere near where I sat watching the daily life of modern Mexico. In the year 1580, Don Juan de Oñate looked across this valley to the sun-glazed badlands that would someday become the American Southwest. There were people already living in the fertile lands of the river these Spanish newcomers would call the *Rio Bravo del Norte*—"The Wild River of the North." The first inhabitants had escaped the droughts of remote deserts and less predictable streams. In this broad valley they learned to deal with the occasional terrible floods and to harness these sacred waters for their fields. They built homes of warm native earth among huge cottonwood trees. And on quiet summer days they heard the clacking sound of heavy leaves as cooling breezes from the river nuzzled them into motion on a hot afternoon.

The people of the valley fought marauding bands of enemies and these conflicts had become part of their lives. The battles of the past had an ebb and a flow, as an enemy gained strength and then receded to be replaced by a new and different enemy. But as Oñate and his band of settlers gazed across the river toward their own "promised land," the ancient ways would change. The native peoples had heard stories of strange bearded White men, and even a man with black skin who appeared at Zuni Pueblo far to the northwest many years before. There was a group of White men and their strange animals who crossed this land to the north many seasons past and then returned down this same valley heading south. These new men had a fascination for shiny metals that they dug from the earth, and they took desperate measures to get them.

Oñate was a driven man, hated by some and followed by others. It was rumored he had many native slaves working his mines in the distant mountains of Zacatecas. There were stories of the cruelty he inflicted upon them in his consuming greed for personal wealth and position. Unfortunately for the peoples of the valley, many of the stories were true and their lives would soon change forever as he marched north toward their ancient adobe villages. I felt like a witness to all that history as I sat on the edge of the street looking north.

Mark came back outside the bus terminal to sit beside me on the curb and watch the flow of people and traffic. Linda's bus had left for Mexico City about half an hour earlier and we waited for mine to leave. The world moved past without comment and I felt almost invisible as the traffic ignored us. I was reluctant to break the spell, but I would be leaving soon and I was still looking for answers.

"How'd you and Linda meet, anyway?" I was hoping for something I could use the next time a relationship entered my own life, and I didn't recall ever asking Mark that question before. The way things had worked out for me so far didn't seem to show much promise. It was time to find another way of doing things, and they had clearly been more successful than me at this relationship thing.

Mark laughed as he recalled the details of meeting his future mate.

"She worked in a bank back in Albany where she got her bachelor's. We had been friendly but I didn't even know her last name. It was a nice warm summer day and I went to cash a check. There were three people in her line and I was last. When I got to the front she smiled and said 'Hi!' I slid a check beneath the glass door that read, 'How about a nooner?'"

"No! You didn't!" I laughed and turned to look at Mark.

He nodded, "It was a stupid thing to do, but I didn't really think she'd be interested in me, anyway, and I guess I was afraid she'd tell me to get lost if I just asked her out. It was one of those dumb stunts that guys pull when they don't know what else to do. If you don't know what to do, at least do something stupid. You know what I mean?"

I stared at Mark with a goofy grin on my face.

"She smiled and glanced at the other teller," Mark continued, "then she looked back at me. I was trying to keep my cool but I felt my face getting red and I swallowed hard and I already regretted treating her in such a jerky way."

My mouth was open, inhaling a gust of dusty air from the street. Two large buses roared past no more than two feet away from our knees. Their tires looked suddenly huge as we sat there on the curb.

"She looked back at the other teller and said, 'I'm going for my lunch break now.'

"We went to a sandwich shop and just talked and I realized she was the most interesting person I'd ever met." Mark paused for a moment to clear his throat and turned away to stare at the oncoming traffic while he pulled an old blue handkerchief from his back pocket and wiped his moistening eyes. His nose was starting to run just a little and he dabbed at it with the handkerchief. I think the sudden rush of emotion surprised him. He took a deep breath before he continued.

"That night after work we took a long walk through the older neighborhood where she lived and we discussed politics. It was late when we got back to her apartment. She invited me in and we made love and fell asleep in each other's arms. It gave my life a direction for the first time ever. Just meeting Linda had forced me to consider growing up and I started work on my master's degree the next year while Linda went on to get her master's in education and then her doctorate. After that we spent time working in Venezuela and Puerto Rico together, and we've been partners ever since. She's the kind of woman I always dreamed of when I was a kid. We've seen some interesting places and done amazing things since we met. Things I can'timagine most other women doing."

It was simple as that.

I listened as Mark talked. We had driven all day and spent a lot of time joking around. Now we had time to do nothing but sit on a broken curb and stare at the world and try to talk about something of substance. It was not easy for either of us.

Earlier, when Linda's bus pulled away, I felt a powerful bond with her. She was going to be on that bus for nearly twenty-five hours on the next leg of her own personal exploration. I respected her and Mark for the way they lived, for the way they honored each other. I wondered if I would ever find that in my own life.

We sat there and tried to pretend that Mark hadn't actually been weeping in public for one brief moment. He wiped his nose and forced the faded handkerchief back into his pocket. I don't know what comes over us now and then, why guys will tell another guy things they'll never tell their girlfriends or wives. Men are fragile creatures who live in fear of being hurt, and women never seem to understand that. We're close-mouthed, and wives are frustrated when they can't get deeply into the heart of the guy they've married. But sometimes it just spills out. Guys will put their feelings and emotions on the table for some other guy to look at. To dissect in public. I don't know why we do that.

Maybe I should have told Annie a lot more than I ever did about how I felt, and to hell with whether she made light of it, because she was a wounded animal herself. I don't know why it didn't happen that way, but it didn't.

Mark and I had become closer in the last few minutes than either of us imagined and I felt we were together at the edge of a healing ocean. Or maybe we were at the edge of a deep chasm. We'd never be the same friends again. Not in the same way, no matter where our paths went from here.

Mark stared thoughtfully into the traffic.

I reminded him of the time we came across an unfortunate misspelling at a candy store in an antiseptic Uptown mall. I looked at the tempting offerings and noticed a large case filled with chocolate-coated nut assortments and the sign above a tray of lumpy brown candy almost made me choke. The sign read "Pecan Turdles." Next to it was another sign for "Almond Turdles." My jar dropped and I nodded to the sign as Mark grinned and shook his head. It was hard to imagine a more descriptive name for brown and lumpy candy in a display window. We ordered a bagful of Almond Turdles and left the store laughing.

Another big Dina bus pulled out of the terminal and headed down the road leading south.

"I'm envious of you." Mark broke the silence, and I was surprised to hear him say that. "You have some great adventures ahead and you seem to notice the richness and the detail of everything that happens. I wish I could just get away for a while and go with you. Just the two of us, to explore Mexico together for a while. But I can't because I have contracts to finish. I miss traveling in Mexico with Linda like we did years ago, but I can't seem to find the time anymore. You know what I mean?"

It wasn't a question that Mark wanted me to answer, so I sat and listened.

"You know, life just hasn't turned out the way I thought it would." Mark continued, "A few years back, I thought we'd be manning the barricades, Linda and I, destroying the corrupt corporate state and building a better nation. The need was so obvious back then, and it seemed so urgent at the time. But now I spend most of my time worrying about contracts and making the damn house payment and putting groceries on the table. What kind of bullshit is that anyway?

"I never should have listened to you in the first place, you bastard." He jabbed me in the ribs with a laugh and we wrestled momentarily in the street-side dust. "Remember when you talked us into buying a house instead of renting from that absentee capitalist slumlord? You were right that we weren't getting anywhere just renting, but Linda and I had to go buy a dilapidated inner-city Victorian to make some kind of goddamned political statement about reclaiming the inner city. And then we started an urban commune to boot. As if we didn't have enough trouble to deal with already.

"So far, I think we've rebuilt most of the damn house," he laughed and shook his head, "and every time I think the neighborhood has hit bottom and it can't get any worse, something else terrible happens. Like when that nice old brick building behind us burnt down and now we've got a glass-strewn vacant lot just across the alley from our back yard. The owner put a sign out there last year: 'Soon on this Site, etc., etc...' and there was a picture of some little apartments and trees and kids playing on the sidewalk. It was probably going to end up just another slummy apartment block, but the picture looked alright. He made the sign out of cheap particle board and somebody whacked it with a broken piece of concrete block. Now what's left of it still hangs there from the post, and the rest is lying face down in the dirt. The piece that's still on the pole says 'Soon on this Site...' and that's all. It's really kind of the most appropriate metaphor for everything that never seems to happen in our part of town. You know: 'Soon on this site nothing much will happen.' Half of our neighbors are too dirt-poor to do anything—even if they wanted to. Most of the time it seems like nobody's got enough money or imagination to make any kind of positive change."

Mark shook his head as he realized he was not going to change the neighborhood and lead an urban rebirth movement with paint brush and lawn rake in hand. The problems were more complex than that, and more complex than any of us imagined in our halcyon days. Like the rest of us who decided to leave the rhetoric behind and start to take real action, he had become another minor player with a bit part in the human adventure. We began this adventure differently so many years ago and now we were mired in the same messy details, unable to regain the high ground where we once seemed to stand above it all. From up there we saw things clearly. From there the answers had seemed obvious.

In Franz Kafka's novel, *The Castle*, the surveyor named K sees the castle looming dark and cold in the snow from the crest of a small hill before he enters the town that surrounds it like a tightly-drawn shawl. Yet the closer he gets to the castle, the less he sees of its high walls until it is hidden completely from view in a warren of winding streets clogged with huge drifts of snow that finally stop him. The novel never actually ends and K is left in a morass of hidden passages, and he never sees the castle again.

When Mark and I and Linda were younger we thought we wouldn't fall into the obvious traps of an older generation. We were too smart for that. There was more to life, a more noble purpose. There had to be.

"What's your long-range plan anyway, Mark?" I asked, "Are you at least semi-happy with what you're doing these days?" Long-range plans had never been on the agenda for either of us in the past, but I was starting to feel like I might need to think about one.

"Funny you should ask." Mark looked down. He scraped a pattern in the dirt with his boot heal before he spoke. I stared across the street and waited while he framed an answer.

"I've been thinking about going to law school," he finally said. "Sometimes I feel life has gotten too easy. I think I need to do something to annoy the bastards again. Maybe I'll specialize in defending interracial gay couples that burn American flags."

I laughed. It was typically Mark to figure out a way to make his own life a lot more difficult. I'm sure Linda knew this was coming. Their home life had been too peaceful lately.

I had no interest in attending law school. I wasn't sure I'd ever finish the degree I'd started in philosophy, or English lit., or whatever my major was by now. I stared back down at the street without thinking about much of anything.

"I know that mess with Annie is bothering you." Mark gently brought up the subject I had been dodging all day driving south through the stark and dramatic lands of the high desert. I looked at the dusty asphalt between my feet and swallowed hard. I had no idea what to say and I just wished the whole subject would fade into the past. And I knew it wouldn't.

"I know it's hard to think about it this way," he continued when I couldn't talk, "but you're going to find someone out there who's maybe a little older and wiser, like you've become now. And she's made her share of mistakes too and she's also wondering how to not go through all that again. She's going to want to start over without carrying the burden of the mistakes she's made. And the two of you are going to do great things together. Things that would not have been possible before, with Annie."

I smiled, still looking at the street between my boots. Mark was covering for me again, as he'd done other times in the past. I thought about what Mark said and I wanted it to be true.

"And when you find her," Mark was relentless, "she'll be smarter than Annie, and with a fraction of the problems. And she'll be more interesting because you'll be more interesting. It's hard to imagine, but I think you're on the verge of actually getting your shit together."

It was brutal, but true. I'd wasted a lot of my life hoping for someone to define me instead of doing that myself. It was time I had a reason to be here. It was time to craft my own world out of life. And then maybe I'd find an interesting relationship. They were empty words at this point, but I tried to focus on them like a mantra.

A self-sufficient life was lonely, but it was something I prided myself on in the days before I met Annie. I was doing well enough then, before I began to rely on her. Before I changed and we both lost the vision that brought us together.

I let Mark's comments pass in the swirling dust of Juarez traffic, although I was thinking a lot about them. "Yeah, I hope you're right," was all I could come up with.

When Annie left on that plane for Seattle, I knew it was the last time I would ever see her. We happened to meet on the street just before she left. She said, "I'm leaving for Seattle tomorrow."

I told her to give my best to her sister, and then she walked away. As I watched her leave, I knew she was doing me a favor. She had become an addiction that I would never overcome on my own. But I never told her that. And I was afraid I could never admit it to myself.

My life so far had played like a series of tawdry short stories, each with its own unhappy ending. The smiles were there, the laughs were there, but they were transparent, revealing an inner emptiness. There was no common thread in it beyond simple existence. Beyond the fact of one more empty soul among millions trapped in a certain place, in a certain time.

The traffic passed as we waited for my southbound bus. Many of the poor people of Mexico had collected in this unforgiving city that lapped against the southern edge of the "first world," trapped here on the margin of their own impoverished society. They pushed heavy carts laden with fruit or building materials or clothing. These people had no time to waste thinking of how they should be changing the world when they needed to make it through the long day ahead of them. I started to wonder if I had too much time on my hands to think about my trivial problems when I should get on with life and do something useful. I recalled an old mechanic who once told me, "If you can't be brilliant, at least try to be useful."

"OK, that's enough about Annie. She's gone now, and she's no longer an obstacle in your path. Forget about her. What about you?" Mark had turned to me. "Have you decided what you're going to do when the bus leaves? Have you thought about where you'll go? We didn't really talk about that yet, did we? Mexico's a big place and there's a lot waiting beyond the horizon just down that dusty road. I have a feeling there are adventures out there waiting for you."

I had been listening to Mark talk about the way his life had gone and I was surprised when he asked me about my plans for this trip. And actually I was wondering the same thing. I thought about Linda's long trip through Mexico on an all-night express bus alone. I began to see clear contrasts between their purposeful lives and the rubble of mine. They had been telling me that all morning without meaning to, and I was beginning to understand. A feeling of liberation came over me as I sat beside a dirty road in Ciudad Juarez.

Something important had already happened on this trip. Something had broken free back in Las Cruces, and a weight had been lifted from my shoulders. I would have time to think this out after I boarded the bus, if I even wanted to, and I reconsidered Mark's question.

"No. I don't really have a plan." I stared into the shimmering heat of a dusty afternoon, still searching for an answer but satisfied now with the direction I was taking, "I think I'll just head down to Chihuahua and see what happens from there. Hell, maybe I'll even write a book about it someday."

"A book?" Mark secretly wanted to be a writer, but writing was not easy for him. "What kind of book? What are you going to write about?"

"I don't really know," I said. "Maybe explore my Unified Theory of Youthful Indiscretion."

"Sounds like your autobiography," Mark laughed. It was a book that neither of us thought would ever happen, just another part of the larger joke that our lives had become. And anyway, it was time to catch my bus.

Mexico VI

I awakened to the crack of a small wave falling onto the shore just outside my room, the sound echoing through the cathedral calm of a crisp cool quiet morning. I was alone on a deserted shore somewhere at the edge of the world. Gone was the roar of wind-driven afternoon breakers, the violence of water against the land, reducing fragile shells to arcs of brilliant sand.

And gone, too, was the endless human debate that drives our lives, left far behind. And the quiet that now filled the void was rich and profound.

In the stillness of a growing dawn I studied a web of faint cracks in the dirty plaster ceiling as I thought about the experiences I'd had since I crossed the Mexican border on my journey to this beach just outside the dirty port town of Tampico and how my life had changed already. I now saw the world in a different way. It was a rough ride but a fascinating journey into a different world, and I had never even considered returning to the border. The trip had taken me deep into the heart of a land that now felt even more intriguing and yet somehow familiar, although it still remained foreign to me.

There were no easy answers. But I now knew the answers had always been somewhere deep within myself. My time beneath the Mexican sun had given me the freedom to think clearly, and the perspective of distance that I needed to find my own answers, wherever they may be. The portion of my history that included Annie was over now, a fading memory that no longer dominated my life. I was no longer resentful or troubled by it and I felt the stronger for it. Soon I might return to the broad valley of the Rio Grande. The important thing was that I had forgiven myself for our failures.

I lay there for a few minutes longer and drank deeply of this special moment before rising slowly to the day. I stepped outside and walked through soft and yielding sand to the glistening, deserted shore. The cool breath of night had kissed the earth at my feet and I stood silently breathing in the dawn beneath a gray morning overcast. I looked out upon a quiet sea as the still damp air lightly touched my forehead and hung loosely on my shoulders. And I listened to the sussing and moaning of the waters, calling me.

I dove deep into the warm and fertile waters of the Gulf of Mexico, cleansing the final layers of fever from my body and lifting the longing from my heart. The gentle caress of warm and infinite waters flowed across my restored muscles and washed my very soul. The pores of my skin drank deeply of its richness as the water seemed to cleanse my whole being. The dark-shadowed past was prologue to this moment, this quiet and better moment. Alone now in her gentle waters, I sank beneath the quietly rolling surface and became as one with the rich soul of Mexico.

COFFEE CAN BREAD

(Poor People's Campaign, 1968)

INGREDIENTS

1 pkg dry yeast
1 1/2 tsp salt
2 cups whole wheat flour
2 cups unbleached white flour
1/2 cup butter
1/2 cup water
1/2 cup milk
1/2 cup brown sugar or molasses
1/2 cup chopped nuts (almonds, pecans, or walnuts)
1/2 cup raisins
2 eggs

PREPARATION

1. Combine dry (first 4) ingredients, set aside.

2. Melt butter in a large stainless steel or glass bowl and add the water and milk.

3. Stir in the dry ingredients, add the nuts, raisins, and eggs and mix to make a stiff dough.

4. Knead on a floured surface until smooth and elastic.

5. Divide in two and place in two well-buttered 1-lb coffee cans. Cover and let rise until dough reaches 1 inch from top. Uncover and bake at 375° for 30 to 35 minutes.

ACKNOWLEDGMENTS

The birthing of a novel is a cumbersome process, and good help is important when nearing the end. These essential assistants aren't the ones actually writing, but they jolt the work forward and find any grating errors that were overlooked during the author's mad dash through the tangled thickets of verbiage.

Carolyn Meyer, David Johnson, and Mark Rudd provided early and passionate feedback into this writing project. Maybe they liked the manuscript, or maybe they hated it—and they told me so. I thank them all for that.

Emilie Vardaman, Richard Meyer, Barrett Price, Helen Muller, Gloria Brandt, Judy Luis, Paul Watson, Bill Little, Mary Beth Acuff, Deb Green, and Jon Kaplan have given good feedback and encouragement on my various writings over the years. Thank you for staying engaged.

Jan Vala applied her laser focus to the many errors committed by the author. She credits her Catholic school upbringing and, "…a nun standing behind me ready to pounce…" whenever she saw something amiss. Bev Kolosseus brought her intense English professor diligence to the task and has given many essential insights and corrections, after twice surviving the arduous reading process.

Cici Kinsman provided excellent and much-appreciated design review and assistance.

A special thanks to Luke and Kyle, who gave me a ride.

And Carolyn, my partner, has been indispensable during the long process. Without her constant encouragement, insightful critique, and talented design skills, this manuscript would still be languishing.

Credit is grudgingly given to the 2020 virus lockdown for a strong kick to keep this dying mule struggling up the long hill to completion.

Needless to say, any errors remaining are my own.

ABOUT THE AUTHOR

Author Perry Robert Wilkes lived in New Mexico's beautiful Rio Grande Valley for fifty years. He holds a Bachelor of Arts degree from the School of Architecture at the University of New Mexico, and specializes in passive solar residential design and energy efficiency. He taught passive solar workshops throughout New Mexico and the Southwest in the 1980s and served for many years on the board of the New Mexico Solar Energy Association. He is a past president of the Downtown Neighborhoods Association.

His writings on culture, urban issues, and architecture have been published in the *New Mexico Independent*, *Century Magazine*, the *RGSC Foghorn*—and even include an Op-Ed in the *Albuquerque Journal*! His prior book entitled *I Always Meant to Tell You* (2003) is a memorial to his brother's family.

Wilkes travels in Mexico, South America, the Russian Far East, and Europe, encountering local people on various forms of public transportation, while photographing and writing about his travels. His in-depth travel dispatches are found online at: https://dispatches.wilkeskinsman.com.

He currently resides in a small town in Sonora, Mexico, where the road ends at the fabled Sea of Cortez.

Also by Perry Robert Wilkes
from Liberación Press

Mexico 1974–75
I Always Meant to Tell You

Travel Dispatches & other stories
https://dispatches.wilkeskinsman.com